THE
LYLE
OFFICIAL
ANTIQUES
REVIEW 1988

THE
LYLE
OFFICIAL
ANTIQUES
REVIEW 1988

COMPILED & EDITED BY
ANTHONY CURTIS

Perigee Books
are published by
The Putnam Publishing Group
200 Madison Avenue
New York, NY 10016

The Library of Congress has catalogued this
serial title as follows:
The Lyle official antiques review.
   [Galashiels, Scot.]
   v. illus. 23 cm.
Annual.
Began with 1971/72 issue. Cf. New serial titles.
   1. Art objects—Collectors and collecting—Catalogs.
NK1133.L9   745.1   74-640592
                       MARC-S
Library of Congress   74[8309]
ISBN 0-399-51397-3

The publishers wish to express their sincere thanks to the following for their
involvement and assistance in the production of this volume:

Karen Douglass (Art Editor)
Janice Moncrieff (Assistant Editor)
Annette Curtis
Susan Cameron
Nichola Fairburn
Tanya Fairburn
Sally Dalgliesh
Frank Burrell
Robert Nisbet
Eileen Burrell

INTRODUCTION

This year over 100,000 Antique Dealers and Collectors will make full and profitable use of their Lyle Official Antiques Review. They know that only in this one volume will they find the widest possible variety of goods — illustrated, described and given a current market value to assist them to BUY RIGHT AND SELL RIGHT throughout the year of issue.

They know, too, that by building a collection of these immensely valuable volumes year by year, they will equip themselves with an unparalleled reference library of facts, figures and illustrations which, properly used, cannot fail to help them keep one step ahead of the market.

In its eighteen years of publication, Lyle has gone from strength to strength and has become without doubt the pre-eminent book of reference for the antique trade throughout the world. Each of its fact filled pages are packed with precisely the kind of profitable information the professional Dealer needs — including descriptions, illustrations and values of thousands and thousands of individual items carefully selected to give a representative picture of the current market in antiques and collectibles — and remember all values are prices actually paid, based on accurate sales records in the twelve months prior to publication from the best established and most highly respected auction houses and retail outlets in Europe and America.

This is THE book for the Professional Antiques Dealer. 'The Lyle Book' — we've even heard it called 'The Dealer's Bible'.

Compiled and published afresh each year, the Lyle Official Antiques Review is the most comprehensive up-to-date antiques price guide available. THIS COULD BE YOUR WISEST INVESTMENT OF THE YEAR!

ANTHONY CURTIS

CONTENTS

ANTIQUES REVIEW

ANTIQUES REVIEW

ANTIQUES REVIEW

Acknowledgements

Abridge Auctions, *(Michael Yewman), Market Place, Abridge, Essex*
Anderson & Garland, *Anderson House, Market Street, Newcastle NE1 6XA*
Ball & Percival, *132 Lord Street, Southport*
Banks & Silvers, *66 Foregate Street, Worcester*
Barbers Fine Art Auctioneers, *(Chobham Ltd.), The Mayford Centre, Smarts Heath Rd.,
    Mayford, Woking*
Bearnes, *Rainbow, Avenue Road, Torquay*
Bermondsey Antiques Market, *Tower Bridge Road, London*
Biddle & Webb, *Ladywood Middleway, Birmingham B16 0PP*
Bloomsbury Book Auctions, *3 & 4 Hardwick Street, London*
Boardman Fine Art Auctioneers, *Station Road Corner, Haverhill, Suffolk*
Bonham's, *Montpelier Gardens, Montpelier Street, London*
Bracketts, *27-29 High Street, Tunbridge Wells*
J. R. Bridgford & Sons, *1 Heyes Lane, Alderley Edge, Cheshire*
British Antique Exporters, *206 London Road, Burgess Hill, W. Sussex*
Wm. H. Brown, *Westgate Hall, Grantham, Lincs*
Lawrence Butler & Co., *Butler House, 86 High Street, Hythe, Kent CT21 5AJ*
Capes, Dunn & Co., *The Auction Galleries, 38 Charles Street, Manchester 1*
Chancellors Hollingsworths, *31 High Street, Ascot, Berkshire SL5 7HG*
Christie's, *8 King Street, St. James's, London*
Christie's (International) S.A., *8 Place de la Taconnerie, 1204 Geneva*
Christie's, *502 Park Avenue, New York, N.Y. 10022*
Christie's (Monaco) S.A.N., *Park Palace, 98000 Monte Carlo*
Christie's (Hong Kong) Ltd., *3607 Edinburgh Tower, 15 Queen's Rd., Hong Kong*
Christie's, *Cornelis Schuystraat 57, 1071 JG, Amsterdam*
Christie's East, *219 East 67th Street, New York, N.Y. 10021*
Christie's & Edmiston's, *164/166 Bath Street, Glasgow*
Christie's S. Kensington, *85 Old Brompton Road, London*
Coles, Knapp & Kennedy, *Georgian Rooms, Ross-on-Wye, Herefordshire*
Cooper Hirst, *Goldway House, Parkway, Chelmsford CM20 7PR*
County Group Estate Agents, *The Auction Sale Rooms, 102 High St., Tenterden, Kent*
Dacre, Son & Hartley, *1-5 The Grove, Ilkley, Yorkshire*
Dee & Atkinson, *The Exchange Saleroom, Driffield, Yorkshire*
Dickinson, Davy & Markham, *Elwes Street, Brigg, S. Humberside DN20 8LB*
Dreweatts, *Donnington Priory, Newbury, Berkshire RG13 2JE*
Hy. Duke & Son, *Weymouth Avenue, Dorchester, Dorset*
Du Mouchelles Art Galleries, *409 E. Jefferson, Detroit, Michigan 48226*
Elliott & Green, *40 High Street, Lymington, Hants*
R. H. Ellis & Sons, *44-46 High Street, Worthing, Sussex*
Frank H. Fellows & Son, *Bedford House, 88 Hagley Road, Edgbaston, Birmingham*
John D. Fleming & Co., *8 Fore Street, Dulverton, Somerset TA22 9EX*
Fox & Sons, *41 Chapel Road, Worthing*
Geering & Colyer, *22-24 High Street, Tunbridge Wells*
Goss & Crested China, *(N. J. Pine), 62 Murray Road, Horndean*
Andrew Grant, *59-60 Foregate Street, Worcester*

ANTIQUES REVIEW

Graves, Son & Pilcher, *71 Church Road, Hove, Sussex*
Giles Haywood, *The Auction House, St. John's Road, Stourbridge, W. Midlands DY8 1EW*
Heathcote Ball & Co., *The Old Rectory, Appleby Magna, Leicestershire*
Hobbs & Chambers, *'At the Sign of the Bell', Market Place, Cirencester GL7 1QQ*
John Hogbin & Son, *8 Queen Street, Deal, Kent*
Edgar Horn, *49-50 South Street, Eastbourne, Sussex*
Jacobs & Hunt, *Lavant Street, Petersfield, Hants*
Lalonde Fine Art, *The Auction Room, Oakfield Road, Bristol BS8 2BE*
W. H. Lane & Son, *64 Morrab Road, Penzance, Cornwall*
Lawrence Fine Art, *South Street, Crewkerne, Somerset TA18 8AB*
Locke & England, *Walton House, 11 The Parade, Leamington Spa*
Lots Road Chelsea Auction Galleries, *71 Lots Road, London*
Thomas Love & Son, *South St. John Street, Perth*
Mallams, *24 St. Michael's Street, Oxford*
May, Whetter & Grose, *Cornubia Hall, Par, Cornwall*
Morphets, *4-6 Albert Street, Harrogate, Yorkshire HG1 1JL*
Neales of Nottingham, *192 Mansfield Road, Nottingham*
D. M. Nesbit & Co., *7 Clarendon Road, Southsea, Hants*
Onslows, *123 Hursley, Winchester, Hants*
Outhwaite & Litherland, *Kingsway Galleries, Fontenoy Street, Liverpool L3 2BE*
Parsons, Welch & Cowell, *The Argyle Salerooms, Argyle Road, Sevenoaks, Kent*
Phillips, *Marylebone Auction Rooms, Hayes Place, London*
Phillips, *65 George Street, Edinburgh*
Phillips, *98 Sauchiehall Street, Glasgow*
Phillips, *Blenstock House, 7 Blenheim Street, New Bond St., London*
Phillips, *The Old House, Station Road, Knowle, Solihull, W. Midlands*
Phillips & Jolly's, *The Auction Rooms, 1 Old King Street, Bath*
Prudential Fine Art Auctioneers, *Millmead Auction Rooms, Guildford, Surrey*
John H. Raby & Sons, *21 St. Mary's Road, Bradford*
Reeds Rains, *Trinity House, 114 Northenden Road, Sale, Manchester M33 3HD*
Russell, Baldwin & Bright, *Ryelands Road, Leominster, Herefordshire*
Sandoe, Luce Panes, *Chipping Manor Salerooms, Wotton-under-Edge*
Robt. W. Skinner Inc., *Bolton Gallery, Route 117, Bolton, Mass.*
H. Spencer & Sons Ltd., *20 The Square, Retford, Notts.*
David Stanley Auctions, *Stordan Grange, Osgathorpe, Leics. LE12 9SR*
Street Jewellery, *10 Summerhill Terrace, Newcastle-upon-Tyne*
Stride & Son, *Southdown House, St. John's Street, Chichester, Sussex*
G. E. Sworder's & Sons, *19 North Street, Bishops Stortford, Herts*
Osmond Tricks, *Regent Street Auction Rooms, Clifton, Bristol BS8 4HG*
Vidler & Co., *Auction Offices, Cinque Ports St., Rye, Sussex*
Wallis & Wallis, *West Street Auction Galleries, Lewes, Sussex BN7 2NJ*
Ward & Partners, *16 High Street, Hythe, Kent*
Warner, Sheppard & Wade, *16-18 Halford Street, Leicester*
Peter Wilson Fine Art Auctioneers, *Victoria Gallery, Market Street, Nantwich CW5 5DG*
Woolley & Wallis, *The Castle Auction Mart, Castle Street, Salisbury*
Worsfolds Auction Galleries, *40 Station Road West, Canterbury*

ANTIQUES
REVIEW 1988

THE Lyle Official Antiques Review is compiled and published with completely fresh information annually, enabling you to begin each new year with an up-to-date knowledge of the current trends, together with the verified values of antiques of all descriptions.

We have endeavoured to obtain a balance between the more expensive collector's items and those which, although not in their true sense antiques, are handled daily by the antiques trade.

The illustrations and prices in the following sections have been arranged to make it easy for the reader to assess the period and value of all items with speed.

You will find illustrations for almost every category of antique and curio, together with a corresponding price collated during the last twelve months, from the auction rooms and retail outlets of the major trading countries.

When dealing with the more popular trade pieces, in some instances, a calculation of an average price has been estimated from the varying accounts researched.

As regards prices, when 'one of a pair' is given in the description the price quoted is for a pair and so that we can make maximum use of the available space it is generally considered that one illustration is sufficient.

It will be noted that in some descriptions taken directly from sales catalogues originating from many different countries, terms such as bureau, secretary and davenport are used in a broader sense than is customary, but in all cases the term used is self explanatory.

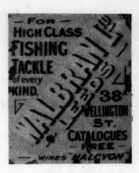

Royal Ediswan Lamps enamel advertising sign, 28 x 20in. (Onslow's) $82

A painted metal figure in 18th century costume, the body shaped as a bottle bearing a Guinness lable. (Christie's) $173

An advertising sign for Walbran Ltd., Leeds for High Class Fishing Tackle of every Kind, 30 x 24in. (Onslow's) $9

A pictorial tinplate sign for Green's Lawn Mowers, 18 x 24in. (Onslow's) $165

An enamel advertising sign for Puritan soap, 24 x 36in. (Onslow's) $33

An enamel advertising sign for Fry's Pure Breakfast Cocoa, 36 x 24in. (Onslow's) $13

Fry's Chocolate, pictorial Five Boys enamel sign, mounted on wood frame, 30 x 36in. (Onslow's) $150

A W. D. & H. O. Wills Westward Ho! Smoking Mixture, enamel sign, 36 x 18in. (Onslow's) $52

An enamel advertising sign for Royal Ediswan The King of Lamps, 28 x 20in. (Onslow's) $195

A painted wooden imitation 'Heinz Salad Cream' bottle, 48in. high. (Christie's) $282

A pictorial enamel advertising sign for Mew's, Isle of Wight, 40 x 28in. (Onslow's) $75

A pair of advertising plaques by T. J. & J. Mayer. (Phillips) $1,600

A pictorial advertisement for Ransomes' Lawn Mowers, The Best in The World, The Automatons and Anglo-Paris, 16½ x 21½in. (Onslow's) $210

An enamel advertising sign for Smilax cigarettes, 36 x 24in. (Onslow's) $45

A painted metal figure of a cockerel, plinth inscribed 'Courage, London & Country Brewers', 12½in. high. (Christie's) $141

An Eat Quaker Oats enamel sign, mounted on wood frame, 42 x 24in. (Onslow's) $27

After Gamy — Garros Gagne le Grand Prix de l'Aero Club, hand-colored lithograph, 17¾ x 35¾in. (Onslow's) $75

A 1:24th scale wood and metal model of the Royal Aircraft Factory SE5a, built by R. Walden, 1976. (Onslow's) $260

A flying scale model of the Gloster Gladiator single seater fighter Serial No. K.8032 with external details, finished in silver with R.A.F. markings, wingspan 56in. (Christie's) $581

1942 Vickers Supermarine Spitfire Mk. IX, constructor's number BR601, wingspan 36ft. 11in., length 31ft.4in. (Christie's) $111,390

Geoffrey Watson — Women's Royal Air Force, published by Employment Exchange, 30 x 20in. (Onslow's) $498

Blackpool Aviation Meeting, 1910, a silver cup with three reeded handles on acanthus legs, 8½in. diam. (Christie's) $1,551

Schneider Trophy, 1931, Official Souvenir Programme, together with two others. (Christie's) $155

Studio of Roy Nockolds — Supersonic, signed, on board — 16 x 20in. (Onslow's) $83

William Munro, Marine Aircraft design, 1st edition, plates, diagrams, some folding, 1933. (Onslow's) $377

Studio of Roy Nockolds — Hawker Fury 1 Serial No. K2074, signed and dated 1940, watercolor, 15 x 19in. (Onslow's) $51

After Gamy — Grand Prix de la Champagne, hand-colored lithograph, 17¾ x 35¾in. (Onslow's) $83

James Goulding, Vickers Vimy, airbrush drawing, signed, on board, five elevations, 21 x 15in. (Onslow's) $60

Bleriot Monoplane Type XI, engine 15 h.p. 3—cylinder air cooled 'Fan' type Anzani, wingspan 25ft., length 26ft. (Christie's) $18,330

W. G. Barrett — The Schneider Trophy, published by Pools Advertising Service Ltd., 30 x 20in. (Onslow's) $75

Geoffrey Watson — Special Shell Aviation Petrol, No. 356, published by Vincent Brooks Day & Son, 30 x 45in. (Onslow's) $166

The Aerial Derby, published by The Dangerfield Printing Co., London, '15, on linen, 29¾ x 20in. (Onslow's) $270

Peter Endsleigh Castle — Supermarine Spitfire Mk 1 AZH — N3277 over countryside, watercolor and gouache, 6 x 12in. (Onslow's) $90

Studio of Roy Nockolds — Sopwith Transport Ditched in the Sea near Shipping, signed, on board — 20 x 30in. (Onslow's) $30

Northwest coast polychrome wood face mask, carved and incised cedar, 9½in. high. (Robt. W. Skinner Inc.) $2,500

Southwestern coiled basketry bowl, Apache, woven in willow and devil's claw, 10¾in. diam. (Robt. W. Skinner Inc.) $450

Woodlands wood face mask, Seneca False Face Soc., 14in. high. (Robt. W. Skinner Inc.) $475

Classic Navajo chief's blanket, woven in single strand homespun and ravelled yarn, 82 x 62in. (Robt. W. Skinner Inc.) $30,000

A Verneh horse blanket, the blue field with rows of stylized animals, 5ft.5in. x 4ft.7in. (Christie's) $1,163

Navajo Yei rug, woven with two rows of opposing skirted Yeibachi figures in red, white and black on a natural gray ground, 66 x 96in. (Robt. W. Skinner Inc.) $950

Southwestern coiled basketry tray, Apache, 22½in. diam. (Robt. W. Skinner Inc.) $1,100

Navajo pictorial Germantown weaving with full yarn tassels on corners, 58 x 92in. (Robt. W. Skinner Inc.) $200

Southwestern polychromed jar, Acoma, 13¼in. diam. (Robt. W. Skinner Inc.) $1,100

Woodlands husk face mask, composed of bands of braided cornhusks, 11½in. high. (Robt. W. Skinner Inc.) $1,000

Southwestern coiled basketry bowl, Apache, woven in devil's claw, 14½in. diam. (Robt. W. Skinner Inc.) $700

Cherokee polychrome wood face mask, Boogerman Dance Mask, made by Will West Long, 16in. high. (Robt. W. Skinner Inc.) $550

Plains beaded hide blanket strip, Sioux, sinew sewn, 66in. long. (Robt. W. Skinner Inc.) $1,100

.Southwestern American Indian tempera painting signed Robert Chee, 15½ x 18½in. (Robt. W. Skinner Inc.) $550

Early 19th century Northern Plains pipe tomahawk, 18in. long. (Robt. W. Skinner Inc.) $3,400 £2,377

Navajo woman's manta, homespun, 33½ x 42in. (Robt. W. Skinner Inc.) $2,600

Southwestern polychrome male figure, Yuma, attached card reads 'Bought 1892 Albuquerque, New Mexico', 8¾in. high. (Robt. W. Skinner Inc.) $650

Navajo pictorial weaving, woven on a natural gray ground with geometric design motifs, 47 x 76in. (Robt. W. Skinner Inc.) $800

A pair of 19th century Japanese
iron stirrups abumi, inlaid overall with silver flowers and foliage,
interiors of red lacquered wood.
(Wallis & Wallis) $393

One of a pair of officer's
embossed gilt shoulder
scales of the Bengal Artillery.
(Wallis & Wallis) $293

A post 1902 officer's gilt and
silvered waist belt plate of
The 22nd Frontier Force
(Sam Browne's Cavalry).
(Wallis & Wallis) $177

A breastplate probably adapted in the early 19th century.
(Wallis & Wallis) $302

A pair of 17th century Indian
arm guards bazu band made
for a princeling, 10in. (Wallis
& Wallis) $286

Part of a Japanese suit of
armor.   (Wallis & Wallis)
$2,402

An American cowboy leather
saddle, circa 1875, body
blind stamped Moran Bros.,
Miles City M.T. (Montana
Territory). (Wallis & Wallis)
$1,930

An officer's full dress sporran of
The Argyll & Sutherland
Highlanders, in its tin case with
chamois leather lining. (Wallis &
Wallis) $668

An early 19th century Indo-
Persian gold damascened steel
shield dhal, 13¼in.. (Wallis &
Wallis) $224

A 17th/18th century mail coat with short sleeves. (Christie's) $267

An officer's full dress sporran of The Black Watch, gilt cantle with thistle border and St. Andrew in center, white goatshair. (Wallis & Wallis) $164

A Victorian Grenadier Guards officer's gilt and silvered waist belt clasp. (Wallis & Wallis) $122

A Victorian officer's full dress sabretache of The 18th Hussars, the inner flap with trade label of Hawkes & Co., Piccadilly. (Wallis & Wallis) $830

A 17th century Indian chiselled steel arm defence bazu band, 13in. (Wallis & Wallis) $91

A Continental articulated breastplate, circa 1700, of swollen form with medial ridge. (Wallis & Wallis) $302

A 17th century Continental breastplate with twin studs for fastening and shoulder straps. (Wallis & Wallis) $214

A Victorian Cavalry officer's silver mounted full dress shoulder belt and pouch of The 20th Hussars. (Wallis & Wallis) $402

One of a pair of Georgian officer's gilt bullion epaulettes of The 6th Dragoon Guards, circa 1825. (Wallis & Wallis) $374

Early 17th century pikeman's breastplate together with associated simulated five lame tassets. (Christie's) $846

An early 19th century Russian Bandsman's coatee of dark gray cloth with red facings, decorated with crimson and white lace. (Wallis & Wallis) $151

Part of an Imperial Russian diplomatic/court uniform. (Christie's) $841

A Georgian copy of a fully articulated and fluted 16th century Maximilian full suit of armor. (Wallis & Wallis) $7,150

Rifle Volunteers (probably 4th Norfolk Rifle Vol. Corps. circa 1872) Bugle-Major's uniform. (Christie's) $336

A Victorian full dress uniform of a Major-General, circa 1865. (Wallis & Wallis) $715

East Suffolk Militia officer's short-tailed scarlet coatee with yellow facings and white metal domed buttons. (Christie's) $720

A retainer's suit of 19th century Japanese armor with a wakizashi in a shagreen scabbard. (Outhwaite & Litherland) $667

An officer of The 2nd Bn. Highland Light Infantry's white cloth undress 'drill-jacket', together with a khaki service dress jacket. (Christie's) $259

An officer's full dress uniform items of The 10th Royal Hussars, together with metal uniform case. (Christie's) $2,142

A miniature suit of armor, 34in. (Wallis & Wallis) $402

The King's (Liverpool Regt.) 6th (Rifle) Bn. officer's busby, full dress tunic, Mess jacket and waistcoat, together with Captain's service dress. (Christie's) $720

DAGGERS

A late Victorian hunting dagger in the style of a Bowie knife, clipped back blade 7½in., stamped W. Thornhill & Co., London, one-piece natural staghorn hilt with silver pommel. (Wallis & Wallis) $100

A Bowie type knife, probably circa 1900, slender blade with false edge, white metal crosspiece with swollen finials, in its tooled green morocco leather sheath with white metal mounts. (Wallis & Wallis) $139

A Nazi S.A. dagger by Wilh. Wagner, Solingen Merschied, German silver mounts, in its metal sheath with single suspension strap, buckle and belt clip. (Wallis & Wallis) $128

A late 19th century S. American bush knife, massive Bowie shaped blade 12¼in., stamped no. 910–G, nickel hilt with eagle's head pommel and scale grip, in its tooled leather sheath. (Wallis & Wallis) $211

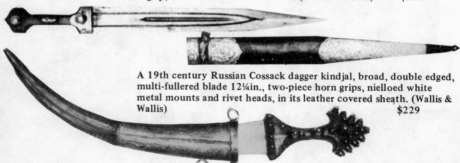

A 19th century Russian Cossack dagger kindjal, broad, double edged, multi-fullered blade 12¼in., two-piece horn grips, nielloed white metal mounts and rivet heads, in its leather covered sheath. (Wallis & Wallis) $229

A silver mounted Wahabite dagger jambiya, curved tapered double edged blade 16in., silver hilt chased with foliage and scale, in its sheath with silver top and brass bottom. (Wallis & Wallis) $612

An Eastern dagger with jade handle, carved lion's head pommel, in shagreen sheath with engraved metal mounts, overall length, 11in. (Chancellors Hollingsworths) $168

26

DAGGERS

A very rare 1856 pattern Naval officer's dirk, 35.5cm. blade by Galt, Portsmouth, with saw back edge, gilt mounted patent solid hilt with lion's head pommel, contained in its gilt mounted leather scabbard. (Phillips) $489

A Bowie knife, circa 1880, single edged clipped back blade 10¼in., stamped Arnachellum, Salem, one-piece staghorn hilt with silver lining to pommel shaped for thumb, in its blind tooled leather sheath. (Wallis & Wallis) $275

A post-1902 Scottish piper's dirk Mk.III, plain clipped back blade 12in., corded wood hilt mounted with German silver piquet studs, plated mounts, crown to pommel, in its patent leather covered wooden sheath. (Wallis & Wallis) $244

An Indian khanjar, recurved double edged polished blade with raised rib 12in., steel ferrule of shaped form with stylized twin scroll guard, pale green jade hilt, in its leather covered sheath. (Wallis & Wallis) $310

An Ottoman dagger, circa 1800, probably from the Caucasus, straight bi-fullered double edged blade 8¾in., one-piece ivory hilt carved with raised bands at forte, in its silver mounted cloth covered sheath with silver tape and wire sewn seam. (Wallis & Wallis) $62

A Mohammedan knife moplah from Malabar, sickle-shaped blade 12in., with chiselled decoration, bone hilt with turned and shaped brass ferrule, in its leather cover. (Wallis & Wallis) $135

An 18th century Persian dagger Kard, very finely watered polished single edged hollow ground blade 8¾in., of Kirk Nardaban pattern, steel grip-strap and bolsters, two-piece polished ivory grips. (Wallis & Wallis) $100

DAGGERS

A Nazi 2nd pattern Luftwaffe officer's dagger, by Holler, gray metal mounts, orange grip, in its gray metal sheath with original hanging strap and belt clip. (Wallis & Wallis) $125

An early 19th century Balinese kris, straight double edged blade with narrow central fuller and etched watered pamir, one-piece bone hilt, in its two-piece carved wooden sheath. (Wallis & Wallis) $232

A silver mounted Nepalese kukri, blade 11½in., brass mounted bone hilt, in its leather sheath with silver mounts. (Wallis & Wallis) $200

A Nazi Army officer's dagger, plated mounts, white celluloid grip, bullion dress knot, in its plated sheath with original hanging straps.   (Wallis & Wallis) $153

A cut-away exhibition knife, 39cm. curved blade signed on the ricasso Joseph Rogers & Sons, 6 Norfolk Street, Sheffield, England, gilt mounted hilt and diagonally ribbed ivory grip. (Phillips) $336

A 19th century S. Indian dagger, recurved double edged blade 6½in., shaped horn hilt mounted with brass, incorporating grotesque animal's head pommel, with bulging eyes. (Wallis & Wallis) $211

A Nazi Army officer's dagger, plated mounts, orange grip, in its plated sheath with original hanging straps and bullion dress knot. (Wallis & Wallis) $128

A post war Polish dress dagger, blade 9in., etched with Polish eagle, Honor I Ojczyna and scrolls, square brass hilt with straight crosspiece, yellow composition grip, squared brass pommel and mounts, in its black leather covered steel sheath. (Wallis & Wallis) $288

A Nazi Naval officer's dress dagger, double edged blade 10in., gilt hilt with eagle and swastika pommel and white celluloid covered grip, in its lacquered brass scabbard. (Wallis & Wallis) $191

An Indian Dravidian horn dagger, 12¾in., the integral grip with cut disc infilled with white clay decoration. (Wallis & Wallis) $67

An Indian dagger bichwa with bi-furcated blade 8in., loop shaped brass hilt with broad knuckle bow. (Wallis & Wallis) $85

A 19th century silver and gold mounted khanjar, the handle mounted in silver. (Parsons, Welch & Cowell) $539

A Nazi S.S. officer's 1936 model dagger, by Bertram Reinh., with German silver mounts, in its metal sheath with plated mounts and hanging chains with belt clip. (Wallis & Wallis) $981

A khanjar, 22cm. watered blade, milky white jade hilt with a floral pattern in gold, cabochon rubies and diamonds, contained in its cloth covered scabbard. (Phillips) $2,448

HELMETS

A post-1902 officer's blue cloth spiked helmet of The Bedfordshire Regt. (Wallis & Wallis) $271

A post-1902 trooper's helmet of The Life Guards, with white metal and brass helmet plate and plume. (Wallis & Wallis) $1,198

A post-1902 other rank's blue cloth ball-topped helmet of The Royal Army Medical Corps. Vols. (Wallis & Wallis) $170

A Prussian Jager Zu Pferd other rank's steel helmet, plated helmet plate and spike, date inside 1916. (Wallis & Wallis) $755

A trooper's helmet of The 1st (Royal) Dragoons, with black hair plume and rosette. (Wallis & Wallis) $514

An other rank's blue cloth spiked helmet of The 1st United States Infantry, circa 1900. (Wallis & Wallis) $158

A Nazi period black patent leather covered police shako, with aluminium helmet plate and mounts. (Wallis & Wallis) $57

A cabasset, circa 1600, formed in one-piece, 'pear stalk' finial to crown, brass rosettes around base. (Wallis & Wallis) $170

A French grey cloth kepi of the Swiss police, Bern maker's mark inside. (Wallis & Wallis) $15

A post-1902 officer's blue
cloth ball-topped helmet of
The Royal Army Medical
Corps. Vols. (Wallis & Wallis)
$236

A U.S. Military Academy
shako with gilt helmet plate,
numeral 5 within garter,
circa 1900. (Wallis & Wallis)
$177

An Victorian officer's blue
cloth ball-topped helmet of
The Vol. Medical Staff Corps.
(Wallis & Wallis) $325

A Bavarian Infantry officer's
pickelhaube, gilt helmet
plate, fluted spike and
mounts. (Wallis & Wallis)
$688

A French grey cloth covered
helmet of the Swiss police,
with gilt and enamel helmet
plate. (Wallis & Wallis)
$33

A Saxony Infantryman's
pickelhaube, gray metal
helmet plate, spike and
mounts. (Wallis & Wallis)
$286

An officer's peaked forage
cap of The Norfolk Regt.,
in its tin case. (Wallis &
Wallis) $391

A cabasset, circa 1600, in one-
piece, 'pear stalk' finial to
crown. (Wallis & Wallis)
$156

A French shako of the Garde
Republicaine, circa 1910,
black cloth with brass bound
peak. (Wallis & Wallis)
$43

HELMETS

A Bavarian Cavalryman's NCO's pickelhaube with lacquered brass helmet plate and leather backed chinscales and mounts. (Wallis & Wallis) $436

A French Mounted Gendarmerie brass helmet, circa 1900. (Wallis & Wallis) $505

A Wurttemberg Infantry Reservist officer's pickelhaube with gilt helmet plate and silvered Landwehr cross. (Wallis & Wallis) $666

A Nazi khaki cloth covered tropical helmet, with both metal shield Army badges. (Wallis & Wallis) $83

A Prussian Infantryman's Ersatz pickelhaube, gilt brass helmet plate, brass mounts and leather lining and chinstrap. (Wallis & Wallis) $177

A whitened French Fire Brigade or police helmet, of military pattern. (Wallis & Wallis) $15

A Victorian other rank's blue cloth ball-topped helmet of The Vol. Medical Staff. (Wallis & Wallis) $177

A German World War I Military 1916 steel helmet, first type triple padded lining. (Wallis & Wallis) $489

A fireman's brass helmet, by Merryweather. (Wallis & Wallis) $340

HELMETS

An Oldenberg Infantryman's pickelhaube, brass helmet plate with white metal arms imposed, with leather lining and chinstrap. (Wallis & Wallis) $273

A post war U.S. Naval officer's peaked cap with gilt and silvered badge and gilt side buttons. (Wallis & Wallis) $24

A Prussian Reservist Artillery officer's pickelhaube, gilt helmet plate, gilt mounts and with silk lining. (Wallis & Wallis) $604

A French officer's Fire Brigade helmet, blackened skull with white metal mounts, chrome and enamel coat-of-arms badge. (Wallis & Wallis) $27

An Edward VII trooper's helmet of The King's Own Norfolk Imperial Yeomanry. (Wallis & Wallis) $357

A khaki tropical helmet of The N. Rhodesia Police, with chromed ERII badge and dark blue puggaree. (Wallis & Wallis) $45

A Bavarian Engineer officer's pickelhaube, with silvered helmet plate, spike and leather and silk lining. (Wallis & Wallis) $429

A German state police black patent leather shako, bearing plate helmet plate and aluminium mounts. (Wallis & Wallis) $36

A post-1902 officer's blue cloth ball-topped helmet of The Royal Army Medical Corps. (Wallis & Wallis) $207

An officer's 1871 pattern helmet of The 3rd (Prince of Wales's) Dragoon Guards. (Wallis & Wallis) $1,630

An Indian Army officer's 1871 pattern helmet of The Scinde Horse. (Wallis & Wallis) $2,689

An other rank's helmet of The 3rd (Prince of Wales's) Dragoon Guards. (Wallis & Wallis) $554

A Prussian Guard Pioneer Bn. officer's pickelhaube. (Wallis & Wallis) $1,141

A plated French Sapeurs Pompiers helmet, bearing brass mounts and helmet plate. (Wallis & Wallis) $51

An officer's pickelhaube of The 3rd Bn. of The 92nd Brunswick Infantry. (Wallis & Wallis) $1,304

An officer's 1834 pattern helmet of The 1st or Royal Regt. of Dragoons. (Wallis & Wallis) $750

A Georgian officer's 1818 Roman, pattern helmet of The 7th (or Princess Royal's) Dragoon Guards. (Wallis & Wallis) $4,238

A Saxony Infantry officer's pickelhaube with gilt and silvered helmet plate. (Wallis & Wallis) $786

HELMETS

A post-1902 trooper's lance-cap of The 16th (The Queen's) Lancers. (Wallis & Wallis) $423

A Prussian Cuirassier officer's helmet, gilt eagle badge, chinscales and German silver fluted spike. (Wallis & Wallis) $2,502

A late Victorian officer's lance-cap of The 9th (Queen's Royal) Lancers. (Wallis & Wallis) $1,548

A Prussian Guard Artillery officer's pickelhaube, gilt guard eagle badge with enamelled center. (Wallis & Wallis) $1,144

A French Restoration period helmet of the Garde Nationale. (Wallis & Wallis) $1,430

A Military 1897 Wurttemberg Infantry officer's pickelhaube, brass helmet plate, spike and mounts. (Wallis & Wallis) $684

A City of London police blue cloth covered helmet, crested type with blackened brass mounts. (Wallis & Wallis) $114

A French model 1845 Second Empire Dragoon officer's helmet. (Wallis & Wallis) $2,860

An officer's 1843 pattern helmet of The 4th Royal Irish Dragoon Guards. (Wallis & Wallis) $3,423

A .30in. Luger semi-automatic pistol by Mauser, no. 10.002421, retailed by Interarms, 10½in., barrel 6in., with wooden grips, in its factory carton with stripping tool and booklet. (Wallis & Wallis) $372

A 5 shot 54-bore Adams model 1851 self-cocking percussion revolver, no. 13014, 12½in., barrel 6¾in., London proved, sprung hammer safety, one-piece chequered walnut grip with sprung cap trap. (Wallis & Wallis) $221

A .450/455 center fire double action 6-shot Webley & Scott target model revolver, no. 445960, barrel 7½in., brown bakelite grips, butt strap stamped Xlent, lanyard ring. (Wallis & Wallis) $356

A .455in. Webley Mark I double action center fire revolver, no. 1676, 9in., barrel 4in., molded bakelite grips. (Wallis & Wallis) $166

A Belgian 6 shot 11mm. double action pin fire revolver, 10½in. overall, barrel 6in., Liege proved, scroll engraved frame and cylinder, loading gate and ejector rod on right side, bag-shaped butt with chequered walnut grips. (Wallis & Wallis) $279

A 6 shot 80-bore single action long spur open frame transitional percussion revolver, 11½in. overall, octagonal barrel 5¼in., engraved Reilly, New Oxford St., London, London proved. (Wallis & Wallis) $312

A 9mm. long barrelled Artillery Luger, no. 818 and 566, 12½in., barrel 8in., dated 1917 at breech, sights to 800 m., swivel safety, frame not slotted for shoulder stock, two-piece chequered wooden grips. (Wallis & Wallis) $196

A 5 shot .31in. Nepperhan Fire Arms Co. single action percussion revolver, 11in. overall, barrel 6in., no. 1363, engraved frame, brass trigger guard, plain wood grips. (Wallis & Wallis) $302

A 6 shot .44in. Smith & Wesson Russian Model single action revolver, 12¼in., barrel 7in., patent dates to 1869, spurred trigger guard, two-piece wooden grips and steel lanyard ring. (Wallis & Wallis) $241

A .177in. Westley Richards 'Highest Possible' air pistol, no. 748, 11½in., barrel 9¾in. to breech, adjustable rearsight, two-piece chequered horn grips, in its original cardboard carton. (Wallis & Wallis) $267

A 6 shot .36in. Colt model 1851 British Military issue single action Navy percussion revolver, 13½in. overall, barrel 7½in., no. 187145, London proved. (Wallis & Wallis) $1,023

A 6 shot .36in. Savage double action Navy percussion revolver, 14½in. overall, barrel 7in., no. 6560, large trigger guard incorporating cocking lever, reciprocating cylinder and wood grips. (Wallis & Wallis) $422

A late 18th century 22-bore Scottish all-steel flintlock belt pistol of military quality, 11in. overall, barrel 7in., ram's horn butt, belt hook on left side, turned steel ramrod. (Wallis & Wallis) $858

A 16-bore East India Co. military flintlock holster pistol, 15½in. overall, barrel 9in., engraved with EIC mark and Henshaw 1802, Tower private proofs. (Wallis & Wallis) $314

A .65in. military pattern flintlock holster pistol, 15in. overall, barrel 9in., with Birmingham proofs, walnut fullstock with regulation brass mounts and swivel ramrod. (Wallis & Wallis) $300

A 22-bore flintlock holster pistol, 14in. overall, sighted octagonal twist barrel 8¼in., with false breech and gold lined touch hole, plain walnut fullstock with slightly flattened chequered butt, steel mounts, horn tipped wooden ramrod. (Wallis & Wallis) $422

A 22-bore Queen Anne type cannon barrelled flintlock holster pistol, 12in. overall, turn-off barrel 5½in., engraved Willets at breech, side action with swan neck cock and L-shaped frizzen spring. (Wallis & Wallis) $550

A .56in. Tower short flintlock Sea Service belt pistol, 16in. overall, barrel officially reduced to 9in. with Tower proofs, the lock stamped with crowned GR and Tower, fullstocked with regulation brass mounts, original steel ramrod and belt hook. (Wallis & Wallis) $572

A Belgian 12-bore military flintlock holster pistol, circa 1840, 15½in. overall, barrel 9in., with Liege proofs, plain slightly rounded lock with swan neck cock, plain fullstock with no provision for ramrod. (Wallis & Wallis) $128

PISTOLS

A 40-bore Scottish all-steel Highland Dress flintlock belt pistol, circa 1830, 10½in. overall, barrel 6½in., with polygonal muzzle and breech, flat lock with roller on frizzen spring. (Wallis & Wallis) $1,007

A brass barrelled 22-bore flintlock holster pistol, circa 1780, 13in. overall, barrel 7½in. with Tower private proofs. (Wallis & Wallis) $372

A 16-bore flintlock holster pistol, by Barbar, circa 1740, 16in., stepped swamped barrel 10in., London proved, maker's mark I.B. beneath star. Fullstocked, lock engraved Barbar, unbridled frizzen and brass furniture. (Wallis & Wallis) $290

A 36-bore silver plated all-steel Scottish Highland Dress flintlock belt pistol, circa 1820, 10½in. overall, barrel 6½in., with 12 sided breech, ball trigger, ram's horn butt with pricker and turned steel ramrod. (Wallis & Wallis) $536

A 14-bore percussion boxlock sidehammer belt pistol, 11in. overall, octagonal twist barrel 5½in., Birmingham proved, scroll engraved frame, hammer and trigger guard, swivel ramrod, belt hook, chequered walnut butt with flared end. (Wallis & Wallis) $201

A 16-bore East India Co. military percussion holster pistol, 15½in. overall, barrel 9in., with London proofs, plain flat lock stamped with rampant lion, fullstocked with regulation brass mount. (Wallis & Wallis) $279

A Caucasian 20-bore flintlock holster pistol, 18in. overall, barrel 10½in., with spurious proof marks at breech, flat lock with date 1829. (Wallis & Wallis) $715

A 16mm. French military flintlock holster pistol, dated 1817, 9½in., barrel 5in., fullstocked, regulation lock engraved Manuf. Royal Mauberge, brass pan, frizzen face roughened with a punch, regulation steel mounts and ramrod. (Wallis & Wallis) $688

A .56in. Tower Sea Service percussion belt pistol, 11½in. overall, barrel 6in., with Tower proofs, plain walnut stock and regulation brass mounts. (Wallis & Wallis) $257

A silver mounted 18-bore flintlock holster pistol, circa 1765, 14½in. overall, barrel 9in. with London and maker's proofs, plain fullstock with bulbous butt and steel trigger guard. (Wallis & Wallis) $459

A 28-bore percussion boxlock side hammer belt pistol, circa 1850, 10¼in. overall, octagonal barrel 5½in., engraved Blissett, London, scroll engraved frame and hammer, belt hook on left of frame, London proved. (Wallis & Wallis) $134

A French 20-bore model 1842 percussion Gendarmerie pistol, 9½in. overall, barrel 5in., dated 1849 at breech, back action lock, three-quarter stocked with plain steel mounts. (Wallis & Wallis) $309

A late 18th century 14-bore flintlock holster pistol, 14½in. overall, sighted octagonal barrel 9¼in., plain fullstock and rounded butt, engraved brass mounts, including trigger guard with pineapple finial. (Wallis & Wallis) $302

A flintlock boxlock pocket pistol, 6½in. overall, turn-off barrel 1½in., with fern leaf engraved muzzle, Birmingham proved, scroll engraved frame with I. Mace, Reading, in ovals, hidden trigger and top thumb safety. (Wallis & Wallis) $627

An officer's 16-bore percussion holster pistol, by E. London, originally made as flintlock circa 1820, 14½in. overall, heavy octagonal twist barrel 9in. engraved at breech with skull and crossbones. (Wallis & Wallis) $550

A 20-bore French model 1837 percussion Naval pistol, 11½in. overall, barrel 6½in., stamped Mle. 1837 on breech tang, back action lock, halfstocked with brass barrel band, trigger guard and buttcap. (Wallis & Wallis) $437

A .56in. Tower percussion Sea Service belt pistol, 11½in. overall, barrel 6in. with Tower proofs, the lock engraved with crowned VR and Tower 1846, fullstocked with regulation brass mounts, swivel ramrod, lanyard ring on buttcap. (Wallis & Wallis) $286

A flintlock boxlock three-barreled pistol, 7.5cm. turn-off barrels, frame engraved with trophies of arms and signed Twigg, London, pan selector on left, sliding safety, slab sided wood butt. (Phillips) $550

A Belgian bronze barrelled and bronze framed flintlock boxlock pocket pistol, 6½in. overall, barrel 2½in., with raised muzzle ring, Liege proved. (Wallis & Wallis) $226

41

POWDER FLASKS

A gun sized copper powder flask, 6¼in., plain lacquered body, nozzle adjustable from 2 to 2¾ drams. (Wallis & Wallis) $114

An early 18th century Scandinavian carved powder horn, 8½in. overall. (Wallis & Wallis) $843

A copper pocket powder flask, 3½in., shaped body, brass top fixed nozzle with gnurled band. (Wallis & Wallis) $105

An 18th century staghorn powder flask, 10½in. overall, with two horn hanging loops. (Wallis & Wallis) $178

A 19th century copy of a German 17th century musketeer's triangular powder flask, 11in. high. (Wallis & Wallis) $28

A 17th century Italian fluted steel powder flask, 7in. overall. (Wallis & Wallis) $471

A 3-way copper pistol flask of the type cased with late duelling pistols. (Wallis & Wallis) $154

A Spanish 18th century powder flask, made from a section of Ibex or similar horn, 10½in. overall. (Wallis & Wallis) $114

A copper gun sized powder flask, 8in., patent brass top, graduated nozzle. (Wallis & Wallis) $171

A copper powder flask 'Panel' (R.504), lacquered brass universal pattern charger unit. (Wallis & Wallis) $113

An early 19th century brass mounted rifleman's powder horn, 11in. overall, charger for 1 to 4 drams. (Wallis & Wallis) $45

An engraved bone Continental powder flask, circa 1600, 6¾in. tall. (Wallis & Wallis) $326

An 18th century engraved bone powder flask, 8¼in. overall, with six hanging rings. (Wallis & Wallis) $150

A large copper gun sized powder flask, 8¼in., embossed overall with basket weave, nozzle graduated 3 to 4 drams. (Wallis & Wallis) $89

An 18th century staghorn powder flask, 9in. overall, wooden charger and iron hanging loops. (Wallis & Wallis) $114

A pistol sized copper powder flask, 4¾in., lacquered brass top stamped 'Dixon & Sons', with adjustable nozzle. (Wallis & Wallis) $122

An 18th century staghorn powder flask, 7½in. overall, with small down turned nozzle and iron hanging loops. (Wallis & Wallis) $42

A 17th century Italian brass mounted steel powder flask, 7in. overall, with belt hook. (Wallis & Wallis) $343

ARMS & ARMOR

A 10-bore military style percussion musket, 51½in. overall, barrel 36in., with Birmingham proofs, the flat lock deeply stamped with crown and Tower proof, fullstocked with regulation brass mounts, steel ramrod and sling swivels. (Wallis & Wallis) $226

A .577in. Enfield 3 band military percussion rifle, 55½in. overall, barrel 39in., with Tower proofs, folding ladder rearsight, fullstocked, with steel barrel bands retaining locking springs, sling swivels and original steel ramrod. (Wallis & Wallis) $543

A brass barrelled flintlock blunderbuss, 39.5cm. two-stage barrel inscribed No. 59 Lombard St., London, plain lock signed W. Bond, full-stocked with brass mounts. (Phillips) $872

A .577in. Snider breech loading rifle, 49in., barrel 30in., military proofs, ladder rearsight to 900 yds., fullstocked, regulation steel mounts, bayonet lug on barrel, stock stamped with Enfield storekeeper's marks and sale marks. (Wallis & Wallis) $332

A mid 19th century 26-bore military style flintlock trade musket or fusil, 54½in. overall, slender barrel 39in., with Birmingham proofs, fullstocked with regulation style brass mounts, sling swivels. (Wallis & Wallis) $257

A 20-bore Continental percussion Jaeger rifle, 46½in., octagonal barrel 31½in., halfstocked, foliate border engraved lock, brass furniture and carved cheekpiece. (Wallis & Wallis) $614

RIFLES

An American made P.53 Enfield 3-band military percussion rifle, 55½in.
overall, barrel 39in., with stepped elevating rearsight, fullstocked with
three steel barrel bands, brass mounts and steel ramrod. (Wallis & Wallis)
$852

A mid 18th century Continental iron barrelled military flintlock musketoon,
46½in. overall, barrel 31in. with horizontal elliptical muzzle, rounded banana
shaped lock, fullstocked with plain iron mounts. (Wallis & Wallis) $528

A 12-bore double-barreled back action percussion sporting gun, by C; Townley
of Lancaster, 46½in., browned twist barrels 30in., halfstocked, dolphin hammers,
foliate engraved steel furniture with pointer on trigger guard. (Wallis & Wallis)
$371

A .303in. Enfield Mk. 1 bolt action Cavalry carbine, no. 2374, 40in.,
barrel 21in., the butt with Birmingham 1902 and broad arrow mark.
(Wallis & Wallis) $257

A 10-bore Militia Brown Bess flintlock musket, circa 1800, of the Whitehaven
Local Militia, 55in. overall, barrel 39in., with Tower private proofs. (Wallis &
Wallis) $858

A .303in. No. 5 Mk. 1 bolt action jungle carbine, no. 00371, 40¼in.,
barrel 20½in., including flash hider, the frame stamped F.R. 1960 R.F.I.
(Wallis & Wallis) $143

A double-barreled 16-bore boxlock ejector sporting gun, by W. Powell , Birmingham, no. 12999, 45in., barrels 28in., top lever opening, chequered small and fore-end. (Wallis & Wallis) $437

A 6.5mm. Swedish Mauser bolt action military rifle, no. HK 383341, 49½in., barrel 29in., elevating rearsight to 600m., plain wood fullstock, with its cleaning rod. (Wallis & Wallis) $71

A French 12-bore model 1822 military musket converted to percussion, 56in. overall, barrel 40½in., dated 1831 at breech, fullstocked with three barrel bands, iron mounts, sling swivels, original iron ramrod. (Wallis & Wallis) $302

A .65in. Enfield pattern 1859 smooth-bore musket for Indian native infantry, 54½in. overall, barrel 39in., with fixed rearsight and plain triangular foresight, fullstocked, with three barrel bands, regulation brass mounts. (Wallis & Wallis) $203

An American .40in. percussion target rifle, no. 1840, 49in. overall, heavy octagonal barrel 32¾in., including 1in. false muzzle, with traces of P. Smith, Buffalo, elevating ratchet rearsight, plain rosewood halfstock. (Wallis & Wallis) $386

A .577in. Enfield 2 band military percussion rifle, 49in. overall, barrel 33in., with Tower proofs, folding ladder rearsight, fullstocked, brass mounts, sling swivels, steel ramrod. (Wallis & Wallis) $513

A double-barreled 12-bore Needham's Patent breech loading needle fire sporting gun, no. 1082, 47½in., twist barrels, 28¾in. to breeches, halfstocked, foliate engraved furniture, engraved silver escutcheon, chequered small and bolted fore with horn tip. (Wallis & Wallis) **$765**

A .577in. Enfield 3-band military percussion rifle, 54in. overall, barrel 39in., with elevating rearsight, fullstocked with brass mounts, sling swivels and original steel ramrod. (Wallis & Wallis) **$443**

A double-barreled 21-bore percussion rifle, 72cm. damascus sighted barrels, signed John Dickson & Son, 60 Princes Street, Edinburgh, folding leaf rear sights to 200 yds., complete with its brass tipped wooden ramrod, in its oak case. (Phillips) **$994**

A .177in. Britannia barrel break air rifle, no. 513, 36in., barrel 21in., stamped with 30 to 60 yds. on leaf rearsight. (Wallis & Wallis) **$196**

An American .38in. percussion 'Plains' sporting or target rifle, circa 1840, 49in. overall, heavy octagonal barrel 33in., with fixed sights and stamped at breech H. Jarecki Erie PA. (Wallis & Wallis) **$357**

A 20-bore double-barreled French silver mounted flintlock sporting gun, 48in. barrels 31½in., halfstocked, locks engraved Dupont a Paris, with Canon Tordu faintly on barrels. Silver furniture hallmarked with maker's mark LD. (Wallis & Wallis) **$943**

ARMS & ARMOR

A 10-bore Volunteer Brown Bess military flintlock musket, 55½in. overall, barrel 39in., with Tower private proofs, fullstocked, with regulation pattern brass mounts apart from oval escutcheon and flat sideplate. (Wallis & Wallis) $634

A .577in. 3 band single shot Snider rifle, 55½in., barrel 37in., Turkish stamp on breech block, graduated rearsight, ladder bears Arabic numbering, steel and brass furniture, fullstock. (Wallis & Wallis) $98

A .451in. Whitworth's Patent hexagonal bore percussion target rifle, 52½in. overall, barrel 36in., with Birmingham proofs, folding rack and pinion rearsight to 1200 yds., adjustable fore-sight, bolted lock, walnut fullstock. (Wallis & Wallis) $1,585

A 24-bore single-barreled percussion sporting rifle by Wm. Holland, 43½in., rebrowned octagonal twist barrel 27in., with leaf sights, halfstocked, steel furniture, scrolled trigger guard, chequered small white metal forecap. (Wallis & Wallis) $371

A double-barreled 12-bore x 2½in. nitro proved top lever opening boxlock non-ejector sporting gun, by Charles Boswell, 46½in., steel barrels 30in., chequered small and fore of stock, auto safe. (Wallis & Wallis) $719

A .44in. Cal. Colt Lightning rifle, no. 56456, 43in., round barrel 26in., chequered wood pump action, wood butt, patent dates to Feb. 22. 1887. (Wallis & Wallis) $362

RIFLES

A .45in. Martini Enfield 2 band single shot military rifle, no. A 825, 48½in., barrel 33in., polished wood fullstock, barrel band bayonet lug, long underlever various stampings on butt (some Eastern). (Wallis & Wallis) $181

A double-barreled 12-bore x 2½in. nitro proved top lever self-opening Lancaster's Patent hammerless ejector sporting gun. no. 12031, 45½in., steel barrels 28in., auto safe, chequered small and fore. (Wallis & Wallis) $780

A 12-bore Russian Crimean War period military percussion musket, 57in. overall, barrel 41½in., converted from flintlock, the lock stamped C.T.P.N.K. 1838, fullstocked with brass mounts. (Wallis & Wallis) $371

A .577in. Snider breech loading rifle, 55½in., barrel 36½in., Birmingham proved, ladder rearsight to 800 yds., regulation brass mounts, steel barrel bands and brass tipped steel cleaning rod. (Wallis & Wallis) $218

A .577in. Snider breech loading rifle, 55in., barrel 36in., Birmingham proved, ladder sight to 800 yds., lock stamped BSACo., regulation brass mounts, steel barrel bands and steel cleaning rod. (Wallis & Wallis) $135

A .55in. British Military Contract Sharp's patent breech loading percussion carbine, 35½in. overall, barrel 18in., with Tower proofs at breech, four folding leaf rearsights. (Wallis & Wallis) $906

ARMS & ARMOR

A last pattern Edward VII Naval cutlass, straight blade 27½in., Enfield and Ordnance stamps at forte, issue mark for 1903, solid steel bowl guard, diced black leather grips. (Wallis & Wallis) $92

An 1821 pattern Heavy Cavalry trooper's sword, curved single edged blade 36½in., solid steel bowl guard, steel mounts, ribbed leather covered grip, in its steel scabbard. (Wallis & Wallis) $543

A French officer's Courtsword, circa 1820, straight single edged blade 31in., gilt hilt with shell guard chiselled with classical figures, lion's head quillon, knight's helmet pommel, diced ebony grip inset with standing figure of Victory. (Wallis & Wallis) $149

A Victorian 1827 pattern Rifle Vol. officer's sword, blade 33in., by Firmin & Sons, with steel hilt and wirebound fishskin covered grip, in its leather covered Field Service metal scabbard. (Wallis & Wallis) $178

A George V 1827 pattern Rifle Vol. officer's sword, blade 31½in., plated hilt, white metal wirebound fishskin covered grip, in its black leather Field Service scabbard. (Wallis & Wallis) $279

A George V 1854 pattern Coldstream Guards officer's sword, blade 33in., by Henry Wilkinson, plated hilt, wirebound fishskin covered grip, in its leather covered Field Service scabbard. (Wallis & Wallis) $226

An 1821 pattern Militia Artillery officer's sword, curved fullered polished blade 35½in., regulation steel hilt, woven wirebound sharkskin covered grip, in its steel scabbard with two hanging rings. (Wallis & Wallis) $128

Late 19th century American Society sword, curved fullered single edged blade, 27½in., copper gilt triple bar guard, lion's head pommel, wirebound sharkskin covered grip, in its steel scabbard. (Wallis & Wallis)
$153

A Victorian officer's sword of The 6th Dragoon Guards, as carried 1877-1912, curved blade 34in., pierced steel guard and mounts, copper wirebound fishskin covered grip, in its steel scabbard. (Wallis & Wallis)
$543

A French ANXI Cuirassier sword, straight double fullered blade 38½in., with spear point, brass hilt with triple bar guard, brass wirebound leather covered grip, in its steel scabbard. (Wallis & Wallis)
$188

A Victorian trooper's sword of The 3rd Bengal Cavalry, straight single edged blade 35in., stamped Wilkinson, Pall Mall, diced black leather grip, in its leather scabbard with steel mounts. (Wallis & Wallis)
$310

An Elizabeth II R.A.F. officer's sword, blade 32in., by Wilkinson Sword, gilt hilt, eagle's head pommel, bullion dress knot, gilt wirebound fishskin covered grip, in its leather scabbard with three gilt mounts. (Wallis & Wallis) $271

A French 1822 pattern Heavy Cavalry trooper's sabre, slightly curved blade 39in., broad and short fullers, brass hilt with triple bar guard, ribbed leather covered grip, in its steel scabbard. (Wallis & Wallis) $181

A George V R.A. officer's sword, blade 34in., by Henry Wilkinson, no. 53269, with wirebound fishskin covered grip in its leather covered Field Service scabbard. (Wallis & Wallis)
$163

ARMS & ARMOR

An o-wakizashi, signed Nobutaka (of Owari, late 16th century), 51cm. long, koshirae, pine-needle design saya with three ribbed shakudo seme and elongated kojiri. (Christie's) $1,504

A Bronze Age sword, 26in. overall, swollen blade of elliptical section with stepped edges, incomplete tang pierced for attachment. (Wallis & Wallis) $446

A 14th century katana attributed to Tegai Kanenaga of Yamato, 68.3cm. long, the saya with horn kojiri and koiguchi. (Christie's) $3,168

A handachi wakizashi, the blade inscribed Suishinshi Hakuyu Nyudo Masahide saku, 49.5cm. long, koshirae, mijingai-nuri saya with impressed brown leather koshimaki and sahari-ishimeji fittings. (Christie's) $4,435

A daisho with fine Higo-style koshirae, probably by Bizen Kiyomitsu, with a date, Teiwa ninen (1346), but 16th century, 71.5cm. long. (Christie's) $7,128

A tachi with unsigned 19th century Bizen blade, 70.7cm. long, with shari-nashiji scabbard with aoimon and umemon, with silvered metal mounts and gilt crane menuki. (Christie's) $4,118

A 19th century Persian all-steel shamshir, watered steel blade 28½in., inlaid with two brass maker's cartouches, steel hilt with down-turned zoomorphic quillons. (Wallis & Wallis) $135

A Bronze Age sword, 16½in. overall, tapered blade of elliptical section with stepped edges, swollen tang retaining two large bronze rivets for retaining hilt. (Wallis & Wallis) $864

52

SWORDS

A wakizashi, by Yokoyama Sukenaga, dated Tempo kunen (1838), 48.6cm. long, with kuroronuri saya and brocade bag. (Christie's) $6,019

A Bronze Age sword, 16½in. overall, very slightly swollen blade with raised broad flattened rib, swollen tang with eroded areas representing twin rivet holes. (Wallis & Wallis) $446

Late 16th century katana with fine shakudo fittings, 68.1cm. long, koshirae, kuroronuri saya decorated with a dragon in hiramakie and with mokkogata shakudo-nanakoji tsuba. (Christie's) $3,009

A silver mounted dha, 54cm. blade, silver wrapped hilt with bands of filigree decoration, large fluted silver pommel, contained in its wood scabbard. (Phillips) $367

A 19th century Saudi Arabian saif with curved steel blade, the silver mounted hilt and scabbard with formal engraving, overall 34in. (Parsons, Welch & Cowell) $616

Late 14th century sun-nobi tanto blade with carved ebony and ivory koshirae, inscribed Hiromitsu, but probably Soshu school, 34.7cm. long, the saya, 19th century. (Christie's) $1,425

An Indian shamsir, 76cm. blade damascened in silver at the forte with foliage, gilt metal hilt, contained in its gilt scabbard. (Phillips) $198

Early 17th century o-wakizashi, signed Kanesaki (of Mino), 52.6cm. long, with kuroronuri saya decorated in hiramakie with three tiny frogs in flight from a large serpent, the hilt with buffalo horn kashira and shiiremono fuchi. (Christie's) $1,425

ARMS & ARMOR

A Nazi Army officer's sword, plated curved blade 32in., by Holler, gilt
metal hilt with stirrup knucklebow, oak leaf decoration, army eagle
langet, copper wirebound black grip, in its black painted steel scabbard.
(Wallis & Wallis) $162

An early 18th century Spanish transitional rapier, flattened diamond
shaped blade 30¾in., stamped En Toledo, large shell guards,
knucklebow and recurved quillons with baluster devices, and steel
wirebound grip.   (Wallis & Wallis) $327

A Nazi Police officer's sword, blade 31in., by Emil Voos Solingen,
retaining all its original plating, plated hilt, aluminium wirebound
blackened wood grip with inset Police badge, in its plated mounted
black painted scabbard. (Wallis & Wallis) $321

A late 17th century broadsword, thin tapering double edged
blade 35in. with fullers at forte, large single shell guard with
thumb loop to side, swollen faceted pommel and woven
steel wirebound grip. (Wallis & Wallis) $357

An 1827 Naval pattern Victorian officer's sword of the
P. & O. Steam Navigation Co., slightly curved single
edged blade, 28½in., by Hogg, St. James' St., London.
(Wallis & Wallis) $586

A Georgian Dragoon officer's sword, circa 1780, straight single
edged double fullered blade 32in., copper gilt hilt, faceted
ovoid pommel, silver wirebound grip, in its leather scabbard.
(Wallis & Wallis) $542

ARMS & ARMOR

A Victorian 1831 pattern General's mameluke sabre, curved clipped back blade 33in., by Ranken & Co., Calcutta, with ivory grips, in its brass scabbard. (Wallis & Wallis) $312

A Georgian 1803 pattern General's sword, curved blade 29in., copper gilt hilt with slotted guard, lion's head pommel, copper wirebound grip, in its leather scabbard with three copper gilt mounts. (Wallis & Wallis) $542

An early 19th century European Cavalry trooper's sabre, plain single edged curved blade 31½in., plain steel hilt with double loop guard, ribbed leather covered grip, in its steel scabbard. (Wallis & Wallis) $100

A Persian 19th century sword shamshir, curved blade 31½in., with two bands of gold damascened inscriptions. Steel grip strap, crosspiece and pommel, two-piece horn grips, in its leather covered scabbard. (Wallis & Wallis) $307

An 1897 pattern George VI Infantry officer's sword, blade 31in., by Wilkinson, no. 68386, plated hilt, wirebound fishskin covered grip, leather dress knot, in its leather covered Field Service scabbard with Sam Browne frog. (Wallis & Wallis) $325

An English Cavalry backsword, circa 1750, straight slightly tapering double fullered single edged blade, 33½in., iron basket guard with plain pommels, flattened circular panels and wooden grip. (Wallis & Wallis) $447

TSUBAS

A 19th century Aorigata
iron tsuba, signed Hojusai
Masakage, 7.3cm.
(Christie's) $1,742

A 17th century Hayashi tsuba,
the ume-no-ki or plum tree
design with gilt-nunome-zogan,
7.5cm. diam. (Christie's)
$601

A rounded square Shibuichi-
Migakiji tsuba, circa 1800,
6.9cm. (Christie's)
$871

An 18th century circular iron
tsuba, signed Bushu ju Masatsune, 7.5cm. diam., and a 17th
century tsuba. (Christie's)
$601

A 17th/18th century oval
copper Shoami tsuba,
6.9cm. (Christie's)
$285

A circular pierced iron Sukashi
tsuba, signed Masatsune, chiselled with corn, 7.7cm. (Wallis &
Wallis) $149

A 19th century circular iron
Migakiji tsuba, 7.4cm. diam.,
and an iron tsuba. (Christie's)
$475

A late Kamiyoshi style tsuba,
hanagiri and ume in yosukashi,
8cm. diam., and a mokkogata
tsuba. (Christie's) $506

An oval iron tsuba, carved
in relief with a flowering
lotus in a stream, 8.2cm.
(Wallis & Wallis) $126

TSUBAS

A 16th/17th century pierced circular iron tsuba, Kyoto School, 8.1cm. (Wallis & Wallis) $119

A 19th century oval Shakudo-Nanakoji tsuba, 7.2cm. (Christie's) $1,346

An 18th century Rokumokko iron tsuba, six butterflies in ikizukashi, 8.1cm. diam., and an oval iron tsuba. (Christie's) $300

A circular pierced iron Akasaka sukashi tsuba, depicting Lake Biwa beneath the moon, 7.8cm. (Wallis & Wallis) $104

A circular pierced iron choshu tsuba, chiselled with chrysanthemum growing by a fence, 8.6cm. (Wallis & Wallis) $149

A circular pierced iron tsuba, carved with thistles and an insect, 7.6cm. (Wallis & Wallis) $74

A pierced iron tsuba, signed Bushu ju Masakuni, chiselled with flowering cherry blossom, 7.6cm. (Wallis & Wallis) $149

A 19th century oval iron tsuba, ikizukashi, signed Choshu Hagi ju Tomoaki, 7cm., and a circular Shoami tsuba, and an oval iron Namban tsuba.(Christie's) $601

A 19th century oval copper Ishimeji tsuba with fitted silver rim, 7.5cm. (Christie's) $712

A Japanese polearm yari, trident head 18.4cm., signed Bushu Noju, Masakane Suki, tempered, the wings pierced for suspension of prayers. Overall length 97in., top inlaid with mother-of-pearl segments and with copper mounts. (Wallis & Wallis) $157

An early 19th century Persian qjar chiselled steel axe, 29¼in., crescent head 8in. chiselled on each side with large cartouche of Islamic script, Steel haft of alternate octagonal and roped sections with bulbous finials. (Wallis & Wallis) $164

A brass and turned wooden tipstave, 11in., cylindrical brass top surmounted by gnurled ball with flaming brass device, turned wooden grip. (Wallis & Wallis) $226

A Nazi Wehrmacht dress bayonet, plated blade 9½in., by Horster, plated mounts, stylized 'eagle's head' pommel, staghorn grip, in its black painted steel scabbard with leather frog. (Wallis & Wallis) $103

A French partizan, circa 1700, 55½in., head 13½in., central blade with raised ribs, down turned and upturned crescents, wavy side pieces. The steel haft is a 42in. barrel from a Brown Bess. (Wallis & Wallis) $128

An early Fiji missile club ulas, 15in., of patinated hardwood, with swollen head, slightly flared grip, carved with zig-zag decoration in relief. (Wallis & Wallis) $54

A 19th century Persian steel axe, 30in., crescent head 7¼in., chiselled with cartouches of Islamic script. Steel haft filed with faceted and whorled sections. (Wallis & Wallis) $244

A Nazi Police dress bayonet, plated blade 12½in., by Carl Eickhorn, white metal mounts, staghorn grips with police emblem, 'eagle's head' pommel, in its leather scabbard with white metal mounts and a dress knot. (Wallis & Wallis) $192

An 18th century Indian 'Elephant knife' bhuj from Sind, 25¼in. overall, broad recurved blade 7½in. with false edge, on its steel haft, the copper gilt lotus pommel unscrews to reveal an 11in. stiletto. (Wallis & Wallis) $260

A 19th century Persian steel axe, 30in., crescent head 6½in., steel haft filed with facets and spiral lines in alternate sections. (Wallis & Wallis) $206

A U.S. M.1917 Bolo bayonet, blade 10½in., by Plumb, Phila., 1918, with wood grip, in its canvas covered scabbard, the leather tip stamped 1917. (Wallis & Wallis) $96

A Victorian universal pattern painted Police truncheon, 18½in., with post 1837 crowned Royal Arms and 'Police'. (Wallis & Wallis)$42

A 19th century Persian qjar etched steel axe, 34in., crescent head 8¼in., etched with two mounted horsemen clashing with shamshirs, dhals, axes, severed limbs. Square section top spike, hollow zoomorphic backpiece, steel haft with swollen pommel. (Wallis & Wallis) $114

An 18th century Austrian parade lance, leaf shaped head 8¼in. etched Vivat Gothenburg above the Imperial eagle, baluster socket with long straps on later 42in. section of haft. (Wallis & Wallis) $151

A William IV turned wooden tipstave, 13¾in., black painted with gilt and red WR, crowned IV. (Wallis & Wallis) $72

A sword bayonet for the Jacobs double barrelled rifle, double edged, fullered blade, 30in., pierced steel guard, double hole in quillon, diced leather grips. (Wallis & Wallis) $351

ARMS & ARMOR

A 19th century Sudanese mace Shishpar, 19½in., of all steel construction, six bladed swollen head with top spike. Octagonal haft with crocodile skin covered pommel. (Wallis & Wallis) $130

An 18th century Madrasi Khandah hilted all steel mace, 34½in., head of 8 flanges, shaped with long, fluted quatrefoil section top spike and fluted steel haft. (Wallis & Wallis) $217

An old Maori carved wood club meri, 14½in., the back carved with a standing figure in the round, with protruding tongue pointing sideways. (Wallis & Wallis) $293

A German target crossbow, heavy steel bow of 89.5cm. span, walnut stock with brass mounts including scroll trigger guard, peephole rear sight, double set triggers, 83.5cm. overall. (Phillips) $581

A Maori hand club Meri or Patu, made from the jaw bone of sperm whale, 14¾in., thin swollen blade with thickened flared grip, pierced for wrist cord. (Wallis & Wallis) $511

A model cannon, turned bronze barrel 7½in., engraved 'Relic of Royal George. Sunk 1782 Raised 1840', swollen muzzle and cascabel. (Wallis & Wallis) $128

An 18th century Fiji missile club Ulas, 16½in., swollen multi-ribbed head with bulbous top, flared grip. (Wallis & Wallis) $163

An African Shona knife, 15in., straight double edged blade 10in., with off-set sides, wooden hilt and sheath with carved geometric decoration, woven brass wire bindings. (Wallis & Wallis) $81

A clockwork wheeled toy of a bisque swivel headed ballerina of Parisienne type, French, circa 1880, 17in. high. (Christie's)
$2,112

An automaton figure of a clown with painted composition face and black and white costume, 18in. high, with glass dome. (Christie's)
$2,044

Late 19th century 'Boy Feeding Pig' automaton, the bisque head marked Jumeau SGDG 4, 18¾in. high. (Robt. W. Skinner Inc.)
$2,600

A clockwork cabbage automaton containing a white rabbit, French, circa 1900, 6½in. high. (Christie's)
$475

A 20th century singing bird automaton, Switzerland, box height 1¾in. and 4.1/8in. wide. (Robt. W. Skinner Inc.)
$600

A gilt metal and composition bird-cage containing a feathered bird automaton on a perch, 12½in. high. (Christie's)
$1,232

A singing bird automaton with clock, Swiss, probably by Jacquet Droz, circa 1785, 20in. high. (Christie's)
$44,000

A 19th century clockwork lady knitting automaton, Germany, 21in. high. (Robt. W. Skinner Inc.)
$1,800

Mid 19th century Swiss musical automaton of singing birds, on oval base, 60cm. high. (Christie's)
$1,980

A George III inlaid mahogany barometer, by P. Cattaneo, late 18th century, 38in. high. (Christie's) $1,045

A 19th century mahogany stick barometer, the plate signed Burton, London, 41½in. high. (Christie's) $2,310

A mid Victorian papier-mache barometer, 38in. high. (Christie's) $471

A 19th century mahogany wheel barometer, the 10in. dial signed Lione & Somalvico, 44in. high. (Christie's) $693

A late 18th century mahogany stick barometer, the brass plate signed Watkins, London, 94cm. high. (Phillips) $1,116

A Sheraton period wheel barometer, by J. B. Roncheti. (Woolley & Wallis) $5,904

An early 19th century crossbanded mahogany and boxwood strung stick barometer, signed Pozzi & Co., 97cm. high. (Phillips) $542

An early 19th century mahogany wheel barometer, the 8½in. diam. dial signed Negretty & Co. (Phillips) $651

A late 19th century rosewood wheel barometer, level signed D. Osborn, 38in. high. (Christie's) $700

A late Georgian mahogany stick barometer, the silvered plate signed Gally, Cambridge, 39in. high. (Christie's) $847

A late 19th century rosewood wheel barometer, the 10in. dial signed Crosta & Co., London, 40¾in. high. (Christie's) $292

A 19th century Standard Station barometer, engraved no. 282, Burrow, Malvern. (Phillips) $434

A 19th century French crossbanded mahogany wheel barometer, Paris 1740, 110cm. high. (Phillips) $1,162

Late 18th century mahogany stick barometer, plate signed G. Adams, 39¼in. high. (Christie's) $1,694

An early 19th century mahogany Sheraton shell wheel barometer, 8in. diam. silver dial signed Lione, Somalvico & Co., 100cm. high. (Phillips) $457

A 19th century mahogany stick barometer, signed O. Cornitti & Son Fecit, London, 95cm. high. (Phillips) $1,085

'Science revealing herself to Nature', a bronze figure cast from a model by E. Barrias, 60cm. high. (Christie's) $4,910

A 19th century French bronze group of two snipe, signed J. Moigniez, with a golden patina, 24cm. high. (Christie's) $1,116

The racing driver, a bronze figure cast from a model by Saalmann, stamped Echte Bronze, 28.5cm. high. (Christie's) $2,376

'Sheltering from the Rain', a bronze and ivory group cast and carved from a model by D. Chiparus, 26cm. high. (Christie's) $2,534

A late 19th century French bronze statuette of Phryne, signed P. Campagne, 60cm. high. (Christie's) $3,030

A late 19th century French bronze statuette of Diana, signed Denecheau, 60cm. high overall. (Christie's) $6,380

The Waiter, a bronze figure cast from a model by Engelhart, inscribed 1904, 26.5cm. high. (Christie's) $475

A 19th century French bronze model of a prancing stallion, cast from a model by C. Fratin, 26cm. high. (Christie's) $2,233

Water Carrier, a bronze figure cast from a model by Franz Seifert, 25.8cm. high. (Christie's) $601

A bronze figure of Eve, incised Oliver Sheppard, 1924, 51cm. high. (Phillips) $1,950

A mid 19th century French bronze group of a child with a swan, signed J. Pradier, 83.5cm. high. (Christie's) $7,656

A late 19th century Italian bronze statuette of a youth seated on a bollard, signed Ch. Brunin, Roma, 60cm. high. (Christie's) $1,355

A late 19th century English bronze bust of G. F. Watts, signed and dated A. Gilbert, 1888, 16.5cm. high. (Christie's) $1,276

One of a set of four ormolu and simulated bronze wall lights of Empire style, fitted for electricity, 17in. high. (Christie's) $1,652

A late 19th century French bronze bust of Napoleon as Emperor, signed and dated on the side R. Colombo, 1885, 48.5cm. high. (Christie's) $2,392

Dancer with Tambourine, a gilt bronze figure cast from a model by Agathon Leonard, 55.5cm. high. (Christie's) $5,702

A mid 19th century English bronze statuette of the Duke of Wellington on Horseback, cast from a model by Alfred, Count d'Orsay, 41cm. high. (Christie's) $1,355

A late 19th century French bronze statuette of Hebe, signed Steiner, 94cm. high. (Christie's) $3,828

BRONZE

'Exotic Dancer', a gilt bronze and ivory figure cast and carved from a model by A. Gory, 37.5cm. high. (Christie's) $3,304

'Danseuse de Thebes', a bronze and ivory figure cast and carved from a model by C. J. Roberte Colinet, 25.8cm. high. (Christie's) $12,393

Mandolin Player, a bronze and ivory figure cast and carved from a model by F. Preiss, signed, 59cm. high. (Christie's) $31,395

A 19th century animalier group of a stag, doe and fawn, on oblate ovoid base, incised Barye and F. Barbedienne Fondeur, 27cm. high. (Phillips) $2,160

A bronze figure, cast from a model by Bruno Zach, 15½in. high. (Christie's) $1,368

A Lorenzl gilt bronze dancing girl, poised on one leg, 15in. high. (Christie's) $1,238

A bronze and ivory bust cast and carved from a model by P. Mengin, 8½in. (Christie's) $332

Pair of 19th century bronze and ormolu three-light figural candelabra, 55cm. high. (Phillips) $1,512

A bronze figure cast from a model by F. Liebermann, depicting a putto astride a cockerel, 40cm. high. (Christie's) $1,487

An Art Deco bronze group of a male and female nude, 65cm. high. (Christie's) $3,304

'Nubian Dancer', a bronze and ivory dancing girl, cast and carved after a model by D. H. Chiparus, 15½in. high. (Christie's) $18,120

'Oriental Dancer', a bronze figure cast from a model by C. J. Roberte Colinet, 19½in. high. (Christie's) $2,718

A bronze group cast from a model by Guirande of a dancing lady, 62.9cm. high. (Christie's) $2,313

'Maid of Orleans', a bronze figure cast after a model by Raoul Larche, 14in. high. (Christie's) $906

A bronze figural lamp, cast from a model by O. S. W. Schimmelpfennig, 9¼in. high. (Christie's) $785

A large Lorenzl silvered bronze figure of a dancing girl, 28½in. high. (Christie's) $2,718

Pair of Regency ormolu and bronze candlesticks with Chinamen holding nozzles, on white marble pedestals, 8½in. high. (Christie's) $1,435

Flute Player, a bronze and ivory figure cast and carved from a model by F. Preiss, 48.5cm. high. (Christie's) $28,090

BRONZE

A gilt bronze figure of a girl with a dog in her arms, on variegated square marble base, 30cm. high. (Christie's) $2,534

A 19th century animalier bronze figure of a mountain goat, incised J. Moigniez, 26cm. high. (Phillips) $990

'Dancer with Thyrsus', a bronze figure cast from a model by Pierre le Faguays, 27.2cm. high. (Christie's) $1,742

A bronze hunting group 'Gone Away', 51cm. high, the base incised Elkington. (Phillips) $5,100

One of a pair of ormolu candlesticks, the shafts formed as kneeling naked maidens with lion skin cloaks, circa 1830, 10in. high. (Christie's) $1,404

A late 19th century English silvered bronze group of Adam and Eve After the Fall, cast from a model by Chas. Bell Birch, dated 1875, 40cm. high overall. (Christie's) $1,515

La Sibylie, a bronze bust cast from a model by E. Villanis, with Societe des Bronzes de Paris foundry mark, 72cm. high. (Christie's) $3,484

One of a pair of Regency ormolu and bronze twin-light candelabra, 13in. high. (Christie's) $1,982

One of a set of three William IV bronze argand lamps with flame finials, fitted for electricity, 28¼in. high. (Christie's) $3,139

BRONZE

A late 19th/early 20th century French bronze statue of Diana the Huntress, the base signed Mercie, 111cm. high. (Christie's) $12,760

A 19th century animalier bronze figure of a chamois, incised J. Moigniez, 24cm. high. (Phillips) $600

Egyptian Dancer, a gilt bronze and ivory figure cast and carved from a model by C. J. Roberte Colinet, 42.5cm. high. (Christie's) $28,512

A late 19th century Spanish bronze group of an Arab with two lion cubs, signed Vallmitjana abarca, 36cm. high. (Christie's) $1,276

One of a pair of 19th century French bronze torcheres of Cupid and Psyche, 94cm. high. (Christie's) $6,061

Morning Walk, a parcel gilt bronze and ivory group cast and carved after a model by A. Becquerel, 26.8cm. high. (Christie's) $1,900

A bronze group cast from a model by C. Kauba, on a variegated square marble base, signed, 14.3cm. high. (Christie's) $554

One of a pair of early 19th century bronze and ormolu candelabra, the glass sconces hung with pendant lustre drops, 31cm. high. (Phillips) $930

One of a pair of mid 19th century bronze candlesticks, the shafts modelled as up-turned sea serpents, 10½in. high. (Christie's) $1,321

One of a pair of late Regency patinated bronze and ormolu urns, 11in. high. (Christie's) $2,831

A bronze group of two hounds on leafy oval base, by P. J. Mene, 18in. long. (Graves Son & Pilcher) $1,585

A bronze figure of a naked man, 'The Sluggard', cast after a model by Frederic Lord Leighton, 56.5cm. high. (Phillips) $4,608

A painted bronze and ivory figural lamp, 'Oriental Waiter', 48cm. high, signed on base F. Preiss. (Phillips) $2,880

A Tiffany Studios bronze and glass inkwell, 18cm. diam., stamped Tiffany Studio New York, 69391. (Phillips) $518

One of a pair of ormolu three-branch wall lights, fitted for electricity, 22in. high. (Christie's) $2,655

Pierrot, a bronze and ivory figure cast and carved after a model by Gibbert, 15.4cm. high. (Christie's) $5,287

A 17th/18th century inlaid bronze two-handled archaistic vessel, gui, 41cm. wide. (Christie's) $1,573

A 19th century French bronze model of a charging bull, cast from a model by Antoine-Louis Barye, 19 x 30cm. (Christie's) $3,366

One of a pair of Louis XVI bronze and ormolu figural candelabra, 70cm. high. (Phillips) $4,608

Late 19th century bronze model of a rhinoceros on marble stand, 48cm. long. (Christie's) $4,998

One of a pair of 19th century large bronze garden vases, 77.5cm. high. (Christie's) $2,030

One of a set of five ormolu twin-branch wall lights of Louis XVI design, 25in. high. (Christie's) $6,560

One of a pair of patinated bronze models of lions, early 19th century, 11½in. wide. (Christie's) $1,551

'The Swing', a bronze and ivory figure cast and carved from a model by Jaeger, 10½in. high. (Christie's) $1,963

An early 20th century French bronze group of two horses, cast from a model by P. Tourgueneff, 41 x 58cm. (Christie's) $1,683

A bronze group cast from a model by A. Boucher of three athletic youths, signed and with Siot-Paris foundry stamp, 50cm. high. (Christie's) $5,289

A gilt bronze figure of a crouching lion, Tang Dynasty, 8cm. wide. (Christie's) $9,438

A bronze of 'Faneur', after Charles-Octave Levy, Salon de Beaux-Art, 1885, 22.5/8in. high. (Robt. W. Skinner Inc.) $700

One of a pair of bronze deer with brown patina, 34½in. high. (Christie's) $2,860

An English bronze statuette of Peter Pan, cast from a model by Sir G. Frampton, the base dated GF 1915, 48cm. high. (Christie's) $15,147

A bronze flattened pilgrim vase, bienhu, Warring States/Han Dynasty, 37cm. wide. (Christie's) $2,516

A bronze group of a man and a poodle, 59cm. high, inscribed D. de Chemellier. (Phillips) $936

A 19th century inlaid bronze charger, Japan, 12.5/8in. diam. (Robt. W. Skinner Inc.) $650

A bronze group of two crows perched on a tree stump, Meiji period, 58.5cm. high. (Christie's) $3,124

Huntress, a silvered bronze figure cast from a model by G. None, Paris, 34cm. high. (Christie's) $1,887

Bronze standing figure of a satyr, 2ft. tall. (Lots Road Galleries) $1,440

BRONZE

An Art Deco bronze and ivory Grecian figure on marble plinth, 11¾in. high. (Capes, Dunn & Co.) $841

A bronze and ivory figure of a dancer cast and carved from a model by Gerdago, 10½in. high. (Christie's) $6,160

A gilt bronze and ivory figure cast and carved from a model by Lorenzl, 11in. high. (Christie's) $800

An archaic bronze food vessel, gui, Shang Dynasty, 22.5cm. diam., wood stand, fitted box. (Christie's) $117,975

A 20th century English bronze statuette of The Sluggard, cast from a model by F. Leighton, 51.5cm. high. (Christie's) $5,386

An archaic bronze bell, nao, mid-1st Millenium B.C., 40cm. high, fitted box, wood stand and bell striker. (Christie's) $3,146

One of a pair of 19th century French bronze figures depicting a fisher girl and hunter, signed Boyer, 14in. high. (Capes, Dunn & Co.)$725

Lioness, a bronze figure cast after a model by Demetre Chiparus, 57.8cm. long. (Christie's) $1,494

One of two bronze models of athletes on rectangular bases, 8.75in. and 9.5in. high. (Woolley & Wallis) $437

A 19th century French bronze group of a Satyr with Nymph and Baby Satyr, in the style of Clodion, 68cm. high. (Christie's) $2,019

A 16th/17th century late Ming bronze group cast as Budai, 32.5cm. wide. (Christie's) $2,831

A Preiss bronze and ivory figure, 'Grecian with Torch', on marble base, 11in. high. (Capes, Dunn & Co.) $1,595

Late 19th century Austrian bronze of a Bedouin on Camel, 10in. high. (Robt. W. Skinner Inc.) $700

An early 19th century ormolu table cruet on four dolphin supports, 48cm. high. (Phillips) $1,285

A gilt bronze and ivory group cast and carved from an original by A. Hussmann, 18.50cm. high. (Phillips) $1,080

A painted bronze and ivory figure, 'Hush', 42cm. high, inscribed D. H. Chiparus. (Phillips) $3,888

Europa and the Bull, a bronze figure cast from a model by H. Muller, 25.4cm. high. (Christie's) $1,022

A green patinated bronze figure, modelled as a faun holding a panther cub, cast from a model by M. Hoffman, 44.50cm. high, circa 1915. (Phillips) $1,152

A 13th/14th century Korean gilt bronze figure of a standing Buddha, Koryo Dynasty, 21.5cm. high. (Christie's) $4,719

A 19th century French bronze relief of a startled stallion, cast from a model by C. Fratin, 26 x 37cm. (Christie's) $2,624

Mid 19th century bronze of a boy playing catchball, 'Preparing to Throw', cast from a model by J. Durham, 37.5cm. high. (Christie's) $1,262

Late 19th century champleve enamel on bronze covered jar, China, 17.3/8in. high. (Robt. W. Skinner Inc.) $600

One of a pair of Charles X ormolu five-light candelabra, 32½in. high. (Christie's) $3,124

A late 19th century French or Italian bronze equestrian statuette of Napoleon, cast from a model by Pinedo, 40cm. high. (Christie's) $1,262

A 20th century English bronze bust of the Viscount Northcliffe, cast from a model by Courtnay Pollack, 52cm. high. (Christie's) $639

One of a pair of 17th/18th century partially gilt bronze censers and covers, 32cm. high. (Christie's) $7,550

A bronze finish spelter hall lamp of a Teutonic knight in 16th century armor, 4ft.4in. high. (Woolley & Wallis) $720

One of a pair of bronze models of athletes running and throwing the discus, 8.5in. and 9.5in. high. (Woolley & Wallis) $392

A 19th century French bronze group of a Greek shepherd teaching a child to play the flute, cast from a model by Coinchon, 41.5 x 34cm. (Christie's) $757

A silvered bronze group, 'Carthage', after a model by T. Riviere, 56cm. high. (Phillips) $2,880

A late 19th century French bronze model of The Vaineueur Du Derby, cast from a model by P. J. Mene, 26 x 24cm. (Christie's) $2,524

A painted bronze and ivory figure, 'Champagne Dancer', 41.50cm. high, inscribed on bronze F. Preiss. (Phillips) $3,600

A 19th century English bronze model of a stag eating oak leaves off a withered tree, from the Coalbrookdale Foundry, 40 x 46cm. (Christie's) $1,093

Early 20th century bronze bust of Woman, signed Wigglesworth, stamped Gorham Co. Founders, 13¾in. high. (Robt. W. Skinner Inc.) $800

An early 19th century French romantic bronze portrait plaque of Albert Bertin, cast from a model by A. Etex, 43 x 32cm. (Christie's) $1,514

Late 19th century bronze lobed koro on karashishi mask and scroll tripod feet, 61cm. high. (Christie's) $1,405

BRONZE

An Art Deco bronze figure, by Fesler Felix, modelled as a naked girl with an elaborate headdress and belt, 37cm. high. (Phillips) $319

A late 19th century French bronze statuette of a Huntsman with a Pointer, cast from a model by Pierre Jules Mene, 47cm. high. (Christie's) $3,366

Mid 19th century bronze of a boy playing catchball, 'Preparing to Catch', cast from a model by J. Durham, 40cm. high. (Christie's) $1,262

A late 19th century French bronze model of a lioness carrying a cub in her mouth, cast from a model by A. N. Cain, 61 x 84cm.(Christie's) $4,880

A painted bronze and ivory figure, 'Oriental Dancer', 40.20cm. high, inscribed on the marble Chiparus. (Phillips) $6,624

A 19th century cast bronze figure of horse and dog, 'Angelo' on base, signed P. Lenordez, France, 20.1/8in. long. (Robt. W. Skinner Inc.) $950

One of a pair of late 19th century bronze baluster vases, decorated in iroe hirazogan and takazogan, 32.5cm. high. (Christie's) $702

A late 19th century English bronze statue of Physical Energy, by G. F. Watts. (Christie's) $42,075

Bear Hug, a bronze figure cast after a model by F. Rieder, 30.8cm. high. (Christie's) $2,044

BRONZE

A French bronze group of the Accolade, after Pierre-Jules Mene, 43.5 x 69cm. (Christie's) $4,785

Early 20th century large bronze architectural ornament, America, 65in. wide. (Robt. W. Skinner Inc.) $2,200

A bronze figure of a panther cast from a model by M. Prost, dark patina, 18.7cm. high. (Christie's) $1,404

Pair of early 20th century Tiffany bronze dore and opalene jewel pricket candlesticks, 12.3/8in. high. (Robt. W. Skinner Inc.) $2,800

A pair of large bronze models of standing geese, 58cm. and 78cm. high. (Christie's) $2,030

'Dancer with Thyrsus', a parcel gilt bronze figure cast after a model by Pierre Le Faguays, 27.6cm. high. (Christie's) $2,313

Late 19th century cast bronze of hunting dog, signed Dubucand, France, 11in. long. (Robt. W. Skinner Inc.) $200

Pair of late 18th century Italian neo-classical gilt metal candlesticks, possibly Torinese, 21in. high. (Christie's) $1,874

A bronze oxyrhynchus fish with uraeus and horned solar disc, a suspension loop behind, 9cm. long, Late Period. (Phillips) $229

A late 19th century French bronze statuette of Mercury asleep, monogrammed and dated CCH 1898, 107cm. long. (Christie's) $3,190

Late 19th century bronze model of a prowling tiger on wood stand, 53cm. long. (Christie's) $859

An early Victorian bronze inkstand with two vase-shaped inkwells, one glass liner cracked, 17in. wide. (Christie's) $413

One of a pair of inlaid bronze mask and ring handles, Warring States/Western Han Dynasty, the masks 9.5cm. wide, the rings 9cm. diam. (Christie's)$86,515

A pair of bronze models of seated rats holding chestnuts, signed on the bases, Shosai chu, Meiji period, approx. 17cm. long. (Christie's) $1,562

Pair of Regency ormolu and bronze candelabra, each with chinoiserie figures holding parasol nozzles, 11½in. high. (Christie's) $7,656

One of a pair of ormolu three-branch wall lights in the rococo taste, 26½in. high. (Christie's) $2,343

'A Savage Drinking from a Stream', a bronze figure cast from a model by J. De Roncourt, 81.2cm. wide. (Christie's) $1,258

One of a pair of bronze and marble bookends in the form of kneeling nudes, 5½in. high. (Capes, Dunn & Co.) $108

A George III mahogany
brass bound bucket, the
tapering side with a door
and carrying handle, 13¼in.
high. (Christie's) $702

A George III oval mahogany
Irish peat bucket with swing
handle and liner, 14in. wide.
(Prudential Fine Art)
$873

One of two Regency brass
bound mahogany peat
buckets with ribbed bodies
and brass handles, 15½in.
high. (Christie's)
$4,804

A George III mahogany
brass bound peat bucket
with brass liner, 11¾in.
high. (Christie's)
$1,730

A George III mahogany brass
bound coal bucket of navette
shape, the slatted sides with
swing handle and liner, 14½in.
wide. (Christie's) $3,102

A George III brass bound
mahogany coal bucket with
brass handle and liner, 13in.
wide. (Christie's)
$786

A Regency mahogany brass
bound peat bucket with
tapering sides and carrying
handle with later tin liner,
16in. high. (Christie's)
$1,663

One of a pair of George III
mahogany brass bound
plate buckets with later tin
liners, 15in. diam.
(Christie's) $1,573

One of two George III brass
bound mahogany buckets of
navette form with detachable
brass liners, 13½in. high.
(Christie's) $1,848

CADDIES & BOXES

Victorian amboyna veneered
sewing box, inlaid with
mother-of-pearl stringing,
12 x 9in. (Peter Wilson)
$197

Shaker butternut sewing
box, the drawers with ebonized diamond escutcheon
and turned ivory pull, New
England, circa 1820, 7½in.
wide. (Robt. W. Skinner Inc.)
$7,750

A Regency tortoiseshell
tea caddy with gilt metal
lion handles, 12½in. wide.
(Christie's) $660

A large 18th century lac
burgaute peach-shaped
box and cover inlaid in
shell, 43.5cm. wide.
(Christie's) $1,179

A mid Victorian black, gilt
and mother-of-pearl japanned
papier-mache purdonium,
20in. wide, and another.
(Christie's) $1,573

A Victorian brass and velvet
'perambulator' sewing box,
possibly America, circa 1880,
7½in. long. (Robt. W. Skinner
Inc.) $400

Early 19th century Chinese
Export black and gold lacquer
games box, 15in. wide.
(Christie's) $1,551

A George III partridgewood
tea caddy with Lever patent
lock, 9½in. high. (Christie's)
$1,337

Early 19th century roironuri
suzuribako, decorated in gold
hiramakie, takamakie and
hirame, 24.8 x 22.9cm.
(Christie's) $7,497

Mid 19th century black painted chest, the interior lined with mid 19th century newspaper, New England, 19¼in. wide. (Christie's) $1,540

A wooden, painted gesso and gilded casket, by W. Cayley-Robinson, 35cm. wide. (Phillips) $1,224

A mid Victorian black and gilt japanned papier-mache cigar box with hinged lid, 7⅜in. wide. (Christie's) $125

One of a set of eight Regency parcel gilt and scarlet japanned tea cannisters, 18in. high. (Christie's) $7,550

Birmingham tortoiseshell snuff box with gilt metal mounts, 2½in. diam., circa 1800. (Peter Wilson) $98

One of a pair of Federal mahogany and mahogany veneer inlaid knife boxes, America or England, circa 1790, 14½in. high. (Robt. W. Skinner Inc.) $950

A 17th century needlework casket, all decorated with silver wire and silkwork, 23cm. wide. (Phillips) $1,368

A 19th century French gold mounted tortoiseshell jewel casket, 5in. high. (Christie's) $8,250

Early 19th century wallpaper hat box, 'A Peep at the Moon', America, 12½in. high, 17in. wide. (Robt. W. Skinner Inc.) $200

A Victorian walnut dome top tea caddy with ornate brass key escutcheon, cartouche and corners, 8.7in. wide. (Woolley & Wallis) $230

Regency Tole Peinte coal bin on claw feet. (Lots Road Galleries) $720

A 19th century pine Scandinavian bride's box, 11½in. high, 21½in. wide. (Christie's) $495

One of a pair of George III black shagreen cutlery boxes, one with gilt fittings, the other with silvered fittings, 13½in. high. (Christie's) $660

A Regency tortoiseshell veneered rectangular tea chest with wire inlay, 7in. long. (Woolley & Wallis) $445

A George III fruitwood tea caddy formed as an apple, 5in. high. (Christie's) $1,179

A Regency gilt metal mounted scarlet leather casket, each of the doors with a musical Chinaman, 12in. wide. (Christie's) $1,318

One of a pair of George III mahogany cutlery urns, the foliate domed covers with urn finials, 29½in. high. (Christie's) $3,412

A 17th century needlework casket, the front and side panels of raised and stuffed stumpwork, England, 10¾in. wide. (Robt. W. Skinner Inc.) $2,600

A Flemish gilt metal mounted ebony casket with partly fitted interior, 17in. wide. (Christie's) $2,811

A George III satinwood and marquetry tea caddy with divided interior, 8in. wide. (Christie's) $792

A 17th century German black painted and parcel gilt strong-box with carrying handles, 27in. wide. (Christie's) $781

A 19th century suzuribako decorated in gold and silver hiramakie, nashiji and hirame on a maki-bokashi ground, 26 x 23.1cm. (Christie's) $5,467

A George III treen (applewood) tea caddy formed as a large apple with hinged cover and ebonized stem, 6in. high. (Christie's) $4,653

A late 16th century French walnut and parcel gilt casket with fitted interior, 20in. wide. (Christie's) $2,811

A 19th century English Colonial camphorwood and ebony chest, 32½in. wide. (Parsons, Welch & Cowell) $1,771

A Norwegian painted pine scala, 19in. wide. (Christie's) $281

An early Victorian gentleman's dressing case, the contents hall-marked, maker Thos. Diller, London, 1840, 11oz. weighable silver. (Woolley & Wallis) $923

An early Victorian black, gilt and mother-of-pearl japanned papier-mache tea caddy, 15¾in. wide. (Christie's) $975

A Regency rosewood and boulle tea caddy of sarcophagus shape, the interior with blue glass mixing bowl 12½in. wide. (Christie's) $239

Mid 19th century chinoiserie decorated lacquer sewing box, containing ivory implements, China, 14½in. wide. (Robt. W. Skinner Inc.) $550

Upson family tole document box, the front and sides with floral band decoration, Conn., circa 1820, 9¼in. long. (Robt. W. Skinner Inc.) $1,000

A mid Victorian black and gilt japanned tole purdonium, with shovel, 12½in. wide. (Christie's) $597

An Indo-Chinese gilt lacquer box profusely decorated in alto relievo, 2ft.4in. wide. (Capes, Dunn & Co.) $522

A Regency black japanned tole coal box on cabochon feet, 24in. wide. (Christie's) $629

A Victorian brass bound coromandel wood dressing case, the silver mounts mostly by C. Rawlings and Wm. Summers, 1845, two bottle tops 1853, case 15 x 10¾in. (Christie's) $2,359

A George III satinwood, marquetry and painted octangular tea caddy with hinged top, 6½in. wide. (Christie's) $957

A Zeiss Ikon Miroflex, 9 x 12cm. format, with 15cm. f 4.5 Tessar lens, 19cm. long, circa 1935. (Christie's) $77

A Leica IIIg camera No. 686682 with a Leitz Summaron f3.5 3.5cm. lens, a Leitz Elmar lens, a Soogz lens hood, an Ablon trimming template and a Tuvoo Universal viewfinder. (Christie's) $655

A Newmand & Sinclair 35mm. cinematograph camera No. 616 with accessories. (Christie's) $418

A 9 x 12cm. ?Ernemann tropical folding plate camera in brass reinforced teak casing with Bolter and Stammer, Hanover label, with lens and Compur shutter. (Christie's) $154

A tropical Contess-Nettel 10 x 15cm. Deck-Rullo camera with teakwood body, circa 1927. (Christie's) $737

A Thornton-Pickard half-plate Ruby camera with a Ross 8½ x 6½ rapid symmetrical No. 39577, d.d.s., focusing cloth in canvas case. (Christie's) $147

A panoramic camera, the Eastman Kodak No. 4 Panoram-Kodak, model D, circa 1910, 10¼in. long. (Christie's) $55

A chrome Nikon S2 camera no. 6175567, with a black Nikkor-S f1.4 5cm. lens, with two others. (Christie's) $524

An Eastman Kodak Co. No. 2 Brownie camera Model D in original maker's box, made circa 1901-33. (Christie's) $65

CAMERAS

A Le Coultre Compass camera No. 2629 with a CCL 3B Anastigmat f3.5 35mm. with plate back and roll film back. (Christie's) $983

A Zeiss Ikon Contax I camera No. AU80899 with a Zeiss Tessar f2.8 5cm. lens. (Christie's) $557

An Andre Debrie 16mm. Sinmor professional cine camera Model No. 46 Series C, with accessories. (Christie's) $998

A Wratten & Wainwright 13 x 18cm. tailboard camera with a Ross 8 x 5 Rapid symmetrical lens. (Christie's) $311

A brass reproduction Petzval-Type daguerreotype camera, signed Voigtlander & Sohn in Wien, no. 084, circa 1956, 12¼in. long. (Christie's) $2,530

A Rectaflex Rotor three-lens turret 35mm. s.l.r. camera. (Christie's) $983

A Zeiss Ikon 4.5 x 6cm. Ermanox Reflex camera No. M99925 with a Carl Zeiss-Ernemann Ernostar lens, lens cap and two s.m.s. in fitted case. (Christie's) $2,093

A 10 x 12in. brass and mahogany field camera with an alloy-bound Marion & Co. No. 5 Rectilinear and Waterhouse stops, all in a case. (Christie's) $278

A 10 x 12in. G. Hare tailboard camera in brass and mahogany with red square cut bellows with a Gasc & Charconnet, Paris, 7in. lens, together with another three. (Christie's) $245

An Ilford Witness camera no. 5226, with a Dallmeyer Super-Six anastigmat f1.9 2in. lens. (Christie's) $688

A 45 x 107mm. Ica Poly-skop camera with a pair of Zeiss Tessar lens, in a fitted case. (Christie's) $138

The Al-Vista Panoramic camera by the Multi Scope & Film Co., 11in. long, circa 1900. (Christie's) $77

A Kodak Ltd. Boy Scout Kodak camera in green enamelled finish No. 99805. (Christie's) $131

A Zeiss-Ikon/Ica Polyskop camera No. J91894 with a pair of Zeiss Tessar f4.5 6.5cm. lens. (Christie's) $299

A red-dial Leica IIIf camera No. 795893 with self-timer and other accessories, all in a Leitz fitted case.(Christie's) $901

A Voigtlander 4¼ x 1.5/8in. Verascope-style leather covered stereo camera with a pair of Heliar f4.5 lens, in fitted case. (Christie's) $154

A 7¼ x 7¼in. sliding box wet-plate camera and a Jamin, Paris, lens with rack and pinion focusing and metal lens cap. (Christie's) $1,449

A Marion & Co. 1¼ x 1¼in. Metal Miniature camera with a Petzval-type lens. (Christie's) $2,130

A double stroke Leica M3 camera No. 785381, with four lenses and accessories. (Christie's) $1,065

A Multiscope and Film Co. No. 4B Al-Vista Panoramic camera with lens No. 3054, in leather case. (Christie's) $262

A quarter-plate Sinclair Una hand and stand camera with a Newman & Sinclair 'Accurate' shutter and Goetz Celor lens. (Christie's) $573

A mid 19th century Bohemian cranberry pink six-light chandelier made for the Indian or Turkish market, 48in. high. (Christie's) $11,781

Late 19th century six-light antler chandelier, 48in. high. (Christie's) $1,178

An Art Deco glass and chromium plated metal chandelier of star form, circa 1930, 71cm. wide. (Christie's) $26,928

A late Regency ormolu three-light chandelier with ostrich feather corona, fitted for electricity, 22½in. high. (Christie's) $1,240

An ormolu six-light chandelier of Regence style, 27½in. high. (Christie's) $1,874

Late 19th century Meissen six-light chandelier, fitted for electric light, 74cm. high. (Christie's) $4,375

A French Art Deco spelter chandelier, the opalescent glass shades molded with cell pattern, 72cm. high. (Christie's) $792

A 17th century brass six-branch chandelier with scrolled branches, fitted for electricity, 20in. high. (Christie's) $4,404

Early 19th century parcel gilt and ebonized six-light chandelier, 33½in. high. (Christie's) $3,722

AMERICAN

Teco pottery brown molded vase, bullet shape on four elongated V feet, Illinois, 1909, 8½in. high. (Robt. W. Skinner Inc.)
$1,800

Saturday evening girl's decorated cream pitcher, Boston, circa 1910, signed S.E.G., 191-5-10 I.G., 3in. high. (Robt. W. Skinner Inc.) $850

Late 19th century Dedham pottery mottled pink vase, incised H.R. Jr., for Hugh Robertson, 8¾in. high. (Robt. W. Skinner Inc.)
$1,200

Late 19th century majolica garden seat, 17¾in. high, 12in. diam. (Robt. W. Skinner Inc.) $950

One of a pair of Tucker porcelain pitchers, Phila., 1826-39, 9in. high. (Christie's) $2,420

Early 20th century Dedham crackleware metal shape vase, 8½in. high. (Robt. W. Skinner Inc.) $1,100

Van Briggle pottery copper clad vase, Colorado, 5½in. high. (Robt. W. Skinner Inc.)
$1,200

Late 19th century Dedham pottery experimental vase, pink star drip design on green, 10¼in. high. (Robt. W. Skinner Inc.)
$5,500

Late 19th century Walley pottery 'Devil' mug, impressed WJW, 5½in. high, 4in. diam. (Robt. W. Skinner Inc.) $350 £245

AMERICAN

Roseville decorated matt umbrella stand, Ohio, circa 1910, no. 724, 20in. high. (Robt. W. Skinner Inc.) $1,300

Early 20th century Saturday evening girl's decorated pitcher, Boston, signed S.E.G. 276-1-10, 9½in. high. (Robt. W. Skinner Inc.) $4,000

Grueby pottery two-color butterscotch vase, Boston, circa 1905, 11in. high. (Robt. W. Skinner Inc.) $2,300

A porcelain pitcher, by The Union Porcelain Works, Greenpoint, N.Y., designed by Karl Mueller, circa 1880, 9¼in. high. (Christie's) $2,420

Early 20th century Dedham pottery rabbit figural flower frog, 6¼in. high. (Robt. W. Skinner Inc.) $700

Early 20th century Dedham pottery large milk pitcher, Rabbit pattern, 8½in. high. (Robt. W. Skinner Inc.) $325

Late 19th century Dedham pottery volcanic oxblood vase, 7.1/8in. high. (Robt. W. Skinner Inc.) $6,600

Late 19th century Chelsea Keramic Art Works oxblood vase, 8¼in. high. (Robt. W. Skinner Inc.) $650

Wheatley pottery vase, Ohio, circa 1905, matt green in Grueby manner, 10¾in. high. (Robt. W. Skinner Inc.) $650

ARITA

Late 17th century Arita blue and white oviform ewer with loop handle, the silver mount 19th century, 25cm. high. (Christie's) $1,718

A European silver mounted Arita teapot and domed cover decorated in iron-red, green and black enamels, circa 1700, 19.6cm. long. (Christie's) $859

One of a pair of 19th century Arita blue and white globular bottle vases, 62.5cm. high. (Christie's) $18,744

An ormolu mounted Japanese Arita baluster jar and cover painted in the Imari palette, the porcelain late 17th century, 35in. high. (Christie's) $5,935

A large Arita polychrome model of Buddha, Meiji period, 46cm. high. (Christie's) $624

Late 17th century Arita oviform ewer with loop handle decorated in underglaze blue, 21cm. high. (Christie's) $1,405

Late 17th/early 18th century Arita octagonal blue and white vase and cover, 56cm. high. (Christie's) $1,874

An 18th century Japanese Arita charger, 18in. diam. (Dreweatts) $1,224

An Arita globular apothecary bottle decorated in underglaze blue, iron-red, green, yellow and black enamels, circa 1680, 27.3cm. high. (Christie's) $4,686

BELLEEK

A Belleek oval basket with pierced trellis sides and everted looped rim, first period, 27cm. wide. (Christie's) $470

A Belleek porcelain trefoil basket, osier pattern, 5in. diam. (Hobbs & Chambers) $238

A Belleek basket and cover of oval shape with three strand basket weave base, 8½in. wide. (Peter Wilson) $1,510

A Belleek cornucopia vase on shell molded base, 9¼in. high. (Christie's) $382

Late 19th century Belleek figure of a young lady dressed in a classical style pink robe, 14¼in. high. (Outhwaite & Litherland) $1,131

A Belleek Parian bust of 'Clytie', the socle with Belleek black printed marks, first period, 29.5cm. high. (Christie's) $1,280

A Belleek Parian figure entitled 'The Prisoner of Love', after the model by G. Fontana, 65cm. high. (Christie's) $7,114

A Belleek porcelain nautilus shell vase, 9in. high. (Christie's) $146

A Belleek figure of 'Erin Awakening from her Slumbers', modelled by Wm. B. Kirk, 42.5cm. high. (Phillips) $2,016

BERLIN

Late 19th century Berlin bowl and cover, blue scepter mark, 10.5in. diam. (Woolley & Wallis) $858

A KPM wall plate, with hand-painted decoration of a bare-breasted Junoesque figure, blue printed KPM mark, 40.5cm. diam. (Christie's) $578

A Berlin faience 'Schnabel-kanne' with original pewter mounts, attributed to the Wolbeer factory, dated AB 1712, 37cm. high. (Phillips) $5,852

A Berlin green-ground oviform pot pourri vase, circa 1810, 31cm. high. (Christie's) $5,970

A Berlin rectangular plaque painted with Diana and Bacchus, impressed scepter and KPM marks, circa 1865, 27.5 x 22cm. (Christie's) $2,524

One of a pair of late 18th century Berlin ornithological wall pockets, 21cm. high. (Christie's) $3,142

A Berlin rectangular plaque painted after Domenichino with a portrait of Sybil, circa 1865, 14.5 x 11cm. (Christie's) $757

A Berlin iron-red ground two-handled cup, cover and stand, blue scepter mark, circa 1830. (Christie's) $1,515

A Berlin rectangular plaque painted after Holbein, impressed KPM and scepter marks, circa 1865, 25 x 18.5cm. (Christie's) $1,276

BOW

A Bow figure of a recumbent lion painted in 'Muses' style with streaked and washed brown fur, circa 1750, 9.5cm. wide. (Christie's) $5,068

One of a pair of Bow figures of a gardener and companion , circa 1762, 20cm. high. (Christie's) $1,029

A Bow blue and white cylindrical piggin, 6.5cm. diam., and a spoon, 9.5cm. long, circa 1760. (Christie's) $760

A Bow octagonal plate printed in Venetian or brick red with 'The Young Archers', 7in. diam. (Dreweatts) $2,218

A Bow sweetmeat figure modelled as a monkey seated beside a rococo scroll molded bowl, circa 1758, 14cm. high. (Christie's) $1,029

A Bow plate printed with Aeneas and Anchises fleeing from Troy, 1756-58, 7½in. diam. (Dreweatts) $2,030

A Bow figure of Air modelled as a nymph in pale blue lined yellow shawl, circa 1758, 23.5cm. high. (Christie's) $1,346

A pair of Bow candlestick figures of a gallant and his companion, 10½in. high. (Graves Son & Pilcher) $936

One of a pair of Bow candlesticks, each modelled as Cupid with a dog at his side, anchor and dagger marks in iron-red, circa 1770, 26.5cm. high. (Christie's) $1,584

A Bristol delft posset pot and cover decorated in the Chinese style with flowers in blue, circa 1710-30, 8in. high. (Dreweatts) $2,320

A Bristol delft polychrome farmhouse plate painted with a cockerel, circa 1740, 18cm. diam. (Christie's) $1,219

A Bristol polychrome posset pot and cover decorated in the Chinese style with flowers in red, blue and green, circa 1710-30, 9in. high. (Dreweatts) $4,640

Two Bristol delft dishes, the centers painted with a bird perched on a branch, circa 1740, approx. 33cm. diam. (Christie's) $1,029

A Bristol campana shaped vase with double rope twist handles and frilled rim, circa 1750, 6¾in. high. (Dreweatts) $3,335

A Bristol delft circular dish, the center painted with an Oriental lady, blue 7 mark, circa 1740, 33cm. diam. (Christie's) $1,425

A Bristol delft blue-dash Adam and Eve small charger, circa 1710, 30.5cm. diam. (Christie's) $1,188

A Bristol delft blue and white cylindrical mug with broad strap handle, circa 1730, 12cm. high. (Christie's) $1,355

A large Bristol delft dish, decorated in blue with two figures in a punt, circa 1760, 13in. diam. (Dreweatts) $377

BRITISH

A creamware globular teapot
and cover with entwined
strap handle, painted in the
manner of D. Rhodes, circa
1770, 14.5cm. high.
(Christie's) $3,484

Victorian majolica strawberry
dish molded in the form of
two nests holding sugar bowl
and creamer, 10¾in. wide.
(Hobbs & Chambers)
$231

A Linthorpe 'Peruvian' vessel,
designed by Dr. C. Dresser,
17cm. high, impressed 296.
(Phillips) $1,296

Bennington scroddled ware
wash bowl and pitcher; bowl
13½in. diam., pitcher
10.7/8in. high, 1853-58.
(Robt. W. Skinner Inc.)
$300

An English rectangular plaque,
painted by James Rouse,
signed and dated 1830, with
Lord Byron watching Mary
Anne Chaworth, 11.5 x
14.5cm. (Phillips)
$708

One of a pair of late 19th/
early 20th century porcelain
wine coolers, English, 8.7/8in.
high. (Christie's) $660

A flambe pottery bowl, by
Bernard Moore, 8¼in. diam.,
and a Chinese carved wood
stand. (Reeds Rains)
$356

A Caughley eye bath, printed
in blue with portions of the
'Fisherman' pattern, 5.5cm.
high. (Phillips) $1,001

A Crown Ducal 'Manchu'
pattern bowl, designed by
Charlotte Rhead, 25.5cm.
diam. (Phillips) $137

A pottery model of a pig,
designed by Louis Wain,
12cm. high, impressed Rd.
no. 033320, Made in England.
(Phillips) $130

A Bretby tobacco jar and
cover, inscribed 'Nicotiank',
16.5cm. high. (Phillips)
$94

A Linthorpe pottery jug
designed by Christopher
Dresser, 9in. high, and a
dish. (Christie's) $230

A Linthorpe pottery vase, designed by
C. Dresser, the central neck surrounded
by five onion shaped forms, 4in. high.
(Christie's) $604

A John Hassell 'Egg Man', modelled as a
policeman, Boy Scout and country yokel,
6in. high. (Christie's) $226

A Brannam pottery figure
of a standing frog holding
a giant lily leaf, in shades of
blue and green, 12¼in. high.
(Christie's) $792

An inscribed globular buff-
ground jug with scroll handle,
painted in the manner of
Absolon of Yarmouth, circa
1790, 10cm. high. (Christie's)
$633

A Foley 'Intarsio' tobacco
jar and cover, 14.3cm. high,
no. 3458, Rd. no. 364386
(SR). (Phillips) $203

BRITISH

A George IV yellow ground jug, printed in red and colored, depicting 'A Visit from Richmond to Carlton House', 15.5cm. high. (Phillips) $847

A ceramic sculpture of a ram, by Rosemary Wren, 13.5cm. high. (Christie's) $54

A pearlware inscribed oviform jug with loop handle, painted in the manner of Absolon of Yarmouth, circa 1790, 18.5cm. high. (Christie's) $2,851

Five pieces of Gray's pottery advertising Ross's Soft Drinks, decorated in several colors. (Lots Road Galleries) $171

A Caughley baluster shaped jug with scroll handle and mask spout, 7in. high, C mark in blue. (Dreweatts) $348

A Portobello money box in the form of a Wesleyan Chapel, flanked by two putti, 16.5cm. high. (Phillips) $924

An English porcelain candlestick figure of 'Girl on a Horse' type modelled as an exotic pheasant, circa 1765, 21cm. high. (Christie's) $3,960

BRITISH

A Yorkshire pearlware sauce-boat in the form of a duck, circa 1790, 19cm. long. (Christie's) $1,188

A Carlton Ware Limited Edition punch bowl, molded in relief with a frieze of Henry VIII, his wives and children, 21cm. high. (Phillips) $489

A Longton Hall white figure of a recumbent horse of Snowman type, circa 1750, 17cm. wide. (Christie's) $1,267

An English majolica ware model of a dolphin forming the base for a table or lamp, 93cm. high. (Phillips) $1,386

Three of five Art Deco Ashtead pottery wall plates. (Phillips) $337

A creamware inscribed ovi-form jug with the inscription Jane Strickelton Armley followed by a rhyme, pro-bably Leeds, circa 1800, 13cm. high. (Christie's) $348

A Linthorpe pottery moon-flask, designed by C. Dresser, 7½in. high. (Christie's) $136

One of a pair of English porcelain groups of leopards and cubs naturally colored, circa 1835, 11cm. wide. (Christie's) $2,534

Part of a Susie Cooper pottery fruit set, comprising a bowl, 22.4cm. diam., and twelve plates, 22.6cm. diam. (Phillips) $145

CANTON

One of a pair of Canton famille rose two-handled vases with pelican handles. (Christie's) $632

Early 19th century Chinese Canton decorated famille verte bowl, 11.5in. diam. (Woolley & Wallis) $573

A Canton famille rose two-handled vase with a linen fold body and neck, 25in. high. (Christie's)$758

A Cantonese vase of ovoid form with Buddhist lion handles, 86cm. high, Daoguang. (Osmond Tricks) $832

Pair of Cantonese famille rose vases of ovoid form with Buddhist lion handles, 37cm. high, Daoguang. (Osmond Tricks) $960

One of a pair of 19th century Canton baluster vases, 24in. high. (Parsons, Welch & Cowell) $935

A Beijing or Canton enamel and gilt bronze two-handled tripod censer and pierced domed cover, Qianlong seal mark, 40cm. high.(Christie's) $2,671

A Canton enamel octagonal boxed supper set and cover, mid Qing Dynasty, 34cm. wide. (Christie's) $666

A Canton coffee pot, the domed cover with gilt finial, 9¾in. high. (Reeds Rains) $418

CARDEW

An Abuja stoneware casserole
and cover, by Michael
Cardew, with two strap
handles, circa 1960, 31.2cm.
diam. (Christie's)
$1,156

An Abuja stoneware teapot
with screw top, by Michael
Cardew, circa 1958, 10cm.
high. (Christie's) $627

A stoneware deep footed
bowl, by Michael Cardew,
circa 1975, 33.2cm. wide.
(Christie's) $597

A stoneware stemmed bowl,
by Michael Cardew, with
crescent lug handles, circa
1975, 17.1cm. high.
(Christie's) $141

An earthenware dish, by
Michael Cardew, impressed
MC and Winchcombe Pottery
seals, circa 1930, 35.1cm.
diam. (Christie's)$660

A large stoneware oviform
jar, by Michael Cardew, with
four lug handles and short
cylindrical neck, circa 1970,
39.6cm. high. (Christie's)
$627

An early earthenware motto
jug, by Michael Cardew,
circa 1925, 15.5cm. high.
(Christie's) $578

An Abuja stoneware slip-
glazed plate, by Michael
Cardew, covered in a dark
brown glaze over an olive-
green celadon, 25.7cm. diam.
(Christie's) $148

A stoneware two-handled
crock and cover, by Michael
Cardew, circa 1975, 38.5cm.
high. (Christie's) $865

CARDEW

A stoneware deep bowl, by Michael Cardew, impressed MC and Wenford Bridge seals, circa 1970, 28.7cm. diam. (Christie's) $660

One of a pair of Abuja stoneware circular dishes and covers, by Michael Cardew, circa 1960, 10.5cm. diam. (Christie's) $148

A large earthenware bowl, by Michael Cardew, covered in a brown glaze stopping short of the foot, circa 1930, 37.2cm. diam. (Christie's) $495

One of a pair of stoneware plates, by Michael Cardew, circa 1979, 24.4cm. diam. (Christie's) $314

An Abuja stoneware oviform jar with three lug handles, by Michael Cardew, circa 1960, 19.5cm. high. (Christie's) $743

A stoneware plate, by Michael Cardew, with panels of sgraffito, blue and iron-brown painted decoration against a grayish-white ground, circa 1970, 26.9cm. diam. (Christie's) $180

One of a pair of Abuja stoneware soy sauce pots with screw covers, by Michael Cardew, circa 1959, 9.5cm. high. (Christie's) $330

An earthenware ewer, by Michael Cardew, 26cm. high, also a basin en suite, circa 1935. (Christie's) $471

An earthenware motto jug by Michael Cardew, circa 1925, 18cm. high. (Christie's) $943

A Chelsea peach-shaped
cream jug with puce stalk
handle, circa 1750, 11cm.
wide. (Christie's)
$6,019

A Chelsea figure of a standing cow, her coat with purple
markings, red anchor mark,
circa 1756, 11.5cm. wide.
(Christie's) $2,692

A Chelsea fluted oval salt or
strawberry dish, incised
triangle mark, 1745-49,
12.3cm. wide. (Christie's)
$2,851

A Chelsea 'crayfish' salt after
a silver original by N. Sprimont,
painted in the workshop of Wm.
Duesbury, 1745-49, 12.5cm.
wide. (Christie's)
$20,592

A scent bottle of 'Girl in a
Swing' type modelled as a
youth and companion, the
base inscribed C'est L'Amour
Qui m'Inspire, circa 1755,
10.5cm. high. (Christie's)
$2,534

A Chelsea peach-shaped dish
painted in the Kakiemon
palette, circa 1750, 20cm.
wide. (Christie's)
$4,435

A Chelsea shell salt, painted
in the workshop of Wm.
Duesbury, incised triangle
mark, 1745-49, 7.5cm. wide.
(Christie's) $2,692

A pair of Chelsea masqueraders,
gold anchor marks at back,
circa 1765, 30cm. high.
(Christie's) $2,059

A Chelsea fluted teabowl
painted in a vivid Kakiemon
palette with birds perched
and in flight, 1750-52, 5cm.
high. (Christie's)
$1,900

CHELSEA

A Chelsea Hans Sloane botanical dish of lobed heart shape, 27cm. long, red anchor mark. (Phillips) $2,926

A Chelsea group of two goats, painted in the workshop of Wm. Duesbury, raised red anchor mark, circa 1751, 16.5cm. wide. (Christie's) $14,256

A Chelsea mottled claret-ground shaped oval dish, 33.5cm. wide, and another 34cm. wide, circa 1760. (Christie's) $1,900

A Chelsea acanthus leaf molded cream jug with bamboo styled handle, crown and trident mark in blue, circa 1749, 8.4cm. high. (Christie's) $6,336

Pair of Chelsea figures of Great Spotted Cuckoos, one with raised red anchor mark, circa 1750, 19cm. high. (Christie's) $6,652

A scent bottle of 'Girl in a Swing' type modelled as Wm. Shakespeare, circa 1755, 8.5cm. high. (Christie's) $570

A Chelsea peach-shaped cream jug painted in the Vincennes style with a bouquet of flowers, circa 1750, 11cm. wide. (Christie's) $6,652

Pair of Chelsea Derby candlestick figures of a gallant and his companion, 6½in. and 6in. high, no nozzles. (Graves Son & Pilcher) $830

A Chelsea chicken box and a cover, circa 1756, 9cm. wide. (Christie's) $1,267

CHELSEA

A Chelsea double scent bottle modelled as a parrot and a rooster, circa 1755, 7cm. high. (Christie's) $2,692

A Chelsea cinquefoil teabowl painted in the Kakiemon palette with The Lady in a Pavilion Pattern, 1750-52, 5.5cm. high. (Christie's) $1,504

A 'Girl in a Swing' gold mounted cylindrical etui, 1751-54, 11.5cm. high. (Christie's) $2,851

A Chelsea lobed teaplant beaker painted in a vivid famille rose palette, 1745-49, 7.5cm. high. (Christie's) $5,702

A Chelsea decagonal plate painted in a Kakiemon palette with phoenix perched and in flight, circa 1752, 19.5cm. diam. (Christie's) $2,534

A Chelsea acanthus leaf molded white chocolate pot on four feet, 1745-49, 24cm. high overall. (Christie's) $1,346

A Chelsea gold mounted scent bottle naturalistically modelled as a pineapple, circa 1755, 6.5cm. high. (Christie's) $1,584

A Chelsea fluted saucer dish painted in a vivid Kakiemon palette with phoenix perched and in flight, circa 1752, 18cm. diam. (Christie's) $9,820

A Chelsea cane handle modelled as a lady's head, 1745-49, 7cm. high. (Christie's) $2,217

CHELSEA

A copper gilt mounted etui of 'Girl in a Swing' type, circa 1755, 12.5cm. long. (Christie's) $1,188

A Chelsea flared fluted beaker painted in the Kakiemon palette, 1750-52, 7cm. high. (Christie's) $1,742

One of a pair of Chelsea gold mounted scent bottles modelled as a friar and nun, circa 1756, 9cm. high. (Christie's) $1,188

A Chelsea goat and bee jug of conventional type, incised triangle mark, 1745-49, 11cm. high. (Christie's) $5,385

A Chelsea silver shaped plate painted in the Kakiemon palette with The Red Tiger Pattern, 1750-52, 23cm. diam. (Christie's) $6,336

A Chelsea flared and fluted coffee cup with scroll handle, circa 1750, 7.5cm. high. (Christie's) $2,692

Late 19th century Chelsea Keramic Art Works square molded vase, 7½in. high, 4in. diam. (Robt. W. Skinner Inc.) $450

A Chelsea plate with Gots-zkowsky erhabene Blumen, circa 1753, 24cm. diam. (Christie's) $633

A Chelsea gold mounted scent bottle naturalistically modelled as a peach, circa 1755, 7cm. high. (Christie's) $1,188

CHINESE

A large Chinese bottle-shaped porcelain vase, 25in. high. (Parsons, Welch & Cowell) $477

A rose-verte armorial dish, circa 1735, 14in. diam. (Christie's) $3,436

A 17th century Dehua blanc-de-chine figure of Guandi, 24cm. high, fitted box. (Christie's) $2,044

One of a pair of 19th century rose medallion garden seats, China, 19in. high. (Robt. W. Skinner Inc.) $5,250

A Yue Yao circular box and cover, Five Dynasties, 7cm. diam. (Christie's) $1,494 £1,045

A slate panel carved in high relief through a buff surface to the darker ground, late Qing Dynasty, 34 x 28cm., wood stand. (Christie's) $1,258

A dragon saucer dish painted in iron-red and gilt , unenclosed Guangxu six-character mark and of the period, 34cm. diam. (Christie's) $943

A 19th century large pottery Foo dog and stand, China, 29in. high with stand. (Robt. W. Skinner Inc.) $1,600

A large Export armorial dish painted in shades of blue, yellow, iron-red, green and gilt, circa 1740, 17in. diam. (Christie's) $4,686

CHINESE

A flambe glazed bottle vase, impressed Qianlong seal mark and of the period, 45.5cm. high. (Christie's)
$4,719

A Doucai saucer dish, Qianlong seal mark and of the period, 52cm. diam. (Christie's)
$13,370

A transitional Wucai gu-shaped beaker vase, circa 1640, 41.2cm. high. (Christie's) $2,831

An 11th/12th century Annamese jar and shallow domed cover, Thanh Hoa, 21cm. high. (Christie's)
$597

Pair of modern Chinese ducks, on punchwork base, each 9½in. high. (Christie's) $440

A phosphatic-splashed ovi-form ewer, Tang Dynasty, 16cm. high. (Christie's)
$4,719

One of four late 18th century Chinese Export soup plates, 8.7/8in. diam. (Christie's)
$1,870

A 17th/18th century Dehua blanc-de-chine figure of Guanyin, 40cm. high. (Christie's) $2,674

An Annamese blue and white dish, 15th century, 15in. diam. (Christie's)
$1,327

Early 19th century Oriental Export porcelain punch bowl, China, rim diam. 14¾in., 6in. high. (Robt. W. Skinner Inc.) $2,100

One of a pair of Doucai bowls, Daoguang seal marks and of the period, 14.3cm. diam. (Christie's) $3,146

19th century Chinese square cut corner 'Thousand Butterfly' porcelain salad bowl, 10¼in. diam. (Robt. W. Skinner Inc.) $750

One of a pair of Oriental square porcelain vases, 12in. high. (Chancellors Hollingsworths) $275

A straw-glazed and painted figure of a richly caparisoned horse, Sui Dynasty, 32cm. high. (Christie's) $5,033

A flambe glazed rectangular pear-shaped vase, impressed Qianlong seal mark and of the period, 30cm. high. (Christie's) $1,415

One of a pair of blue and white baluster vases with elephant handles, 14th century, 21.9cm. high. (Christie's) $4,876

One of a pair of blue and white armorial dishes, circa 1752, 13¼in. diam. (Christie's) $14,839

One of a pair of 19th century rose Mandarin porcelain temple jars with mask and ring handles, China, 17½in. high. (Robt. W. Skinner Inc.) $1,600

CLARICE CLIFF

A Clarice Cliff Latona pottery oviform vase, painted with green, purple, white and orange flowers, 16.5cm. high. (Phillips) $216

A large Clarice Cliff circular plaque from a design by Frank Brangwyn, in polychrome, 17in. diam., painted inscription No. 3. (Christie's) $2,416

A Clarice Cliff Bizarre pottery mask, kite-shaped, 28cm. long. (Christie's) $1,793

A Clarice Cliff Fantasque pottery jug with loop handle, 23cm. high, printed factory marks. (Phillips) $201

A Clarice Cliff Bizarre cubist breakfast set painted with geometric designs in red, blue, green and ochre, circa 1931. (Christie's) $835

A Clarice Cliff Fantasque pottery vase, painted in brown, black green, yellow and orange with a cottage and trees, 20.3cm. high. (Phillips) $216

A Clarice Cliff 'Fantasque' pottery vase of flared form, 13.9cm. high, together with a Presnec pot and cover. (Phillips) $182

A Clarice Cliff 'Inspiration' charger, 'The Knight Errant', 45.5cm. high. (Phillips) $1,728

A Clarice Cliff Fantasque lotus jug, 25cm. high, printed factory marks. (Phillips) $648

COALPORT

A Coalport (John Rose) oviform vase, painted with a silhouette portrait of George III, circa 1810, 20.5cm. high. (Christie's) $443

A Coalport blue and white oval two-handled soup tureen and cover, transfer-printed with pagodas on river islands, circa 1800, 37cm. wide. (Christie's) $474

One of a pair of Coalport oviform jugs, circa 1800, 20cm. high. (Christie's) $1,439

A Coalport (John Rose & Co.) Great Exhibition plate, 1851, 26cm. diam. (Christie's) $1,267

A Coalport spirally molded oviform jug, circa 1800, 22.5cm. high. (Christie's) $406

One of a pair of Coalport iron-red-ground flared bucket-shaped flower pots and stands, painted by Thos. Baxter, circa 1805, approx. 13cm. high. (Christie's) $3,801

COPELAND

Copeland bust of Comte d'Orsay. (Lots Road Galleries) $86

Bust of Venus. (Lots Road Galleries) $72

A white bust of a gentleman. (Lots Road Galleries) $50

HANS COPER

A stoneware goblet form vase, by Hans Coper, circa 1975, 13.7cm. high. (Christie's) $5,977

A black glazed stoneware stemmed cup form, by Hans Coper, circa 1960, 13.1cm. high. (Christie's) $3,578

A stoneware goblet-shaped vase, by Hans Coper, with waisted oval section rim, circa 1970, 24.9cm. high. (Christie's) $9,583

A stoneware black bulbous bottle, by Hans Coper, circa 1965, 14.7cm. high. (Christie's) $8,651

A waisted cylindrical stoneware vase, by Hans Coper, circa 1958, 17.3cm. high. (Christie's) $3,965

A stoneware shouldered bottle vase, by Hans Coper, circa 1970, 20.8cm. high. (Christie's) $8,262

A stoneware goblet vase, by Hans Coper, circa 1952, 15.2cm. high. (Christie's) $5,505

A stoneware spherical vase, by Hans Coper, with horizontal flange, 1951, 19cm. high. (Christie's) $11,566

A monumental stoneware 'thistle' vase, by Hans Coper, circa 1965, 57.4cm. high. (Christie's) $44,044

DELFT

A Bristol delft dish, decorated in green, red and blue with the Mimosa pattern, circa 1740, 13¾in. diam. (Dreweatts) $282

A delft posset pot with scroll handles, the waisted body decorated in blue, circa 1720, 5½in. high. (Dreweatts) $275

A delft plate, the cartouche enclosing the initials G H E and date 1714, 8½in. diam., English or Dutch. (Dreweatts) $362

An English delft pierced basket of circular shape raised on bun feet, probably Wincanton or Bristol, 27cm. diam. (Phillips) $3,850

Mid 18th century Dutch Delft polychrome equestrian figure of Prince William of Orange, blue script mark of De Lampetkan, 15cm. high. (Christie's) $475

Late 17th century London delft blue-dash tulip charger, 34cm. diam. (Christie's) $1,188

Early 18th century Delft Dore circular plate, iron-red APK, 146, 614 mark of Pieter Adriaenson Koeks, 24.5cm. diam. (Christie's) $1,346

A London delft dry drug jar, circa 1720, 6in. high. (Dreweatts) $507

Early 18th century Delft Dore circular dish, iron-red APK mark of P. A. Koeks, 30.5cm. diam. (Christie's) $3,801

DELFT

An English delft oak leaf charger with blue-dash rim edged with a yellow band, 34cm. diam. (Phillips) $1,771

A Dutch Delft polychrome shaped plaque modelled and painted with a bird perched in a cage, mid 18th century, 34.5 x 42.5cm. (Christie's) $3,960

A delft plate decorated in blue with a cartouche over the rim, Dutch or English, 1698, 10in. diam. (Dreweatts) $435

An English delft polychrome Royal portrait plate, William and Mary, 22cm. diam. (Phillips) $3,234

Early 18th century Dutch Delft blue and white seated Magot, 18cm. high. (Christie's) $1,188

A London delft blue-dash oak leaf charger, circa 1675, 33.5cm. diam. (Christie's) $4,118

A large delft dish, decorated in blue, green and brown, probably Brislington, circa 1730, 13in. diam. (Dreweatts) $188

One of a pair of London delft blue and white wet-drug jars, named for S. E. Spin, Ceru and S. Papau.Err, circa 1740, 17cm. high. (Christie's) $665

Early 18th century Delft Dore circular plate, iron-red APK monogram of Pieter A. Koeks, 23cm. diam. (Christie's) $3,168

DERBY

A Derby figure of Jupiter, scantily draped in a turquoise-lined pink flowered cloak, circa 1765, 27.5cm. high. (Christie's) $1,188

Part of a Derby dessert service painted in the manner of Wm. Cotton, Robert Bloor & Co., circa 1815. (Christie's) $2,851

A Derby hairdressing group, modelled as a gallant beside a lady dressing her hair, crown, crossed batons and D mark in iron-red, circa 1830, 18cm. high. (Christie's) $633

A Derby 'dry-edge' group of a goat and kid, decorated in the workshop of Wm. Duesbury, Andrew Planche's period, circa 1752, 12cm. wide. (Christie's) $6,652

A Derby seamstress group, modelled as a gallant standing beside a maid repairing his stockings, Robert Bloor & Co., circa 1830, 16.5cm. high. (Christie's) $712

Part of a Crown Derby china teaset, Japan pattern with rouge-de-fer blue, gilt and green decoration, 58 pieces. (Graves Son & Pilcher) $1,585

A Derby shoe-black group, modelled as a gallant, his shoes being polished by a maid, incised No. 81, Robert Bloor & Co., circa 1830, 18.5cm. high. (Christie's) $950

A Derby baluster pot pourri vase and pierced domed cover, Wm. Duesbury & Co., circa 1760, 19cm. high. (Christie's) $633

A Derby sweetmeat figure modelled as a lady seated, Wm. Duesbury & Co., circa 1760, 17cm. high. (Christie's) $823

DERBY

A Derby figure of Jupiter holding a thunderbolt, circa 1770, 29cm. high. (Christie's) $712

One of a pair of Derby fluted lozenge-shaped dishes, the centers painted in the manner of Steele with fruit, circa 1810, 28.5cm. wide. (Christie's) $1,584

A Derby figure of John Milton leaning on a pile of books, Wm. Duesbury & Co., circa 1765, 29cm. high. (Christie's) $570

A Crown Derby squat vase and cover with two mask handles, circa 1884, 5in. high, printed mark in blue. (Dreweatts) $290

A Derby owl, its plumage in yellow, brown and pink perched astride a tree-stump, circa 1765, 6.5cm. high. (Christie's) $1,108

A Derby white 'dry-edge' figure of Winter modelled as a scantily draped putto, Andrew Planche's period, circa 1752, 10.5cm. high. (Christie's) $712

A Derby figure of Shakespeare in yellow-lined purple cloak, Wm. Duesbury & Co., circa 1765, 27.5cm. high. (Christie's) $570

One of a pair of Derby pear-shaped vases and covers of tapering form, Wm. Duesbury & Co., circa 1760, 18cm. high. (Christie's) $1,188

A Derby white figure of St. Philip, Wm. Duesbury & Co., circa 1760, 25.5cm. high. (Christie's) $871

DOULTON

A Royal Doulton vase by
Mark V. Marshall, incised
artist's monogram JMJ
247, circa 1910, 51cm.
high. (Christie's)
$7,603

A Royal Doulton miniature
face mask, 'Jester', possibly
HN1611, 7.7cm. long, c.m.
(Phillips) $886

A Doulton stoneware vase
designed by F. Butler,
47.8cm. high. (Christie's)
$1,321

A Royal Doulton Flambe
model of a bulldog, 14.2cm.
high, c.m.l. & c., impressed
date 10.26, no. 135.
(Phillips) $1,430

A Royal Doulton earthenware
figure, 'One of the Forty',
possibly HN646, designed by
H. Tittensor, 18.1cm. high,
c.m.l. & c., shape no. 319.
(Phillips) $2,431

A Royal Doulton Chang
jar and cover, by Harry Nixon,
8in. high. (Christie's)
$1,008

A Royal Doulton stoneware
garden ornament, by Francis
C. Pope, 48.5cm. high, c.m.l.
(Phillips) $228

A Doulton ewer and biscuit
barrel, both with plated lids.
(Lots Road Galleries)
$115

A Doulton Lambeth stone-
ware jug decorated by H. and
F. Barlow and Mark V.
Marshall, 24.5cm. high, r.m.
& e. (Phillips) $886

DOULTON

One of a pair of Royal Doulton Lambeth stoneware baluster vases, by H. Barlow and Florence Roberts, 27.4cm. high, c.m.l. & c., dated shield 1902. (Phillips) $715

A Royal Doulton face mask, 'Jester', probably HN1630, 28.5cm. long, c.m.l.& c., date code for 1937, incised 933. (Phillips) $200

A Doulton Lambeth vase, by Emily Stormer, 24.5cm. high, c.m. dated 1877, artist's monogram numbered 825. (Phillips) $200

A Royal Doulton Cecil Aldin Series Ware jardiniere, the decoration from the 'Old English Scenes', 18cm. high, c.m.l. & c. (Phillips) $243

A Royal Doulton model, 'Kingfisher', 10.5cm. high, c.m.l. & c. (Phillips) $42

A Royal Doulton Flambe model of an elephant, 16.8cm. high, c.m.l. & c., signed Noke. (Phillips) $157

A Royal Doulton stoneware model of a dog, by Gilbert Bayes, 49.5cm. high. (Phillips) $858

A Royal Doulton figure of a bulldog draped in the Union Jack, 7in. high, printed marks. (Christie's) $748

A Doulton Lambeth Silicon Ware oviform vase, by Edith D. Lupton and Ada Dennis, 20.5cm. high, dated 1885. (Phillips) $271

DOULTON

A Royal Doulton pottery character jug modelled as The Gondolier, 8in. high, D6589. (Christie's) $377

Royal Doulton Flambe Buddha, signed Noke, 8in. high. (Hobbs & Chambers) $576

Royal Doulton pottery musical character jug modelled as Owd Mac, 6¼in. high, D5889. (Christie's) $679

A Doulton Lambeth stoneware vase, by Mark V. Marshall, 25cm. high, r.m. artist's monogram no. 3. (Phillips) $386

A Royal Doulton 'Tango' pattern porcelain part coffee set, coffee pot, 20.75cm. high, c.m.l. & c., impressed dates 1.1.35 and 2.1.35. (Phillips) $314

A Doulton Lambeth Faience tile panel, 61.5 x 20.6cm., printed c.m. on reverse of each. (Phillips)$314

A Royal Doulton blue and white oval plaque, printed with a mother and child picking flowers, 14in. wide. (Christie's) $332

A Royal Doulton pottery character jug modelled as The White Haired Clown, 6¼in. high, D6322. (Christie's) $755

A Royal Doulton Flambe figure modelled as a seated Buddha, 6¾in. high, possibly by C. J. Noke. (Christie's) $875

DOULTON

A Royal Doulton figure, 'The Ballet Dancer', probably designed by L. Harradine, 19cm. high, c.m.l. & c., date code for 1943. (Phillips) $1,029

A Doulton stoneware jardiniere with molded decoration of a band of masks of comedy and tragedy, 19cm. high. (Christie's) $660

A Royal Doulton figure, 'Teresa', HN1683, designed by L. Harradine, 14cm. high, c.m.l. & c., date code for 1936, introduced 1935, withdrawn 1938. (Phillips) $1,144

A Doulton Burslem porcelain fruit set, by Walter Slater, each piece painted in natural colors with dandelion buds and clocks, flowers and leaves, b.r.m. & c., England, Rd. no. 72067. (Phillips) $572

Royal Doulton Dewar's whisky moonflask, printed design no. 181, circa 1919, 8in. high. (Peter Wilson) $282

A Royal Doulton Holbein Ware plaque, by Walter Nunn, 11.4 x 18.3cm. image area, c.m.l. & c. (Phillips) $572

A Doulton Lambeth Faience moonflask, decorated by Hannah Barlow, 9½in. high. (Christie's) $504

DOULTON

A Doulton Lambeth jug, by Arthur B. Barlow, 17cm. high, o.m. dated 1873, artist's monogram no. 777. (Phillips) $171

One of a pair of Royal Doulton Cecil Aldin Titanian glazed Series Ware vases, 15.5cm. high, c.m.l. & c., printed D 4525. (Phillips) $157

A Doulton Lambeth stone-ware garden seat, possibly designed by Mark V. Marshall, 51.5cm. high. (Phillips) $1,287

A Royal Doulton Flambe model of a pair of penguins, 15cm. high, c.m.l. & c. (Phillips) $114

A Royal Doulton face mask, 'Sweet Anne', HN1590, design attributed to L. Harradine, 20.2cm. long, c.m.l. & c., impressed date 4.7.33. (Phillips) $357

A Royal Doulton advertising model of a bulldog, 14.7cm. high, c.m.l. & c., Rd. no. 645658. (Phillips) $858

A Royal Doulton miniature face mask, possibly by L. Harradine, HN1614, 7cm. high, c.m. (Phillips) $429

A Doulton Lambeth figural group by George Tinworth, 14.1cm. high, r.m., dated 1881. (Phillips) $943

'The Red-Haired Clown', a Royal Doulton character jug, 6¼in. high, and Mr. Pickwick, 4in. high. (Christie's) $1,728

DOULTON

A Doulton Lambeth stoneware biscuit barrel, by Florence and Lucy Barlow, 20cm. high, r.m. 1883. (Phillips) $686

A Royal Doulton figure, 'Folly', HN1750, designed by L. Harradine, 25cm. high, c.m.l. & c., date code for 1937, introduced 1936, withdrawn 1949. (Phillips) $715

A Royal Doulton Chang vase, by Henry Noke, covered overall in a thick trailing multi-colored glaze, 7½in. high. (Dreweatts) $1,044

A Royal Doulton figure, 'Doreen', 5¾in. high. (Outhwaite & Litherland) $507

A Royal Doulton pottery musical jug modelled as Old Charley, 6in. high, D5858. (Christie's) $528

A large Royal Doulton Flambe model of a fox, glazed in black and red, 23.6cm. high, c.m.l. & c., signed Noke. (Phillips) $171

A Royal Doulton earthenware globular vase, 21.8cm. high, c.m.l. & c. (Phillips) $78

Royal Doulton 'Fox in Red Frock Coat', HN100, 16cm. high, c.m.l. & c. (Phillips) $300

A Royal Doulton miniature face mask, 'Jester', possibly HN1609, 7.5cm. long, c.m. (Phillips) $1,029

A famille rose punch bowl, circa 1765, 13½in. diam. (Christie's) $2,697

One of a pair of 19th century large famille rose urns on pierced wooden stands, 23½in. high. (Christie's) $1,980

A Chinese famille rose and blue and white bowl, 5¾in., seal mark of Daoguang and of the period. (Dreweatts) $1,040

A famille rose armorial oblong octagonal dish, circa 1775, 12¾in. wide. (Christie's) $2,499

One of two late 19th century famille rose covered jars, 6¾in. high. (Christie's) $660

A Chinese famille rose, shaped oval meat dish, Qianlong, 17in. long. (Dreweatts) $1,595

A famille rose armorial dish painted at the center with a coat-of-arms and crest, circa 1730, 11in. diam. (Christie's) $1,093

A famille rose gilt ground wig stand and cover, gilt Jiaqing seal mark and of the period, 27.9cm. high. (Christie's) $2,831

Late 18th century famille rose Canton enamel circular segmented supper set formed as eight fan-shaped dishes, 18in. diam. (Christie's) $1,015

FAMILLE VERTE

A 19th century Chinese baluster vase decorated with famille verte panels of figures on a powder-blue-ground, 24in. high. (Dreweatts) $551

A famille verte oval incense basket and cover with high strap handle, Kangxi, 12.5cm. wide. (Christie's) $3,360

A famille verte square bottle, Kangxi, 8¼in. high, fitted as a lamp. (Christie's) $749

A famille verte saucer dish painted with rockwork issuing flowering peony and camellia, Kangxi, 27cm. diam. (Christie's) $1,260

A famille verte pear-shaped vase, reverse painted with a long-tailed bird on rockwork, Kangxi, 19.5cm. high. (Christie's) $1,848

One of a pair of famille verte saucer dishes, Chenhua six-character marks within a double circle, early 18th century, 39cm. diam. (Christie's) $12,584

An 18th century famille verte rouleau vase, 44cm. high. (Christie's) $2,831

A 19th century Chinese famille verte plaque, 17 x 12.5in. (Woolley & Wallis) $372

An 18th/19th century famille verte group formed as a large Buddhistic lion, 12½in. high. (Christie's) $499

Mid 18th century Aire
Faience blue and white
trompe l'oeil waved circular
dish, 24cm. diam.
(Christie's) $3,142

A Mennecy teapot and cover
of globular shape with
double ogee handle and
flower finial, 9.5cm. high,
incised DV mark. (Phillips)
$1,108

One of a pair of French
Faience oval two-handled
glass coolers, circa 1760,
28cm. wide. (Christie's)
$1,130

A Moustiers shaped circular
plate, manganese GOL and
cross mark of Olerys and
Laugier, circa 1740, 25cm.
diam. (Christie's)
$1,130

A pair of Mennecy figures
of a young man and woman,
circa 1740, 17.5cm. high.
(Christie's) $2,851

Mid 18th century Rouens
Faience circular plate of
panier de fleurs pattern,
24.5cm. diam. (Christie's)
$1,632

A Chantilly Kakiemon
square box and cover,
iron-red hunting horn
mark, circa 1740, 25cm.
high. (Christie's)
$23,760

One of a pair of Vincennes
two-handled small seaux in
the Meissen style, blue
interlaced L marks enclosing dots, circa 1752,
13.5cm. wide. (Christie's)
$15,048

A Mennecy white pot pourri
vase, incised DV mark on
base, circa 1740, 12cm. high.
(Christie's) $285

FRENCH

One of a pair of documentary Vincennes white hunting groups, La Chasse au Sanglier and La Chasse au Loup, after Oudry, modelled by J. Chabry, circa 1752, 31.5cm. and 32cm. wide. (Christie's) $134,640

A Vincennes bleu lapis conical teapot, blue interlaced L marks and painter's mark of Thevenet, circa 1753, 11cm. high. (Christie's) $1,742

A Moustiers shaped oval dish painted in shades of manganese with Berainesque dwarves, birds and a fox, circa 1740, 33cm. diam. (Christie's) $1,884

A St. Cloud white beaker, cover and saucer with silver gilt mounts, circa 1730. (Christie's) $950

An Art Deco porcelain spirit flask and stopper, 'Joueur de Golfeur', 27.5cm. high. (Phillips) $391

A Vincennes circular bowl, blue crowned interlaced Ls enclosing the Bourbon fleur-de-lys, circa 1752, 32.5cm. diam. (Christie's)
$11,880

A large turquoise glazed ceramic frog, 65cm. high, probably French from Sarreguemines. (Phillips) $1,123

Late 17th century garniture of three Nevers bleu persan vases, 37cm. and 59cm. high. (Christie's) $7,128

One of a pair of Vincennes bleu lapis pots and covers, circa 1754, 7cm. high. (Christie's) $792

GERMAN

A Kloster-Veilsdorf figure 'of Cadi-Leskier, modelled by Pfranger, circa 1770, 14cm. high. (Christie's) $5,028

A Nymphenburg shaped octa-foil saucer dish from the Hof service, impressed P2, circa 1760, 27cm. diam. (Christie's) $4,085

A German white figure of a young boy, probably Wegley or Cassel, circa 1765, 10cm. high. (Christie's) $158

A Ludwigsburg rococo oval two-handled tureen and cover, blue crowned inter-laced C mark and impressed IP, circa 1765, 32cm. wide. (Christie's) $3,801

A Weimar ceramic porcelain oviform chocolate jug, 19cm. high, printed factory mark Leuchtenburg. (Phillips) $72

An 18th century German porcelain gold mounted rectangular snuff box and cover with waisted sides, 8.5cm. wide. (Christie's) $4,118

A Furstenberg figure of a bird seller modelled by Desoches, blue script F mark, circa 1775, 16cm. high. (Christie's) $1,584

A German porcelain wine barrel supported on a wood stand, circa 1880, the barrel 30cm. wide. (Christie's) $1,512

A pair of late 19th century German figures of a gardener and companion, overglazed blue crossed swords mark and incised numerals, 46cm. high. (Christie's) $558

GERMAN

A Cassel white figure of a putto standing nude with loin cloth on tree-stump base, incised IR on base, circa 1770, 9.5cm. high. (Christie's) $1,900

A Bayreuth blue and white circular dish, circa 1730, 22cm. diam. (Christie's) $1,193

A Frankenthal Janus-headed figure, blue crowned CT and AB monogram marks, incised S2, circa 1765, 17cm. high. (Christie's) $1,346

Late 18th century German oblong octagonal snuff box and cover, probably Nymphenburg, 8cm. wide. (Christie's) $6,019

A German Faience enghalskrug of baluster form, the front with initials 'IGS 1730', 34.5cm. high. (Phillips) $5,236

A Niderviller Faience shaped hexafoil dish, circa 1775, 25cm. diam. (Christie's) $8,170

A Hochst group of the garlanded sleeper, modelled by J. P. Melchior, blue wheel mark and incised SX, circa 1770, 19cm. wide. (Christie's) $3,960

A Kelsterbach pipe bowl with silver mounts and hinged cover, 1767-68, 7cm. high. (Christie's) $3,142

A Frankenthal chinoiserie group of lovers, blue crowned CT mark and 74, 17cm. wide. (Christie's) $1,029

GERMAN

A Hochst figure of a young girl holding a basket of pears, modelled by J. P. Melchior, circa 1770, 13cm. high, and another of a girl holding a basket of apples, 10cm. high. (Christie's) $871

A Frankenthal group of a seated young man and two young women, modelled by K. G. Luck, dating from 1778, 23cm. wide. (Christie's) $3,960

A Hochst figure of a boy in white tunic with puce edging, modelled by J. P. Melchior, blue wheel mark, circa 1770, 14.5cm. high. (Christie's) $1,267

A Hochst figure of a boy holding a dog by its tail, modelled by J. P. Melchior, blue wheel mark, circa 1770, 13.5cm. high. (Christie's) $1,267

A Hochst baluster coffee pot and cover, blue wheel mark and incised IN, circa 1765, 18cm. high. (Christie's) $1,346

A Ludwigsburg chinoiserie group, modelled by J. Weinmuller, incised Geer mark, circa 1770, 34cm. high. (Christie's) $2,534

A Hochst figure of a young boy, modelled by J. P. Melchior, blue wheel mark, circa 1770, 14cm. high. (Christie's) $1,188

A Furstenberg arched rectangular tea caddy, impressed no. 2, circa 1770, 10.5cm. high, silver cover. (Christie's) $1,108

A Hochst figure of a boy eating cherries, modelled by J. P. Melchior, traces of blue mark and incised P No. 1, circa 1770, 11.5cm. high. (Christie's) $871

GERMAN

A Hochst figure of a girl, in puce-edged white clothes, modelled by J. P. Melchior, blue wheel mark and incised HM monogram and no. 176, circa 1770, 14.5cm. high. (Christie's) $792

A Frankenthal group, modelled by K. G. Luck, blue crowned CT mark, circa 1770, 14cm. high. (Christie's) $2,692

A Hochst figure of a nymph, emblematic of intelligence, impressed 2H and iron-red painter's mark IZ of J. Zeschinger, circa 1753/4, 16cm. high. (Christie's) $633

A Ludwigsburg figure of Arion, blue interlaced L mark and impressed I.L.F. 53. and with iron-red painter's mark of Sausenhofer, circa 1765, 15cm. high. (Christie's) $380

A Hochst baluster hot-milk jug and cover with artichoke finial, incised HI on base, circa 1760, 14.5cm. high. (Christie's) $570

A Furstenberg figure of a stonemason standing, blue script F mark, circa 1775, 11cm. high. (Christie's) $443

A Hochst figure of a boy, modelled by J. P. Melchior, blue wheel mark and incised HI and other marks, circa 1765, 17.5cm. high. (Christie's) $3,009

A Furstenberg group of Perseus, modelled by Desoches, blue script F mark, circa 1780, 26.5cm. high. (Christie's) $554

A Ludwigsburg standing figure of Flora, circa 1775, 26.5cm. high. (Christie's) $253

GERMAN

Late 19th century German figure of a monkey, decorated in gray and yellow glazes, 46cm. high. (Christie's) $638

A Frankenthal group of a performing bear dancing to a hurdy-gurdy played by one of two boys, circa 1770, 19.5cm. high. (Christie's) $4,399

A Hochst figure of a young man, modelled by J. P. Melchior, incised HM monogram and No. 3, circa 1765, 16cm. high. (Christie's) $1,742

A Limbach group of a family, puce LB monogram mark, circa 1775, 23cm. high. (Christie's) $443

A Siegburg pale gray stoneware schnelle with hinged pewter cover, dated 1566, 21cm. high, (repair to base). (Christie's) $1,188

A Frankenthal group of a young woman embracing an elderly man, modelled by K. G. Luck, circa 1778, 15.5cm. high. (Christie's) $3,168

A Frankenthal figure of a horn player, modelled by Konrad Link, blue crowned CT monogram mark and date mark for 1767, 16.5cm. high. (Christie's) $3,168

A German porcelain rectangular plaque painted with a portrait of Ruth, circa 1880, 20.5 x 13.5cm. (Christie's) $757

A Ludwigsburg figure of Columbine from the Commedia dell'Arte modelled by Franz Anton Pustelli, circa 1760, 10.5cm. high. (Christie's) $3,142

GERMAN

A Furstenberg figure of Bagolin modelled by A. S. Laplau, circa 1775, 12cm. high. (Christie's) $3,456

A Nymphenburg oil and vinegar stand with two bottles and hinged covers, circa 1765, the bottles 18cm. high. (Christie's) $12,571

A Ludwigsburg figure of a youth seated on a rocky out-crop, circa 1770, 19cm. high. (Christie's) $665

A Frankenthal group of four putti emblematic of the Seasons, blue crowned CT mark and dating for 1779, 16.5cm. high. (Christie's) $1,188

Late 17th century Frankfurt blue and white enghalskrug, 24cm. high. (Christie's) $1,267

A Ludwigsburg group of two putti, blue interlaced C's and impressed IO marks, circa 1765, 17cm. high. (Christie's) $554

An Art Deco Schwarzburger Werkstatten porcelain figure, 56cm. high, signed O. Kramer .29. (Phillips) $1,872

An Erfurt cylindrical tankard with pewter foot, circa 1740, 20.5cm. high. (Christie's) $1,346

A Rosenthal porcelain figure, 'Korean Dancer', designed by C. Holzer-Defanti, 40cm. high, printed factory marks for 1929. (Phillips) $576

GOLDSCHEIDER

A Goldscheider figure, from a model by Lorenzl, 13in. high. (Christie's) $226

A wall mask attributed to Goldscheider, modelled as the head of a young girl, orange and green on a flesh-colored ground, 27.3cm. high. (Christie's) $158

A Goldscheider pottery figure of a dancing girl, designed by Lorenzl, 16in. high. (Christie's) $1,057

A Goldscheider pottery figure, modelled as a sailor holding a girl, 30cm. high. (Christie's) $537

A Goldscheider pottery 'Negro' wall mask, 26.5cm. high. (Phillips) $228

An Art Nouveau Goldscheider pottery figure, modelled as a girl wearing long flowing robes, designed by E. Tell, 65cm. high. (Phillips) $691

'Butterfly Girl', a Goldscheider figure after a model by Lorenzl, 7in. high. (Christie's) $634

A Goldscheider pottery double face wall plaque, the two females in profile, 12in. high. (Christie's) $596

A Goldscheider pottery group after a model by Lorenzl, of a flamenco dancer and a guitar player, 17in. high. (Christie's) $893

GOSS & CRESTED CHINA

An Arcadian Nurse and Wounded Tommy, 108mm. long, with Arms of City of Winchester. (Goss & Crested China Ltd.) $114

Shelley Bi-plane, No. 344, with fixed propeller, 150mm. long, bearing a transfer of Peterborough. (Goss & Crested China Ltd.) $99

A lion standing with Wembley Exhibition arms, date 1924-5, 135mm. long. (Goss & Crested China Ltd.)
$405

A three-handled loving cup, 5in. high. (Christie's)
$143

A Savoy Stokes Bomb, 95mm. (Goss & Crested China Ltd.)
$306

Jersey fish basket, arms of Saltash, large size, 58mm. (Goss & Crested China Ltd.)
$24

Parian bust of W. H. Goss, impressed legend and printed mark, 6½in. high. (Christie's) $159

Portland Lighthouse with black band, arms of Leeds, 120mm. high. (Goss & Crested China Ltd.)
$107

Roman Tetinae, International League Model for 1924, printed mark. (Christie's)
$72

A gray pottery horse torso and head formed in two parts, Han Dynasty, 53cm. long. (Christie's) $11,011

A green-glazed pottery hill jar and cover on three bear feet, Han Dynasty, 23cm. high. (Christie's) $1,179

A large painted gray pottery horse torso and head, Han Dynasty, 48.5cm. long. (Christie's) $22,022

A gray earthenware door post, Warring States/Han Dynasty, 82cm. high. (Christie's) $2,988

A green-glazed pottery vase molded with taotie and fixed ring handles, Han Dynasty, 33cm. high. (Christie's) $2,145

A massive green-glazed red pottery watch-tower, in four sections, Han Dynasty, 134cm. high. (Christie's) $22,022

A painted gray pottery cocoon-shaped jar, some earth encrustation, Han Dynasty, 26.5cm. wide. (Christie's) $1,101

A green-glazed red pottery jar, Han Dynasty, 36cm. high. (Christie's) $2,359

A green-glazed red pottery hill jar and related cover, Han Dynasty, 22cm. high. (Christie's) $943

IMARI

An Imari circular deep bowl decorated in various colored enamels and gilt on underglaze blue, Meiji period, 25cm. diam. (Christie's) $1,405

One of a pair of Imari models of a man partly clad in a kimono seated astride a large carp, circa 1700, approx. 26cm. long. (Christie's) $5,935

Late 19th century Imari deep bowl decorated in typical colors and gilt on underglaze blue, 25cm. diam. (Christie's) $749

An 18th century Imari figure of an actor decorated in various colored enamels and gilt on underglaze blue, 47cm. high. (Christie's) $2,186

One of a pair of Imari models of a cockerel and hen, Genroku period, 28cm. and 24cm. high. (Christie's) $6,996

An 18th century Imari globular bottle vase with tall neck, 23.5cm. high. (Christie's) $2,098

An Imari oviform jar and cover decorated in iron-red enamel and gilt on underglaze blue, Genroku period, 48cm. high. (Christie's) $3,847

Late 19th century Genroku style Imari dish decorated in various enamels on underglaze blue, 57cm. diam. (Christie's) $11,715

An Imari model of a bijin decorated in colored enamels on underglaze blue, Genroku period, 38cm. high. (Christie's) $4,547

IMARI

One of a pair of Imari jars and covers, Genroku period, 53cm. high. (Christie's) $7,810

A Japanese Imari soup plate painted with 'La Dame au Parasol', circa 1735, 9¼in. diam. (Christie's) $2,186

Late 17th/early 18th century molded Imari pear-shaped coffee pot, 44cm. high. (Christie's) $1,874

A large Imari plaque with a scalloped border, decorated in underglaze blue and over glaze red and green enamels, 16in. diam. (Outhwaite & Litherland) $232

Late 17th century Ko-Imari koro modelled as a kirin, 23cm. high. (Christie's) $2,343

A large Imari dish decorated in iron-red, green, aubergine, black enamels and gilt on underglaze blue, Genroku period, 53.5cm. diam. (Christie's) $6,560

One of a pair of Imari Tokkuri decorated in typical colors and gilt, 23cm. high. (Christie's) $1,249

Large Imari porcelain jardiniere, Japan, 18in. high, 21¼in. diam. (Robt. W. Skinner Inc.) $1,700

Late 17th century Imari gin cask modelled as a bijin seated on a stylized cart, 40cm. high. (Christie's) $4,061

138

IMARI

One of a pair of Japanese
Imari bottle vases, circa 1900,
12in. high. (Peter Wilson)
$1,128

Late 18th/early 19th century
Imari foliate rimmed blue
and white bowl, 37cm. diam.
(Christie's) $1,874

Late 17th century Imari
conical coffee pot with loop
handle, 34cm. high.
(Christie's) $1,562

Late 19th century Imari
dish painted in underglaze
blue, iron-red, colored
enamels and gilt, 78.6cm.
diam. (Christie's)
$4,373

One of a pair of late 17th
century Imari trumpet-shaped
beaker vases, 30cm. high.
(Christie's) $3,436

An Imari dish decorated in
iron-red, green, black,
aubergine enamels and gilt
on underglaze blue, Meiji
period, 53cm. diam.
(Christie's) $2,499

One of a pair of Imari
models of leaping carp,
Genroku period, 25cm. high.
(Christie's) $4,998

Late 19th century Imari
foliate rimmed jardiniere,
38cm. high. (Christie's)
$2,186

One of a pair of late 17th
century Imari models of a
cockerel and hen with a
chick, 16cm. high.
(Christie's) $3,748

A Deruta majolica albarello, inscribed 'Ghoma di Lava', on a scroll surrounded by grotesques and leaf forms, 18.5cm. high. (Phillips) $492

A Faenza circular tondino of Cardinal's hat form, circa 1525, 25cm. diam. (Christie's) $21,384

A 17th century Castel Durante baluster armorial pharmacy bottle, 22cm. high. (Christie's) $2,534

Early 18th century Castelli circular tondo painted with St. Francis of Assisi, 20cm. diam., (minor rim chip). (Christie's) $506

A 16th/17th century Italian majolica blue glazed, two-handled baluster vase with dolphin handles, 27cm. high. (Christie's) $1,267

An 18th century Castelli circular tondo, 24.5cm. diam., (rim chips). (Christie's) $554

A Doccia baluster coffee pot and cover with bird's head mask spout, circa 1780, 22cm. high. (Christie's) $443

A Savona or Albissola majolica syrup jar, from the workshop of Luigi Levantino, with short spout and loop handle, 19cm. high. (Phillips) $739

A Le Nove white group of a dancing gallant and companion, circa 1780, 16cm. high. (Christie's) $538

ITALIAN

A Montelupo majolica circular dish, painted in blue, ochre and green with an equestrian figure, 32cm. high. (Phillips) $770

A Doccia teacup and saucer, circa 1765. (Christie's) $475

A Montelupo majolica circular dish, with an equestrian figure carrying a flag, 31.5cm. diam. (Phillips) $847

Late 16th century Palermo waisted albarello, 26.5cm. high. (Christie's) $792

A pair of mid 18th century Castelli circular tondi, 20cm. diam. (Christie's) $2,692

A dated Montelupo albarello of dumb-bell shape, the reverse dated 1561, 21cm. high. (Phillips) $847

Late 18th century bassano shaped circular dish, 34cm. diam. (Christie's) $1,193

A Montelupo wet drug jar with ovoid body and two green dolphin handles, 33cm. high. (Phillips) $1,047

A Savona blue and white pierced tazza, blue lighthouse mark, circa 1700, 35.5cm. diam. (Christie's) $1,108

Mid 18th century Castelli documentary circular plate painted with Lot and his daughters, 17.5cm. diam. (Christie's) $316

A Capodimonte oviform teapot with scroll handle and spout, blue fleur-de-lys mark, circa 1750, 14.5cm. wide. (Christie's) $1,188

A Gubbio lustre tondino, painted in red and yellow lustre and in green and blue, circa 1530, 22cm. diam. (Christie's) $7,603

Early 17th century Palermo oviform vase, 27.5cm. high. (Christie's) $1,188

Late 17th century pair of Sicilian figures of Adam and Eve, 26cm. high, (minor glaze loss). (Christie's) $1,425

A Castelli rectangular plaque painted with Abraham sacrificing a lamb, circa 1720, 27 x 20.5cm. (Christie's) $1,425

A Gubbio lustre plate painted in ruby lustre, blue and green, circa 1530, 25cm. diam. (Christie's) $14,256

A 1950's Italian china Galle figure of a kneeling semi-dressed female figure, 18in. high. (Reeds Rains) $775

Late 18th century Castelli circular plate, blue G.M. mark, 18cm. diam. (Christie's) $348

JAPANESE

CHINA

A porcellanous stem dish, by Shoji Hamada, the cup with pentafoil bowl, circa 1922, 7.8cm. high. (Christie's) $1,817

A Kakiemon model of a bijin decoated in iron-red, blue, green, yellow and black enamels, circa 1680, 36cm. high. (Christie's) $14,058

A Kakiemon bowl with molded rim, circa 1680, 21.5cm. diam. (Christie's) $15,620

A Kakiemon oviform ewer of Islamic form, Kanbun/ Empyo period (1663-81), 33cm. high. (Christie's) $11,715

One of a pair of Kakiemon-type foliate blue and white shallow dishes, late 17th century, 34cm. diam. (Christie's) $15,391

A Kakiemon model of a standing bijin decorated in iron-red, blue, green, aubergine and black enamels and gilt, circa 1680, 41cm. high. (Christie's) $7,870

A stoneware bottle-shaped vase, by Shoji Hamada, circa 1930, 37.4cm. high. (Christie's) $1,982

Late 19th century Satsuma hexagonal oviform jar on tripod feet, 22.5cm. high. (Christie's) $4,547

A Kakiemon hexagonal jar and domed cover, Empo/ Jokoyo period (1673-1687), 32cm. high. (Christie's) $96,195

A stoneware press molded rectangular bottle, by Shoji Hamada, covered in panels of tenmoku and dark turquoise glaze, circa 1960, 25.1cm. high. (Christie's) $1,982

A stoneware jug, by Shoji Hamada, covered in a grayish-green glaze decorated in iron-brown brushwork with scrolling foliage, circa 1922, 8.3cm. high.(Christie's) $231

Late 19th century Kinkozan tapering cylindrical vase decorated in various colors and gilt on glazed blue, 24.5cm. high. (Christie's) $1,562

A stoneware bowl on shallow foot, by Shoji Hamada, covered in a tenmoku glaze with brushwork decoration, circa 1921, 18cm. diam. (Christie's) $908

A stoneware bottle vase, by Shoji Hamada, covered in a lustrous black glaze with areas of running iron-brown, circa 1922, 24.6cm. high. (Christie's) $578

Late 19th century Kyoto square dish with canted corners, 15.7cm. sq. (Christie's) $937

A stoneware carved jar and cover, by Shoji Hamada, circa 1922, 10.5cm. high. (Christie's) $908

A 19th century Kiyomizu rounded rectangular koro, 23cm. high. (Christie's) $546

A stoneware globular vase with two strap lug handles, by Shoji Hamada, circa 1922, 15.9cm. high. (Christie's) $527

A small stoneware jar, by Shoji Hamada, circa 1920, 7.3cm. high. (Christie's) $263

Late 19th century Seifu blue and white plate, 21cm. diam. (Christie's) $702

Late 18th century bowl and cover modelled as a seashell with smaller shells, probably Hirado, 14.4cm. wide. (Christie's) $656

Late 19th century Shofu oviform vase with everted rim, 22cm. high. (Christie's) $343

A stoneware molded rectangular tray, by Shoji Hamada, with printed label Made in Japan, circa 1960, 2.5cm. (Christie's) $743

A stoneware press molded rectangular bottle vase, by Shoji Hamada, circa 1960, 23.5cm. high. (Christie's) $7,931

A Raku roughly potted jar and cover, by Keiko Hasegawa, 19.8cm. high. (Christie's) $527

A 19th century large Kyoto-Satsuma oviform vase, signed Nihon Kyoto Kinkozan zo, 83cm. high. (Christie's) $3,124

One of a pair of late 19th century Hirado saucer-shaped dishes, each decorated in Kutani style, 61.2cm. diam. (Christie's) $5,467

A George Jones game-pie dish and cover, impressed maker's monogram GJ, George Jones within crescent moon and registration lozenge for 1873, 37cm. long. (Christie's) $2,871

A George Jones strawberry set, comprising a tray and two detachable containers, impressed maker's monogram GJ and registration lozenge for 1875, 23cm. high. (Christie's) $925

A George Jones sweetmeat dish, molded monogram GJ and Stoke-on-Trent and impressed registration lozenge for 1868, 30cm. diam. (Christie's) $1,036

A George Jones flower holder modelled as three wicker baskets, with molded registration lozenge for 1872, 27.8cm. high. (Christie's) $765

Pair of George Jones majolica garden seats of cylindrical form, circa 1874, 18.1/8in. high. (Robt. W. Skinner Inc.) $9,500

A George Jones figure of a camel, impressed with monogram GJ and Kumassie, 23.2cm. high. (Christie's) $1,515

A George Jones majolica ware punch bowl, modelled as Mr. Punch, 21.5cm. diam. (Phillips) $1,800

A George Jones vase, the handles formed as be-ribboned rams' heads, molded maker's monogram GJ and Stoke-on-Trent, 34cm. high. (Christie's) $1,595

A George Jones majolica cheese dome and stand. (Dreweatts) $604

KANGXI

An Imperial famille verte coral-red ground bowl, underglaze blue Kangxi yuzhi mark within a double square and of the period, 11cm. diam. (Christie's) $26,880

A famille verte bowl and cover, Kangxi, 13.5cm. wide, wood stand. (Christie's) $1,176

A famille verte bowl, encircled Kangxi six-character mark and of the period, 14.8cm. diam. (Christie's) $685

A blue and white and underglaze copper red fish bowl, Kangxi, 40cm. diam. (Christie's) $3,775

An iron-red and gilt oviform vase with slender trumpet neck, Kangxi, 28cm. high. (Christie's) $303

A famille verte saucer dish, encircled Kangxi six-character mark and of the period, 24.8cm. diam. (Christie's) $2,856

A famille verte saucer dish, painted in the Kangxi manner, encircled Tongzhi six-character mark and of the period, 18.6cm. diam. (Christie's) $247

A blue and white vase, with period six-character Kangxi mark, 14½in. high. (Christie's) $1,210

A blue and yellow saucer dish, Kangxi six-character mark and of the period, 25.1cm. diam. (Christie's) $2,359

A porcelain circular box and cover, by Bernard Leach, with St. Ives seals, 7.8cm. wide. (Christie's) $1,188

A stoneware tea caddy, by Bernard Leach, circa 1970, 16cm. high. (Christie's) $440

A circular stoneware plate with everted rim decorated by Bernard Leach, 39.2cm. diam., circa 1954. (Christie's) $2,643

A tall stoneware jug, by Bernard Leach, with ribbed rim and strap handle, 28.8cm. high. (Christie's) $495

An oviform stoneware vase, by Bernard Leach, impressed BL and St. Ives seals, circa 1960, 27.6cm. high. (Christie's) $2,045

A tapering stoneware cylindrical vase, by Bernard Leach, circa 1960, 34.2cm. high. (Christie's) $1,074

A stoneware rectangular slab bottle, by Bernard Leach, impressed St. Ives seal, circa 1960, 19.5cm. high. (Christie's) $826

A porcelain footed bowl, by Bernard Leach, circa 1955, 25.7cm. diam. (Christie's) $3,775

A stoneware rectangular slab bottle, by Bernard Leach, circa 1965, 19cm. high. (Christie's) $865

LEACH

A stoneware cut-sided bowl, by Bernard Leach, circa 1965, 25cm. wide. (Christie's) $1,415

An early stoneware rectangular tea caddy, by Bernard Leach, circa 1925, 15.2cm. high. (Christie's) $503

A stoneware teabowl, by Bernard Leach, circa 1969, 14.1cm. diam. (Christie's) $707

A stoneware pilgrim plate with everted rim, decorated by Bernard Leach, 32.2cm. diam. (Christie's) $6,940

A stoneware 'Leaping Deer' vase, by Bernard Leach, impressed St. Ives seal, 35cm. high. (Christie's) $7,435

A circular stoneware plate with everted rim, decorated by Bernard Leach, circa 1957, 32cm. diam. (Christie's) $826

A stoneware oviform vase, by Bernard Leach, circa 1957, 32cm. high. (Christie's) $1,074

A stoneware rectangular slab bottle, by Bernard Leach, circa 1960, 18.5cm. high. (Christie's) $2,674

A tall stoneware elongated oviform vase with flattened sides, by Bernard Leach, circa 1960, 18.5cm. high. (Christie's) $1,258

LENCI

A Lenci centerpiece modelled as a young naked girl, 46cm. high. (Christie's) $1,258

A Lenci figure modelled as a naked girl reclining on a tartan blanket, black painted Lenci marks, 30.7cm. long. (Christie's) $1,258

A Lenci ceramic figure, the young girl in geometric patterned dress, 9½in. high, painted marks. (Christie's) $422

LIVERPOOL

A Liverpool delft blue and white globular bottle painted with a mother and child in a garden, circa 1760, 24cm. high. (Christie's) $762

Late 18th century Naval Liverpool pitcher, England, 11in. high (several chips on rim and a crack on spout seams). (Robt. W. Skinner Inc.) $2,100

A Liverpool Herculaneum green-ground tapering ovi-form vase, circa 1810, 24cm. high. (Christie's) $931

One of four late 18th century Liverpool dinner plates, 10in. diam. (Robt. W. Skinner Inc.) $550

A Christian Liverpool bottle vase of plain pear shape with a slightly flared rim, 28cm. high. (Phillips) $1,925

An inscribed Liverpool delft puzzle jug, the rim with three spouts and hollow handle, circa 1750, 8in. high. (Dreweatts) $3,190

LOWESTOFT

A Lowestoft creamboat of low Chelsea ewer shape, painted in blue with floral swags, 5.5cm. high. (Phillips) $246

A Lowestoft cream jug of barrel shape, painted in underglaze blue with a diaper and scroll cartouche, 7cm. high. (Phillips) $554

A Lowestoft teapot and cover, printed in underglaze blue with the 'Pagoda and Man Crossing a Bridge' pattern, the cover with the 'Wolf and Exotic Bird', 10.5cm. high. (Phillips) $847

A Lowestoft cream jug of slender pear shape, painted by the Tulip Painter, 8.5cm. high. (Phillips) $585

An inscribed Lowestoft 'trifle' mug with single-spur handle, 14cm. high. (Phillips) $7,700

A Lowestoft 'pencilled' cream jug of slender shape, painted with a scene of a chinaman crossing a bridge, 9cm. high. (Phillips) $446

A Lowestoft sparrow-beak jug, painted in underglaze blue with a bold flower spray, 8.5cm. high. (Phillips) $215

A Lowestoft sparrow-beak jug, painted in colors with a floral spray with scattered sprigs, 8.5cm. high. (Phillips) $354

A Lowestoft sparrow-beak jug, painted in blue with pagodas and flowering plants, 9cm. high. (Phillips) $215

CHINA

Queen Caroline: a small lustre pottery cream jug, printed in black with portrait and national flora, 8cm. high. (Phillips) $480

A Zsolnay Pecs lustre group, modelled as two polar bears on a large rock in a green and blue golden lustre, 4½in. high. (Christie's) $400

A Pilkington Royal Lancastrian lustre vase, designed by W. Crane and painted by Wm. S. Mycock, 27cm. high. (Phillips) $1,584

Early 19th century Sunderland lustre pottery jug, 4¾in. high. (Reeds Rains) $131

A Sunderland lustre oviform jug, 9½in. high, circa 1830. (Christie's) $496

A Pilkington's Lancastrian jar and cover, the body decorated by Richard Joyce, 6in. high, date mark for 1911. (Christie's) $576

A Pilkington Lancastrian baluster vase with everted rim, decorated by Walter Crane, 26.6cm. high. (Christie's) $792

Pair of mid 19th century copper lustre jugs with blue band decoration and painted figures of Queen Victoria and Prince Albert, 5½in. high. (Reeds Rains) $372

A lustre Pilkington 'Royal Lancastrian' oviform vase, painted by Richard Joyce, 30.5cm. high. (Phillips) $960

MARTINWARE

A Martin Bros. stoneware bird, 27.5cm. high, the head dated 1891 and the base 1890. (Phillips) $2,880

A large Martin Bros. stoneware jardiniere of tapering cylindrical shape, 32cm. high. (Christie's) $960

A Martin Bros. stoneware bird with detachable head, 9¾in. high, London and Southall, 1902. (Reeds Rains) $6,975

A Martinware stoneware gourd vase, the oviform body incised and cross hatched at the neck with green, 9½in. high. (Christie's) $547

A Martin Bros. stoneware double face jug in buff colored glaze, 7in. high, London and Southall, 1903. (Reeds Rains) $1,395

A Martinware stoneware single handled jug, the incised decoration in shades of brown, green and blue on a cream ground, 8¾in. high. (Christie's) $316

A Martin Bros stoneware two-handled spirit flask, 9½in. high, London and Southall, 1901. (Reeds Rains) $1,085

A Martin Bros. stoneware model of a bird, 36cm. high, the head only dated 1898. (Phillips) $4,896

A Martin Bros. stoneware jug painted with fish and sea monsters on mottled blue ground, 10¼in. high, London and Southall 1897. (Reeds Rains) $1,085

Part of a Mason's Ironstone dinner service, pattern no. 2604, approx. 90 pieces, retailed by Higginbotham and Son, Dublin. (Worsfolds) $5,232

A Mason's ironstone circular jardiniere, the handles in the form of bears, 42cm. diam. (Phillips) $1,152

A Mason's patent ironstone jug decorated in the Chinese taste, 32cm. high. (Lawrence Fine Art) $672

Mason's style jug and foot bath. (John D. Fleming & Co.) $1,411

A comprehensive Mason's ironstone dinner service, decorated in famille rose style, 72 pieces. (Phillips) $6,468

MEISSEN

A Meissen circular saucepan with shaped handle, circa 1740, 18.5cm. wide. (Christie's) $712

A Meissen snuff box and cover, modelled as a recumbent pug-dog, with contemporary copper gilt mounts, circa 1755, 8cm. long. (Christie's) $10,296

A Meissen circular bowl, blue crossed swords mark and Pressnummer 21, circa 1750, 16.5cm. diam. (Christie's) $871

A Meissen chinoiserie plate; the center painted by C. F. Herold, circa 1728, 22cm. diam. (Christie's) $13,828

A Meissen small Kakiemon hexagonal baluster vase, circa 1735, 10cm. high. (Christie's) $5,970

A Meissen ornithological sugar basin and cover, Pressnummer 6, 1745-50, 11.5cm. diam. (Christie's) $2,136

A Meissen rectangular tea caddy and cover painted in Silbermalerei with chinoiserie figures, circa 1740, 13.5cm. high. (Christie's) $4,713

A Meissen group of a pug bitch suckling her puppy, after a model by Kaendler, 21.5cm. high, crossed swords mark. (Phillips) $677

One of a pair of Meissen baluster pots and covers, one with Pressnummer 37, circa 1740, 9cm. high. (Christie's) $3,456

MEISSEN

A Meissen figure of a Dutchman in dancing attitude, circa 1740, 17cm. high. (Christie's) $506

A Meissen model of a town house of two storeys and an attic, circa 1748, 18cm. high. (Christie's) $6,913

A Meissen figure of an Austrian fusilier, blue crossed swords mark at back, circa 1765, 23.5cm. high. (Christie's) $3,168

A Meissen group of Bacchus, blue crossed swords and dot and 3 mark, circa 1770, 22cm. high. (Christie's) $792

A Meissen Fabeltiere baluster candlestick, blue crossed swords mark and impressed Former's marks, circa 1735, 24cm. high. (Christie's) $5,970

A Meissen baluster hot milk jug and cover with contemporary silver hinge, circa 1740, 14cm. high.(Christie's) $1,571

A Meissen Jagd cup and cover, circa 1733, 42cm. high. (Christie's) $20,113

A Meissen fluted large saucer dish with scalloped rim, circa 1735, 15.5cm. diam. (Christie's) $1,884

A Meissen figure of a lemonseller from the Cris de Paris series, circa 1755, 13.5cm. high. (Christie's) $1,188

MEISSEN

A Meissen figure of Scapin from the Commedia dell' Arte Series modelled by J. J. Kaendler and P. Reinicke, circa 1744, 13.5cm. high. (Christie's) $5,068

A Meissen yellow-ground cylindrical chocolate pot and cover, Pressnummer 21, circa 1740, 15cm. high. (Christie's) $2,010

A Meissen figure of a bread seller, modelled by P. Reinicke and J. J. Kaendler, circa 1755, 19.5cm. high. (Christie's) $3,484

A Meissen turquoise-ground baluster hot milk jug and cover, circa 1740, gilder's mark C. (Christie's) $1,507

A Meissen chinoiserie two-handled pilgrim flask/scent bottle, the sides painted by J. G. Horoldt, circa 1728, 9cm. high. (Christie's) $5,028

A Meissen group of four children scantily clad, blue crossed swords and incised numeral and impressed marks, circa 1880, 17cm. high. (Christie's) $1,093

A Meissen figure of an oars-man, blue crossed swords, star and 4 mark at back, circa 1780, 13.5cm. high. (Christie's) $1,188

A Meissen Kakiemon plate painted with the Flying Fox and Brocade pattern, circa 1740, 24cm. diam. (Christie's) $2,010

A Meissen figure of a gardener, blue crossed swords at back and impressed 1756, 11cm. high. (Christie's) $237

MEISSEN

A Meissen circular sugar bowl and cover, gilt 85 mark, circa 1740, 10cm. diam. (Christie's) $2,010

A Meissen blue and white baluster teapot and domed cover, the porcelain 1725-30, the gilding almost contemporary, 18cm. wide. (Christie's) $2,010

A Meissen cartouche-shaped snuff box and cover, the interior of the base entirely gilt, circa 1730, 7.5cm. wide. (Christie's) $7,128

A Meissen Hausmalerei shell-shaped bowl, painted by F. F. Mayer von Pressnitz, circa 1750, 19cm. wide. (Christie's) $1,130

A Meissen figure of Cupid, blue crossed swords, impressed and incised numeral marks, circa 1880, 19.5cm. high. (Christie's) $673

A Meissen pentagonal saucer painted with the Red Dragon pattern, circa 1730. (Christie's) $691

A Meissen rectangular tea caddy and cover, circa 1735, in fitted case, 11cm. high. (Christie's) $3,456

A Meissen group of Europa and the Bull, circa 1880, 22.5cm. high. (Christie's) $1,093

A Meissen circular sugar bowl and cover with flower-bud finial, blue crossed swords mark, circa 1750, 10.5cm. diam. (Christie's) $1,029

MEISSEN

A Meissen chinoiserie oval sugar box and cover, blue crossed swords mark and incised W, circa 1730, 12cm. wide. (Christie's) $16,342

A Meissen KPM chinoiserie baluster teapot and domed cover, circa 1723-25, 15.5cm. wide. (Christie's) $11,314

A Meissen cartouche-shaped snuff box and cover, circa 1745, 7.5cm. wide. (Christie's) $8,712

A Meissen KPM chinoiserie two-handled bowl and cover, circa 1725, 13cm. wide. (Christie's) $26,399

A Meissen group of nude girls standing beside a tree stump, circa 1880, 18.5cm. high. (Christie's) $673

A Meissen rectangular waisted snuff box and cover, with hinged silver mount, circa 1760, 8cm. wide. (Christie's) $2,851

A Meissen dish with barbed rim, circa 1735, 37.5cm. diam. (Christie's) $1,571

A Meissen chinoiserie hot milk jug and cover, circa 1735, in fitted case, 15cm. high. (Christie's) $2,387

A Meissen saucer dish from the Bamberg Service, blue crossed swords and K mark for Kretschmar, circa 1730, 21.5cm. diam. (Christie's) $2,059

Early/mid 18th century blue and white moonflask molded and painted in early Ming taste, 31cm. high. (Christie's) $1,887

One of a pair of Ming blue and white vases, meiping, circa 1500, 24.5cm. high. (Christie's) $3,932

A late Ming blue and white frog kendi modelled as a seated frog, Wanli, 16cm. high. (Christie's) $2,202

A late Ming blue and white barrel-shaped garden seat with lion mask handles, Wanli, 38cm. high. (Christie's) $3,146

A late Ming blue and white saucer dish with foliate rim, Wanli, 52cm. diam. (Christie's) $3,775

A late Ming blue and white gu-shaped vase, Wanli, 9¾in. high. (Christie's) $1,483

A late Ming blue and white baluster jar, encircled Wanli six-character mark and of the period, 34cm. high. (Christie's) $14,943

A Ming blue and white stem cup, encircled Wanli six-character mark at the center and of the period, 10cm. diam. (Christie's) $14,157

A late Ming polychrome square table screen probably for the Japanese market, Tianqi, 17.4cm. sq. (Christie's) $4,089

MINTON

A Minton parian figure of Florinda, after John Bell, 13¼in. high, 1848. (Parsons, Welch & Cowell) $138

A Minton mushroom teapot, gourd-shaped, yellow body with naturalistic polychrome coloring, impressed Minton with date code for 1862, 14.8cm. high. (Christie's) $638

A Minton parian figure of Dorothea, after John Bell, 13¾in. high, registration tablet for 1872. (Parsons, Welch & Cowell) $323

Minton Art Deco hexagonal garden seat, 18in. tall, marked No. 1364. (Worsfolds) $604

A Minton centerpiece with flower form base divided into six segmented compartments, date code for 1865, 36.5cm. high. (Christie's) $4,785

A Minton majolica vase, impressed Minton 1558 date code for 1870, 17.9cm. high. (Christie's) $538

A majolica teapot in the form of a monkey, probably Minton, 10¼in. high. (Reeds Rains) $518

Pair of Minton candlesticks, impressed Minton and with date code for 1862, 41.2cm. high. (Christie's) $1,116

A Minton vase, designed by Dr. C. Dresser, U-shaped on four splayed feet, 19.2cm. high. (Christie's) $1,817

MINTON

A Minton jug, impressed Minton 474 and with date code for 1870, 32cm. high. (Christie's) $797

A large Minton oval platter on four bracket feet, glazed in green, yellow, brown and white, impressed Minton 927 O and date code for 1870, 61cm. long. (Christie's) $1,595

One of a pair of Minton jugs, each one impressed Minton 596, one with date code for 1867, one for 1870, 24.5cm. high. (Christie's) $319

A Minton figure modelled as a bare-foot maiden in a full-length robe, naturalistic polychrome coloring, impressed date code for 1857, 44.7cm. high. (Christie's) $717

A large Minton jardiniere with bearded ram's head handles, aubergine with naturalistic polychrome coloring, date code for 1851, 36cm. high. (Christie's) $1,276

A Minton jardiniere and stand, designed by Albert Carrier de Belleuse, jardiniere impressed Mintons 990 and with date code for 1872, base impressed Minton 2227, 168cm. high. (Christie's) $19,140

One of a pair of garden seats modelled as crouching monkeys holding coconuts and supporting cushions on their heads, 46.5cm. high. (Christie's) $15,950

A Minton plant trough, rectangular shape with rounded bottom on attached bracket support, 35.8cm. high. (Christie's) $10,367

One of a pair of Minton vases of swollen baluster shape, impressed Minton 827 and 827A, 35.5cm. high. (Christie's) $2,233

MINTON

A Minton two-handled vase, naturalistic polychrome coloring on pale blue ground, impressed Minton and with date code for 1870, 40.7cm. high. (Christie's)
$1,276

A Minton fish platter and cover, the cover modelled as a carp, impressed Mintons 1979 and with date code for 1903, 61cm. long.(Christie's)
$3,030

One of a pair of Minton 'Tower' jugs, impressed 1231 and with date codes for 1868(?), 34.5cm. high. (Christie's) $957

A Minton sweet chestnut dish and spoon, impressed marks Minton 594N and date mark for 1867, 24.5cm. diam. (Christie's) $1,515

A Minton jardiniere with a molded frieze of figures, pale blue and white with a pink interior, impressed Minton 534, 29cm. high. (Christie's) $957

A Minton porcelain figure of a putto seated upon a conch shell, impressed Mintons 1539 and with date code for 1873, 43.5cm. high. (Christie's) $1,435

A Minton wall plaque, ochre and cobalt blue on a turquoise ground, impressed Minton 1668 and with date code for 1873, 51cm. long. (Christie's)
$829

A Minton figure modelled as a boy in rustic garb, his arm round the neck of a donkey, impressed Minton 196, 20cm. high. (Christie's) $478

One of a pair of Minton pedestal form garden seats, naturalistic polychrome coloring on an olive ground, 43cm. high. (Christie's)
$3,190

MOORCROFT

A Moorcroft wheatear motif vase with green and purple tones on an off-white ground, 13½in. high. (Locke & England) $691

A Moorcroft pottery dark pink glazed box and cover, designed for Liberty & Co., 3¾in. high. (Christie's) $422

A Moorcroft pottery vase, the body decorated in the leaf and blackberry pattern, 6in. high. (Christie's) $115

A Moorcroft 'Spanish' pattern pot pourri of oviform with screw cover, 10.2cm. high. (Phillips) $261

A Moorcroft MacIntyre Florian ware four-piece teaset, in shades of blue and white, teapot, 4½in. high. (Christie's) $387

One of a pair of Moorcroft Art pottery vases, painted with red and ochre poppies, 10½in. high. (Biddle & Webb) $662

A Moorcroft two-handled box and cover, decorated in the 'Claremont' pattern, 6½in. high. (Christie's) $691

A pair of Moorcroft vases, bodies painted in the pomegranate pattern, 15in. high, impressed marks, signed in green. (Christie's) $716

A Wm. Moorcroft pottery circular plaque, trailed and enamelled with anemonies in red and yellows on a yellow ground with blue center. (Biddle & Webb) $631

One of two blue and white sauceboats of European silver shape, circa 1750, 21cm. wide. (Christie's) $6,009

One of twelve provincial blue and white bowls painted with a stylized landscape, circa 1750, 15cm. diam. (Christie's) $1,638

One of twelve blue and white bowls painted with the 'Scholar on Bridge' pattern, circa 1750, 19cm. diam. (Christie's) $4,643

One of twelve plates painted with the 'Boatman and Six-Flower Border' pattern, circa 1750, 23cm. diam. (Christie's) $3,003

A Martaban olive-brown glazed oviform jar, circa 1750, 29cm. high. (Christie's) $3,012

One of two blue and white dishes, the borders each with three clusters of flowering branches, circa 1750, 42cm. diam. (Christie's) $15,295

One of two blue and white oval butter tubs and shallow domed covers, circa 1750, 11.5cm. wide. (Christie's) $8,739

One of four Chinese Imari spittoons, circa 1750, 12.3cm. diam. (Christie's) $4,096

A blue and white oblong octagonal tureen and cover, circa 1750, 33.5cm. wide. (Christie's) $6,009

A blue and white chamber pot painted with peony and bamboo issuing from rock-work, circa 1750, 18.5cm. diam. (Christie's) $2,293

One of two enamelled globu-lar teapots and shallow domed covers, circa 1750, 21.5cm. wide. (Christie's) $1,529

A blue and white bowl-shaped jug, the handle with a flower spray at right angles to the spout, circa 1750, 21cm. wide. (Christie's) $2,293

One of twelve blue and white plates painted with 'The Boatman and Six-Flower Border' pattern. (Christie's) $8,194

A copper red and celadon glazed figure of a standing dignitary, circa 1750, 18.3cm. high. (Christie's) $30,045

A large blue and white deep dish painted with four fan-tailed fish, circa 1750, 45cm. diam. (Christie's) $10,924

A blue glazed figure of a seated boy, circa 1750, 11.5cm. high. (Christie's) $2,075

A blue and white oval tureen, cover and stand, heavily en-crusted, circa 1750, the stand 41cm. wide. (Christie's) $4,643

A blue and white 'piggy-back' group formed as a standing lady and a small boy, circa 1750, 19.8cm. high. (Christie's) $14,203

One of two blue and white circular tureens and shallow domed covers, circa 1750, 23.5cm. wide. (Christie's) $14,203

One of two blue and white globular teapots and shallow domed covers, circa 1750, 21cm. wide. (Christie's) $3,277

One of two chamber pots, circa 1750, 15.5cm. wide, 12.5cm. diam. (Christie's) $3,754

Part of a set of twelve Chinese Imari teacups and saucers painted with the 'Chrysanthemum Rock' pattern, circa 1750. (Christie's) $12,018

A white glazed figure of a pheasant, circa 1750, 26.3cm. high. (Christie's) $2,621

One of two underglaze blue and gilt dishes painted with the 'Three Pavilions' pattern, circa 1750, 39.5cm. diam. (Christie's) $6,009

An underglaze blue and enamelled cylindrical mug with loop strap handle, circa 1750, 13.5cm. high. (Christie's) $2,075

One of two blue and white spittoons, the interior with a border of trellis pattern, circa 1750, 12.6cm. diam. (Christie's) $3,277

One of two cylindrical condiment jars and shallow domed covers, with a wide loop handle, circa 1750, 11.5cm. wide. (Christie's) $6,009

A Paris tea kettle, cover and stand, iron-red monogram mark of Louis-Stanislas-Xavier, circa 1780, 30cm. wide. (Christie's) $2,387

One of a pair of Paris center-pieces, modelled as biscuit figures of Cupid, circa 1820, 32.5cm. high. (Christie's) $957

A Paris gold-ground cabinet-cup and saucer, circa 1815. (Christie's) $1,178

A Paris (Schoelcher) tea service in the Empire taste, the salmon-pink grounds painted in sepia with vases of fruit flanked by putti seated on foliage scrolls and anthemion on wide bands beneath richly gilt borders, the interiors richly gilt, puce script marks, circa 1820. (Christie's) $4,147

One of a pair of late 19th century Paris porcelain urns, 10½in. high. (Christie's) $440

A Paris yellow-ground ewer and oval basin, circa 1820, the ewer 26.5cm. high, the basin 32cm. wide. (Christie's) $797

A Paris porcelain coffee pot of pear form with strap handle, 9½in. high. (Christie's) $323

PRATTWARE

A Pratt type Toby jug modelled as a rotund gentleman seated, entitled 'Tobey', 9¾in. high, circa 1790. (Christie's) $930

A Prattware flask of circular form with a portrait of The Duke of York and the reverse Louis XVI and Marie Antoinette, 5in. high, circa 1794. (Christie's) $186

A Prattware Toby jug, his pipe by his left side, 24cm. high. (Phillips) $720

A Prattware oval jug molded with two bust portraits of The Miser, 5½in. high, circa 1795. (Christie's) $281

A pair of Prattware oval plaques, molded in relief with busts of Louis XVI and Queen Marie Antoinette, 18cm. high. (Phillips) $631

Early 19th century Prattware figure of a young maiden with hand outstretched, 9½in. high. (Reeds Rains) $217

A Prattware model of a Gothic Chapel with central tower and spire, 24cm. high. (Phillips) $893

A Prattware oval plaque, molded in high relief with two lions colored in ochre and brown, 28.5cm. long. (Phillips) $800

A Prattware cottage money box in the form of a two-storeyed house with blue tiled roof, 12.5cm. high. (Phillips) $646

LUCIE RIE

A squat stoneware bottle vase, by Lucie Rie, covered in thick pitted grayish white glaze with traces of lavender-blue, circa 1970, 16.5cm. high. (Christie's) $1,404

A stoneware footed bowl, by Lucie Rie, covered in a white glaze, 15cm. wide. (Christie's) $396

A porcelain bottle vase, by Lucie Rie, circa 1982, 24.2cm. high. (Christie's) $2,831

A porcelain sgraffito and inlaid bottle vase, by Lucie Rie, circa 1972, 16.3cm. high. (Christie's) $1,179

An early sgraffito stoneware vase, by Lucie Rie, circa 1953, 22.6cm. high. (Christie's) $6,292

A stoneware sgraffito bottle vase, by Lucie Rie, circa 1972, 24.6cm. high. (Christie's) $2,123

A monumental tall stoneware tapering cylindrical vase, by Lucie Rie, circa 1955, 36.5cm. high. (Christie's) $1,569

A stoneware cylindrical vase, by Lucie Rie, circa 1972, 13.1cm. high. (Christie's) $393

A large stoneware sgraffito goblet shaped vase, by Lucie Rie, with cylindrical flower holder, circa 1955, 19.8cm. high. (Christie's) $1,569

ROCKINGHAM

A Rockingham miniature inkwell in the form of a shoe, C13 and griffin mark in iron-red, 1826-30, 12.5cm. wide. (Christie's) $601

A Rockingham model of a dog recumbent on a maroon colored base, 9.5cm. long. (Phillips) $928

A Rockingham toast rack from the service made for the Earl of Radnor, 19cm. long. (Phillips) $800

A Rockingham plate, the center painted with fruit and flowers, puce griffin mark and pattern no. 562, circa 1835, 23.5cm. diam. (Christie's) $348

A documentary Rockingham biscuit figure of Paysan Basque Des Environs De Bayonne, 1829, 21cm. high. (Christie's) $633

A Rockingham plate, the center painted by J. Wager Brameld with Cole Titmouse and Goldfinch, circa 1835, 23cm. diam. (Christie's) $760

A Rockingham biscuit figure of a Tyrolean girl, incised no. 13, circa 1830, 18.5cm. high. (Christie's) $871

A Rockingham green-ground bombe-shaped rectangular inkstand, puce griffin mark, circa 1835, 31cm. wide. (Christie's) $4,118

A Rockingham figure of a cobbler, after the model by Cyffle, incised no. 39, 1826-30, 14.5cm. high. (Christie's) $1,188

ROCKINGHAM

A Rockingham onion-shaped table scent bottle and stopper, C12 in red, puce griffin mark, circa 1835, 15cm. high. (Christie's) $554

A Rockingham figure of a shepherd, incised no. 4, 1826-30, 21.5cm. high. (Christie's) $554

A Rockingham pastille burner, the cover with C12 in iron-red, the stand with red griffin mark, 1826-30, 9.5cm. high. (Christie's) $475

A Rockingham spill vase painted with a church in a mountainous wooded river landscape, C8 in gold and puce griffin mark, circa 1835, 11.5cm. high. (Christie's) $633

A Rockingham blue-ground pin tray, the center painted in the manner of Edwin Steele, circa 1835, 9.5cm. wide. (Christie's) $506

A Rockingham green-ground cylindrical vase, painted by John Randall, C13 in red, puce griffin mark, circa 1835, 11cm. high. (Christie's) $950

A Rockingham cabinet cup and stand with two gilt scroll handles, circa 1835, the stand 11.5cm. diam., the cup 10cm. high. (Christie's) $760

A Rockingham biscuit bust of Frederick Augustus, Duke of York, circa 1827, 16.5cm. high. (Christie's) $1,108

A Rockingham cylindrical patch box and screw-on cover painted in the manner of Edwin Steele, 1826-30, 10cm. diam. (Christie's) $1,188

ROOKWOOD

Rookwood standard glaze ewer with sterling silver overlay, Ohio, 1892, 10¼in. high. (Robt. W. Skinner Inc.) $2,800

Rookwood pottery tall portrait vase, Cincinnati, 1894, decorated with figure entitled 'Spirit of the Summit', 14½in. high. (Robt. W. Skinner Inc.) $4,100

Rookwood standard glaze jug, with Palmer Cox figure, Ohio, 1891, artist's initials H.E.W., 6in. high. (Robt. W. Skinner Inc.) $950

Rookwood standard glaze vase with sterling silver overlay, Ohio, 1892, initialled K.C.M. for Kate C. Matchette, 6½in. high. (Robt. W. Skinner Inc.) $2,300

Rookwood pottery scenic vellum plaque, signed C. Schmidt, 1921, 12½ x 8½in. (Robt. W. Skinner Inc.) $800

A Rookwood earthenware vase, decorated by Leonore Asbury, sizemark XXI and Rookwood mark for 1914, 21cm. high. (Christie's) $408

Rookwood pottery silver overlay vase, initialled HEW for Harriet Eliz. Wilcox, 1894, 5.5/8in. high. (Robt. W. Skinner Inc.) $1,300

One of a pair of Rookwood stoneware bookends, modelled as sphinx holding books, light brown glaze, 18cm. high. (Christie's) $190

A Rookwood silver overlay vase, impressed artist's monogram SS, 12.5cm. high. (Christie's) $792

CHINA

ROYAL DUX

A Royal Dux bust, the young Art Nouveau maiden gazing to the left, raised pink triangle mark, 20in. high. (Christie's) $943

A Royal Dux centerpiece with figure of a water nymph kneeling on an abalone shell, 15½in. high. (Reeds Rains) $387

A Royal Dux group of a flute player and dancer both wearing Orientally inspired costume, 12in. high, raised pink triangle mark. (Christie's) $261

A Royal Dux porcelain group of classical figures, the boy in wolf-skin, and girl wearing a gown, 26in. high. (Dacre, Son & Hartley) $1,094

Pair of small Royal Dux figures. (Cooper Hirst) $527

A Royal Dux porcelain group of a peasant man and woman, on leaf decorated base, 22¾in. high. (Dacre, Son & Hartley) $432

RUSSIAN

A biscuit group of three tipsy men standing on an oval base, by Gardner, printed and impressed marks, 23.5cm. high. (Phillips) $1,078

A biscuit figure of a man fishing through ice, by Gardner, printed and impressed marks, 26.5cm. high. (Phillips) $492

A biscuit group of two bearded men, by Gardner, printed and impressed marks, 22cm. high. (Phillips) $677

SATSUMA

Late 19th century Satsuma model of a recumbent karashishi, 34cm. long. (Christie's) $1,874

Late 19th century Satsuma teapot and cover modelled as a stylized bird, 18cm. long. (Christie's) $1,249

A 19th century Satsuma shaped oval box and cover, signed Tokozan, 24cm. wide. (Christie's) $1,562

Late 19th century Satsuma trumpet-shaped two-handled vase decorated in various colored enamels and gilt, 37.5cm. high. (Christie's) $4,897

Late 19th century large oviform Satsuma vase in various colored enamels and gilt, 48cm. high. (Christie's) $7,810

One of a pair of Satsuma vases, Japan, circa 1880, 14½in. high. (Robt. W. Skinner Inc.) $300

Late 19th century Satsuma model of a courtier, signed Dai Nihon, 22.5cm. high. (Christie's) $1,311

A Japanese Satsuma bowl painted with panels of figures at various pastimes, 4¾in. diam. (Christie's) $474

Late 19th century Satsuma temple jar with carved teak cover, Japan, 13.1/8in. high. (Robt. W. Skinner Inc.) $950

SEVRES

A Sevres baluster cream jug, blue interlaced L marks enclosing the date letter N for 1766, 12.5cm. high. (Christie's) $285

One of three 19th century Sevres porcelain gilt mounted jardinieres, one oval 10½in. wide and a pair of cache pots, 6in. diam. (Reeds Rains) $961

A Sevres circular sugar bowl and cover, blue interlaced L marks enclosing the date letter O for 1767, 11cm. high. (Christie's) $380

A 19th century Sevres style ormolu mounted covered urn, France, 32½in. high. (Robt. W. Skinner Inc.) $2,600

A Sevres Dejeuner comprising a teapot and cover, circular sugar bowl and cover, four cups and saucers and a tray, date letter D for 1756 on the tray. (Christie's) $3,960

One of a pair of Sevres apple-green ground vases and covers, circa 1770, 35cm. high. (Christie's) $5,068

A Sevres blue-ground baluster jug and cover with gilt metal mount, blue interlaced L marks enclosing the date letter H for 1760, 19cm. high. (Christie's) $1,267

A Sevres two-handled seau a liqueur rond, blue inter-laced L marks enclosing the date letter U for 1773, 13cm. high. (Christie's) $3,801

One of a pair of Sevres apple-green ground baluster pot pourri vases and covers, date letter K for 1763, 22cm. high. (Christie's) $10,296

SEVRES

A Sevres green-ground circular
sugar bowl and cover, blue
interlaced L's enclosing the date
letter I for 1761 and the painter's mark Aloncle, 12cm. high.
(Christie's) $554

A Sevres oviform teapot
and cover with gilt dentil
rims, circa 1765, 16cm.
wide. (Christie's)
$475

A large Sevres (hard-paste) two-
handled blue nouveau and
Louis XVI ormolu jardiniere,
date letter GG for 1784, 52cm.
wide. (Christie's)
$41,184

A Sevres hop-trellis fluted
cup and saucer, circa 1765.
(Christie's) $475

A Sevres pattern gilt metal
mounted, royal blue ground,
two-handled pot pourri vase
and domed cover, circa 1888,
29in. high. (Christie's)
$2,073

A Sevres hard-paste cup and
saucer, blue crowned interlaced L mark enclosing date
letter U for 1773. (Christie's)
$554

One of a pair of late 19th
century Sevres pattern
oval pot pourri vases and
covers with winged caryatid
handles, imitation interlaced
L marks, 40.5cm. high.
(Christie's) $1,914

A Sevres hard-paste green-
ground soup tureen and cover,
gilt interlaced L marks and HP
mark of Prevost, circa 1785,
30cm. wide. (Christie's)
$1,584

One of a pair of late 19th
century Sevres pattern royal
blue-ground oviform vases
and fixed covers with gilt
bronze mounts, 42cm. high.
(Christie's) $1,116

A Sevres two-handled seau a bouteille, blue interlaced L marks enclosing the date letter D for 1756 and with painter's mark of Rosset, 23cm. wide. (Christie's)
$1,506

A Sevres shaped oval basin, date letter F for 1758, 31.5cm. wide. (Christie's) $1,194

A Sevres shaped circular plate made to match 'des Asturies' service, 24cm. diam. (Christie's) $1,469

A Sevres bleu celeste square tray with pierced scroll border, circa 1757, 14.8cm. sq. (Christie's) $1,469

A Sevres bleu nouveau coffee cup and saucer, painter's mark of Morin, date letter N for 1766. (Christie's)
$1,561

A Sevres mocha set, blue interlaced L marks enclosing the date letter G for 1759 and painter's mark of Catrice. (Christie's) $734

One of two Sevres two-handled feuille-de-choux seaux a bouteille, with painter's marks of Tardy and Tandart, 26cm. wide. (Christie's) $1,837

A Sevres pattern royal blue-ground jewelled coffee can and saucer, imitation interlaced L marks, circa 1865. (Christie's) $398

A Sevres rose pompadour square tray, blue interlaced L marks enclosing the date letter E for 1757 and painter's mark of Noel, 14.5cm. sq. (Christie's)
$6,492

A Jian Yao deep bowl with russet streaks over a black glaze thinning to a chocolate-brown at the rim, S. Song Dynasty, 12.9cm. diam. (Christie's) $1,258

A Ding Yao bottle potted in the form of a contemporary metal prototype, N. Song Dynasty, 25cm. high, fitted box. (Christie's) $94,380

A Jun Yao bowl, the sides under a lightly-crackled lavender glaze, S. Song Dynasty, 11.3cm. diam. (Christie's) $3,932

A Cizhou carved oviform jar, Song Dynasty, 26cm. high, fitted box. (Christie's) $7,865

A Ding Yao dish carved with a feathery lotus spray and scrolling leaves, N. Song Dynasty, 20.7cm. diam., fitted box. (Christie's) $23,595

A Cizhou small baluster jar, Song Dynasty, 12.3cm. high, fitted box. (Christie's) $3,932

A Ding Yao dish, Northern Song Dynasty, 11.2cm. diam., fitted box. (Christie's) $1,047

A Yingqing fluted baluster vase with S-scroll handles on the flaring neck, Song Dynasty, 17.2cm. high. (Christie's) $629

A Henan black glazed conical bowl, Song Dynasty, 14cm. diam., fitted box. (Christie's) $1,333

A Spode blue-ground garniture of five vases painted with pink and gilt flowering prunus branches, puce marks and pattern no. 3975, circa 1820. (Christie's) $760

George III Spode part tea service, each piece hand-enamelled on a white ground showing thumb nail decoration, heightened in gilt. (Peter Wilson) $719

A Spode pearlware Greek Pattern part dinner service printed in blue and iron-red with classical figures at various pastimes within shaped cartouches reserved on berried-foliage grounds, circa 1810. (Christie's) $30,096

Late 18th century Spode blue and white pottery oval footbath, 18in. wide. (Reeds Rains) $1,267

A Spode miniature teapot and cover with gilt spout, red mark and pattern no. 1166, circa 1820, 5cm. high. (Christie's) $677

A Spode circular box and cover, pattern no. 1166, circa 1820, 7.2cm. diam. (Christie's) $1,270

STAFFORDSHIRE

A Staffordshire figure of a sheep, recumbent to the left, circa 1780, 15cm. wide. (Christie's) $443

Staffordshire soup tureen, England, circa 1845, marked 'Texian Campaigne', with ladle and undertray, J.B. mark on base, 10in. high. (Robt. W. Skinner Inc.) $3,900

A Staffordshire saltglaze globular teapot and cover, painted in the famille rose palette, circa 1750, 10.5cm. high. (Christie's)
$712

A 19th century Staffordshire pottery portrait figure of Wm, Shakespeare, 9in. high. (Reeds Rains) $139

A Brownfield teaset, comprising a platter, teapot, sugar bowl, milk jug, four cups and saucers, platter 41cm. diam. (Christie's) $303

One of a pair of early 19th century Staffordshire pottery figures of putti, 6in. high. (Reeds Rains) $201

A 19th century Staffordshire pottery portrait figure of the Rev. John Wesley, 7in. high. (Reeds Rains) $116

Pair of mid 19th century Staffordshire pottery equestrian groups of the Prince and Princess of Wales, 7½in. high. (Reeds Rains)
$279

A Staffordshire figure of Napoleon on a floral encrusted rocky plinth, 8½in. high, circa 1825. (Christie's) $154

STAFFORDSHIRE

CHINA

A Staffordshire pearlware figure of a girl, circa 1790, 17cm. high. (Christie's) $316

A Staffordshire saltglaze agateware cat, with irregular blue markings and brown striations, circa 1750, 13.5cm. high. (Christie's) $2,692

A Staffordshire Toby jug, smoking a pipe and holding a jug, circa 1770, 23.5cm. high. (Christie's) $2,217

A Staffordshire saltglaze octagonal plate, transfer-printed in iron-red with the fable of The Lion and The Fox. (Christie's) $4,118

A Staffordshire figure of an Alcibiades hound, on a black marbled base edged in green and turquoise, circa 1810, 42cm. high. (Christie's) $2,059

A 19th century Staffordshire 'cottage' ornament, modelled as a double fronted house, 10in. high. (Parsons, Welch & Cowell) $83

A Staffordshire saltglaze bear-jug and cover, circa 1755, 24cm. long. (Christie's) $3,009

An amusing Staffordshire sheep creamer, their fleeces washed in ochre, 10.5cm. long. (Phillips) $1,540

A Staffordshire porcellaneous pastille burner in two sections, modelled as a hexagonal cottage, 11cm. high. (Phillips) $308

STAFFORDSHIRE

CHINA

A jardiniere modelled as a rectangular plant holder of wooden slats, impressed Brown, Westhead Moore, 33cm. high. (Christie's) $2,392

A Staffordshire saltglaze solid agateware cat, circa 1750, 12.5cm. high. (Christie's) $3,484

A Staffordshire figure of a boy leaning against a tree-stump with a dog at his side, circa 1790, 16.5cm. high. (Christie's) $348

A 19th century Staffordshire 'cottage' ornament in the form of a double turreted chapel, 9in. high. (Parsons, Welch & Cowell) $55

A Staffordshire saltglaze pear-shaped cream jug and cover, painted in a bright famille rose palette, circa 1750, 12.5cm. high. (Christie's) $1,267

A Staffordshire saltglaze plate, transfer-printed in iron-red with the fable of the Two Travellers and The Bear. (Christie's) $712

One of a pair of Queen Anne silver mounted stoneware tankards, attributed to Staffordshire, 13cm. and 13.5cm. high. (Phillips) $1,416

A Staffordshire small oval combined patchbox and nutmeg grater, with gilt metal mounts, circa 1765, 1.7/8in. long. (Christie's) $629

A Staffordshire group of a sheep and a lamb standing calmly together on a shaped rectangular base, 10cm. high. (Phillips) $616

A Rhenish stoneware baluster
tankard with English silver
neck mount, circa 1700, 19cm.
high. (Christie's) $554

A small stoneware inkpot,
by Shoji Hamada, 1923,
5.4cm. high. (Christie's)
$1,101

A stoneware four gallon crock,
by J. Norton & Co., Vermont,
circa 1880, 14in. high. (Robt.
W. Skinner Inc.) $1,700

A stoneware asymmetrical
bulbous vase, by Jennifer
Lee, covered in a matt oat-
meal glaze, 19.5cm. high.
(Christie's) $90

A stoneware plate, by Henry
Hammond, covered in a gray
pitted and fleck glaze with
iron-brown brushwork, circa
1958, 26cm. diam. (Christie's)
$214

A stoneware footed vase, by
Ewen Henderson, circa 1972,
27cm. high. (Christie's)
$707

A celadon stoneware globular
vase, by Norah Braden,
covered in a grayish-green
glaze with wax resist decoration, 21cm. high. (Christie's)
$578

A stoneware sake bottle vase,
by S. Ichino, impressed Ichino
character and St. Ives seals,
17.4cm. high. (Christie's)
$47

A stoneware pinched and
coiled bulbous vase, by
Betty Blandino, impressed
BB seal 1985, 31cm. high.
(Christie's) $247

STONEWARE

A Bunzlau brown stoneware heptagonal flask with pewter mounts and cover, 1643, 18.5cm. high. (Christie's) $1,346

A large Abuja stoneware bowl, by Alhassan Tanko, 36cm. diam. (Christie's) $330

'Dark Sky with Clouds', a stoneware vase form, by Ivo Mosley, 40.4cm. high. (Christie's) $440 £308

Mid 19th century three gallon stoneware jug, stamped 'S. Hart — Fulton', 13½in. high. (Robt. W. Skinner Inc.) $425

A stoneware mug, by Katharine Pleydell-Bouverie, impressed Cole, circa 1930, 11.5cm. high. (Christie's) $157

A massive stoneware asymmetrical vase, by Ewen Henderson, with everted rim, 56cm. high. (Christie's) $1,569

A stoneware spherical bottle by the Mashiko School, 21.3cm. high. (Christie's) $97

A stoneware figure of an eagle, inscribed M. Schilkin, Arabia, 44.2cm. high. (Christie's) $125

A stoneware elongated oviform asymmetrical vase, by Jennifer Lee, 20.6cm. high. (Christie's) $35

Stoneware butter churn, marked 'John Burger, Rochester', circa 1860, 19in. high. (Robt. W. Skinner Inc.) $29,000

A stoneware press-molded jar and cover, by S. Ichino, covered in a semi-translucent olive-green glaze, 20cm. high. (Christie's) $47

A Siegburg gray stoneware schnelle, dated 1576, 27cm. high. (Christie's) $3,168

A large slab-built stoneware vase, inscribed James Tower 85, 54.6cm. high. (Christie's) $550

One of a pair of stoneware candlesticks, 22cm. and 21.5cm. high, registration lozenge for 1876, silver collars, London, 1884. (Phillips) $290

A Nottingham stoneware puzzle-jug with a lustrous brown glaze, incised date 1715, 12cm. high. (Christie's) $3,484

A German Westerwald stoneware jug, circa 1750, 22cm. high. (Christie's) $6,009

A spherical stoneware bowl, by Val Barry, covered in a greenish-gray matt glaze, with brown speckling, 18.7cm. high. (Christie's) $231

A stoneware double gourd-shaped bottle vase, by Poh Chap Yeap, circa 1975, 16.6cm. high. (Christie's) $78

STONEWARE

A European stoneware gray glazed slender baluster jug with plain loop handles, circa 1750, 26cm. high. (Christie's) $1,091

A stoneware press-molded rectangular bottle, by Shoji Hamada, circa 1967, 20.1cm. high. (Christie's) $2,516

A Westerwald armorial blue and gray stoneware baluster jug with hinged pewter cover, 25cm. high. (Christie's) $871

Late 17th century Westerwald gray stoneware cylindrical tankard, 15cm. high, (hair crack in base). (Christie's) $665

A stoneware crane-necked bottle vase, by Hiroyuki Ichino, 28.2cm. high. (Christie's) $503

'Chest', a large slab-built stoneware vase, incised James Tower 83, 54cm. high. (Christie's) $865

A stoneware pilgrim flask, by Malcolm Pepper, circa 1975, 32.8cm. high. (Christie's) $188

'Swan Pot', a stoneware jug, by Vicki Read, painted artist cypher and dated 72 Winslow, 26.4cm. high. (Christie's) $114

A Westerwald blue and gray stoneware oviform tankard, circa 1800, 35.5cm. high. (Christie's) $396

STONEWARE

A stoneware rounded rectangular bowl, by Karl Scheid, dated 67, 19.5cm. wide. (Christie's) $495

A Yixing brown stoneware globular teapot and domed cover, circa 1750, 19cm. wide. (Christie's) $2,183

A stoneware deep bowl, by John Ward, with foliate rim, 36.2cm. diam. (Christie's) $197

A massive stoneware flattened bottle, by Joanna Constantinidis, impressed C seal 1982, 54.5cm. high. (Christie's) $1,101

Pair of late 19th century almost life-sized stoneware models of a courtier and a courtesan, probably Kyoto ware, 149cm. high. (Christie's) $10,153

A Henri van de Velde stoneware amphora vase, covered in a sang-de-boeuf translucent glaze separating in parts to reveal beige-colored body, 23.5cm. high. (Christie's) $8,712

An early marbled stoneware lamp holder formed as a wide flanged recessed dish, Tang Dynasty, 11cm. diam. (Christie's) $2,516

A Yixing pale brown stoneware rectangular cylindrical teapot, circa 1750, 22.5cm. wide. (Christie's) $2,456

A stoneware chamberstick, by K. Pleydell-Bouverie, 8.9cm. high, and a bowl, circa 1975, 5.9cm. high. (Christie's) $70

TANG

A yellow and amber-glazed shallow cup, Tang Dynasty, 10cm. diam. (Christie's) $1,573

A buff pottery figure of an expectant mother, Tang Dynasty, 25.5cm. high. (Christie's) $1,101

A large glazed tripod globular jar of Yue type, Tang Dynasty, 28cm. wide, 23.5cm. high. (Christie's) $6,606

A painted red pottery figure of a camel, Tang Dynasty, 48.6cm. high. (Christie's) $1,887

A pair of large Sancai standing figures of Court Dignitaries, Tang Dynasty, approx. 85cm. high. (Christie's) $29,887

An unglazed russet pottery standing camel, Tang Dynasty, 63cm. high. (Christie's) $5,033

A phosphatic-splashed black-glazed wrist rest, Tang Dynasty, 11cm. wide. (Christie's) $1,573

A Sancai buff pottery figure of a standing horse, Tang Dynasty, 47cm. high. (Christie's) $23,595

A green and white-glazed stoneware ewer with double loop handle, Tang Dynasty, 21.5cm. high. (Christie's) $2,831

TERRACOTTA

A 19th century terracotta garden ornament, probably France, 25½in. diam., 25½in. high. (Robt. W. Skinner Inc.) $750

A pair of 19th century Continental terracotta figures of a peasant girl and a boy, 90cm. and 91cm. high. (Phillips) $2,700

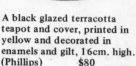

A black glazed terracotta teapot and cover, printed in yellow and decorated in enamels and gilt, 16cm. high. (Phillips) $80

A late 18th century French terracotta bust of a man wearing The Order of St. Esprit, in the style of Pajou, 20in. high. (Christie's) $2,811

A set of three black glazed terracotta jugs of graduated size, printed in yellow with portraits and vases of enamelled flowers. (Phillips) $160

A terracotta wall bracket in the form of a grotesque boar's head, 53cm. high. (Phillips) $540

VENICE

An 18th century Venice (Cozzi) white veilleuse, cover and stand, 27cm. high. (Christie's) $1,267

A Venice (Cozzi) teabowl and saucer, iron-red anchor marks, circa 1775. (Christie's) $1,346

Late 16th century Venice Istoriato two-handled, oviform vase and tall waisted cover, 44cm. high, overall. (Christie's) $950

A Vienna (Du Paquier) deep shaped quatrefoil dish painted in Schwartzlot, circa 1730, 22cm. diam. (Christie's) $1,382

A Vienna group of a shepherdess, blue beehive marks, circa 1770, 16.5cm. wide. (Christie's) $506

One of a pair of late 19th century Vienna plaques, painted by F. Koller, 19in. diam. (Woolley & Wallis) $1,430

A Vienna red lacquer oval snuff box and cover, circa 1800, 17.5cm. wide. (Christie's) $8,712

A Vienna ceramic centerpiece, by George Klimt, 20cm. wide. (Christie's) $235

A Vienna pink-ground oval snuff box and cover, with copper gilt mount, blue beehive mark, circa 1780, 8.5cm. wide. (Christie's) $871

A Vienna (Du Paquier) plate painted in underglaze blue, enamel colors and silver, circa 1730, 23cm. diam. (Christie's) $1,884

A Vienna figure of Venus, impressed beehive mark, circa 1760, 15cm. high.(Christie's) $627

A Vienna (Du Paquier) lobed circular dish, circa 1730, 34.5cm. diam. (Christie's) $6,652

WEDGWOOD

A Wedgwood polished black basalt intaglio seal, 3.5cm. diam. (Phillips) $662

A Wedgwood three-color jasper dice-pattern cylindrical jardiniere, 9cm. high, and a stand, circa 1790. (Christie's) $1,439

A Wedgwood lilac and white jasper teacup and saucer, circa 1790. (Christie's) $609

A Wedgwood & Bentley black basalt oviform two-handled vase and cover, circa 1775, 40cm. high. (Christie's) $2,851

One of a pair of Wedgwood solid lilac jasper cylindrical vases molded in white relief with Corinthian columns, circa 1785, about 15.5cm. high. (Christie's) $950

A Wedgwood black basalt encaustic-decorated oviform two-handled vase painted with Jupiter, circa 1800, 30cm. high. (Christie's) $1,101

A Wedgwood caneware oviform jug and cover, 22cm. high, and a saucer dish, circa 1815. (Christie's) $931

Pair of Wedgwood caneware oviform vases, impressed marks and B, circa 1815, 16cm. high. (Christie's) $287

A Wedgwood garden seat of rounded hexagonal shape, impressed Wedgwood, 46cm. high. (Christie's) $1,355

WEDGWOOD

A Wedgwood creamware pierced circular basket and stand painted in puce camaieu by J. Bakewell, circa 1768, basket 18.5cm. diam. (Christie's) $2,710

A Wedgwood salmon platter, naturalistic coloring on a brown ground, impressed Wedgwood, 64cm. long. (Christie's) $1,595

A Wedgwood oval medallion, modelled by Wm. Hackwood, 2.5cm. diam. (Phillips) $748

A Wedgwood black basalt encaustic decorated vase, painted in red and enriched in white with Apollo and Diana, late 18th century, 24cm. high. (Christie's) $2,217

One of a pair of Wedgwood black basalt tritons, impressed lower-case mark and K, circa 1785, 28cm. high. (Christie's) $3,726

A 19th century Wedgwood jasper model of the Portland Vase, 10½in. high. (Reeds Rains) $792

One of a pair of Wedgwood & Bentley black basalt oviform two-handled vases and covers, circa 1775, 38cm. high. (Christie's) $11,088

Pair of Wedgwood black basalt encaustic decorated oviform two-handled vases and one cover, circa 1800, 37.5cm. high. (Christie's) $5,702

One of a pair of Wedgwood & Bentley black basalt ewers with dolphin handles, circa 1775, 41.5cm. and 42.5cm. high. (Christie's) $4,752

WEDGWOOD

Wedgwood pearlware nautilus compote and undertray, circa 1872, 9in. high, 10¾in. long. (Robt. W. Skinner Inc.) $650

A Wedgwood/Whieldon hexagonal teapot and cover in chinoiserie style, 16cm. high. (Phillips) $2,400

A Wedgwood green and white jasper cylindrical teapot and cover, circa 1800, 9.5cm. high. (Christie's) $542

A Wedgwood & Bentley 'porphyry' vase and cover, the shield-shaped body applied with gilt mounting, 47.5cm. high. (Phillips) $6,468

Pair of Wedgwood black basalt encaustic decorated vases, painted in red with Hercules and Hercules seated on a lion skin before a sphinx, 18th century, 24cm. high. (Christie's) $4,435

One of a pair of Wedgwood black basalt wine and water ewers after the models by J. Flaxman, date code for 1868, 39cm. high. (Christie's) $2,032

Late 19th century Wedgwood blue ground jasper jardiniere, 10in. diam. (Peter Wilson) $190

An Art Deco Wedgwood animal figure, modelled as a duiker, designed by J. Skeaping, 23.5cm. high. (Phillips) $187

Pair of Wedgwood cream glazed octagonal plates each painted by E. Lessore, 8¾in. diam. (Christie's) $400

WEDGWOOD

A Wedgwood creamware globular teapot and cover, painted in the atelier of D. Rhodes, circa 1770, 13.5cm. high. (Christie's)
$3,726

Stilton cheese dish and cover in the style of Wedgwood, circa 1900, 12in. high. (Lots Road Galleries)
$160

A Wedgwood blue and white jasper cylindrical teapot and cover, circa 1790, 10.5cm. high. (Christie's) $847

One of a pair of Wedgwood blue and white jasper cylindrical altar vases, circa 1785, 13.5cm. high. (Christie's)
$1,016

A Wedgwood black basalt encaustic decorated vase, painted in red and enriched in white with a lady and attendants, late 18th century, 24cm. high. (Christie's) $2,217

A large Wedgwood black basalt pot pourri vase and cover with loop handles, 12in. high. (Parsons, Welch & Cowell) $784

A Wedgwood caneware custard cup and cover with rope twist handle, 7.5cm. high. (Phillips) $1,040

A Wedgwood 'Fairyland' lustre 10in. circular bowl of inverted bell shape. (Parsons, Welch & Cowell)
$1,312

An Art Deco Wedgwood animal figure, modelled as a fallow deer, designed by J. Skeaping, 21.5cm. high. (Phillips) $230

WEDGWOOD

A Wedgwood green and white jasper teabowl and saucer, circa 1790. (Christie's) $1,101

One of two Wedgwood caneware flared circular flowerbowls and pierced liners, circa 1815, 20.5cm. and 18.5cm. high. (Christie's) $542

A Wedgwood lustre charger, by Alfred and Louise Powell, 31.5cm. wide. (Christie's) $380

WHIELDON

A Whieldon wall pocket of waisted form molded with bearded mask beneath a manganese glaze, circa 1760, 22.5cm. high. (Christie's) $1,585

A Whieldon spirally molded wall pocket, circa 1750, 24cm. high. (Christie's) $2,059

Late 18th century Whieldon pattern square shaped pottery tea caddy, 4in. high. (Reeds Rains) $259

WOOD

A Ralph Wood Toby jug, in brown jacket and hat, circa 1770, 25cm. high. (Christie's) $1,346

A Ralph Wood figure of a recumbent ram, on an oval green rockwork base molded with foliage, circa 1770, 18.5cm. wide. (Christie's) $3,801

A Ralph Wood Toby jug of conventional type, circa 1770, 25.5cm. high. (Christie's) $2,692

WORCESTER

One of a pair of Royal Worcester vases and covers, by A. Lewis, in the Hadley style, shape no. 1911, date codes for 1904, 30cm. high. (Phillips) $800

A Worcester partridge tureen and cover, circa 1765, 15cm. wide. (Christie's)
$1,185

A Royal Worcester ovoid vase and cover, by John Stinton, shape no. G998, date code for 1907, 33cm. high. (Phillips)
$1,262

An ormolu mounted Worcester vase and cover, 45cm. high, square mark in blue, the porcelain circa 1770, the mounts probably early 19th century. (Phillips) $2,079

A Worcester baluster mug transfer-printed in black by R. Hancock with Parrot Pecking at Fruit, circa 1760, 12cm. high. (Christie's)
$5,759

One of a pair of late 19th century Worcester porcelain vases, Grainger period, 9.3/8in. high. (Christie's)
$550

Royal Worcester Persian ewer, cream ground with gilt painted and polychrome enamelled decoration, date mark code for 1886. (Peter Wilson) $380

A Worcester small cylindrical mug transfer-printed in black by R. Hancock with The King of Prussia, date 1757, 9cm. high. (Christie's)
$1,185

One of a pair of Royal Worcester vases and covers, painted by R. Sebright, 13½in. high. (Reeds Rains)
$576

WORCESTER

A Worcester faceted teapot and cover painted in a famille rose palette with The Beckoning Chinaman Pattern, circa 1758, 16cm. high. (Christie's) $1,267

A Worcester two-handled sauceboat with lobed lips at each end, circa 1756, 19cm. long. (Phillips) $1,001

A Worcester blue and white pleated oval sauceboat with scroll handle, circa 1758, 19.5cm. wide. (Christie's) $443

A Chamberlain's Worcester green-ground part dessert service, the centers painted with bouquets within gilt wells, within apple-green borders and shaped gilt gadrooned rims, impressed marks and script marks in red, circa 1830. (Christie's) $2,851

A Royal Worcester oviform ewer, the body painted by John Stinton, date code for 1911, pattern no. 1309, 41cm. high. (Christie's) $1,504

Two of four Royal Worcester 'ivory' wall brackets emblematic of the Seasons, circa 1880, approx. 26cm. high. (Christie's) $1,029

A Royal Worcester vase, by George Owen, shape no. 1527, date code for 1922, 11cm. high. (Phillips) $3,080

WORCESTER

A Worcester blue and white
molded oval sauceboat,
blue crescent mark, circa
1768, 20cm. wide. (Christie's)
$601

A Worcester teapot and cover
of globular form, painted in
underglaze blue with the
'Indian Fisherman', 13cm.
high, circa 1755. (Phillips)
$3,542

A Worcester tapering ovi-
form teapot and cover with
faceted spout and scroll
handle, circa 1758, 14cm.
high. (Christie's)
$1,267

A Flight, Barr & Barr Worcester
armorial vase and cover, attributed to Thos. Baxter, 19cm.
high. (Phillips) $4,928

A Worcester blue-ground
small mug painted with exotic
birds, blue crescent mark,
circa 1770, 8.5cm. high.
(Christie's) $1,504

A Chamberlain's Worcester
coral-red-ground crested
jug painted with a view of
Worcester, circa 1805.
(Christie's) $1,425

A Royal Worcester melon-
shaped biscuit barrel and
stand, circa 1895. (Coles,
Knapp & Kennedy)
$332

A Worcester, Flight, Barr &
Barr, urn-shaped two-handled
vase and cover, circa 1820,
46cm. high. (Christie's)
$2,376

A Chamberlain's Worcester
armorial plate, decorated
with the arms of Allan,
9¼in. diam. (Dreweatts)
$348

WORCESTER

A Worcester cos lettuce leaf molded sauceboat, the stalk handle with fruit and foliage terminal, circa 1760, 18.5cm. wide. (Christie's) $633

One of a pair of Worcester partridge tureens and covers, circa 1760, 18cm. wide. (Christie's) $2,371

One of a pair of Worcester yellow-ground pierced oval two-handled baskets, blue square seal marks, circa 1768, 18.5cm. wide. (Christie's) $6,969

A Worcester blue-scale tapering hexagonal vase and domed cover, circa 1770, 33cm. high. (Christie's) $8,470

A Worcester blue and white bottle and a basin transfer-printed with The Pinecone and Foliage pattern, circa 1775, bottle 22cm. high, basin 27.5cm. diam. (Christie's) $1,439

A Worcester blue-ground inverted baluster vase painted by J. H. O'Neale, circa 1770, 34cm. high. (Christie's) $3,049

A Hadleys Worcester vase painted by J. W. Sedgley, printed green mark and date code for 1905, 10in. high. (Outhwaite & Litherland) $290

A Worcester quartrefoil two-handled basket, pierced cover and stand, circa 1760, basket 20cm. wide. (Christie's) $1,524

Royal Worcester vase and cover painted by Ricketts, 11in. high. (Reeds Rains) $713

Late 19th century Dresden Christmas ornament of a silver two-wheeled basket cart drawn by Billy goat, 3¾in. long. (Robt. W. Skinner Inc.) $450

Late 19th century Dresden Christmas ornament, white poodle with red silk ribbon, 3¼in. long. (Robt. W. Skinner Inc.) $225

Late 19th century Dresden Christmas ornament of a silver cannon on wheeled carriage, 3½in. long. (Robt. W. Skinner Inc.) $200

Late 19th century Dresden Christmas ornament of a three-masted ship, 4½in. high, 4.7/8in. long. (Robt. W. Skinner Inc.) $190

Late 19th century Dresden Christmas ornament of a silver champagne bottle candy container, 3.5/16in. high. (Robt. W. Skinner Inc.) $100

Late 19th century Dresden Christmas ornament of a rooster, brown wash over gold, 3.1/8in. high. (Robt. W. Skinner Inc.) $140

Late 19th century Dresden Christmas ornament of a sitting silver retriever, 2¾in. high. (Robt. W. Skinner Inc.) $300

Late 19th century Dresden Christmas ornament of a gold and rose iridescent cockatoo in a hoop, 3.3/8in. high. (Robt. W. Skinner Inc.) $175

Late 19th century Dresden Christmas ornament of a silver three-quarter flat jockey on horse, 2in. high. (Robt. W. Skinner Inc.) $150

BRACKET CLOCKS

A George III mahogany striking bracket clock, by Ellicott, London, 16in. high. (Christie's) $3,146

A George III bracket clock with enamel dial, by Robt. Henderson, 15½in. high. (Graves Son & Pilcher) $10,570

A Regency mahogany and gilt brass mounted bracket clock, the brass dial signed Robt. Wood, London, 43cm. high. (Phillips) $1,740

A Regency mahogany striking bracket clock, the painted dial signed Collett, Chelsea, 15½in. high. (Christie's) $1,630

An 18th century Austrian ebonized quarter striking bracket clock with gilt metal handle, 12in. high. (Christie's) $2,359

A late 17th century ebony veneered bracket timepiece, by Henry Jones, London, 36cm. high. (Phillips) $5,472

A Georgian fruitwood bracket clock, signed on a cartouche Henry Heve, London, 43cm. high. (Phillips) $2,448

A late Stuart tortoiseshell veneered case for a miniature bracket clock, 10in. high. (Christie's) $1,415

An 18th century ebonized and gilt brass mounted quarter chiming bracket clock, signed Wm. Webster, 52cm. high. (Phillips) $4,176

BRACKET CLOCKS

A scarlet lacquer striking bracket clock, the brass dial signed Jas. Smith, London, 20in. high. (Christie's) $1,540

Late 18th century George III mahogany bracket clock for the Canadian market, signed Fras. Dumoulin a Montreal, 16½in. high including handle. (Christie's) $2,640

A George II striking mahogany bracket clock, date aperture and plaque signed Tho. Hall, Rumsey, 19½in. high. (Christie's) $2,692

A Queen Anne ebonized timepiece bracket clock, signed Fromanteel, London, 14¼in. high. (Christie's) $2,988

An early George III 8-day bracket clock with verge striking movement by Wm. Allam, 15.5in. high. (Woolley & Wallis) $11,808

Late 18th century ebonized striking bracket clock, signed A. Van Eeden, Haarlem, 20in. high. (Christie's) $1,650

A mid Georgian ebonized striking bracket clock, the dial signed Stepn. Rimbault, London, 19½in. high. (Christie's) $2,283

An 18th century ebonized bracket clock, signed S. de Charmes, London, 39cm. high. (Phillips) $1,872

A Georgian ebonized bracket clock, signed Tho. Wagstaffe, London, 50cm. high. (Phillips) $1,872

BRACKET CLOCKS

A late Georgian mahogany musical bracket clock, chime/not chime lever signed Rivers & Son, Cornhill, London, 24in. high. (Christie's) $4,566

A Regency ebonized bracket clock, the dial signed W. French, Royal Exchange, London, 40cm. high. (Phillips) $1,267

A George II green japanned striking bracket clock, the dial signed Fra Dorrell, London, 18¼in. high. (Christie's) $9,306

A William III ebonized quarter striking bracket clock, with gilt metal handle to ogee basket top, 14in. high, excluding later feet. (Christie's) $2,359

A Regency period bracket clock, the brass inlaid lancet case of Egyptian styling, circa 1810, 20in. high. (Reeds Rains) $2,015

A George III mahogany bracket clock, the arched brass dial signed Benjn. Ward, London, 52cm. high. (Phillips) $4,350

A Regency mahogany bracket clock, Gothic shaped case, by Payne, London, 24in. high. (Coles, Knapp & Kennedy) $1,887

Early 19th century George III mahogany striking bracket clock, signed Edw. Tomlin, Royal Exchange, London, 15½in. high. (Christie's) $2,200

An 18th century ebony and gilt brass mounted bracket clock, signed on a cartouche Cha: Cabrier, London, 57cm. high. (Phillips) $3,168

BRACKET CLOCKS

An Austrian fruitwood quarter striking bracket clock, signed B. Schmidt, 20in. high. (Christie's) $1,346

A George III ebonized miniature striking bracket clock, signed Williams, 168 Shoreditch on Arabic chapter disc, 14½in. high overall. (Christie's) $3,775

A mid Georgian scarlet japanned quarter striking, musical and automaton bracket clock in the style of G. Grendey, 37in. high. (Christie's) $77,550

A documentary Louis XIV bronze mounted tortoiseshell religieuse, signed Gaudron a Paris, the case inscribed L.B., circa 1710, 18in. high. (Christie's) $5,500

A 19th century rosewood and inlaid bracket timepiece, 32cm. high. (Phillips) $748

A Charles II ebonized striking bracket clock, backplate signed R. Pingo Neare The Pallmall, Londini in a lambrequin, 13½in. high. (Christie's) $2,988

An early George III padouk-wood automaton organ clock, by Wm. Vale, London, 37in. high. (Christie's) $12,692

An early George III ebonized striking bracket clock with brass handle, dial signed Sam. Toulmin, Strand, London, 18½in. high. (Christie's) $1,258

A Continental tortoiseshell bracket timepiece, basically circa 1700, 16in. high. (Christie's) $2,186

CARRIAGE CLOCKS

A brass grande sonnerie carriage clock with split compensated balance to lever platform, 5¾in. high. (Christie's) $943

A gilt metal grande sonnerie oval carriage clock with enamel dial, 6.1/8in. high. (Christie's) $2,516

A gilt metal striking carriage clock by Paul Garnier, one-piece case with lifting front glass, 5in. high. (Christie's) $2,044

A gilt metal striking carriage clock with decorative swagged Arabic chaptered enamel dial, 6½in. high. (Christie's) $629

A 19th century English time-piece, the backplate signed French Royal Exchange, London, 17.5cm. high. (Phillips) $7,540

A silver plated striking carriage clock with split compensated balance to gilt lever platform, 6½in. high. (Christie's) $865

A gilt metal striking carriage clock, inscribed Examined by Dent and with presentation inscription dated 1877, 7in. high. (Christie's) $755

A 19th century English gilt brass quarter striking carriage clock, the dial signed James McCabe, Royal Exchange, London 2677, 19cm. high. (Phillips) $4,350

A French 19th century gilt brass carriage clock, bearing the Drocourt trademark, and signed for Klaftenberger, Paris, 17cm. high. (Phillips) $493

CARRIAGE CLOCKS

A gilt metal striking carriage clock for the Chinese market, stamp of Japy Freres, 5¾in. high. (Christie's) $1,022

A gilt metal striking oval carriage clock with uncut bimetallic balance to silvered lever platform, plain oval case, 5½in. high. (Christie's) $865

A gilt brass quarter striking carriage clock with cut bimetallic balance to lever platform, 6in. high. (Christie's) $786

An English striking carriage clock, mottled plates signed Chas. Frodsham, 9in. high. (Christie's) $7,827

A Franche Comte gilt metal striking carriage clock for the Chinese market, 6½in. high. (Christie's) $1,022

A gilt metal and enamel striking carriage clock, ivorine dials within multi-colored champleve enamel mask, 7in. high. (Christie's) $3,617

An ormolu quarter striking pendule d'officier with Turkish chaptered enamel dial signed Courvoisier et Compe., 8½in. high. (Christie's) $2,359

A brass cased quarter striking carriage clock, the backplate signed L. Leroy & Cie, 6in. high. (Christie's) $1,304

A 19th century French gilt brass carriage clock, the enamel dial signed for J. F. Bautte, Geneve, 17cm. high. (Phillips) $2,900

CARRIAGE CLOCKS

A gilt brass grande sonnerie carriage clock, 7¾in. high. (Christie's) $2,200

A gilt metal striking oval carriage clock for the Oriental market, stamp of Japy Freres, 6in. high. (Christie's) $1,900

A gilt metal striking carriage clock, stamp of Henri Jacot, 5¾in. high. (Christie's) $1,267

An oval engraved gilt brass grande sonnerie carriage clock, 7½in. high. (Christie's) $2,420

A French gilt brass carriage clock, the lever movement striking on a gong, 21cm. high. (Phillips) $1,324

A Victorian brass inlaid, rosewood carriage clock, dial signed Craighead & Webb, 9¼in. high. (Christie's) $2,217

An early multi-piece striking carriage clock with lever narrow platform, strike and alarm on bell, 5¾in. high. (Christie's) $815

A Swiss gilt brass striking carriage clock with chronometer escapement, circa 1830, 7in. high. (Christie's) $9,350

A 19th century French brass carriage clock, signed on the backplate Ollivant & Botsford,. Paris & Manchester, 17cm. high. (Phillips) $464

CARRIAGE CLOCKS

A gilt metal striking carriage clock with modern lever platform, stamp of Henri Jacot, 4¾in. high. (Christie's) $950

A brass striking carriage clock with strike/repeat on gong, stamp of Henri Jacot, 4.7/8in. high. (Christie's) $570

A French brass carriage timepiece, the enamel dial signed Le Roy & Fils, in a gorge case, 9.5cm. high. (Phillips) $633

A lacquered brass grande sonnerie carriage clock, 7in. high. (Christie's) $1,320

Breguet Neveu & Compie., No. 3992: a silver quarter striking carriage clock with alarm, 5½in. high. (Christie's) $33,264

A lacquered brass petite sonnerie carriage clock with enamel dial, corniche case, 5¼in. high. (Christie's) $865

A gilt metal striking carriage clock with center seconds for the Chinese market, 6in. high. (Christie's) $1,022

A gilt metal strking oval carriage clock with scroll handle and on rosso antiquo marble stand, 5½in. high, excluding stand. (Christie's) $2,044

A lacquered brass grande sonnerie carriage clock with calendar, by Drocourt, No. 12276, 7in. high. (Christie's) $2,640

LANTERN CLOCKS

An early 18th century brass lantern clock, dial signed Smorthwait in Colchester, 37cm. high. (Phillips) $1,824

A George I bracket timepiece movement, backplate signed L. Bradley, London, dial 6in. x 8¼in. (Christie's) $1,312

A 17th century Stuart brass and steel lantern clock, by J. Ebsworth 'in Bethlehem', London, 'fecit', 16in. high. (Robt. W. Skinner Inc.) $1,400

A late 17th century brass lantern clock, the dial signed Edward Stanton, London, 39cm. high. (Phillips) $1,872

A 19th century Japanese lantern clock with red enamel dial, 28cm. high. (Phillips) $3,360

An 18th century Continental brass lantern clock of small size, 27cm. high. (Phillips) $1,656

A brass lantern clock, dial signed Lawrence Debnam in Froome, 34cm. high. (Phillips) $1,520

Mid 18th century brass lantern clock for the Turkish market, signed Isaac Rogers, London, 14in. high. (Christie's) $935

An Edwardian lantern clock in the 17th century taste, London, 1902, 6½in. high. (Christie's) $1,241

LANTERN CLOCKS

A brass lantern clock, signed Thomas Knifton in Lothbury, London, 15in. high. (Christie's) $3,643

A Japanese brass lantern clock, the posted frame 30-hour iron movement with double foliot verge escapement, 11½in. high. (Christie's) $2,120

An English lantern clock, dial signed Nicholas Coxeter, 14½in. high. (Christie's) $6,160

A N. European striking lantern clock, dated 1672, 8in. high. (Christie's) $2,992

A Germanic iron chamber clock, the posted frame 30-hour movement with fabricated wheels, 22in. high. (Christie's) $4,118

A Japanese striking lantern clock with alarm, 15in. high. (Christie's) $3,872

A lantern clock with engraved dial plate, 15in. high. (Christie's) $1,496

A brass lantern clock with pendulum verge escapement, signed Stephen Tracy, London, 15in. high. (Christie's) $1,015

A late Stuart brass quarter chiming carillon lantern clock, dial signed Edw. Hemins of Bister, 15in. high. (Christie's) $6,160

LONGCASE CLOCKS

A late Stuart walnut and marquetry longcase clock, dial signed Peter Mallett, London, 7ft.6in. high. (Christie's) $11,088

An 18th century mahogany longcase clock, by Charles Haley. (Parsons, Welch & Cowell) $2,038

A Georgian mahogany longcase clock, signed Wm. Webster, London, 91in. high. (Christie's) $1,718

A late Georgian mahogany longcase clock, dial signed Robert Martin, Glasgow, 6ft. 11in. high. (Christie's) $943

George III oak longcase clock, by J. Ivory, Dundee, 7ft. 6in. high. (Capes, Dunn & Co.) $1,007

A 17th century walnut month going longcase clock, by John Knibb, Oxford, 2.08m. high. (Phillips) $18,720

Federal mahogany inlaid tall case clock, by J. Bailey, Mass., circa 1790, 93in. high. (Robt. W. Skinner Inc.) $18,000

A Georgian mahogany longcase clock, the 12in. dial signed Will. Phelps, Putney, 2.28m. high. (Phillips) $4,176

LONGCASE CLOCKS

Federal cherry inlaid tall case clock, back of dial inscribed 'Wm. Prescott', circa 1790, 91¾in. high. (Robt. W. Skinner Inc.)
$12,000

A George III mahogany longcase clock, the silvered chapter ring signed Rich. Penny, London, 2.08m. high. (Phillips)
$1,885

A George III Lancashire mahogany longcase clock, signed H. Fisher, Preston, 7ft.5in. high. (Christie's)
$2,851

A late Stuart Provincial walnut longcase clock, dial signed Thos. Cruttenden in Yorke, 6ft. 11½in. high. (Christie's)
$3,460

An early George III dark green japanned longcase clock, dial signed Benjamin Baddy, London, 8ft. 7in. high. (Christie's)
$18,612

A George II green and chinoiserie lacquered longcase clock, by Wm. Lambert, London, 7ft.2in. high. (Capes, Dunn & Co.)
$1,377

A 19th century mahogany regulator, the dial signed James, Saffron Walden, 1.87m. high. (Phillips)
$4,320

A 19th century mahogany regulator with 12in. circular painted dial, 2.09m. high. (Phillips)
$3,456

LONGCASE CLOCKS

Mid 18th century George III mahogany tall case clock, signed 'Isaac Hewlett, Bristol', 93.1/8in. high. (Christie's)
$5,500

A Chippendale mahogany tall case clock, works by Thos. Stretch, Phila., circa 1750-65, 92½in. high. (Christie's)
$16,500

A Chippendale mahogany tall case clock, dial signed by Thos. Wagstaffe, London, case Phila., 1760-90, 87¾in. high. (Christie's)
$19,800

A mid Georgian black japanned longcase Act of Parliament clock, 31in. dial signed Will. Threlkeld, London, 6ft.10in. high. (Christie's)
$2,202

Mid 18th century Dutch floral marquetry longcase clock, signed Lourens Eichelar, 8ft. 5in. high. (Christie's)
$6,050

George III mahogany longcase clock with swan-neck pediment, 7ft.10in. high. (Hobbs & Chambers)
$886

An 18th century walnut longcase clock, by Marm'd. Storr. (Parsons, Welch & Cowell)
$3,020

An 18th century mahogany longcase clock, signed G. Binch, Manchester, 94in. high. (Reeds Rains)
$1,440

LONGCASE CLOCKS

A George II burr walnut calendar longcase clock, the dial signed George Merttins, Londini, 8ft. high. (Christie's) $7,128

A George III Salisbury mahogany veneered 8-day longcase clock, the dial inscribed Edw. Marsh, 7ft.8in. high. (Woolley & Wallis) $2,288

A George III Lancashire mahogany longcase clock, the dial signed Saml. Collier, Eccles, 8ft. 2in. high.(Christie's) $3,960

A George III Scottish mahogany longcase clock, the brass dial signed Jas. Mylne, Montrose, 7ft.3in. high. (Christie's) $2,217

A George III mahogany 8-day striking longcase clock, dial inscribed Jno. Morse, 6ft.9in. high. (Woolley & Wallis) $3,718

A Chippendale walnut tall case clock, dial signed by Thos. Crow, Delaware, circa 1770, 89¼in. high. (Christie's) $6,820

The Longstreet Family Federal inlaid mahogany tall case clock, dial signed by Aaron Lane, circa 1790, 94in. high.(Christie's) $41,800

A George III mahogany veneered 8-day striking longcase clock, inscribed James Vigne, London, 8ft.2in. high.(Woolley & Wallis) $4,320

LONGCASE CLOCKS

A William and Mary walnut and marquetry month going longcase clock, the 11¼in. dial signed Wm. Jourdain, 7ft. 3in. high. (Christie's) $13,861

A Chippendale mahogany tall case clock, dial signed by Joseph Hollingshead, circa 1750, 93½in. high. (Christie's) $3,850

Late 19th century mahogany quarter chiming longcase clock, signed Maple & Co., London, 2.54m. high. (Phillips) $3,625

An 18th century walnut longcase clock, brass dial signed Hen. Massey, London, 2.46m. high. (Phillips) $2,610

A George III mahogany longcase clock, the dial signed Rich. Winch, Hackney, 2.46m. high. (Phillips) $2,610

Walnut tall case clock, New England, circa 1780, 88in. high, back of dial inscribed 'G.R.'. (Robt. W. Skinner Inc.) $2,000

A Georgian mahogany longcase clock, the brass dial signed Thos. Nevitt, 2.14m. high. (Phillips) $3,190

A Georgian mahogany quarter chiming longcase clock, the dial signed Wm. Dutton, London, 2.09m. high. (Phillips) $9,860

LONGCASE CLOCKS

An American carved walnut longcase regulator, signed Howard & Davis, Makers — Boston, circa 1851, 8ft.0½in. high. (Christie's) $24,200

A Continental 18th century mahogany longcase clock with 11in. brass dial, 2.62m. high. (Phillips) $1,740

A late 17th century walnut and panel marquetry longcase clock, signed Jos. Buckingham in ye Minories, 2.16m. high. (Phillips) $8,410

A 19th century mahogany longcase clock, the dial signed Barraud, Cornhill, London, 1.98m. high. (Phillips) $841

A George III mahogany longcase clock, dial signed Wm. Farrar, Pontefract, 8ft.2in. high. (Christie's) $1,573

A 19th century mahogany longcase clock, signed Simmons, Coleman St., 2.01m. high. (Phillips) $2,465

An early 18th century walnut longcase clock, signed Dan. Delander, London, 2.54m. high. (Phillips) $5,510

Country cherry tall case clock, by A. & C. Edwards, Mass., circa 1794, 92in. high. (Robt. W. Skinner Inc.) $1,000

LONGCASE CLOCKS

Early 19th century
Country Federal
cherry tall case clock,
by R. Whiting, Conn.,
89in. high. (Robt. W.
Skinner Inc.)
$2,300

Country painted pine
tall clock, by Simeon
Crane, Mass., circa
1810, 86¼in. high.
(Robt. W. Skinner
Inc.) $5,750

Federal cherry inlaid
tall case clock, pro-
bably Conn., circa
1790, 93in. high.
(Robt. W. Skinner
Inc.) $4,000

A George III style
mahogany long-
case clock, dial
plate signed Henry
Jarman, London,
7ft.10½in. high.
(Christie's)
$3,460

A Dutch walnut
longcase clock,
dial signed Andris
Vermeulent,
Amsterdam, 7ft.
high. (Christie's)
$4,404

Federal birch inlaid
tall case clock, New
England, circa 1780,
90in. high. (Robt. W.
Skinner Inc.)
$3,200

A walnut longcase
clock, the chapter
ring signed Edn.
Stanton, London,
6ft.4in. high.
(Christie's)
$5,218

An Art Nouveau
oak longcase clock,
by J. Gruber,
253cm. high.
(Christie's)
$3,304

LONGCASE CLOCKS

A George I walnut longcase clock, by Jos. Windmills, London, 7ft.8in. high. (Christie's) $10,696

A Queen Anne walnut year-going longcase clock, by Daniel Quare, London, 7ft.6in. high. (Christie's) $31,460

A Federal inlaid cherrywood tall case clock, dial signed by Seth Thomas, Conn., circa 1800, 90in. high. (Christie's) $8,250

A Charles II walnut and parquetry long-case clock, 10in. dial signed C. Gretton, London, 6ft.3in. high. (Christie's) $9,438

A green japanned longcase clock, the brass dial signed Jos. Windmills, London, 8ft.4in. high. (Christie's) $3,261

A Charles II wal-nut month-going longcase clock, dial signed Thos. Tompion, 6ft.4in. high. (Christie's) $66,066

A Federal inlaid maho-gany tall case clock, dial signed by Wm. Cummens, Mass., circa 1800, 96in. high. (Christie's) $16,500

A Chippendale cherry-wood tall case clock, dial signed by Thos. Harland, Conn., circa 1775, 95in. high. (Christie's) $12,100

MANTEL CLOCKS

An ormolu strut clock, in the manner of Thos. Cole, the silvered dial signed Hunt & Roskell, London, 5½in. high. (Christie's) $1,223

A German gilt brass square timepiece alarm signed Ang. Metzke Soran, 3¼in. square. (Christie's) $3,424

Federal mahogany pillar and scroll clock, E. Terry & Sons, Conn., circa 1825, 31in. high. (Robt. W. Skinner Inc.) $650

A Victorian strut clock with enamel dial signed Baudin Freres, Geneve, 8in. high. (Christie's) $792

A George III gilt metal alabaster and white mantel clock, the backplate signed J. Burrows, Goodge Street, London, 19in. high. (Christie's) $495

Mid 19th century Black Forest carved walnut figural clock, 28¾in. high. (Robt. W. Skinner Inc.) $2,900

Federal mahogany pillar and scroll clock, by Ephraim Downes, Conn., circa 1825, 31in. high. (Robt. W. Skinner Inc.) $750

An electric mantel timepiece, the movement with enamel dial signed Dollond, London, 44cm. high. (Phillips) $864

A gilt metal clock, by Thos. Cole, London, simulating a watchstand in the form of a miniature chiffonier set, 5¼in. high. (Christie's) $6,197

MANTEL CLOCKS

Federal mahogany pillar
and scroll clock, by Ephraim
Downs for G. Mitchell, Conn.,
circa 1820, 31in. high. (Robt.
W. Skinner Inc.) $850

An early English alarm 'table'
clock, the movement signed
Eduardus East, Londini,
3¾in. diam. of dial.
(Christie's)
$10,600

A small timepiece contained
in an amboyna veneered
lancet case with brass outline, by Thos. Cole, 10in.
high. (Woolley & Wallis)
$1,800

A 19th century French
ormolu and enamel mantel
clock, the case decorated
with polychrome champleve
enamel, 24cm. high.
(Phillips) $406

A Regency English bronze
and gilt bronze mantel
timepiece, 30cm. high.
(Phillips) $648

An Empire ormolu mantel
clock, the steel dial signed
Le Roy & fils Hrs du roi,
25in. high. (Christie's)
$1,405

A Regency variegated wood
mantel timepiece, signed
Davd. Magson, 12¾in. high.
(Christie's) $823

Mid 19th century red marble and
patinated gilt bronze industrial
clock, French, 17in. high.
(Christie's) $2,200

An Empire ormolu mantel
clock with enamel dial signed
Le Roy Hr. du Roi a Paris,
14½in. high. (Christie's)
$1,015

MANTEL CLOCKS

A 19th century French ormolu and champleve enamel mantel clock, the gilt dial signed for Howell & James, 43cm. high. (Phillips) $870

Empire mahogany carved mantel clock, by Eli Terry & Son, Conn., circa 1825, 31in. high. (Robt. W. Skinner Inc.) $1,000

A 19th century French ormolu and bronze mantel clock, the dial with enamel numerals, 58cm. high. (Phillips) $1,015

Mid 19th century ormolu mantel clock with circular dial, 17½in. high. (Christie's) $797

A 19th century French ormolu and porcelain mantel clock, the enamel dial signed Grohe A Paris, 28cm. high. (Phillips) $696

A Belgian incised black slate perpetual calendar mantel clock, 16¾in. high. (Christie's) $1,262

An Alfred Dunhill Art Deco marble mantel clock and cigarette case, 23.7cm. high. (Christie's) $871

A Meissen clockcase with a seated figure of Cupid, blue crossed swords and incised numeral marks, circa 1880, 30cm. high. (Christie's) $1,084

A 19th century French ormolu and porcelain mounted mantel clock, 41cm. high. (Phillips) $754

MANTEL CLOCKS

A French 19th century bronze ormolu and red marble mantel clock, the enamel dial signed Guibal A Paris, 57cm. high.   (Phillips) $2,175

A glass and ormolu oval four-glass clock with gong strike, the chapter ring signed Franz Wiess & Sohne Wien, 13in. high. (Christie's) $2,609

A 16th century gilt metal table clock, by Hans Gruber, the whole case well engraved, 23cm. high. (Phillips) $6,380

A Japanese gilt brass striking spring clock, the case engraved with stylized flowers and with turned angle columns, 6in. high. (Christie's) $1,956

Early 19th century Sicilian coral mantel clock with enamel dial, 21in. high. (Christie's) $2,552

An ormolu mounted boulle mantel clock, the enamel dial signed Grohe Paris, 11½in. high. (Christie's) $792

A Paris (Jacob Petit) clockcase and stand of scroll outline, blue JP marks, circa 1835, 37cm. high overall. (Christie's) $1,196

Mantel clock on D-shaped marble base, the clock face surmounted by a bronzed group of lovers. (Lots Road Galleries) $703

An ormolu and white marble four glass clock with perpetual calendar and moonphase dial below time dial, 16¾in. high. (Christie's) $5,348

MANTEL CLOCKS

An early Anglo-Flemish
weight driven clock, circa
1600, 19cm. high.
(Phillips) $1,087

An enamelled Art Deco timepiece,
retailed through Fortnum & Mason,
London, 23.5cm. wide, when open,
with Swiss 8-day movement.
(Phillips) $1,224

French ormolu mounted
boulle bracket clock in
Louis XV style, with strike
(Worsfolds) $1,170

A 17th century gilt brass
table clock, the rectangular
case surmounted by a bell,
17cm. high. (Phillips)
$3,190

A Lalique square-shaped
clock, Inseparables, the clear
and opalescent glass decorated
with budgerigars, 11cm. high.
(Christie's) $1,584

An Empire ormolu mounted
mahogany mantel clock, the
dial signed Gaston Jolly a
Paris, 16in. high. (Christie's)
$1,015

A 16th century gilt metal
drum clock, 6cm. diam.,
together with an alarm
mechanism of drum form.
(Phillips) $2,175

A 17th century South German
gilt metal quarter striking table
clock, the movement signed
J. O. H., for Johann Ott.
Halaicher, 13.5cm. sq.
(Christie's) $3,484

A 19th century ebonized
mantel clock, the dial
signed James McCabe,
Royal Exchange, London,
1717, 26cm. high.
(Phillips) $1,872

MANTEL CLOCKS

An ormolu mounted boulle bracket clock, the chapter ring signed J. Gudin a Paris, 41½in. high. (Christie's) $2,499

A Regency bronze and ormolu mantel clock with enamel dial, 14½in. wide. (Christie's) $3,567

A gilt metal strut clock attributed to Thos. Cole, 5¼in. high. (Christie's) $1,425

A Federal mahogany pillar and scroll clock, by E. Terry & Sons, circa 1835, 31in. high. (Robt. W. Skinner Inc.) $1,200

A Charles X ormolu mantel clock with glazed circular dial, 19in. high. (Christie's) $1,483

An Empire mahogany mantel clock, bearing partial label of Forestville Mfg. Co., circa 1830, 32in. high. (Robt. W. Skinner Inc.) $325

Mid 19th century silvered bronze and ormolu mantel clock, the backplate signed Le Roy a Paris, 26½in. high. (Christie's) $1,093

A Meissen clockcase of shaped outline, the movement with circular dial, blue crossed swords mark, circa 1880, 31cm. high. (Christie's) $2,356

A Galle carved and acid-etched clock, 13cm. high. (Christie's) $4,089

MANTEL CLOCKS

An early 17th century crucifix clock with detachable base, signed under the countwheel B.R. 1631, 35cm. high. (Phillips) $7,250

A 19th century French gilt brass and champleve enamel four glass mantel clock, 25cm. high. (Phillips) $696

Late 19th century lacquered brass and painted metal lighthouse clock, probably French, 22in. high. (Christie's) $2,200

An Empire ormolu mantel clock, the dial signed F. B. Adams, London, 17in. high. (Christie's) $1,249

A 19th century French white marble and ormolu mantel clock, 51cm. high. (Phillips) $691

A 19th century mechanical organ automaton with clock, 26in. high. (Christie's) $13,200

A Black Forest trumpeter clock, the two-train movement striking on a wire gong and playing a fanfare, 48in. high. (Christie's) $2,618

A Regency bronze and gilt bronze mantel timepiece, 31cm. high. (Phillips) $1,425

A 19th century French ormolu mantel clock with circular enamel dial, 35cm. high, together with a base. (Phillips) $580

MANTEL CLOCKS

Mid 19th century banjo time-piece with alarm, signed A. Willard, Jnr., Boston, 33½in. high. (Christie's)
$11,000

William IV period mahogany four glass mantel clock, by W. J. Thomas, London, 12⅝in. high. (Reeds Rains)
$892

A Federal mahogany veneer lighthouse clock, by Simon Willard, Mass., circa 1825, 27½in. high. (Christie's)
$110,000

An Empire white marble clock, signed Robin, H. de l'Empereur, circa 1810, 17¾in. high. (Christie's)
$1,650

A French late 19th century champleve bronze and glass mantel clock, 15½in. high. (Robt. W. Skinner Inc.)
$1,200

Early 19th century Empire pendule a cercle tournant, signed J. J. Lepaute, 19in. high. (Christie's)
$16,500

A 19th century Austrian silver and lapis lazuli decorative mantel timepiece, 22cm. high. (Phillips) $3,744

A French Empire ormolu mantel clock, the movement mounted on a chariot, 44cm. high. (Phillips)
$1,728

An ormolu mantel clock, the glazed dial signed Gosselin a Paris, 16¾in. high. (Christie's) $1,093

MANTEL CLOCKS

A Fin De Siecle silvered and parcel gilt brass windmill clock, 18½in. high. (Christie's) $1,443

An Empire ormolu mantel clock surmounted with a winged putto striking metal on an anvil at a forge, 12½in. wide. (Christie's) $1,408

A Louis XVI ormolu mounted marble pendule a cercle tournant, signed Ant. Coliau a Paris, 15½in. high. (Christie's) $4,400

An Empire ormolu mantel clock with circular enamel dial set within a plinth with Apollo and his lyre, 20½in. high. (Christie's) $1,584

Federal mahogany shelf clock, by Aaron Willard, Mass., circa 1825, 34in. high. (Robt. W. Skinner Inc.) $7,500

An Empire bronze and ormolu mantel clock, the enamel dial signed Lemoine a Paris, 24¼in. high. (Christie's) $2,640

A Regence ormolu mounted boulle bracket clock, dial signed Mynuel a Paris, 32in. high. (Christie's) $2,464

Late 19th century gilt and patinated bronze and marble industrial clock, probably French, 14½in. high. (Christie's) $1,650

An Empire ormolu mantel clock with glazed dial in tapering plinth case surmounted by an oil lamp, 15in. high. (Christie's) $2,816

SKELETON CLOCKS

A small skeleton timepiece, on mahogany base with glass dome, 11in. high. (Christie's) $1,144

A Victorian brass 'Strutt' epicyclic skeleton clock, slate base with plaque signed W. Wigston, Derby, No. 51, W. Strutt Esq. Inv., 10¼in. high. (Christie's) $4,089

A brass skeleton timepiece with spring detent escapement on oval white marble base, 17in. high excluding dome. (Christie's) $2,200

A Eureka electric striking clock, signed Eureka Clock Co. Ltd., London, 11in. high overall. (Christie's) $2,516

A quarter chiming skeleton clock, the pierced plates of open and angular design, 21in. high. (Christie's) $3,261

A brass chiming skeleton clock, on oval oak base with glass dome, English, circa 1900, 24in. high including dome. (Christie's) $5,500

A Victorian brass skeleton clock, 12½in. high, with glass dome. (Christie's) $3,968

An early Victorian brass striking skeleton clock, signed Harrison Darlington, 12¼in. high, excluding dome. (Christie's) $2,164

A brass skeleton timepiece with coup perdu escapement, on oval base with two plinths, 14in. high. (Christie's) $1,650

WALL CLOCKS

An Ithaca walnut calendar clock, 1866, 45in. long. (Robt. W. Skinner Inc.) $1,600

A Louis XVI ormolu cartel clock, the enamel dial signed Brille a Paris, 14in. high. (Christie's) $7,040

A George III black lacquered and chinoiserie decorated tavern wall timepiece, signed Frans. Perigal, London, 1.44m. high. (Phillips) $1,305

À cherry wall regulator timepiece, by Seth Thomas Clock Co., Conn., circa 1880, 36in. long. (Robt. W. Skinner Inc.) $650

French 18th century wall clock with dual striking, by Basnard. (John D. Fleming & Co.) $398

A Dutch marquetry 'Koort-staartklok' with automaton, 19th century, 39in. high. (Christie's) $2,059

A George III giltwood cartel clock with later white dial and timepiece movement, 30in. high. (Christie's) $1,240

An Austrian Biedermeier mahogany quarter striking wall clock, 41½in. high. (Christie's) $2,376

An 18th century Continental carved giltwood cartel clock, 64cm. high. (Christie's) $1,185

WALL CLOCKS

An ormolu cartel clock of Louis XVI style, the enamel dial signed Guibal, Paris, 26in. high. (Christie's) $757

A Georgian giltwood wall dial clock, the 14in. enamel dial signed Geo. Yonge, London, 24in. diam. (Christie's) $2,217

Late 19th century walnut regulator timepiece, by the Chelsea Clock Co., Mass., 35in. high. (Robt. W. Skinner Inc.) $850

The Col. Isaac Gardiner Reed Presentation banjo clock, by Aaron Willard, 1812-16, 35½in. high, including eagle. (Christie's) $121,000

An 18th century Dutch 'Stoelklok', 71cm. high. (Christie's) $1,033

A French cartel clock with eight day movement, 9½in. high. (Capes, Dunn & Co.) $174

A Federal mahogany giltwood and eglomise banjo clock, Mass., 1815-25, 40in. high. (Christie's) $1,430

An 8-day fusee wall clock in mahogany case, the cream painted dial inscribed 'Ganthony'. (Woolley & Wallis) $1,065

Late 19th century walnut regulator timepiece, by The E. Howard Watch & Clock Co., Boston, 40in. high. (Robt. W. Skinner Inc.) $900

WATCHES

A gilt metal and leather covered verge watch, inscribed Quare, London, 2567, 60mm. diam. (Phillips) $580

An 18kt. gold hunter-cased keyless chronograph, the movement signed J. W. Benson, No. 2516, London, 54mm. diam. (Phillips) $1,740

A silver pair cased verge watch, the movement signed Tho. Tompion, London, 2631, 55mm. diam. (Christie's) $4,240

A late 17th century silver pair cased verge watch, signed Tho. Tompion, London 0292, 57mm. diam. (Phillips) $2,610

A Continental gold verge watch, the bridge-cock movement with gold dial and serpentine hands, 55mm. diam. (Christie's) $503

A French gold quarter repeating musical cylinder watch with plain balance, musical disc and gilt cuvette, 59mm. diam. (Christie's) $3,617

An 18kt. gold keyless lever chronograph, the movement signed Nicole & Capt., London, Patent No. 7255, 48mm. diam. (Phillips) $754

A gold keyless lever watch, signed Geo. Edward & Sons on ½-plate gilt movement jewelled to the third, 53mm. diam. (Christie's) $943

An 18th century silver pair cased verge watch, signed G. Bryan, London, 399, 50mm. diam. (Phillips) $609

WATCHES

A gold hunter-cased chronometer, the enamel dial signed French Royal Exchange, London 18567, 51mm. diam. (Christie's) $1,467

An 18kt. gold hunter-cased keyless lever watch, signed Nicole & Capt., London, Patent No. 2932, 44mm. diam. (Phillips)
$464

A French gold and enamel verge watch, the bridge-cock movement signed Hessen a Paris, 38mm. diam. (Christie's) $815

A Continental gold and enamel quarter repeating watch, the movement with ruby cylinder escapement, 37mm. diam. (Phillips) $1,305

A silver cased pocket chronometer by John Arnold, London, 50mm. diam. (Christie's) $13,046

A gold minute repeating lever watch, the ¾-plate movement signed Jos. Penlington, Liverpool, No. 12937, 51mm. diam. (Christie's)
$2,446

A platinum keyless lever dress watch, by Cartier, the signed silver dial with sweep minute hand and with aperture for the hours, 45mm. diam. (Phillips) $2,030

A gold pocket chronometer, the fusee movement signed Wm. Pickman, with enamel dial and gold hands, 54mm. diam. (Christie's)
$1,258

A French gold and gem set verge watch, the case with three-color decoration set with turquoise and rubies, 42mm. diam. (Phillips)
$522

WATCHES

An 18kt. gold openface quarter repeating verge watch with jacquemarts, Swiss, signed on the cuvette Breguet & Fils, no. 23592, 55mm. diam. (Christie's) $2,640

An 18kt. gold openface dress watch, signed Patek Philippe & Co., Geneva, no. 188192, 42mm. diam. (Christie's) $880

A two-color gold openface dress watch, signed Patek Philippe & Co., no. 817759, 45mm. diam. (Christie's) $1,210

An enamelled platinum openface dress watch, signed Patek Philippe & Co., Geneva, no. 810822, 39mm. diam. (Christie's) $1,320

A nielloed silver sector watch, signed Record Watch Co., Tramelan, 60mm. wide. (Christie's) $1,320

A platinum openface dress watch, signed Patek Philippe & Co., Geneva, no. 890237, 43mm. diam. (Christie's) $1,265

A 14kt. gold openface pocket watch, 'Paul Breguette', 17-jewel, in a polished gold case. (Robt. W. Skinner Inc.) $125

An 18th century gold pair cased pocket watch, the fusee movement inscribed John Walker, Newcastle upon Tyne 736. (Parsons, Welch & Cowell) $862

A gold pair cased verge watch, signed Jams. Hagger, London 200, 54mm. diam. (Christie's) $3,643

WATCHES

Late 19th century 14kt. gold openface calendar watch, Swiss, 50mm. diam. (Christie's) $495

An 18kt. gold openface lever watch, signed Patek Philippe & Co., no. 135231, 45mm. diam. (Christie's) $1,540

A 14kt. gold openface lever watch, signed Patek Philippe & Co., Geneva, no. 89566, 50mm. diam. (Christie's) $1,045

An enamelled platinum openface dress watch, signed Patek Philippe & Co., Geneva, no. 814228, 42mm. diam. (Christie's) $1,210

Breguet No. 58: a gold quarter repeating duplex watch, gilt Lepine calibre, 44mm. diam. (Christie's) $3,168

An openface platinum dress watch with 19-jewel movement with gold train, signed Audemars Piguet & Co., no. 36541, 43mm. diam. (Christie's) $990

An 18kt. gold openface dress watch, signed Patek Philippe & Co., Geneva, no. 892815, 47mm. diam. (Christie's) $1,320

An openface gun metal calendar watch with damascened bar pattern lever movement, 62mm. diam. (Christie's) $165

A late 18th century gold and enamel verge watch, the movement signed Gregson A Paris 13123, 50mm. diam. (Phillips) $792

WATCHES

A silver fusee lever watch with winding indicator, signed Smith & Son, London, the case, London, 1899, 52mm. diam. (Christie's) $1,100

A gold hunter-cased cylinder watch, the movement signed Vulliamy, London ruim, 50mm. diam. (Christie's) $619

14kt. gold hunting case pocket watch, 'Elgin', jewelled gilt movement and white porcelain dial. (Robt. W. Skinner Inc.) $225

A slender gold stem wind open faced lever pocket watch, signed Cartier, Paris, 45mm. diam. (Reeds Rains) $1,147

A Swiss gold, enamel and gem set verge watch, the bridgecock movement signed Fres. Bordier, Geneve No. 35751, 44mm. diam. (Christie's) $950

A small 18kt. gold openface five-minute repeating split-second chronograph, signed Tiffany & Co., the movement by P. Philippe, no. 111758, 42mm. diam. (Christie's) $4,950

A gold miniature keyless lever watch, the steel bar movement jewelled to the center and signed for Tiffany & Co., N.Y., 27mm. diam. (Phillips) $493

An 18th century silver and horn pair cased verge watch, signed Conrs. Dunlop, London 3451, the inner case marked London 1762, 52mm. diam. (Phillips) $2,016

14kt. gold hunting case pocket watch, 'Elgin', lever set jewelled nickel movement and white porcelain dial. (Robt. W. Skinner Inc.) $550

WATCHES

A Swiss gilt metal and enamel verge watch, wound through Arabic enamel dial, 54mm. diam. (Christie's) $633

A gold hunter-cased quarter repeating calendar watch, signed L. A. Favre Brandt, Geneve, 53mm. diam. (Christie's) $1,760

An 18kt. gold openface center seconds watch, signed Patek Philippe & Co., Geneva, no. 185202, 46mm. diam. (Christie's) $2,200

A French gold jump hour cylinder watch with plain balance and gold cuvette inscribed Breguet A Paris No. 8416, 50mm. diam. (Christie's) $2,202

A Continental gold quarter repeating ruby cylinder watch, 49mm. diam. (Christie's) $871

A gilt metal pair cased verge stop watch, signed James Wild, Soho, 56mm. diam. (Phillips) $273

A French gold, enamel and pearl verge watch, the bridge-cock movement signed Martin A Paris 11750, 37mm. diam. (Christie's) $2,217

An 18kt. gold openface dress watch, with nickel 17-jewel lever movement, signed Vacheron & Constantin, Geneva, no. 486697, 48mm. diam. (Christie's) $880

A gun metal double dial calendar watch with white enamel dial, 52mm. diam. (Christie's) $385

WRISTWATCHES

A gold self-winding wristwatch with center seconds,
signed Rolex Oyster Perpetual.
(Christie's) $1,760

A platinum wristwatch with
17-jewel movement and
sapphire crown, signed
Breguet, no. 4300.
(Christie's) $2,200

An 18kt. gold wristwatch
with nickel 18-jewel cal.
27-AM400 movement,
signed Patek Philippe & Co.,
no. 731479. (Christie's)
$1,100

An 18kt. gold wristwatch
with nickel 18-jewel cal. 23-
300 movement, signed Patek
Philippe & Co., no. 781179.
(Christie's) $1,210

A gold self-winding wristwatch with calendar, signed
Lucien Picard, Seashark, with
textured 14kt. gold bracelet.
(Christie's) $495

A gold wristwatch, signed
Breguet, no. 3150, with
leather strap and 18kt. gold
deployant buckle. (Christie's)
$2,200

A Swiss gold wristwatch,
gold cuvette inscribed in
Russian, the dial signed
in Cyrillic Pavel Buhre,
39mm. diam. (Christie's)
$1,584

A gold wristwatch with nickel
17-jewel movement, signed
Gruen Watch Co., Curvex
Precision. (Christie's)
$330

An 18kt. gold wristwatch,
signed Patek Philippe & Co.,
retailed by Cartier, with
fitted box. (Christie's)
$1,430

WRISTWATCHES

A gold wristwatch with nickel
21-jewel movement, signed
Lord Elgin, with 14kt. gold
bracelet. (Christie's)
$418

A gentleman's gold wrist-
watch, the movement with
17 rubies, signed Rolex
Precision. (Christie's)
$629

An 18kt. gold wristwatch
with nickel 17-jewel movement, signed Vacheron &
Constantin, no. 421150.
(Christie's) $2,200

A gold self-winding wristwatch
with center seconds, signed
Rolex Oyster Perpetual.
(Christie's) $990

A gold wristwatch with nickel
18-jewel cal. 23-300 movement, signed Patek Philippe &
Co., no. 782328, and a 14kt.
gold watch signed Omega.
(Christie's) $1,760

An 18kt. gold self-winding
wristwatch, signed Patek
Philippe & Co., no. 116018,
with signed 18kt. gold buckle
to leather strap. (Christie's)
$1,540

A gold wristwatch, signed
Audemars Piguet, no. 58098,
with nickel 18-jewel movement. (Christie's)
$935

A gold self-winding wristwatch, signed Piaget, no.
7311215, the leather strap
with 18kt. gold buckle.
(Christie's) $825

An 18kt. gold wristwatch,
signed West End Watch Co.,
with nickel movement jewelled
through the center.(Christie's)
$660

Late 19th century cloisonne enamel globular jar and shallow domed cover, 59.5cm. high. (Christie's) $5,935

A cloisonne enamel and gilt bronze tripod censer and domed cover, Qianlong/ Jiaqing, 39cm. high. (Christie's) $2,516

A Japanese cloisonne enamel baluster vase decorated with butterflies in flight, 4¾in. high. (Christie's) $3,168

Late 19th century Japanese cloisonne urn of baluster form, 19¼in. high. (Christie's) $2,090

A cloisonne enamel and gilt bronze vessel and cover, ding, Qianlong, 49.5cm. high. (Christie's) $5,977

A 17th century cloisonne enamel Hu vase, 48cm. high. (Christie's) $2,516

A cloisonne enamel circular box and flat cover, Qianlong, 32.7cm. diam., wood stand. (Christie's) $3,460

One of a pair of Japanese cloisonne vases, 10in. high. (Reeds Rains) $518

Japanese cloisonne octagonal wall plaque, circa 1900, 24in. diam. (Peter Wilson) $1,762

CLOISONNE

A 16th century Ming cloisonne enamel globular tripod censer, 12.8cm. diam. (Christie's) $2,831

Cloisonne vase decorated with dragons on a dark-blue field, converted to a reading lamp, 19in. high. (Peter Wilson) $158

A Namikawa compressed globular tripod censer and domed cover, circa 1900, 10.3cm. diam. (Christie's) $3,124

One of a pair of Japanese cloisonne vases, each painted with panels of cockerels and hens and birds in flight, 6¼in. high. (Christie's) $632

Pair of rounded rectangular enamelled cloisonne vases, Meiji period wood stands, 30.4cm. high. (Christie's) $879

A fine Ando cloisonne enamel slender oviform vase with short flaring neck, Meiji period, 24.3cm. high. (Christie's) $1,249

A cloisonne enamel foliate shaped box and cover, Meiji period, 9cm. wide. (Christie's) $234

A tall cloisonne vase decorated in various colored enamels on a dark blue ground with a spray of tiger lilies, late 19th century, 33cm. high. (Christie's) $781

A cloisonne enamel candle holder formed as a standing elephant, late Qing Dynasty, overall 33cm. wide. (Christie's) $3,775

A brass bowl, the outer rim decorated with a Moorish design, possibly Turkish, 8½in. diam., and another. (Christie's) $156

Pair of Federal brass andirons, Phila., 1800-10, 29in. high. (Christie's) $3,050

An early 17th century South German gilt brass and copper miniature casket, signed Michel Mann,.7.3cm. wide. (Phillips) $4,608

One of two pairs of brass candlesticks, early 19th century, 9½ and 10¾in. high. (Robt. W. Skinner Inc.) $375

A Nara period copper gilt square plaque decorated in repousse with Amida, 7th/8th century, 11.3 x 11.3cm. (Christie's) $13,992

Early 20th century hammered copper bird cage on stand, 74in. high. (Robt. W. Skinner Inc.) $275

A Robin Banks enamelled copper charger, RB monogram 1986, 39.4cm. diam. (Christie's) $302

A Dutch or Flemish 16th century brass candlestick , 18.8cm. high. (Phillips) $792

A gilt copper turret of hexagonal form, probably Tuscan 15th century. (Phillips) $576

An oval brass planter with gadroon embossed decoration, 13in. high. (Peter Wilson) $300

A pair of brass and iron knife-blade andirons, American, circa 1800, 22¼in. high. (Christie's) $880

Early 19th century copper coal helmet, also a matching shovel, 17½in. high. (Peter Wilson) $616

A Benham & Froud brass and copper adjustable floor oil lamp, 175cm. high. (Christie's) $364

A brass alms dish with raised central dome, 17th century, 17½in. diam. (Christie's) $776

A set of three George III brass fire-irons, 31¼in. long. (Christie's) $775

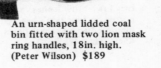

One of a pair of brass and enamelled andirons, 26in. high. (Christie's) $3,344

An urn-shaped lidded coal bin fitted with two lion mask ring handles, 18in. high. (Peter Wilson) $189

Pair of early 19th century brass andirons, New York, signed Bailey, 21½in. high. (Robt. W. Skinner Inc.) $1,400

An 18th century Spanish brass flagon, 8.5in. high. (Woolley & Wallis) $403

Pair of Perry & Co. brass candlesticks, designed by Dr. C. Dresser, with wood handles, 5½in. (Christie's) $1,661

One of a pair of copper and brass vacuum flasks with handles, attributed to W. A. S. Benson, 48cm. high. (Christie's) $364

Pair of early 18th century Continental brass candlesticks, 9in. high. (Christie's) $3,080

Gustav Stickley hammered copper umbrella holder, circa 1905, no. 273, 27¼in. high. (Robt. W. Skinner Inc.) $700

Benedict Art Studios hammered copper wall plaque, N.Y., circa 1907, 15in. diam. (Robt. W. Skinner Inc.) $800

Mid 19th century copper jelly mold, 5in. diam. (Peter Wilson) $155

One of a pair of 19th century brass atheniennes , supported on four ram's head monopodiae on square bases, 45cm. high. (Phillips) $1,944

A late 19th century English brass doorway, each door 209 x 77.5cm. (Christie's) $23,925

Large 19th century brass planter with bird's head ring handles, China, 28in. diam. (Robt. W. Skinner Inc.) $950

A 19th century firegrate with brass detail. (Lots Road Galleries) $331

Early 20th century Arts & Crafts hammered copper wood box with loop handles, 23½in. wide. (Robt. W. Skinner Inc.) $750

Pair of early 18th century brass tapersticks, English, 4½in. high. (Christie's) $2,310

A Regency copper oval samovar, the domed cover with a sphinx finial, 13in. high. (Woolley & Wallis) $317

Pair of Federal brass andirons and matching tools, 1800-20, 17in. high. (Christie's) $1,045

An early 20th century English copper electrotype bust of Eliza Macloghlin, cast by A. Toft from a model by Sir A. Gilbert, dated 1906, 40.5cm. high. (Christie's) $15,950

Mid 19th century copper jelly mold with fluted column decoration, 6in. diam. (Peter Wilson) $155

Pair of 18th century brass table candlesticks with baluster stems, 11in. high. (Hobbs & Chambers) $172

A pair of late 19th century Chinese lady's stilted shoes of red silk with blue silk border. (Phillips) $226

A 16th century man's embroidered cap embellished with sequins and gold lace trim, England, 8in. high. (Robt. W. Skinner Inc.) $10,000

A late 19th century Chinese child's robe of terracotta silk, embroidered in colored silks. (Phillips) $573

A gentleman's banyan of printed worsted, circa 1820's. (Phillips) $1,057

Three-quarter length wrap-over mink coat, silk lined. (Peter Wilson) $705

A late 19th century two-piece gown of mauve, gray and orange silk brocade of striped design, circa 1880. (Phillips) $241

A late 19th century Chinese waistcoat of brown worsted, the black silk border embroidered in blue and ivory silk. (Phillips) $131

A noh costume, Karaori, decorated in various colors on gold twill-weave ground, late Edo period. (Christie's) $26,554

A Moroccan Western Atlas cloak of black wool, of semi-circular form, with narrow hood. (Phillips) $282

A late 19th century Chinese robe of blue silk, embroidered in colored silks and applied gold thread. (Phillips) $1,057

A Nigerian Haussa robe of indigo cotton embroidered in pale blue with knives, roundels and knots. (Phillips) $169

A noh costume, Karaori, late Edo period. (Christie's) $14,839

A mid 19th century dress of cream and brown wool printed in mainly red, green and orange. (Phillips) $253

A 19th century black silk uchikake richly embroidered in gold and color. (Christie's) $4,373

A two-piece gown of ivory silk brocaded in lime and pink silk, maker's label G. Worth, Paris, circa 1900. (Phillips) $1,963

An embroidered vest and pair of embroidered shoes, 18th century, the vest with floral sprays on ivory silk. (Robt. W. Skinner Inc.) $800

A Woodlands hide jacket, lined with printed cotton, decorated with a polychrome beadwork foliate and floral motif, 80cm. long. (Phillips) $351

A late 18th century gentleman's double-breasted waistcoat of yellow silk brocade. (Phillips) $119

DOLLS

An Armand Marseille bisque-headed 'dollie', wood and composition ball jointed body, 24in. high. (Hobbs & Chambers) $285

Early 20th century Lehmann waltzing doll, head with EPL trademark, 9in. high. (Robt. W. Skinner Inc.) $900

A Chad Valley painted felt portrait doll modelled as the Princess Elizabeth, circa 1938, 18in. high, together with another and a koala bear. (Christie's) $471

A pink china shoulder headed doll, the kid body with wooden limbs, 15in. high, circa 1840. (Christie's) $471

A set of composition dolls representing the Dionne quintuplets with doctor and nurse, 7½in. high, the adults 13in. high, by Madame Alexander. (Christie's) $639

A bisque-headed character doll, marked 1488 Simon & Halbig 4, 12½in. high. (Christie's) $2,359

A Simon & Halbig bisque headed doll with composition ball jointed body, 24in. high. (Hobbs & Chambers) $489

A bisque headed character baby doll, 9in. high, marked 142 2/0 by Kestner. (Christie's) $302

Early 20th century Armand Marseille bisque headed Floradora doll, 14in. high. (Hobbs & Chambers) $187

DOLLS

A bisque headed child doll, 8½in. high, marked 1078 S&H. (Christie's) $403

A bisque headed character baby doll, 27in. high, marked SFBJ252 Paris 12. (Christie's) $2,356

A bisque headed character baby doll molded as an Oriental, 9¼in. high, marked 3/0. (Christie's) $639

A French mechanical walking doll, the bisque head with blonde mohair wig, 38cm. high. (Phillips) $1,047

A composition portrait doll modelled as Shirley Temple, 13½in. high, marked S.T. 5/0 CB Germany. (Christie's) $370

Simon & Halbig/Kammer & Reinhardt bisque-headed doll, 1914-27, 26in. high. (Hobbs & Chambers) $789

Late 19th century Heubach 12-Koppelsdoft bisque headed doll, impressed AWW, Germany, 32in. high. (Hobbs & Chambers) $857

A bisque headed doll, C1912, by Franz Schmidt, 12½in. high. (Hobbs & Chambers) $446

A bisque-headed bebe, the jointed body dressed in pink, 19in. high, marked on the head 8 and with the Schmitt of Paris shield mark on bottom. (Christie's) $2,988

A bisque-headed child doll, 22in. high, marked Handwerck 109-11 Halbig on the shoes, NAPAUD 32 rue du 4 Septembre. (Christie's) $1,179

A brown bisque-headed baby doll with brown composition baby's body, 14½in. high, marked AM341/2.5K. (Christie's) $314

A bisque-headed bebe, marked SteA.2 and written in red Steiner A.S.G.D.G. Paris Bourgoin jeun, and a wig, 18in. high. (Christie's) $2,359

A set of Chad Valley Snow White and the seven dwarfs. Snow White with painted cloth face, fixed blue glass eyes and velvet limbs, 17in. high, the dwarfs in original clothes, 9½in. high. (Christie's) $440

A bisque-headed character doll, marked SFBJ236 Paris 6 and embossed 21, 14in. high. (Christie's) $786

A bisque-headed bebe, the fixed wrist jointed composition body dressed in blue, impressed SteA.1, 16in. high. (Christie's) $2,674

A bisque-headed doll with composition body, 17in. high, impressed SFBJ60 Paris O. (Outhwaite & Litherland) $290

A composition headed Japanese doll with closed mouth, inset eyes and black hair wig, 16½in. high, and a composition headed Gosho Ningo. (Christie's) $235

A bisque-headed character child doll, 23in. high, marked K*R Simon and Halbig 117n58, and a boy doll, 22in. high. (Christie's) $1,337

A bisque-headed bebe with jointed composition body, mark 7 stamped in blue on the body Bebe Jumeau Depose, 15in. high. (Christie's) $1,494

A bisque headed character doll with a quantity of other items, including bedding, shoes, a parasol, a box of washing items and twenty-three changes of clothes, 14½in. high, marked F.S. and Co., 1272/352 Deponiert. (Christie's) $1,337

A bisque-headed character boy doll, impressed 7 3072 and with JDK sticker on the body, 20in. high. (Christie's) $865

A bisque shoulder headed doll with closed mouth, solid pate and kid body with bisque arms, 14½in. high. (Christie's) $503

A bisque shoulder headed doll, the stuffed body with bisque limbs, 11½in. high, circa 1860. (Christie's) $1,022

A German oblong enamel snuff box, the white ground body painted in puce with battle scenes, circa 1760, 3¼in. long. (Christie's) $1,321

A German oblong enamel box commemorating the Treaty of Hubertsburg, circa 1763, 3¼in. long. (Christie's) $1,074

A German oblong enamel snuff box with engraved gilt metal mounts, circa 1765, 3¼in. long. (Christie's) $991

A Dunhill enamelled cigarette lighter, 5cm. high, stamped with maker's marks and Pat. No. 143752. (Phillips) $403

Pair of Staffordshire white ground enamel candlesticks, circa 1770, 10.5/8in. high. (Christie's) $1,487

A German enamelled cigarette case, 8.5 x 4.5cm., stamped 800 with crescent and crown and with Austrian import marks. (Phillips) $57

A George III oblong enamel 'New Year's Gift' calendar snuff box in the style of Anthony Tregent, London, 1757, 3¼in. long. (Christie's) $1,022

A Staffordshire oblong enamel tea caddy with gilt metal mounts, circa 1765, 4.3/8in. long. (Christie's) $1,487

A Staffordshire small rectangular enamel snuff box, inscribed on the interior 'Vole Amour a mon Secours', circa 1765, 1¾in. long. (Christie's) $943

An officer's silver (not hall-marked) and enamel cap badge of The Irish Guards. (Wallis & Wallis) $103

A 19th century enamel nef, the hull and sails decorated with the Rape of Europa and other classical scenes, 20cm. long, probably Vienna. (Phillips) $864

A Staffordshire small oval enamel snuff box of tub form, with crimped gilt metal mounts and shaped thumbpiece, circa 1770, 2.5/8in. long. (Christie's) $629

A Staffordshire oblong white ground enamel snuff box with engraved gilt metal mounts, circa 1770, 3½in. long. (Christie's) $1,101

A Staffordshire small oval enamel snuff box, the gilt metal mounts with zig-zag ornament, circa 1765, 1.7/8in. long. (Christie's) $865

A German oblong white ground enamel snuff box, painted in the manner of David Chodowiecki, the scenes mostly after Boucher, Berlin, circa 1760, 3¼in. long. (Christie's) $3,775

A plique-a-jour circular box and cover decorated in translucent enamels, 5.8cm. diam., stamped on base 925. (Phillips) $230

A German circular gold mounted enamel snuff box with waisted sides, circa 1760, 2¼in. diam. (Christie's) $2,643

A Staffordshire oval enamel snuff box of tub-shape, with crimped gilt metal mounts, circa 1770, 2.5/8in. long. (Christie's) $597

A Flemish fan with ivory sticks, the guards inlaid with mother-of-pearl and decorated with silver pique, 26.5cm, long. (Phillips) $479

An ivory brise fan painted and lacquered with a classical scene, 8½in., circa 1730. (Christie's) $3,933

A late 18th century Italian fan with pierced ivory sticks, 28cm. long. (Phillips) $535

La Contre Revolution, a printed fan edged with green silk fringe, 11in., French, circa 1790. (Christie's) $901

A French painted pierced ivory brise fan with tortoiseshell guards decorated with silver pique, early 18th century, 21cm. long. (Phillips) $479

A fan, the dark leaf painted with a Biblical scene of figures drinking from a mountain torrent, 10¼in., Italian, circa 1770, in silk covered box. (Christie's) $1,147

A late 18th century fan with carved, pierced and silvered ivory sticks, 24.5cm. long, and a box. (Phillips) $155

An early 19th century fan with carved shaped ivory sticks, the vellum leaf painted with Flora attended by maidens and suitors, 28cm. long. (Phillips) $513

An early 18th century Flemish fan, the carved ivory sticks decorated with silver pique and mother-of-pearl cloute, 27cm. long. (Phillips) $120

An ivory brise fan painted with a lady fishing, 9in., circa 1730. (Christie's) $5,736

Early 18th century ivory brise fan, the leaf painted with convivial figures in a garden, 8in. (Christie's) $3,605

A fan, the leaf painted with the return of a hero, the verso with chinoiserie, 10in., French, circa 1760, in glazed case. (Christie's) $3,278

A French fan, the leaf painted with elegant figures in a park, the mother-of-pearl sticks carved, pierced and gilt with figures in Turkish dress, 11in., circa 1760. (Christie's) $2,950

A fan, the leaf painted with a court scene, 10in., circa 1770. (Christie's) $655

A fan, the mother-of-pearl sticks carved with the departure of a hero, 10½in., circa 1760. (Christie's) $1,966

A fan, the ivory sticks carved, pierced and gilt with the Altar of Love, 10½in., Italian, circa 1780. (Christie's) $1,346

BEDS

A mahogany lit a bateau, three-quarter size, circa 1830, 43½in. high. (Robt. W. Skinner Inc.) $1,000

Late 19th century ebonized Bentwood cradle, Europe, 52in. long. (Robt. W. Skinner Inc.) $900

An Empire mahogany lit en bateau with box spring mattress, 48in. wide, 86in. long. (Christie's) $4,686

A George III mahogany four-post bedstead, 5ft.2in. wide, 6ft.9in. long, 7ft.6in. high. (Parsons, Welch & Cowell) $6,680

A mahogany four-post bed with box spring and mattress covered in pale green repp, 18th century and later, 82½in. long. (Christie's) $10,367

A giltwood four-post bed with padded arched head-rest, box-spring and mattress, circa 1830, 64in. wide, (Christie's) $10,153

A parcel gilt and cream-painted four-post bed, with padded headboard and yellow repp pleated hangings, box spring and mattress, 83.5in. wide. (Christie's) $1,652

A George III painted cradle with ogee-arched hood and cane-filled sides, 41in. long. (Christie's) $1,328

A Renaissance Revival walnut and burl veneer bed and chest, bearing the label 'E. D. Trymby's, Phila., Penn.', (Robt. W. Skinner Inc.) $3,500

BEDS

Painted Empire maple masonic bed, N.Y., circa 1830, 54in. wide. (Robt. W. Skinner Inc.) $600

An oak bed with panelled headboard on square legs with rollers, late 16th cen-- tury, 52in. wide. (Christie's) $3,344

An Empire mahogany bed, the head and foot-end inlaid with brass musical trophies, 43¾in. wide. (Christie's) $1,562

A late Federal carved cherry-wood four-post bedstead, probably New York, circa 1825, 53¼in. wide. (Christie's) $6,050

A mahogany four-post bed with box-spring and mattress, 59in. wide. (Christie's) $2,772

A Regency parcel gilt and fruitwood four-post bed, 43½in. wide, 96in. high. (Christie's) $6,198

A Regency mahogany and brass campaign bed, with inscribed brass plaque 'Butler's Patent, Catherine St.', 26in. wide. (Christie's) $6,375

A rococo Revival walnut bed, America, circa 1860, 91in. high, 74in. long. and a chest. (Robt. W. Skinner Inc.) $2,700

A Federal carved mahogany four-post bedstead; Mass., circa 1820, 76in. long, 47¼in. wide. (Christie's) $6,600

BOOKCASES

A Regency mahogany dwarf
bookcase with four graduated
shelves above a drawer, 30in.
wide. (Christie's)
$2,851

A satinwood dwarf bookcase
on molded base with brass
paw feet, 55½in. wide.
(Christie's) $5,583

A Regency ormolu mounted,
parcel gilt and rosewood
dwarf bookcase with specimen
marble top, 18in. wide.
(Christie's) $4,032

A mahogany breakfront bookcase with molded dentilled
overhanging cornice, 71½in.
wide. (Christie's)
$3,102

An oak breakfront bookcase,
by A. W. N. Pugin and John
Webb, now painted white,
98in. wide. (Christie's)
$9,438

A George III mahogany breakfront bookcase on splayed
bracket feet, 74½in. wide.
(Christie's) $11,011

A Victorian oak breakfront
library bookcase, the top
section enclosed by four
glazed panel doors, 88in.
wide. (Christie's)
$2,175

A Regency mahogany break-
front bookcase with raspberry
moire silk lined interior,
108in. wide. (Christie's)
$24,816

A late Federal tiger maple
bookcase, in two parts,
possibly New York, 1810-
20, 52½in. wide.(Christie's)
$7,150

BOOKCASES

A George III mahogany bookcase with a pair of glazed
cupboard doors enclosing
shelves, 49in. wide. (Christie's)
$6,979

A Regency purpleheart
pedestal bookcase with
square 17th century Italian
marble top formed in two
segments, 23in. sq.
(Christie's) $31,460

A George IV rosewood dwarf
bookcase with adjustable
open shelves, 44in. wide.
(Christie's) $1,258

An early Victorian oak bookcase in the Gothic style,
92in. wide, 93in. high.
(Christie's) $5,049

A 19th century mahogany
breakfront cabinet with
dentil cornice, 79in. wide.
(Dreweatts) $2,610

A Georgian mahogany breakfront library bookcase on a
plinth base, 2.56m. wide.
(Phillips) $18,460

A German walnut and mar-
quetry bookcase, the open
shelves lined with rust-
colored velveteen, basically
mid 18th century, 64½in.
wide. (Christie's)
$5,467

An early Victorian oak breakfront bookcase, by A. W. N.
Pugin and John Webb, now
painted white, 146in. wide.
(Christie's) $7,078

A George III mahogany bookcase, banded with satinwood,
53in. wide. (Christie's)
$28,314

BOOKCASES

A George III mahogany break-front bookcase with a pair of glazed cupboard doors, 97½in. wide. (Christie's) $8,262

Gustav Stickley open slat-sided bookshelf, circa 1909, 27in. wide. (Robt. W. Skinner Inc.) $800

A George III carved mahogany bookcase on stand with scroll carved hairy paw feet, 1.56m. wide. (Phillips) $3,600

Georgian two-part mahogany bookcase with two glazed doors above two panelled doors, 7ft.10in. high. (Lots Road Galleries) $3,825

Gustav Stickley two-door bookcase, gallery top over doors with eight panes each, circa 1903-4, no. 716, 42in. wide. (Robt. W. Skinner Inc.) $4,500

One of a pair of dwarf mahogany reproduction bookcases with Empire style mounts. (Lots Road Galleries) $362

L. & J. G. Stickley two-door bookcase, style no. 645, circa 1912, 49in. wide. (Robt. W. Skinner Inc.) $2,500

A Regency simulated rosewood dwarf bookcase with four graduated shelves, 30¼in. wide. (Christie's) $4,957

Gustav Stickley leaded two-door bookcase, designed by Harvey Ellis, circa 1904, no. 716, 42¾in. wide. (Robt. W. Skinner Inc.) $2,200

BOOKCASES

A Gustav Stickley oak bookcase, the door with wrought iron lock plate and drop loop handle, 98cm. wide. (Christie's) $1,982

An Isokon book stand, white painted natural wood, with sloping book compartments, 40.3cm. high. (Christie's) $330

A mid Georgian mahogany bookcase with pair of glazed doors with egg-and-dart carved astragals, 73½in. wide. (Christie's) $11,962

A large Regency mahogany breakfront bookcase, the base with six panelled cupboard doors, 176in. wide. (Christie's) $6,061

Gustav Stickley two-door bookcase, gallery top, eight panes in each door, circa 1912, 48in. wide. (Robt. W. Skinner Inc.) $1,900

Gustav Stickley leaded single door bookcase, designed by Harvey Ellis, circa 1904, no. 700, 36in. wide. (Robt. W. Skinner Inc.) $7,500

Gustav Stickley two-door bookcase, circa 1910, no. 716, gallery above eight-pane doors, 42in. wide. (Robt. W. Skinner Inc.) $1,900

L. & J. G. Stickley narrow bookcase with adjustable shelves, circa 1912, no. 652, 22in. wide. (Robt. W. Skinner Inc.) $1,700

Onondaga double door bookcase, by L. & J. G. Stickley, circa 1902-04, 56½in. high. (Robt. W. Skinner Inc.) $1,900

BOOKCASES

A set of George III pierced
fret side mahogany wall
shelves, 19in. wide.
(Woolley & Wallis)
$815

A mid Victorian gilt metal
mounted satinwood and
walnut dwarf bookcase,
109in. wide. (Christie's)
$5,662

A Regency simulated rose-
wood hanging open book-
shelf, 57cm. wide, 75cm. high.
(Phillips) $2,698

Late 18th/early 19th century
George III mahogany two-
part bookcase cabinet in two
sections, 23¼in. wide.
(Christie's) $5,500

A late Federal mahogany
breakfront bookcase, Phila.,
1815-20, 108in. wide.
(Christie's)
$28,600

An early Victorian oak bookcase, by A. W. N. Pugin and
John Webb, now painted
white, 75½in. wide. (Christie's)
$7,078

A Regency rosewood book-
case, the upper part with
open shelves, the lower part
with two glazed doors.
(Lots Road Galleries)
$1,872

A George III mahogany
bookcase, the glazed doors
enclosing shelves, 43½in.
wide. (Christie's)
$3,932

A Regency mahogany book-
case in the Gothic style,
29in. wide. (Christie's)
$7,755

BUREAU BOOKCASES

An early 18th century walnut and featherstrung bureau cabinet, 1.07m. wide. (Phillips) $11,628

Mid 18th century Italian scarlet and gold lacquer bureau cabinet on cabriole legs and hoof feet, 37in. wide. (Christie's) $3,124

A William and Mary walnut banded pollard elm bureau cabinet, 39½in. wide. (Christie's) $12,408

A George III mahogany bureau bookcase, the sloping flap enclosing a fitted interior, 43½in. wide. (Christie's) $5,174

A Scandinavian green painted and parcel gilt secretaire bookcase, basically late 18th century, 47in. wide. (Christie's) $3,124

Edwardian mahogany inlaid bureau bookcase, shell inlay on fall-front, 35in. wide. (Peter Wilson) $1,185

A Victorian painted and decorated pine secretary bookcase, Heywood Bros., painting attributed to E. and T. Hill, circa 1860, 49in. wide. (Christie's) $11,000

A George II padoukwood bureau cabinet, the sloping flap enclosing ten drawers, 34in. wide. (Christie's) $8,530

A George III mahogany bureau bookcase, the leather lined flap enclosing a fitted interior, 50in. wide. (Christie's) $9,740

BUREAU BOOKCASES

A Chippendale walnut bookcase desk, in two sections,
Mass., 1760-80. (Christie's)
$6,050

A mahogany bureau bookcase,
the fall-flap enclosing a fitted
interior, 34in. wide.
(Christie's) $3,509

A George III rosewood and
mahogany bureau bookcase,
the fall-flap enclosing a
fitted interior, 45in. wide.
(Christie's) $7,177

A Queen Anne walnut bureau
bookcase with candle slides,
41½in. wide. (Christie's)
$14,734

A Chippendale style faded
mahogany bureau bookcase
on ogee bracket feet, 4ft.
wide. (Woolley & Wallis)
$3,861

A George II mahogany bureau
cabinet, the fall front enclosing a fitted interior with
drawers, 1.04m. wide.
(Phillips) $7,200

A Chippendale block front
desk and bookcase in two
sections, Mass., 1760-80,
40½in. wide. (Christie's)
$38,500

An 18th century Anglo-
Dutch kingwood, burr yew-
wood and amboyna oyster
veneered bureau cabinet,
1.98m. high. (Phillips)
$4,350

A George III mahogany
bureau bookcase, the leather-
lined fall-flap enclosing a
fitted interior, 49in. wide.
(Christie's) $5,104

BUREAU BOOKCASES

A late 18th/early 19th century Italian scarlet lacquer and gilt bureau cabinet, 89cm. wide. (Phillips) $10,080

A George I walnut and parcel gilt bureau cabinet inlaid with feather banding, 39¼in. wide. (Christie's) $62,040

A Regency mahogany bureau cabinet, the George III base with sloping lid above two short and three long drawers, 45in. wide. (Christie's) $1,900

A late 17th/early 18th century walnut crossbanded bureau cabinet, with fitted interior, 1.25m. wide. (Phillips) $8,928

A George III mahogany bureau bookcase, 46in. wide, 96½in. high. (Christie's) $3,460

A Queen Anne walnut bureau bookcase with a partly-fitted interior, 41½in. wide. (Christie's) $40,326

A George III mahogany bureau bookcase, the fall-flap opening to reveal a fitted interior, 3ft.8in. wide. (Woolley & Wallis) $4,176

A Queen Anne walnut cross-banded and featherstrung bureau cabinet in three sections, 1.08m. wide. (Phillips) $44,640

A walnut bureau cabinet with a pair of mirror glazed doors, 32½in. wide. (Christie's) $7,078

BUREAUX

A George I walnut bureau inlaid with featherbandings, with later fitted interior, 36in. wide. (Christie's) $2,718

A Chippendale maple slant-front desk, New England, 1760-90, 37½in. wide. (Christie's) $3,300

A Chippendale walnut slant-front desk with fitted interior, Rhode Island, 1760-90, 40¼in. wide. (Christie's) $3,850

A Chippendale walnut slant-front desk with a fitted interior, Penn., dated 1779, 41½in. wide. (Christie's) $17,600

Mid 18th century George III mahogany slant-front desk, 36¼in. wide. (Christie's) $4,950

Federal cherry drop-front desk with fitted interior, New England, circa 1800, 39½in. wide. (Robt. W. Skinner Inc.) $1,600

Mid 18th century German rococo miniature walnut veneer slant-front bureau, 18¼in. wide. (Christie's) $1,760

A Chippendale maple slant-front desk, attributed to Nathaniel Dominy IV or V, Long Island, N.Y., 1760-80, 36¼in. wide. (Christie's) $9,900

A George I walnut bureau with leather lined flap enclosing a fitted interior, 36in. wide. (Christie's) $6,292

BUREAUX

A Chippendale walnut slant top desk on claw and ball feet, probably Penn., circa 1780. (Robt. W. Skinner Inc.) $10,000

An Edwardian inlaid mahogany cylinder bureau with decorated urn front, 30in. wide. (Coles, Knapp & Kennedy) $792

An 18th century Dutch marquetry inlaid bombe bureau veneered in mahogany, 4ft.1in. high. (Woolley & Wallis) $6,292

Chippendale tiger maple slant top desk with fall-front, New England, circa 1780, 42in. wide. (Robt. W. Skinner Inc.) $8,250

An early 18th century small walnut bureau. (Parsons, Welch & Cowell) $6,191

A George I walnut bureau with later leather lined flap enclosing a fitted interior, 35½in. wide. (Christie's) $3,102

A Queen Anne walnut bureau with fall-front and stepped fitted interior, 28¾in. wide. (Coles, Knapp & Kennedy) $10,570

Late 18th century George III mahogany slant-top desk with fitted interior, 39in. wide. (Christie's) $4,950

Chippendale tiger maple desk, Rhode Island, circa 1770, exterior with original worn red paint, 36in. wide. (Robt. W. Skinner Inc.) $36,000

BUREAUX

A Queen Anne maple slant front desk, New England, 1750-60, 40in. wide. (Christie's) $6,050

A cedar wood and walnut bureau, the sloping flap enclosing a fitted interior, the sides with carrying handles, 22½in. wide. (Christie's) $1,156

Mid 18th century Chinese Export padoukwood bureau with four serpentine drawers, the back inscribed TH52, 39¾in. wide. (Christie's) $17,061

An inlaid walnut slant front desk, by Thos. Cooper, Long Island, 1770, 40in. wide. (Christie's) $26,400

A Federal mahogany eagle-inlaid slant front desk, 1790-1810, 44¾in. wide. (Christie's) $6,600

Chippendale mahogany slant top desk on ogee bracket feet, Mass., circa 1780, 41in. wide. (Robt. W. Skinner Inc.) $6,000

A Chippendale mahogany reverse-serpentine slant front desk, labelled by Stone and Alexander, Boston, circa 1790, 42in. wide. (Christie's) $13,200

Late 18th century Italian satinwood and marquetry bureau, 50in. wide. (Christie's) $9,372

A walnut bureau inlaid with feather banding, the sloping flap enclosing a fitted interior, 30in. wide. (Christie's) $1,337

BUREAUX

A George I walnut bureau, the leather lined crossbanded sloping flap enclosing a fitted interior, 38in. wide. (Christie's) $15,950

Gustav Stickley drop-front desk with cabinet doors, circa 1902-04, 32¾in. wide. (Robt. W. Skinner Inc.) $3,700

A late George III mahogany cylinder bureau with tambour shutter enclosing a fitted interior, 42in. wide. (Christie's) $1,694

A William and Mary burr walnut bureau, the sloping flap enclosing a fitted interior, 38¼in. wide. (Christie's) $9,251

A George I walnut bureau, the quarter baize lined flap inlaid with chevron banding enclosing a fitted interior, 29¼in. wide. (Christie's) $13,959

A George III mahogany bureau, the leather lined crossbanded sloping flap enclosing a fitted interior, 37in. wide. (Christie's) $1,487

An early Georgian walnut and featherbanded bureau on bracket feet, 33in. wide. (Christie's) $6,048

Federal mahogany inlaid cylinder desk on flared French feet, Maryland, circa 1790, 44in. wide. (Robt. W. Skinner Inc.) $6,000

An early Georgian yewwood bureau with leather lined crossbanded sloping flap, 37½in. wide. (Christie's) $5,505

CABINETS

Late 17th century German walnut and marquetry cabinet, 55¼in. wide. (Christie's) $1,718

A Charles II black and gold lacquer cabinet-on-stand decorated with chinoiserie scenes, 40½in. wide. (Christie's) $20,163

A Spanish walnut cabinet on splayed feet, 29in. wide. (Christie's) $2,030

A William and Mary oyster-veneered walnut cabinet with fitted interior, formerly surrounding a cupboard, lacking stand, 40½in. wide. (Christie's) $1,487

A William and Mary walnut, floral marquetry and inlaid cabinet-on-stand, on later supports, 1.14m. wide. (Phillips) $7,920

A mid 17th century oak side cabinet with inset gray fossil marble top, 52½in. wide. (Christie's) $3,635

A decorated pine side cabinet designed and painted by H. Von Herkomer, 95cm. wide. (Phillips) $2,304

Mid 18th century French chestnut side cabinet, 49in. wide. (Christie's) $2,030

A mahogany Chippendale style cabinet in the Gothic manner, on octagonal reeded supports, 38in. wide. (Outhwaite & Litherland) $17,255

CABINETS

Late 17th century Portuguese rosewood sewing cabinet carved with ripple moldings, 21½in. wide. (Christie's) $3,124

A George III mahogany music cabinet with adjustable top, opening to reveal four sloping flaps, 26in. wide. (Christie's) $4,561

A George I black lacquer cabinet-on-stand, 53½in. wide. (Christie's) $7,444

A late 18th century Milanese rosewood cabinet, with quartered chevron veneered top and front, 47½in. wide. (Dreweatts) $1,160

An Arts & Crafts painted cabinet and bookshelves (top missing), the figures drawn by M. Reed, 61cm. wide. (Phillips) $460

A Regency brass inlaid rosewood side cabinet with mirror glazed panelled doors, 48½in. wide. (Christie's) $13,183

A bamboo and lacquer cabinet with central mirror to the back, the door panels decorated with Chinese warriors. (Lots Road Galleries) $483

A Regency rosewood dwarf cabinet with Bramah lock, 36in. wide. (Christie's) $1,318

One of a pair of Regency ormolu mounted rosewood side cabinets, the doors with pleated cafe-au-lait silk ground, 19in. wide. (Christie's) $3,877

One of a pair of Regency rosewood and parcel gilt dwarf cabinets attributed to Wm. Marsh, 50¼in. wide. (Christie's) $77,550

A 19th century gilt brass mounted black lacquered cabinet on stand, Japan, 32½in. wide. (Robt. W. Skinner Inc.) $2,200

A 17th century ormolu mounted ebonized and Japanese lacquer side cabinet with red marble top, 52in. wide. (Christie's) $23,265

A 19th century carved, painted and parcel gilt cabinet, China, 44¼in. wide. (Robt. W. Skinner Inc.) $2,100

Grain painted pine lawyer's cabinet, the panel doors opening to reveal thirty-eight compartments, New England, circa 1800, 33in. wide. (Robt. W. Skinner Inc.) $2,500

A late 17th/early 18th century Italian ebonized, tortoiseshell and gilt metal mounted cabinet on later stand, 2.05m. high x 1.72m. wide. (Phillips) $14,400

An early Georgian walnut cabinet in two sections inlaid with chevron banding, 119cm. wide. (Christie's) $44,044

Early 20th century Jacobean style cabinet on stand, America, 48in. wide. (Robt. W. Skinner Inc.) $900

A Charles II oak cabinet on square feet, 43in. wide. (Christie's) $1,573

CABINETS

One of a pair of Regency mahogany wall cabinets with glazed fronts, 12½in. wide. (Christie's) $2,044

A mid Victorian ebony and ivory inlaid display cabinet of concave semi-circular shape, designed by O. Jones, 110in. wide. (Christie's) $30,294

A late Victorian black and gilt japanned papier-mache purdonium, on later rosewood bracket feet, 18¾in. wide. (Christie's) $1,573

One of a pair of Regency mahogany dwarf cabinets, the top crossbanded and edged with satinwood, 33in. wide. (Christie's) $32,571

Late 19th century Russian oak cabinet, 33½in. wide, 99in. high. (Christie's) $1,598

One of a pair of rosewood dwarf cabinets with specimen marble tops, 29½in. wide. (Christie's) $7,865

An Italian walnut cabinet with a fall-front panel enclosing a fitted interior, the carvings late 17th century, 27¾in. wide. (Christie's) $1,874

A Renaissance Revival inlaid rosewood cabinet, America, circa 1870, 36½in. wide. (Robt. W. Skinner Inc.) $1,900

An ebonized and ivory inlaid side cabinet, the design attributed to T. E. Colcutt, 137cm. wide. (Phillips) $1,008

CABINETS

A late 17th/early 18th century Chinese coromandel lacquer cabinet on carved giltwood stand, 60cm. wide. (Phillips) $1,584

An early Victorian oak cabinet, by A. W. N. Pugin and John Webb, 52in. wide. (Christie's) $3,775

A Swiss walnut and marquetry cistern cabinet, basically late 17th century, 31in. wide. (Christie's) $3,436

An early Victorian oak cabinet fitted with a pair of gothic panelled doors enclosing seventeen drawers, 43¾in. wide. (Christie's) $943

An Art Deco Epstein & Goldbart cocktail cabinet, mahogany veneered in sycamore, fitted interior, 60½in. high. (Christie's) $770

One of a pair of Regency brass inlaid rosewood side cabinets with mottled black marble tops, 26½in. wide. (Christie's) $5,583

Late 19th century Kinji cabinet decorated in gold hiramakie, hirame and nashiji and inlaid in Shibayama style, 20.8cm. high. (Christie's) $5,935

A Portuguese rosewood cabinet-on-stand with five short and two long drawers, basically late 17th century, 25¼in. wide. (Christie's) $2,343

A 19th century large dark reddish-brown nashiji cabinet, 114 x 96 x 46.5cm. (Christie's) $17,182

CABINETS

A Queen Anne walnut and crossbanded miniature bureau on stand of a later date, 41cm. wide. (Phillips) $3,168

Regency satinwood and ebony collector's cabinet, the ebony handles with ivory centers, 38in. wide. (Christie's) $17,061

A mid 18th century carved mahogany breakfront china cabinet on later stand, in the Chippendale manner, 1m. wide. (Phillips) $3,900

An early Victorian ormolu mounted ebony and pietra dura side cabinet, 43in. wide. (Christie's) $6,699

An Italian walnut pedestal cabinet on bracket feet, 21in. wide. (Christie's) $1,405

An ormolu mounted mahogany cabinet, the base with a pair of shibayama lacquer panel doors, 48¼in. wide. (Christie's) $7,177

One of a pair of Regency ormolu mounted and parcel gilt dwarf rosewood cabinets, the doors backed with pleated green silk, 36in. wide. (Christie's) $21,714

A scarlet and black lacquer cabinet-on-stand, the cabinet 17th century and later, 41in. wide. (Christie's) $3,190

An Art Deco cocktail bar trolley, the bar handle flanked by two inset clear and satin glass panels by Lalique, 88cm. wide. (Christie's) $9,914

CABINETS

Late 18th century George III mahogany cabinet, 63in. wide. (Christie's) $7,150

Late 19th century pine tall cabinet, probably New York, 26½in. wide. (Christie's) $1,100

A Regency ormolu mounted rosewood breakfront dwarf cabinet, the doors backed with pleated silk, 60¼in. wide. (Christie's) $13,042

A Goanese ivory inlaid ebony cabinet-on-stand, the cabinet late 17th century, 19in. wide. (Christie's) $4,752

An Italian ebony and pietra dura cabinet-on-stand with three-quarter balustraded gallery, 47in. wide. (Christie's) $29,920

One of a pair of Empire ormolu mounted cabinets, 25¾in. wide. (Christie's) $11,440

Early 17th century Tuscan walnut cabinet with molded overhanging cornice, 64in. wide. (Christie's) $6,688

Victorian gilt bronze and porcelain mounted walnut side cabinet, circa 1860, 59½in. wide. (Robt. W. Skinner Inc.) $1,400

An Edwardian rosewood inlaid side cabinet, 54in. wide. (Peter Wilson) $1,185

CANTERBURYS

Early 19th century mahogany swept top music canterbury, 22in. wide. (Dreweatts) $899

Regency rosewood canterbury with rectangular top and pierced undulating splayed gallery, 27½in. wide. (Christie's) $2,481

A George IV rosewood music canterbury, 20½in. wide. (Christie's) $2,296

A George III satinwood canterbury, the hinged top with three-quarter gallery. (Christie's) $11,632

Late 18th century George III mahogany canterbury, 19½in. long, 21in. high. (Robt. W. Skinner Inc.) $850

A George IV mahogany and rosewood canterbury with gilt metal gallery, 51cm. wide, stamped Wilkinson. (Phillips) $6,420

A Regency rosewood canterbury on baluster legs, 20½in. wide. (Christie's) $4,247

A Victorian figured walnut canterbury stand, the top with three-quarter gallery, 22in. wide. (Christie's) $1,056

A carved rosewood canterbury, England, circa 1875, 20½in. wide. (Robt. W. Skinner Inc.) $950

FURNITURE

DINING CHAIRS

One of a set of five Regency stained beechwood dining chairs covered with green and pink glazed chintz, and another of later date. (Christie's) $1,483

Two of a set of seven George III design mahogany dining chairs. (Woolley & Wallis) $2,880

One of a set of six Victorian mahogany balloon-back dining chairs with stuff over seats. (Hobbs & Chambers) $1,296

A carved gilt and gesso side chair in the George I style, the vase splat depicting the child Zeus. (Phillips) $497

Two of a set of six Regency period mahogany dining chairs, the padded seats covered in differing classical design needlework. (Woolley & Wallis) $3,289

A Queen Anne carved walnut side chair, Penn., 1740-60, 40½in. high. (Christie's) $3,960

One of an assembled set of six Chippendale maple side chairs, New England, 1760-80, 40½in. high. (Christie's) $1,980

Two of a set of fourteen mahogany dining chairs of George III style, the seats covered in red leatherette. (Christie's) $9,123

One of a pair of late 18th/early 19th century Dutch walnut veneered and marquetry balloon-back dining chairs in the Queen Anne taste. (Phillips) $823

DINING CHAIRS

One of six Victorian rosewood balloon-back chairs with upholstered seats. (Reeds Rains) $1,267

Two of a set of ten George III style mahogany dining chairs. (Christie's) $4,089

One of a pair of mid 18th century George III carved mahogany side chairs, 37¾in. high. (Christie's) $1,760

One of a pair of Chippendale carved mahogany side chairs, Phila., 1765-85, 39in. high. (Christie's) $104,500

Two of a set of six Stickley Bros. dining chairs, including one armchair, circa 1908. (Robt. W. Skinner Inc.) $850

An early Victorian child's black, gilt and mother-of-pearl japanned correction chair. (Christie's) $173

One of a set of five late Federal mahogany side chairs, probably Phila., 1800-10, 31in. high. (Christie's) $2,860

Two of a set of ten mahogany dining chairs in Georgian style, with drop-in seats. (Woolley & Wallis) $3,565

A Charles Thompson, Chippendale, carved mahogany side chair, Phila., 1765-80, 38¼in. high, 23½in. wide. (Christie's) $341,000

DINING CHAIRS

One of a pair of George II mahogany dining chairs on cabriole legs and scrolled toes, 21¾in. wide. (Christie's) $8,530

One of a pair of Louis XVI elm chaises with oval backs and serpentine seats. (Christie's) $2,343

One of a set of five late 18th century George III mahogany shield back side chairs, 37in. high. (Robt. W. Skinner Inc.) $700

One of a set of three George III mahogany dining chairs with shield-shaped backs and trailing flowerhead crestings, stamped HM. (Christie's) $3,877

One of a set of six George III mahogany dining chairs with bowed drop-in seats covered with floral chintz. (Christie's) $8,065

One of a set of four George III satinwood dining chairs upholstered in aubergine watered silk. (Christie's) $3,722

One of two 19th century maple Shaker slat-back tilter chairs, Conn., 40¾in. high. (Robt. W. Skinner Inc.) $1,000

One of a set of twelve grained beech frame sabre leg side chairs with brass mounts and moldings. (Woolley & Wallis) $4,752

A Queen Anne maple side chair, Newport, Rhode Island, 1750-65, 37¾in. high. (Christie's) $2,640

DINING CHAIRS

One of a set of five
Dutch walnut dining chairs
with eared serpentine drop-
in seats. (Christie's)
$5,618

One of four Louis XV carved
and cream decorated side
chairs, having bowed seats on
molded cabriole legs.
(Phillips) $3,744

One of a pair of cherry Queen
Anne side chairs with upholstered seats, Conn. River
Valley, circa 1750, 39¾in.
high. (Robt. W. Skinner Inc.)
$2,900

One of a set of seven
George III mahogany dining
chairs, including a pair of
armchairs, with drop-in
seats. (Christie's)
$4,957

One of a set of three Regency
simulated rosewood dining
chairs mounted with gilt
metal, the split-cane seat on
sabre legs. (Christie's)
$382

One of a set of eight mahogany dining chairs with waved
ladder backs. (Christie's)
$3,412

One of a set of six black
painted Windsor side chairs,
each stamped 'J. R. Hunt,
Maker', circa 1820.
(Christie's) $3,520

One of a set of eight white painted
frame side chairs covered in late
18th/early 19th century tapestry.
(Woolley & Wallis) $5,285

One of a pair of Chippendale
mahogany side chairs, Mass.,
1760-90, 36½in. high.
(Christie's) $17,600

DINING CHAIRS

One of a set of six Regency mahogany dining chairs, the toprails incised with key-pattern and ebonized. (Christie's) $5,287

Federal mahogany inlaid shield-back side chair, Mass., circa 1800, 38¼in. high. (Robt. W. Skinner Inc.) $1,700

One of a pair of mid Georgian mahogany dining chairs with paper scroll toprails and pierced splats. (Christie's) $2,974

A George III mahogany dining chair with bow shaped toprail and vase shaped splat. (Christie's) $991

One of a set of four 18th century painted turned slat-back side chairs, New England, 40in. high. (Robt. W. Skinner Inc.) $3,250

A Chippendale carved walnut side chair, with shell-carved cabriole legs, Phila., 1760-80. (Christie's) $3,080

One of a set of eight Regency mahogany dining chairs, including an open armchair, with drop-in seats. (Christie's) $4,089

A French Art Nouveau oak dining chair, designed by C. Plumet and A. Selmersheim. (Phillips) $489

One of a set of ten Regency simulated rosewood dining chairs with caned seats. (Christie's) $2,636

DINING CHAIRS

A George III mahogany dining chair with bowed padded seat. (Christie's) $1,551

One of a pair of Queen Anne fruitwood side chairs with drop-in needlework seats. (Christie's) $2,233

One of a pair of scarlet lacquered chairs of Queen Anne design on cabriole legs and pad feet. (Christie's) $2,230

One of a set of eight Regency mahogany dining chairs, and a similar pair of armchairs. (Christie's) $3,146

One of a set of nine George III mahogany dining chairs with close-nailed red leather covered seats. (Christie's) $13,959

One of a set of six Regency rosewood (part simulated) dining chairs with brass inlaid toprails. (Phillips) $1,275

One of a set of twelve William IV carved mahogany dining chairs with stuff over seats. (Phillips) $8,064

One of a pair of Louis XV beechwood chaises with cartouche-shaped backs and serpentine seats. (Christie's) $1,405

An Empire mahogany chaise with padded seat covered in green velour. (Christie's) $437

DINING CHAIRS

One of a pair of mid Victorian black, gilt and mother-of-pearl japanned papier-mache occasional chairs. (Christie's) $1,258

Two of a set of eight William IV mahogany dining chairs, including a pair of armchairs. (Reeds Rains) $4,320

One of a set of four arrow-back side chairs, Mass., circa 1815, 35in. high. (Robt. W. Skinner Inc.) $1,900

A Chippendale mahogany side chair on cabriole legs, Mass., 1760-90, 38in. high. (Christie's) $2,200

Two of a set of seven George III carved mahogany shield back dining chairs and one later copy, England, circa 1780. (Robt. W. Skinner Inc.) $6,900

One of a set of six mid 18th century Portuguese carved hardwood dining chairs in the rococo taste. (Phillips) $4,260

One of a pair of William and Mary bannister-back maple side chairs, New England, 1710-40. (Christie's) $1,650

Two of a set of seven Regency mahogany dining chairs, including a pair of armchairs, and a single chair of later date. (Christie's) $4,963

A Chippendale mahogany side chair, Mass., 1760-90, 39¼in. high. (Christie's) $1,430

DINING CHAIRS

One of a set of four late
George III inlaid mahogany
side chairs, 34¾in. high.
(Christie's) $5,500

Two of a set of six Regency
period mahogany dining
chairs. (Woolley & Wallis)
$2,288

One of a set of four Victorian
mahogany dining chairs with
trafalgar seats. (Hobbs &
Chambers) $561

One of an assembled pair of
18th century 'York' maple
side chairs, New England,
41in. high. (Christie's)$770

Two of an assembled set of
nine English, 19th century,
elm and beech wheelback
Windsor chairs, approx. 34in.
high. (Christie's) $4,620

One of two Shaker cherry
ladder-back side chairs,
New Hampshire, circa 1840.
(Robt. W. Skinner Inc.)
$5,250

A Chippendale mahogany
side chair on cabriole legs,
probably New Jersey,
1760-90, 38¾in. high.
(Christie's) $4,400

Two of a set of five late 18th
century George III elmwood
dining chairs, 37in. high.
(Christie's) $3,850

One of a set of eleven Regency
carved mahogany dining chairs
with slip-in horsehair seats.
(Phillips) $6,816

EASY CHAIRS

A mid Victorian walnut open armchair, the cartouche-shaped padded back with gros and petit point needlework panel. (Christie's)
$1,276

A blue PVC inflatable armchair. (Christie's)
$578

A George III parcel gilt and white painted open armchair with oval back, upholstered in puce silk. (Christie's)
$1,551

A George III mahogany open armchair covered in red velvet. (Christie's)
$1,730

One of a pair of George III mahogany open armchairs, covered in buff linen, 23¾in. wide. (Christie's)
$5,428

A Queen Anne style easy chair, upholstered in a red, white and blue bargello patterned fabric. (Christie's)
$1,540

A George III mahogany library armchair with padded back, arm supports and bowed seat upholstered in maroon damask. (Christie's)
$2,636

An early George II mahogany library armchair upholstered in floral yellow damask, on cabriole legs and scrolled feet. (Christie's)
$8,932

A George I mahogany library armchair upholstered in white linen, on cabriole legs and pad feet. (Christie's)
$2,326

EASY CHAIRS

One of a pair of George III gray painted open armchairs covered in pale blue watered cotton, 24in. wide. (Christie's) $2,636

A Gothic Revival walnut chair, America, circa 1870, 39in. wide, and matching arm couch, 87in. long. (Robt. W. Skinner Inc.) $1,700

One of a pair of Louis XVI walnut fauteuils, covered in close-nailed floral needlework. (Christie's) $2,343

One of a pair of Chippendale style easy chairs, 50in. high. (Christie's) $2,640

An upholstered oak armchair with cut out sides, circa 1905, 28¾in. wide. (Robt. W. Skinner Inc.) $1,000

One of two George III mahogany library armchairs with padded rectangular backs, arm supports and seats. (Christie's) $4,032

A George III mahogany open armchair, lacking upholstery. (Christie's) $1,887

Late 18th century George III library chair on Marlborough legs, 40in. high. (Christie's) $2,860

One of a set of four George III gilded mahogany open armchairs in the Louis XVI style. (Christie's) $13,959

EASY CHAIRS

A George III parcel gilt and
white painted open armchair,
covered in a blue, white and
gray floral brocade.
(Christie's) $1,008

An early George III giltwood
bergere upholstered in aquamarine silk. (Christie's)
$1,163

One of a pair of mid 18th
century walnut open arm-
chairs, possibly German.
(Christie's) $6,284

One of a pair of mahogany
open armchairs covered in
olive-green linen. (Christie's)
$3,460

One of a pair of early Victorian
rosewood armchairs, each with
a spoon-shaped back and serpentine seat, on cabriole legs.
(Christie's) $4,712

One of a set of six George III
parcel gilt and cream painted
open armchairs covered in
pale green mercerized cotton.
(Christie's) $32,571

A Federal mahogany wing
chair with serpentine crest,
New York, 1790-1810, 47in.
high. (Christie's) $825

An inlaid rosewood curule-
type armchair, attributed to
Pottier and Stymus, circa
1870, 34in. high, 31in. wide.
(Robt. W. Skinner Inc.)
$1,100

One of a pair of George III
style wing chairs, together
with a matching footstool.
(Christie's) $3,080

EASY CHAIRS

A George III carved, and later gilded, elbow chair with stuffover serpentine seat. (Phillips) $426

One of a pair of mid 19th century ebonized Gothic Revival armchairs, America, 57in. high. (Robt. W. Skinner Inc.) $900

Late 18th century stained beechwood fauteuil upholstered in yellow striped cotton. (Christie's) $468

An early Georgian walnut wing armchair on cabriole legs and pad feet headed by shells. (Christie's) $3,722

A George III mahogany bergere with later brass feet and castors. (Christie's) $9,438

An early Georgian walnut wing armchair, the back and out-scrolled arms and bowed seat upholstered in floral moquette. (Christie's) $3,460

Mid 19th century Louis XV style tapestry upholstered miniature giltwood bergere, France, 19in. wide. (Robt. W. Skinner Inc.) $2,250

A George III mahogany dining armchair with high curved back, out-scrolled arms and squab.(Christie's) $1,887

One of a set of six mid 18th century Italian parcel gilt and green painted open armchairs. (Christie's) $14,839

EASY CHAIRS

One of a pair of late 18th/
early 19th century carved
hardwood fauteuils in the
Louis XV style. (Phillips)
$460

A George III parcel gilt open
armchair with oval padded
back and bowed seat in sky-
blue satin. (Christie's)
$1,473

A Regency mahogany side
chair after a design by Thos.
Hope, with buttoned scroll
back and seat in a molded
frame. (Christie's)
$5,423

One of a pair of George III
giltwood library armchairs,
upholstered in mustard-yellow
cut velvet. (Christie's)
$29,469

A Chippendale period
carved mahogany library
open armchair of Gains-
borough type in the French
taste. (Phillips)
$5,700

One of two Regency maho-
gany bergeres with caned backs,
sides and seats. (Christie's)
$10,857

A mid Georgian mahogany
wing armchair upholstered
in pale yellow floral damask.
(Christie's) $2,313

A Regency mahogany library
bergere upholstered in
buttoned pale green leather.
(Christie's) $2,202

An early Georgian walnut
wing armchair with high
back, upholstered in close-
nailed scarlet velvet.
(Christie's) $7,444

EASY CHAIRS

A walnut wing armchair with waved seat-rail on cabriole legs. (Christie's) $3,190

One of a pair of giltwood bergeres, covered in green floral glazed cotton, circa 1830, possibly Scandinavian. (Christie's) $2,811

A Georgian carved and ebonized elbow chair, in the manner of John Linnell. (Phillips) $489

One of two George III mahogany library armchairs with padded backs, arms and seats, one re-railed, one partly re-railed. (Christie's) $3,304

A William IV library armchair, the back, arms and seat upholstered in pale green leather. (Christie's) $697

A George III mahogany armchair of Gainsborough type, with a stuff over floral gros point needlework back and seat. (Phillips) $1,440

A George III mahogany frame library tub-shaped bergere on ring-turned tapered legs. (Phillips) $2,250

A Regency beechwood bergere, on ring turned tapering legs, lacking candle arms. (Christie's) $1,179

A Queen Anne walnut wing armchair covered in cream linen on cabriole legs. (Christie's) $4,963

EASY CHAIRS

One of a set of five George III stripped beechwood open armchairs. (Christie's) $7,550

One of a pair of Barcelona chairs, designed by Mies van der Rohe, with stainless steel, X-shaped frames. (Christie's) $1,108

One of a pair of early George III giltwood open armchairs with cartouche shaped padded backs, arm rests and seats. (Christie's) $38,775

One of a pair of giltwood bergeres of Louis XV style, seats covered in 18th century Beauvais tapestry. (Christie's) $5,582

Mid 18th century ebonized mahogany open armchair with high removable panel back. (Christie's) $5,423

One of a pair of Louis XVI style carved and polished beech frame fauteuils. (Lots Road Galleries) $570

An early George III mahogany open armchair after a design by T. Chippendale. (Christie's) $49,632

A Regency mahogany reading chair with deeply buttoned green leather upholstery and yoke shaped toprail. (Christie's) $826

A George III mahogany library armchair upholstered in needlework, partly re-railed. (Christie's) $6,380 £4,400

EASY CHAIRS

A Louis XVI stained beech-wood bergere, the back, seat and squab covered in plum velvet. (Christie's)
$1,874

A mid Victorian walnut folding armchair with button upholstered slung seat and back, on sabre legs. (Christie's) $957

Part of a Louis XVI style salon suite of settee, six elbow chairs and two side chairs. (Lots Road Galleries)
$3,600

A mid Victorian walnut tub armchair with padded back and seat, on cabriole legs. (Christie's) $1,196

One of a pair of George III giltwood open armchairs with oval padded backs and bowed seats. (Christie's) $991

A parcel gilt and beechwood fauteuil of neo-classical design, on spirally-turned tapering legs. (Christie's)
$2,073

A walnut wing armchair, the seat upholstered in yellow floral damask, on shell cabriole legs and claw and ball feet. (Christie's) $1,817

A hall porter's mahogany chair with arched buttoned olive green leather canopy seat and arms, 31in. wide. (Christie's) $3,257

One of a pair of early George III mahogany library chairs covered in close-nailed and buttoned yellow damask. (Christie's) $37,224

ELBOW CHAIRS

One of a pair of early George III mahogany open armchairs in the Gothic style, 23½in. wide. (Christie's)
$29,469

Early 19th century Empire painted and parcel gilt armchair, Europe, 35in. high. (Robt. W. Skinner Inc.)
$850

One of a set of nine mahogany Chippendale style open armchairs, 43in. high. (Christie's)
$5,500

A Chippendale walnut armchair, Phila., 1760-80, 38in. high. (Christie's)
$1,430

One of a set of six Regency parcel gilt, painted and simulated rosewood dining chairs, and four en suite of a later date. (Christie's) $8,179

An American Arts & Crafts stained oak rocking chair, in the manner of David Kendal for Phoenix Furniture. (Phillips) $129

A Regency mahogany bergere, the cane-filled back and arms with two pale green leather squab cushions. (Christie's)
$2,831

Gustav Stickley revolving office chair, no. 361, circa 1904, signed with decal in a box, 28in. wide. (Robt. W. Skinner Inc.)
$1,300

L. & J. G. Stickley slat-sided armchair, circa 1912, style no. 408, 26½in. diam. (Robt. W. Skinner Inc.)
$1,200

ELBOW CHAIRS

A satinwood bergere of George III design with caned back, sides and seat with a rust squab cushion. (Christie's) $702

A mid Victorian black, gilt and mother-of-pearl japanned papier-mache open armchair. (Christie's) $1,101

A George III painted satinwood open armchair upholstered in cream silk. (Christie's) $1,628

A George III mahogany elbow chair, the drop-in seat covered in needlework. (Woolley & Wallis) $403

One of a pair of early 19th century yew and elm Windsor armchairs. (Christie's) $2,340

A George III mahogany open armchair, and another similar. (Christie's) $865

One of a pair of Finimar laminated birchwood open armchairs designed by Alvar Alto. (Christie's) $2,044

Late 19th century Victorian steer horn armchair, upholstered in maroon velvet, America. (Robt. W. Skinner Inc.) $1,300

One of a pair of Federal style mahogany lolling chairs, 41¼in. high. (Christie's) $3,520

ELBOW CHAIRS

A Queen Anne walnut corner chair, Penn., 1735-60, 25in. wide. (Christie's) $3,300

A walnut rocking chair, by G. Hunzinger, N.Y., circa 1876, 32in. high. (Robt. W. Skinner Inc.) $250

One of a set of three Adam period carved giltwood elbow chairs with stuffover bowed seats. (Phillips) $6,816

One of a set of eight Regency carved mahogany dining chairs, including a pair of scroll arm elbow chairs. (Phillips) $5,112

One of a set of ten Renaissance Revival walnut dining chairs, circa 1870, 37in. high. (Robt. W. Skinner Inc.) $1,700

One of a set of four Regency ebonized and gilt decorated elbow chairs painted en grisaille. (Phillips) $9,230

A laminated mahogany armchair, circa 1900, 45in. high. (Robt. W. Skinner Inc.) $550

Fancy wicker armchair, by Heywood Bros. & Co., Mass., 39in. high. (Robt. W. Skinner Inc.) $1,300

A George I carved red walnut corner chair on cabriole legs with shell pendant ornament and pointed pad feet. (Phillips) $2,272

ELBOW CHAIRS

One of a set of three George III satinwood open armchairs with shield-shaped backs and triple bar splats. (Christie's) $15,510

A Bentwood rocking recliner, with adjustable back, Austria, circa 1890. (Robt. W. Skinner Inc.) $550

A George IV mahogany armchair with channelled scroll back, stamped W. Hodge, 36½in. high. (Christie's) $2,809

One of a pair of Sheraton ebonized and gilt decorated elbow chairs with cane seats. (Phillips) $3,692

An Adam period giltwood frame armchair with padded shield-shaped back. (Woolley & Wallis) $2,880

One of a set of six Regency mahogany dining chairs, including one armchair inscribed Young upholsterer, 1809 Wm. Teiocks frame maker. (Christie's) $7,975

One of a set of four early Victorian oak open armchairs by Bell & Coupland, Preston. (Christie's) $11,781

One of two Dutch Colonial hardwood burgomaster chairs with drop-in seats. (Christie's) $5,467

One of a set of twelve Regency mahogany dining chairs, including a pair of elbow chairs. (Phillips) $6,816

ELBOW CHAIRS

One of a pair of George III mahogany armchairs with bowed padded seats. (Christie's) $2,016

One of a pair of Spanish walnut open armchairs, partly 17th century. (Christie's) $3,436

One of a pair of avodire and painted open armchairs, each with a shield-shaped back. (Christie's) $4,404

One of a pair of George III mahogany open armchairs with close-nailed yellow brocade covered seats. (Christie's) $7,755

An Empire ormolu mounted mahogany fauteuil, the back and seat upholstered with distressed silk. (Christie's) $3,280

One of a pair of Sheraton style elbow chairs, the back panels embossed with putti. (Lots Road Galleries) $270

Gustav Stickley mahogany bow armchair, circa 1907, no. 336, 36in. high. (Robt. W. Skinner Inc.) $1,600

A James II walnut caned chair with cartouche shaped back and X-framed seat, stamped EW. (Christie's) $826

One of a pair of walnut open armchairs of late 17th century style, covered in ivory and plum velvet. (Christie's) $2,811

ELBOW CHAIRS

A George III mahogany open armchair with shield-shaped back and pierced splat. (Christie's) $2,831

Late 17th century Flemish elm and beechwood open armchair covered in floral needlework. (Christie's) $937

One of a set of eight Regency mahogany dining chairs, including a pair of elbow chairs. (Phillips) $4,050

One of a set of six George III carved mahogany dining chairs in the Sheraton taste, including one elbow chair. (Phillips) $2,850

An Arts & Crafts inlaid oak elbow chair, the central back splat inlaid with a flower motif in pewter and wood. (Phillips) $172

An early 19th century Russian birch open armchair with pig-skin covered seat. (Christie's) $2,343

Part of a suite of Scandinavian cream and green painted furniture in the revived neo-classical style, circa 1880. (Christie's) $3,905

A carved walnut armchair, by G. Hunzinger, N.Y., circa 1869, 32¾in. high. (Robt. W. Skinner Inc.) $400

A mid Victorian open armchair of Gothic style with drop-in seat. (Christie's) $1,473

ELBOW CHAIRS

An early 18th century German giltwood fauteuil, the back and seat upholstered in patterned cut-velvet. (Christie's) $1,874

One of a set of seven George III mahogany dining chairs in the Hepplewhite taste, including one elbow chair. (Phillips) $3,300

Late 18th century Italian green painted and parcel gilt armchair, upholstered in green and white striped silk. (Christie's) $781

A bowback Windsor armchair with saddle seat, New England, circa 1780, 37¼in. high. (Robt. W. Skinner Inc.) $2,600

One of a pair of oak Bentwood open armchairs, each bearing a label 'Patent Pending 25597/1932, Regd Design 781, 637. (Phillips) $489

A George III beechwood open armchair with oval padded back and bowed seat, formerly caned. (Christie's) $743

L. & J. G. Stickley tall back armchair, with spring cushion seat, no. 837, circa 1907, 44in. high. (Robt. W. Skinner Inc.) $500

One of a pair of Regency simulated bronze and parcel gilt bergeres after a design by George Smith, 24in. wide. (Christie's) $80,652

One of a set of six Wiener Werkstatte black stained limed oak dining chairs, designed by J. Hoffmann. (Christie's) $25,344

ELBOW CHAIRS

One of a pair of Dutch mahogany and marquetry open armchairs, together with a double chairback settee. (Christie's) $3,905

One of a set of twelve Chippendale style carved mahogany armchairs, 39½in. high. (Christie's) $15,400

A mahogany open armchair of George I design, with leather upholstered seat. (Christie's) $1,551

One of a pair of parcel gilt and green painted open armchairs. (Christie's) $1,171

An American Arts & Crafts oak reclining chair with reclining mechanism, in the manner of A. H. Davenport of Boston. (Phillips) $216

One of a pair of George III cream and brown painted open armchairs, the caned seat with squab cushion. (Christie's) $4,342

An early Georgian walnut open armchair, the back and seat covered in yellow damask. (Christie's) $2,831

A late 18th/early 19th century ash and elm chair with wide seat and turned legs. (Dreweatts) $986

One of a pair of George III mahogany library armchairs covered in close-nailed blue suede. (Christie's) $23,265

CHESTS-OF-DRAWERS

A Chippendale pine chest-of-drawers, New England, 1760-80, 40in. wide. (Christie's) $880

A Chippendale mahogany chest-of-drawers, New England, 1780-1800, 33½in. wide. (Christie's) $4,620

A Jacobean style oak and walnut chest fitted with four long drawers, 41in. wide. (Christie's) $1,415

A Federal cherrywood serpentine chest-of-drawers, New England, 1790-1810, 42in. wide. (Christie's) $4,620

A Chippendale walnut tall chest-of-drawers on ogee bracket feet, Penn., 1760-90, 43in. wide. (Christie's) $3,300

A George I burr walnut bachelor's chest with crossbanded double hinged top, 34in. wide. (Christie's) $29,469

A 19th century mahogany campaign chest, the drawers with brass inset handles, 3ft. wide. (Hobbs & Chambers) $1,008

A William and Mary painted pine blanket chest, Conn., 1720-40, 41in. wide. (Christie's) $9,350

A Federal inlaid mahogany bowfront chest-of-drawers, New Hampshire, 1790-1810, 40in. wide. (Christie's) $6,600

CHESTS-OF-DRAWERS

A Queen Anne walnut, cross-banded and featherstrung bachelor's chest, on bracket feet, 71cm. wide. (Phillips) $7,810

A William and Mary marquetry and oyster walnut chest, 39in. wide. (Christie's)$7,865

A Chippendale mahogany chest-of-drawers, New England, 1760-80, 42in. wide. (Christie's) $2,420

A Louis Philippe mahogany, marble top chest-of-drawers, circa 1840, 44½in. wide. (Robt. W. Skinner Inc.) $600

Chippendale walnut tall chest-of-drawers with old brass pulls, Penn., circa 1780, 38in. wide. (Robt. W. Skinner Inc.) $4,000

A late 17th century oak chest with four long graduated drawers on side runners, 3ft. 2in. wide. (Woolley & Wallis) $772

Federal mahogany and mahogany veneer bowfront chest-of-drawers, New England, circa 1800, 41in. wide.) (Robt. W. Skinner Inc.) $1,500

Mid 19th century Napoleon III carved mahogany chest-of-drawers, 51½in. wide. (Robt. W. Skinner Inc.) $450

An early George III mahogany chest on later ogee bracket feet, 31½in. wide. (Christie's) $2,030

CHESTS-OF-DRAWERS

Chippendale four-drawer maple chest, New England, circa 1780, 36in. wide. (Robt. W. Skinner Inc.) $900

Late 19th century wood tansu in two parts, 118.5cm. wide. (Christie's) $1,405

A George III mahogany chest of four long graduated drawers, 31in. wide. (Christie's) $2,202

A George III mahogany chest with four graduated long drawers on ogee bracket feet, 38in. wide. (Christie's) $1,982

Chippendale tiger maple chest, New England, circa 1780, 37in. wide. (Robt. W. Skinner Inc.) $6,500

A Federal inlaid mahogany bowfront chest-of-drawers, Massa., 1795-1810, 42in. wide. (Christie's) $1,650

Child's Empire stencil decorated chest-of-drawers, New England, circa 1820, 17¾in. wide. (Robt. W. Skinner Inc.) $950

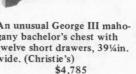

An unusual George III mahogany bachelor's chest with twelve short drawers, 39¼in. wide. (Christie's) $4,785

A George III mahogany campaign secretaire chest with crossbanded top above a fall-front writing drawer, 34in. wide. (Christie's) $2,831

CHESTS-OF-DRAWERS

A George III satinwood bow-fronted chest, the top cross-banded with rosewood, 42in. wide. (Christie's)
$15,510

Decorated blanket chest, Albany County, N.Y., circa 1840, 41¾in. wide. (Robt. W. Skinner Inc.)
$9,000

Shaker birch chest-of-drawers, probably New England, circa 1840, 38½in. wide. (Robt. W. Skinner Inc.) $1,100

An oak Norfolk style chest-of-drawers with brass handles and escutcheons, 30in. wide. (Worsfolds) $2,340

George III mahogany chest-of-drawers with replaced bail handles, England, circa 1770, 46¼in. wide. (Robt. W. Skinner Inc.) $500

A George III mahogany bow-fronted chest of four graduating drawers, 27¾in. wide. (Christie's) $3,146

George III mahogany chest-of-drawers with writing slide, England, circa 1770, 37¼in. wide. (Robt. W. Skinner Inc.) $2,800

An early Georgian burr walnut chest with four crossbanded graduated drawers, 26in. wide. (Christie's) $22,022

Federal mahogany inlaid bow-front chest-of-drawers, N.Y., circa 1790, 41¼in. wide. (Robt. W. Skinner Inc.) $2,200

CHESTS-OF-DRAWERS

A George II mahogany chest with four graduated long drawers, 30in. wide. (Christie's) $2,044

Chippendale cherry serpentine chest-of-drawers with old brasses, Conn., circa 1780, 34½in. wide. (Robt. W. Skinner Inc.) $6,000

A walnut and oyster-veneered chest decorated and inlaid with boxwood lines, part 18th century, 37in. wide. (Christie's) $3,542

A George III mahogany serpentine chest, with writing slide and four graduated long drawers, 37in. wide. (Christie's) $1,982

A William and Mary walnut and seaweed marquetry chest-on-stand, on later bun feet, 98cm. wide. (Phillips) $3,456

A George III mahogany serpentine chest with four graduated long drawers, 40in. wide. (Christie's) $6,514

Chippendale cherry chest-of-drawers with five thumb-molded drawers, 38¼in. wide, circa 1790. (Robt. W. Skinner Inc.) $1,400

A Chippendale blue painted maple chest-of-drawers, New England, circa 1780-1810, 41½in. wide. (Christie's) $5,500

Painted Country Chippendale chest-of-drawers, New England, 36½in. wide. (Robt. W. Skinner Inc.) $2,500

CHESTS-OF-DRAWERS

A George III mahogany serpentine fronted chest-of-
drawers with chased brass
handles, 36½in. wide.
(Dreweatts) $4,205

A Chippendale mahogany
serpentine chest, the top
containing a brushing slide,
1.03m. wide. (Phillips)
$2,850

A mahogany bachelor's chest
with crossbanded rounded
rectangular top, basically 18th
century, 30in. wide.
(Christie's) $20,735

George II mahogany bachelor's
chest, the top with a baize-
lined dressing slide, 31in. wide.
(Christie's) $1,914

A late Georgian mahogany
bowfront chest crossbanded
and inlaid with boxwood
lines, 36in. wide.
(Christie's) $725

A bachelor's walnut chest
with crossbanded hinged top,
31in. wide. (Christie's)
$2,946

Federal mahogany inlaid bowfront chest with original brass
pulls, circa 1790, 40in. wide.
(Robt. W. Skinner Inc.)
$2,300

Chippendale walnut inlaid
tall chest, Penn., 1805,
39in. wide. (Robt. W.
Skinner Inc.)
$5,000

Federal bird's-eye maple and
birch chest-of-drawers, probably New Hampshire, circa
1820, 37¾in. wide. (Robt. W.
Skinner Inc.) $1,600

CHESTS-ON-CHESTS

A George III mahogany tallboy on ogee bracket feet, 43¾in. wide. (Christie's) $3,877

An early George II mahogany tallboy, the base with three graduated long drawers on bracket feet, 41¼in. wide. (Christie's) $2,359

A mid Georgian mahogany tallboy on ogee bracket feet, 44in. wide, 73in. high. (Christie's) $1,982

A George I walnut tallboy with molded cornice, 45½in. wide. (Christie's) $7,975

An early Georgian walnut tallboy on later bracket feet, 41½in. wide. (Christie's) $7,975

A mid Georgian walnut secretaire-tallboy with later back, 41½in. wide. (Christie's) $4,131

A Chippendale maple chest-on-chest, in two parts, probably New Hampshire, 1760-90, 38½in. wide.(Christie's) $13,200

A Chippendale inlaid walnut tall chest-of-drawers, Penn., 1760-90, 44½in. wide. (Christie's) $3,520

A George III mahogany secretaire tallboy, 42½in. wide, 72½in. high. (Christie's) $2,988

CHESTS-ON-CHESTS

An early Georgian walnut and oak tallboy on bracket feet, 41½in. wide. (Christie's) $2,809

A Chippendale maple chest-on-chest, in two parts, New England, 1760-90, 37½in. wide. (Christie's) $26,400

A Queen Anne walnut tall-boy with chamfered cavetto cornice, 42in. wide. (Christie's) $32,571

Chippendale cherry flat top chest-on-chest, Conn., circa 1770, 38¼in. wide. (Robt. W. Skinner Inc.) $11,500

A Queen Anne cherrywood high chest-of-drawers, in two sections, New England, 1740-60, 71½in. high. (Christie's) $11,000

George III carved mahogany chest-on-chest, England, circa 1770, 42in. wide. (Robt. W. Skinner Inc.) $1,700

A George III mahogany tall-boy with key-pattern cornice, 44½in. wide. (Christie's) $2,831

Late 18th century George III inlaid mahogany chest-on-chest, England, 44½in. wide. (Robt. W. Skinner Inc.) $2,200

One of a pair of figured walnut tallboys inlaid with feather-banding, possibly German, 41¼in. wide. (Christie's) $13,959

CHESTS-ON-STANDS

A Queen Anne burr walnut chest-on-stand with feather banded top, 40¾in. wide. (Christie's) $3,460

A Queen Anne mahogany high chest-of-drawers in two sections, Boston, circa 1755, 38in. wide. (Christie's)$46,200

A Queen Anne walnut chest-on-stand inlaid with fruitwood compass medallions, 42in. wide. (Christie's) $2,478

A William and Mary style burr walnut veneered chest-on-stand inlaid with geometric chequered boxwood lines, 44in. wide. (Christie's) $2,156

A William and Mary walnut and marquetry chest-on-stand, 38½in. wide. (Christie's) $3,828

A William and Mary kingwood oyster veneered and rosewood banded chest-on-stand, the stand circa 1840, 49½in. wide. (Christie's) $4,785

A George I pale walnut chest-on-stand, on cabriole legs and pad feet, the stand partly re-veneered and with replaced back, 39¼in. wide. (Christie's) $2,313

A Queen Anne maple and walnut chest-on-frame, in two sections, N.Y. State, 1740-80, 38¼in. wide. (Christie's)
$8,250

A Queen Anne inlaid walnut high chest-of-drawers, in two sections, Mass., 1730-40, 39¼in. wide. (Christie's) $49,500

CHESTS-ON-STANDS

A Chippendale walnut high chest-of-drawers on stand, Penn., 1760-90, 43in. wide. (Christie's) $17,600

Queen Anne walnut and maple highboy on four cabriole legs, New England, circa 1770, 38in. wide. (Robt. W. Skinner Inc.) $13,000

A Queen Anne walnut chest-on-stand with two short and three graduated long drawers, 40in. wide. (Christie's) $9,570

A walnut chest-on-stand, the cupboard door enclosing a fitted interior, flanked by six drawers, 37½in. wide. (Christie's) $1,735

An Anglo-Dutch early 18th century walnut and inlaid chest-on-stand. (Parsons, Welch & Cowell) $785

A William and Mary walnut chest-on-stand with two short and three long graduated drawers, 38½in. wide. (Christie's) $1,887

A Queen Anne cherrywood high chest-of-drawers, Long Island, 1735-70, 40½in. wide. (Christie's) $11,000

A Queen Anne style walnut veneered highboy on hipped cabriole legs with Spanish type feet, England, 62¼in. high. (Robt. W. Skinner Inc.) $1,400

A George I walnut and elm chest-on-stand, 38½in. wide. (Christie's) $2,988

CHIFFONIERS

One of a pair of late Victorian ebonized chiffoniers banded with amboyna, 35¾in. wide. (Christie's) $3,190

A rococo Revival rosewood veneered etagere, America, circa 1860, 51in. wide. (Robt. W. Skinner Inc.) $1,300

A Regency period mahogany chiffonier, the drawers with brass knob handles, 3ft.3in. wide. (Woolley & Wallis) $2,867

A Regency mahogany chiffonier, the two-tiered superstructure with baluster supports and gallery, 24in. wide. (Christie's) $2,552

A mid 19th century rosewood secretaire chiffonier of reverse breakfront form, 7ft.2in. wide. (Parsons, Welch & Cowell) $2,233

A Regency rosewood secretaire chiffonier with shelf and mirror superstructure, 27in. wide. (Graves Son & Pilcher) $987

A George IV rosewood chiffonier, the shelved back inset with a mirror plate, 44in. wide. (Christie's) $1,309

A Renaissance Revival walnut carved sideboard, the panelled back with two oval mirrors, possibly New York, circa 1860, 89½in. high. (Robt. W. Skinner Inc.) $3,300

Early 19th century rosewood chiffonier with two frieze drawers above two panelled doors. (Lots Road Galleries) $703

COMMODES & POT CUPBOARDS

George III mahogany tray-top night cupboard, 1ft.8in. wide. (Hobbs & Chambers) $800

One of a pair of late 18th century North Italian, Milanese, walnut and ivory bedside commodes, 24¼in. wide. (Christie's) $17,600

A George III mahogany bedside commode with rectangular tray top, 21in. wide. (Christie's) $1,108

A Biedermeier mahogany pedestal cupboard with D-shaped top and frieze drawer above a cupboard door and base drawer, 23½in. wide. (Christie's) $1,056

A pair of walnut bedside tables with rectangular tops and waved three-quarter galleries, 16¼in. wide. (Christie's) $3,896

A Biedermeier mahogany pedestal cabinet, the swivelling door enclosing three shelves, 25½in. wide. (Christie's) $1,056

A Renaissance Revival walnut demi-commode, 20in. wide. (Robt. W. Skinner Inc.) $750

A set of Regency mahogany bedside steps with three leather lined treads, a door and a drawer, 28½in. wide. (Christie's) $1,839

Table de nuit, Continental brass inlaid with a drawer, cupboard and marble top, 1ft.8in. wide. (Lots Road Galleries) $672

COMMODE CHESTS

A George III mahogany serpentine commode, 50½in. wide. (Christie's) $8,530

An 18th century Dutch coromandel and satinwood veneered serpentine commode of slight bombe outline, 1.20m. wide. (Phillips) $2,272

An 18th century Maltese walnut veneered serpentine commode, 5ft.5in. wide. (Woolley & Wallis) $1,860

A late 18th century walnut crossbanded and parquetry demi-lune commode in the Louis XVI taste, 1.04m. wide, possibly Italian. (Phillips) $5,814

A D-shaped figured oak commode with two pannelled doors on gadrooned bun feet, 41½in. wide. (Christie's) $1,500

A George III mahogany veneered demi-lune commode, crossbanded, 3ft.7in. wide. (Woolley & Wallis) $1,208

A Dutch mahogany and marquetry commode of bombe form with shaped serpentine top, 35in. wide. (Christie's) $5,632

A 20th century inlaid fruitwood demi-lune commode, with semi-circular variegated onyx top, 48in. wide. (Robt. W. Skinner Inc.) $1,200

A Dutch ormolu mounted mahogany and marquetry commode on cabriole legs. (Christie's) $4,928

COMMODE CHESTS

An ormolu mounted king-
wood commode of Louis XV
style with serpentine breccia
marble top, 48in. wide.
(Christie's) $2,871

An ormolu mounted king-
wood and marquetry
commode of Louis XVI
design, with breakfront
Carrara marble top, stamped
five times Wassmus, 50in.
wide. (Christie's)
$5,104

A Dutch mahogany and
marquetry commode on
later feet, 49in. wide.
(Christie's) $6,560

A Kingwood breakfront
commode with later eared
white marble top, basically
late 18th century, 37½in.
wide. (Christie's)
$3,124

A George III mahogany small
commode, the serpentine top
geometrically veneered and
crossbanded, 29½in. wide.
(Christie's) $8,870

A 19th century French parquetry inlaid commode
cabinet, 2ft.2½in. wide.
(Geering & Colyer)
$403

Mid 18th century Portuguese
rosewood commode of
serpentine outlines with boxwood stringing, 51in. wide.
(Christie's) $4,686

Late Empire figured maho-
gany marble top commode,
circa 1830, 47¾in. wide.
(Robt. W. Skinner Inc.)
$1,100

Late 17th century Italian
rosewood commode profusely
inlaid with ivory, mother-of-
pearl and pewter, 60in. wide.
(Christie's) $7,029

CORNER CUPBOARDS

A Federal walnut corner cupboard, probably Kentucky, 1800-20, 50in. wide. (Christie's) $2,860

George III mahogany bow-front corner cabinet, 44in. high. (Lots Road Galleries) $604

A 19th century Continental painted corner cupboard, 81in. high, 41in. wide. (Christie's) $3,850

George III mahogany standing corner cupboard, 36in. wide. (Reeds Rains) $694

A George III mahogany encoignure in the Louis XV style, of bombe shape with serpentine top, 30½in. wide. (Christie's) $9,861

A satinwood and mahogany inlaid bowfront display cabinet, 31in. wide. (Christie's) $968

George III inlaid mahogany bow-fronted corner cupboard, 2ft.7in. wide. (Hobbs & Chambers) $832

An Edwardian Sheraton design bowfront standing corner cupboard, 29in. wide. (Lalonde Fine Art) $2,604

An early Georgian walnut hanging cupboard, the panelled door enclosing shaped shelves. (Christie's) $2,217

CORNER CUPBOARDS

Federal pine corner cupboard, possibly Penn., circa 1820, 56in. wide. (Robt. W. Skinner Inc.) $2,100

A Chippendale pine hanging corner cupboard, Penn., 1760-85, 46in. high, 26½in. wide. (Christie's) $1,430

Grain painted pine and poplar corner cupboard, possibly Pennsylvania, circa 1830, 83in. high, 55½in. wide. (Robt. W. Skinner Inc.) $3,500

A George III style mahogany standing corner display cabinet inlaid with urns, 33½in. wide. (Christie's) $1,280

An early Georgian oak hanging cupboard, 22in. wide. (Christie's) $702

One of a pair of 19th century N. Italian marquetry and walnut bowfront corner cabinets, 2.45m. high, 82cm. wide. (Phillips) $9,180

A mahogany inlaid corner cupboard with glazed astragal door. (Dee & Atkinson) $392

A mid Georgian oak corner cupboard, 40in. wide, 86½in. high. (Christie's) $3,511

George III oak corner cupboard on stand with original brass fittings. (Hobbs & Chambers) $328

CUPBOARDS

An early George III mahogany bedside cupboard, 22in. wide. (Christie's) $1,861

A 17th century oak cupboard, 38in. wide. (Christie's) $4,804

A small oak court cupboard, basically early 17th century, 27½in. wide. (Christie's) $11,088

A Georgian mahogany linen press with dentilled molded cornice, 4ft. wide. (Parsons, Welch & Cowell) $1,760

A 16th/17th century Spanish walnut cupboard with two pairs of panelled doors, 37½in. wide. (Christie's) $4,250

Country Federal walnut stepback cupboard, circa 1820, 46in. wide, 85½in. high. (Robt. W. Skinner Inc.) $1,900

A 19th century American pine step-back cupboard, 54in. wide. (Christie's) $2,090

An oak and fruitwood food cupboard inlaid with geometric lozenge patterns, late 16th/early 17th century, 35¾in. wide. (Christie's) $7,022

Federal cherry and mahogany veneer mantel cupboard, Penn., circa 1820, 13½in. wide. (Robt. W. Skinner Inc.) $750

CUPBOARDS

A Spanish elm cupboard with two doors pierced with gothic lancets, 25in. wide. (Christie's) $8,870

A George III mahogany bedside cupboard on square molded legs, 21in. wide. (Christie's) $1,258

A walnut court cupboard, in the manner of A. W. Pugin, 147cm. wide. (Christie's) $1,267

An 18th century carved pine tall cupboard on replaced ball feet, 44in. wide. (Robt. W. Skinner Inc.) $1,000

An oak cupboard, partly 16th century with restorations, 35in. wide. (Christie's) $6,468

One of a pair of Austrian oak and leaded glass cupboards, 197.9cm. high, 103.6cm. wide. (Christie's) $1,226

Two-part poplar cupboard, the drawers with brass bail handles, New Jersey, circa 1810, 45in. wide. (Robt. W. Skinner Inc.) $2,700

Painted pine chimney cupboard, Mass., circa 1810, 25in. wide, 78in. high. (Robt. W. Skinner Inc.) $5,700

Early 19th century oak, mahogany cupboard on bracket feet, 50in. wide. (Peter Wilson) $423

DAVENPORTS

A George IV rosewood veneered davenport, the sliding top with a pierced brass gallery, 19.5in. wide. (Woolley & Wallis) $1,389

A mid Victorian mahogany davenport of gothic style, 30in. wide. (Christie's) $3,825

A Victorian walnut davenport, with fret gallery above a writing slide and two small drawers, four side drawers, 22in. wide. (Dreweatts) $2,218

Victorian rosewood davenport, sloping top, fitted interior and four drawers. (Hobbs & Chambers) $1,113

Victorian ebonized davenport with maple banding and incised decoration. (Lots Road Galleries) $474

Mid 19th century Victorian burl walnut davenport desk, 23in. wide. (Robt. W. Skinner Inc.) $800

A Victorian burr walnut veneered piano top davenport with fitted interior, 22in. wide. (Woolley & Wallis) $2,004

A 19th century Irish inlaid yew davenport with fitted interior, 25½in. wide. (Reeds Rains) $3,168

A Regency rosewood davenport with three-quarter gilt metal gallery and leather lined flap, 20½in. wide. (Christie's) $3,542

DAVENPORTS

A rosewood and marquetry inlaid davenport, in the manner of T. Turner of Manchester. (Geering & Colyer) $1,144

Victorian carved and brass inlaid mahogany davenport desk, America, 19th century, 29¼in. wide. (Robt. W. Skinner Inc.) $1,100

A 19th century Burmese carved teak davenport, 26in. wide. (Dacre, Son & Hartley) $775

A Regency mahogany davenport with sliding leather lined sloping flap, enclosing a fitted interior, 20in. wide. (Christie's) $6,353

Early Victorian burr walnut davenport with sliding top, after a design by W. Smee & Sons, London, circa 1850, 1ft.10in. wide. (Capes, Dunn & Co.) $3,024

A Victorian walnut davenport, with pierced brass gallery and rising surface, 2ft.10in. wide. (Geering & Colyer) $1,185

An early Victorian rosewood davenport with pierced three-quarter gallery, with Bramah locks, 21¼in. wide. (Christie's) $3,326

A mid Victorian burr walnut davenport with serpentine piano lid, 39in. wide. (Locke & England) $1,800

A George IV pollard oak davenport with three-quarter pierced brass gallery and leather lined flap, 19½in. wide. (Christie's) $2,674

DISPLAY CABINETS

An Art Nouveau inlaid mahogany vitrine, 114.7cm. wide. (Christie's) $1,074

A mid Victorian ormolu mounted figured walnut side cabinet, 72in. wide. (Christie's) $5,049

An Art Nouveau mahogany display cabinet in Scottish style, with bevelled mirror top above a single leaded glass door, 54in. wide. (Christie's) $1,001

A Louis XIV fruitwood and walnut cabinet with later molded cornice, possibly German, 29in. wide. (Christie's) $4,928

An Edwardian mahogany display cabinet in two parts with swan-neck pediment, blind fret carving and urn finials. (Lots Road Galleries) $1,887

One of a pair of ormolu mounted tulipwood display cabinets, 21¾in. wide, 57½in. high. (Christie's) $7,337

A mid Victorian oak and marquetry cabinet, 55in. wide, 85in. high. (Christie's) $3,828

A Louis Majorelle Art Nouveau walnut and rosewood vitrine, 188cm. high. (Phillips) $3,744

Late 18th century Dutch walnut and marquetry display cabinet, 60in. wide. (Christie's) $17,182

DISPLAY CABINETS

A 19th century Chinese hardwood display cabinet, 32in. wide. (Woolley & Wallis) $883

An Edwardian satinwood and marquetry china cabinet in the Sheraton taste, 1.10m. wide. (Phillips)
$5,760

An English Art Nouveau mahogany display cabinet with bevelled mirror back, 71in. high x 53in. wide. (Christie's) $1,479

A Christopher Pratt & Sons inlaid mahogany display cabinet, 192.6cm. high. (Christie's) $1,262

A scarlet boulle and ebonized breakfront vitrine cabinet, 64in. wide. (Christie's)
$3,509

Late 18th century Louis XVI carved and painted demi-lune vitrine, France, 27½in. wide. (Robt. W. Skinner Inc.)
$1,400

An ormolu mounted king-wood vitrine cabinet with serpentine breccia marble top, 35in. wide. (Christie's)
$2,871

One of a pair of mid Victorian ormolu mounted satinwood side cabinets, 36in. wide. (Christie's) $4,342

A mahogany serpentine front standing corner cabinet with astragal glazed upper section, on ogee bracket feet, 194cm. high. (Osmond Tricks)
$928

DRESSERS

An early Georgian oak high dresser, the molded cornice with three shelves on shaped trestle supports, 61in. wide. (Christie's) $11,088

Late 18th/early 19th century oak shelf rack, 41in.wide. (Peter Wilson) $758

Late 18th century oak three-drawer dresser with rack, 74in. long. (Peter Wilson) $2,054

Mid 18th century George II oak Welsh dresser, 58½in. long. (Robt. W. Skinner Inc.) $2,700

A carved oak Victorian dresser with three drawers in base, 6ft.2in. wide. (Jacobs & Hunt) $800

Late 18th century oak, mahogany banded dresser with rack, 72in. wide. (Peter Wilson) $1,480

A Charles II oak low dresser, 88½in. wide. (Christie's) $14,784

An oak Welsh dresser on square tapering legs, 6ft. wide. (Woolley & Wallis) $2,736

An oak low dresser, the frieze with three fielded drawers, 71½in. wide. (Christie's) $2,956

DUMB WAITERS

A late Georgian mahogany two-tier dumb waiter, 41½in. high. (Christie's) $924

A Regency ormolu mounted mahogany dumb waiter, 27in. diam., 42¾in. high. (Christie's) $8,530

A George III satinwood and mahogany two-tier dumb-waiter with circular cross-banded tray top, 22½in. wide. (Christie's) $3,987

A Regency mahogany two-tier dumbwaiter, 36½in. high. (Christie's) $1,108

A George III mahogany two-tier dumb waiter on tripod support, 2ft.1½in. diam., circa 1760. (Christie's) $1,150

George III mahogany dumb-waiter with three graduated dished shelves, circa 1770, 42½in. high. (Robt. W. Skinner Inc.) $1,100

A mid Georgian mahogany three-tier dumbwaiter with graduated shelves, 43in. high. (Christie's) $1,948

A Regency ormolu mounted mahogany dumb waiter, 26¼in. diam., 45¼in. high. (Christie's) $6,979

A William IV mahogany three-tier dumb waiter, 150cm. high. (Phillips) $2,240

KNEEHOLE DESKS

A mahogany partner's desk with red leather lined top, 71½in. wide. (Christie's) $2,016

Mid 18th century George III crescent-shaped mahogany desk, 81½in. wide. (Christie's) $13,200

A George II mahogany partner's desk with leather lined top and nine drawers, 57½in. wide. (Christie's) $19,387

A mahogany pedestal desk with gilt-tooled green leather lined top, 33in. wide. (Christie's) $1,240

A George II mahogany kneehole desk with arched apron and six short drawers about a recessed enclosed cupboard, 83cm. wide. (Phillips) $2,850

A George III mahogany kneehole dressing chest with cross-banded hinged top, 41½in. wide. (Christie's) $2,831

A George III mahogany partner's pedestal desk, the top with inset baize top, 4ft. 5in. wide. (Woolley & Wallis) $13,680

A William and Mary figured walnut kneehole desk inlaid with feather banding, 33¾in. wide. (Christie's) $6,606

A late Victorian oak library desk, the molded leather lined top above a kneehole, 113in. wide. (Christie's) $2,831

KNEEHOLE DESKS

Early 19th century mahogany partner's desk with leather lined top and six frieze drawers, 60in. wide. (Christie's) $2,831

Early Victorian oak partner's desk, the lock stamped Clarke & Simmons, Birmingham, 71½in. wide. (Christie's) $20,163

A mid Victorian mahogany partner's desk with green leather lined top, 65in. wide. (Christie's) $4,962

A figured walnut kneehole desk crossbanded and inlaid with feather-banding, basically 18th century, 32½in. wide. (Christie's) $4,466

A George III mahogany cylinder desk with three-quarter pierced ormolu gallery, 47½in. wide. (Christie's) $13,557

A George III mahogany military dressing table, the hinged top enclosing a fitted interior, 36in. wide. (Christie's) $2,326

A Heal's sycamore kneehole desk, the rectangular top with semi-circular end, 133.4cm. wide. (Christie's) $633

A mahogany kneehole desk with chequer pattern inlay, 41½in. wide. (Christie's) $1,240

A George I burr walnut kneehole desk with hinged top enclosing a fitted interior with dressing mirror and lidded compartments, 36in. wide. (Christie's) $32,571

LOWBOYS

An early George III mahogany lowboy on cabriole legs and pad feet, 32in. wide. (Christie's) $5,583

An early 18th century gilt and gesso japanned side table on cabriole legs, 82cm. wide. (Phillips) $12,780

An 18th century Scottish red walnut lowboy with carved and scrolled kneehole, 33½in. wide. (Christie's) $2,808

An early Georgian walnut side table with arched and waved frieze, 29in. wide. (Christie's) $6,609

Early 18th century walnut lowboy, 29½in. wide. (Christie's) $2,400

A burr walnut lowboy, featherbanded in ash with quarter veneered molded top, 33½in. wide, basically late 17th century. (Christie's) $2,265

An early Georgian oak side table, the frieze with three drawers on lappeted club legs and pad feet, 34in. wide. (Christie's) $1,706

An early Georgian oak lowboy on cabriole legs and trifid feet, 31¼in. wide. (Christie's) $1,504

A 19th century Dutch walnut and foliate marquetry lowboy, 27in. wide. (Christie's) $1,510

SCREENS

A giltwood three-leaf screen with arched panels applied with silk and painted with paeonies and foliage, each leaf 59 x 22½in. (Christie's) $4,576

Late 19th century fundame two-leaf table screen inlaid in Shibayama style, signed Nobuyuki, each leaf 25 x 14cm. (Christie's) $3,148

An ebonized and marquetry four-leaf screen inlaid in satinwood, beechwood, walnut and stained fruitwood, 190cm. high, 141cm. wide. (Christie's) $2,356

An Empire mahogany cheval firescreen, the screen filled with distressed silk, 24in. wide. (Christie's) $492

An Arts & Crafts mahogany four-fold embroidered screen, 152cm. high. (Christie's) $1,262

A Louis XVI gray painted firescreen with rectangular silk panel, 17¼in. wide. (Christie's) $1,672

An Aesthetic Movement ebonized and painted three-leaf screen, 134.2cm. wide, 143.9cm. high. (Christie's) $1,262

One of two similar mid Georgian mahogany pole-screens, 56in. high. (Christie's) $924

Late 19th century two-leaf table screen, each leaf 33 x 15.5cm. (Christie's) $3,847

SCREENS

A Dutch painted leather six-leaf screen, late 18th century, each leaf 95½ x 21½in. (Christie's) $2,044

An early Victorian rose-wood firescreen with glazed panel, 40in. wide, 63in. high. (Christie's) $826

A painted leather four-leaf screen, each leaf 66 x 19½in. (Christie's) $1,914

A mahogany pole screen with acorn finial, the adjustable panel with a spray of flowers, 23in. wide. (Christie's) $620

An 18th century Chinese coromandel lacquer twelve-leaf screen, each leaf 19in. wide, 93½in. high. (Christie's) $58,938

An Arts & Crafts oak fire-screen, the framework enclosing a panel of Morris & Co. fabric woven with 'The Tulip and Rose', 55.5cm. high. (Phillips) $273

A Regency mahogany four-leaf screen, the divided panels with Chinese wallpaper, slightly distressed, each leaf 78 x 21½in. (Christie's) $12,393

A painted Japanese two-part folding screen, gouache and silver leaf, circa 1860, 55 x 49½in. (Robt. W. Skinner Inc.) $3,400

A Dutch painted leather four-leaf screen decorated with parrots and exotic birds, each leaf 84¼ x 20in. (Christie's) $1,258

SCREENS

An 18th century Dutch polychrome painted leather six-leaf screen, each leaf 22in. wide, 84in. high. (Christie's) $29,887

A Chippendale mahogany polescreen, Mass., 1765-85, 58in. high. (Christie's) $4,950

A Regency black and gold lacquer six-leaf screen, each leaf 108 x 23¾in. (Christie's) $9,616

A mid Victorian black, gilt and mother-of-pearl japanned firescreen, 52in. high. (Christie's) $2,674

A Chinese six-leaf coromandel screen, the panels early 19th century, each leaf 78 x 21½in. (Christie's) $4,147

A silk-embroidered firescreen, attributed to Morris & Co., 97.5cm. high. (Christie's) $316

A 19th century spinach-green jade and hardwood four-leaf screen, each leaf 211 x 43cm. (Christie's) $13,370

Early 19th century Dutch painted four-leaf screen, one panel distressed, each panel 72 x 21in. (Christie's) $2,643

An Indian hardwood three-leaf screen, each leaf 76 x 32in. (Christie's) $774

An early Georgian walnut
secretaire, the convex
frieze drawer and fall-flap
inlaid with chevron lines,
43½in. wide. (Christie's)
$3,304

A mid 19th century ormolu
mounted mahogany secre-
taire with griotte marble
top, 50in. wide. (Christie's)
$4,783

A walnut and yewwood secretaire cabinet, 41½in. wide.
(Christie's) $3,146

A Renaissance Revival walnut
butler's secretary, circa 1860,
40¾in. wide. (Robt. W.
Skinner Inc.) $1,900

Gustav Stickley oak and
wrought iron secretary, designed by Harvey Ellis, circa
1904, 56in. wide. (Robt. W.
Skinner Inc.)
$13,000

An ormolu mounted, par-
quetry and marquetry
secretaire a abattant of
Louis XVI style, on toupie
feet, 30in. wide. (Christie's)
$2,392

Late Empire figured maho-
gany secretary on scroll feet,
circa 1835, 46¼in. wide.
(Robt. W. Skinner Inc.)
$950

A Louis XVI tulipwood and
chequer inlaid secretaire a
abattant with later gilt metal
ornament, 97cm. wide.
(Phillips) $1,950

A Georgian mahogany
secretaire press. (Parsons,
Welch & Cowell)
$1,283

SECRETAIRE BOOKCASES

A Federal mahogany secretary, in three sections, 1800-15, 41½in. wide. (Christie's) $7,150

A Regency mahogany secretaire cabinet, the base with baize-lined secretaire with burr elm fitted interior, 48½in. wide. (Christie's) $5,783

George III mahogany secretaire bookcase, circa 1800, 42½in. wide. (Robt. W. Skinner Inc.) $2,600

A George III carved mahogany secretaire bookcase, 2.45m. high, 1.34m. wide. (Phillips) $7,344

A George III mahogany secretaire cabinet on bracket feet, 48in. wide. (Christie's) $10,164

A Regency yewwood and laburnum crossbanded secretaire bookcase, 1.74m. high, 95cm. wide. (Phillips) $5,184

A George III mahogany secretaire cabinet, 49½in. wide. (Christie's) $14,784

A Regency mahogany secretaire bookcase, the base with fall-front fitted writing drawer, 47½in. wide. (Christie's) $6,688

George III mahogany secretaire bookcase, circa 1810, 44in. wide. (Robt. W. Skinner Inc.) $1,100

SECRETAIRE BOOKCASES

Mid 18th century George III mahogany butler's secretary desk in two sections, 46in. wide. (Christie's) $6,600

A mahogany secretaire bookcase, inlaid with boxwood lines and having satinwood banded borders, 19th century, 43½in. wide. (Christie's) $3,770

A George III mahogany secretaire cabinet with a pair of glazed cupboard doors, 46½in. wide. (Christie's) $3,257

A George III satinwood Weeks secretaire cabinet, the fall-flap enclosing a fitted interior, 38½in. wide. (Christie's) $24,816

A Federal inlaid mahogany breakfront secretary bookcase, Salem, Mass., 1795-1800, 67in. wide. (Christie's) $275,000

A Chippendale carved maple desk and bookcase, Rhode Island, 1750-80, 82in. high, 38in. wide. (Christie's) $26,400

A Federal secretary bookcase, in three sections, N.Y., 1800-10, 37in. wide. (Christie's) $28,600

Late 18th century George III mahogany secretary bookcase, 77½in. wide. (Christie's) $26,400

A George III secretaire bookcase, the top section enclosed by two glazed Gothic astragal doors, 43in. wide. (Christie's) $4,350

SECRETAIRE BOOKCASES

A Regency mahogany secretaire cabinet with a pair of gothic pattern glazed doors, 43in. wide. (Christie's) $2,871

A Federal mahogany inlaid desk/bookcase, probably Mass., circa 1800, 37½in. wide. (Robt. W. Skinner Inc.) $3,300

A George III satinwood secretaire bookcase with circular enamelled ring handles, 30¾in. wide. (Christie's) $65,142

A George III satinwood secretaire bookcase banded with mahogany and inlaid with boxwood lines, trade label of George Simson, 33¾in. wide. (Christie's) $26,367

A George III mahogany secretaire cabinet with a pair of gothic glazed doors enclosing later shelves, 44in. wide. (Christie's) $4,785

A George III mahogany and burr yew secretaire cabinet, 41½in. wide. (Christie's) $13,959

A George III mahogany secretaire bookcase with a pair of gothic glazed doors, 46in. wide. (Christie's) $2,946

A Georgian carved mahogany secretaire breakfront library bookcase in the Chippendale taste, 2.20m. wide. (Phillips) $11,520

A George III mahogany secretaire bookcase with original brass swan neck handles, 3ft.8in. wide. (Woolley & Wallis) $4,576

SETTEES & COUCHES

A Chippendale style stained maple sofa on molded Marlborough legs, 76in. long. (Christie's) $2,860

Late 18th century carved fruitwood settee, 82in. long. (Robt. W. Skinner Inc.) $800

A Victorian walnut chaise longue with buttoned graduated back panel, 83in. long. (Christie's) $2,015

A Victorian chaise longue with carved mahogany show wood frame and cabriole legs and gold damask cover. (Lots Road Galleries) $870

A Regency ebonized and gilt decorated sofa of chaise longue design with upholstered panel back and scroll ends, having cushion seat and bolster. (Phillips) $5,396

A Federal upholstered mahogany sofa on turned reeded legs with birch inlay, Mass., 1790-1810, 79in. wide. (Christie's) $12,100

Late 18th century George III mahogany small sofa on square tapering legs, on brass cuffs, 50in. wide. (Christie's) $3,520

A Louis XVI white painted banquette with rectangular back, bowed seat and squab covered in blue floral chintz, 53in. wide. (Christie's) $1,483

SETTEES & COUCHES

Classical Revival teak sofa with carved lyre legs terminating in turned feet with brass cap castors, China, circa 1840, 86in. long. (Robt. W. Skinner Inc.) $2,000

Late 18th century Louis XVI painted canape, repainted white and gilt, probably Sweden, 86in. long. (Robt. W. Skinner Inc.) $500

A Chippendale mahogany serpentine-back sofa on Marlborough legs with blocked feet joined by stretchers, Phila., 1765-85, 109½in. wide. (Christie's) $605,000

A Federal carved mahogany sofa, attributed to the shop of Duncan Phyfe, N.Y., 1800-20, 80in. wide. (Christie's) $49,500

A Chippendale style stained maple sofa on molded Marlborough legs, upholstered in ivory striped damask, 76in. long. (Christie's) $3,300

Pine bench, probably circa 1900. (Lots Road Galleries) $371

An ebonized sofa with rectangular back, sides and seat covered in a floral brocade with wild animals, 60in. wide. (Christie's) $1,494

A George III mahogany frame settee with a stuff over back and seat. (Phillips) $1,584

SETTEES & COUCHES

A Victorian carved walnut and upholstered double chair-back settee, 5ft.9in. wide. (Parsons, Welch & Cowell) $2,112

William IV rosewood chaise with scroll carved arm and back rail, lotus carved foot, 86in. long. (Reeds Rains) $835

A mahogany daybed upholstered in blue moire, 65in. long, the castors and leg stamped Howard & Sons Ltd., London. (Christie's) $1,278

A George I walnut and beechwood settee covered in petit and gros point floral needle-work, 64in. wide. (Christie's) $58,938

A William and Mary walnut sofa with high double-arched winged back, outscrolled arms and two squab cushions covered in floral needlework. (Christie's) $4,620

A rococo Revival walnut settee on scroll feet, America, circa 1860, 72in. long. (Robt. W. Skinner Inc.) $750

An Indian white marble bench on baluster legs and square feet, 49in. wide. (Christie's) $5,049

A Dutch walnut and marquetry triple chair-back settee with waved arched toprail and three solid splats, 62in. wide. (Christie's) $3,520

SETTEES & COUCHES

A George IV brass inlaid mahogany and rosewood chaise longue with scrolling padded back, sides and foot rest, 82in. wide. (Christie's) $1,817

A carved mahogany tete-a-tete with scrolled and carved back over S-shaped arms above round upholstered seat, America, circa 1900, 41½in. long. (Robt. W. Skinner Inc.)
                    $550

A giltwood daybed in the Theban style, 79½in. wide. (Christie's) $18,876

A Biedermeier satin-birch sofa with padded rectangular box back, 72in. wide. (Christie's)
                    $2,288

A George III carved mahogany scroll end sofa in the French taste, on cabriole legs with scroll feet, 2.15m. wide. (Phillips) $4,032

A George II elm double chair-back settee with rectangular back and pierced strapwork splats, the padded drop-in seat covered with brown repp, 45in. wide. (Christie's) $1,651

A Windsor bench on bamboo turned legs joined by swelled H-stretchers, 75in. long. (Christie's) $825

A mid Victorian center sofa covered in buttoned green velvet with deep fringe on tapering ebonized baluster legs, 40in. wide. (Christie's) $3,304

SIDEBOARDS

A Regency mahogany sideboard, inlaid with bands of brass ovals on an ebonized ground, 88½in. wide. (Christie's) $19,828

Mid 18th century inlaid mahogany sideboard table on molded Marlborough legs, 70in. wide. (Christie's) $7,700

A Renaissance Revival walnut and burl veneer marble top sideboard, bearing label 'E. D. Trymby's, Philadelphia', circa 1860, 56in. wide. (Robt. W. Skinner Inc.) $1,200

Mid 19th century rosewood marble top sideboard, Lewis McKee & Co., Conn., 60in. wide. (Robt. W. Skinner Inc.) $650

A Regency mahogany sideboard with breakfront D-shaped crossbanded top, 63½in. wide. (Christie's) $1,887

Mid 18th century George III inlaid mahogany demi-lune sideboard, 54in. wide. (Christie's) $4,180

Late Georgian figured mahogany breakfront sideboard with lion mask ring handles, 5ft.7in. wide. (Capes, Dunn & Co.) $1,051

A George III mahogany, tulipwood crossbanded and inlaid sideboard with arched apron and fan spandrels, 1.53m. wide. (Phillips) $6,300

SIDEBOARDS

A Regency mahogany pedestal sideboard with crossbanded molded top with rounded inset center, 97in. wide. (Christie's) $10,740

A George III mahogany sideboard with double bowed top, the tablet-centred frieze flanked by two later baize-lined drawers and two deep drawers, 82in. wide. (Christie's) $7,601

Part of a French Art Deco walnut veneered diningroom suite, comprising a dining table, six chairs and two sideboards, 184cm. and 143cm. long respectively. (Phillips) $748

A mahogany bow-fronted sideboard inlaid with boxwood lines, a brass backrail and arched kneehole, 50in. wide. (Christie's) $1,520

A late George III mahogany bowfront sideboard on ring turned tapering legs and feet, 72½in. long. (Christie's) $1,887

A Sheraton period mahogany veneered bow-fronted sideboard with satinwood line inlay and stringing, 4ft.9in. wide. (Woolley & Wallis) $5,863

A George III mahogany sideboard crossbanded with rosewood, 71¾in. wide. (Christie's) $7,865

William IV mahogany pedestal sideboard with shaped gallery, three drawers and two side cupboards and cellarette, 7ft. wide. (Hobbs & Chambers) $338

STANDS

A Federal birch candlestand, original red stain finish, New England, circa 1790, 26¾in. high. (Robt. W. Skinner Inc.) $1,900

L. & J. G. Stickley open magazine rack, circa 1910, 42in. high, 21in. wide. (Robt. W. Skinner Inc.) $1,100

A mid 19th century French bronze tripod with inset circular green marble top, 34½in. high. (Christie's) $4,785

A Gufram hat-stand, designed by Guido Drocco and Franco Mello, modelled as a cactus plant, 1971, 174.5cm. high. (Christie's) $4,296

A George IV mahogany library bookstand with a panelled fall-flap, 45½in. wide. (Christie's) $1,156

Chippendale cherry candle-stand, probably Rhode Island, circa 1770, 25½in. high. (Robt. W. Skinner Inc.) $750

An early Victorian coat stand, by John Webb, on bracket base with metal liner, 64in. wide. (Christie's) $2,044

A pair of Venetian painted and gilded Blackamoor torcheres, 85in. high. (Christie's) $11,715

One of a pair of ormolu mounted cloisonne etageres, each with two rectangular tiers, 20¼in. wide. (Christie's) $5,948

STANDS

One of a pair of walnut torcheres with lobed tray-tops and hexagonal shaped shafts, 10in. wide, 30½in. high. (Christie's) $1,156

Painted Tramp art stand with drawers, possibly New York, 1820-40, 17½in. wide. (Robt. W. Skinner Inc.) $300

Chippendale cherry candle-stand, the shaped top with ovolo corners, circa 1780, 26in. high. (Robt. W. Skinner Inc.) $2,500

A Chippendale style mahogany urn table, 25in. high. (Christie's) $646

An early 18th century Italian carved giltwood stand with a simulated green marble top, 1.10m. high. (Phillips) $1,200

A George II grained pine pedestal, 53¼in. high. (Christie's) $10,081

Gustav Stickley inlaid tiger maple open music stand, circa 1904, no. 670, signed with Eastwood label, 39in. high. (Robt. W. Skinner Inc.) $7,250

A pair of late 18th century Italian parcel gilt and green painted torcheres, 69½in. high. (Christie's) $7,810

A Victorian mahogany folio stand with brass ratcheted adjustable open slatted slopes, 76cm. high. (Phillips) $2,550

STANDS

A Federal mahogany tilt-top candlestand, American, 1790-1810, 26½in. high. (Christie's) $990

A Federal inlaid mahogany corner stand, New York, 1790-1810, 23in. wide. (Christie's) $8,580

A Federal inlaid cherrywood candlestand, Connecticut River Valley, 1790-1810, 26¾in. high. (Christie's) $13,200

A George III style mahogany urn stand, 27in. high, 12in. wide. (Christie's) $1,045

An elephant's foot waste-paper basket with rosewood rim and ivory plaque, 11in. high. (Christie's) $697

A Thonet stained beechwood plant stand, the design attributed to Josef Hoffmann, 119cm. high. (Christie's) $865

Country Chippendale cherry octagonal top candlestand, probably Conn., circa 1760, 24.7/8in. high, 17¼in. diam. (Robt. W. Skinner Inc.) $1,500

A Federal inlaid mahogany corner stand, the top with a pierced brass gallery, probably New York, 1800-15, 34½in. high. (Christie's) $2,860

A William IV walnut pedestal teapoy, the interior fitted with two cannisters and two glass mixing bowls, stamped Gillow, 28½in. high. (Christie's) $1,057

STANDS

A Federal maple candlestand, with circular dished top, New England, 1790-1810, 28½in. high, 17¼in. diam. (Christie's) $5,500

One of a pair of mid Victorian oak and ebonized umbrella stands in the Gothic taste, 66in. wide. (Christie's) $1,009

A carved mahogany galleried kettle stand, the top with open baluster gallery, 30cm. diam., 75cm. high. (Phillips) $2,272

An ormolu mounted king-wood and marquetry pedestal, with mottled purple marble top, stamped Bertram & Son, 46in. high. (Christie's) $1,355

A pair of parcel gilt and painted Blackamoors of a negro and negress, 76¼in. high. (Christie's) $7,029

A George III mahogany reading stand, the adjustable top with hinged ratcheted slope, 70cm. high. (Phillips) $4,320

An early Victorian walnut pedestal teapoy, the hinged panel lid enclosing a fitted interior, 19½in.diam. (Christie's) $431

Limbert octagonal plant stand, style no. 251, circa 1910, 24¼in. high. (Robt. W. Skinner Inc.) $1,000

A mid Victorian black and mother-of-pearl japanned papier-mache music stand, 17¾in. diam. (Christie's) $613

STANDS

A Regency mahogany reading stand with adjustable top, 30½in. wide. (Christie's) $1,381

Limbert round tall pedestal, circa 1906, no. 267, 32½in. high, 14in. diam. (Robt. W. Skinner Inc.) $900

A mid Victorian walnut music stand, the slope on an adjustable brass shaft, 23in. wide. (Christie's) $1,003

An early Victorian walnut folio stand with pierced adjustable twin-flap top, 28in. wide. (Christie's) $5,313

A painted and parcel gilt Blackamoor torchere, carved as a negress, 62½in. high. (Christie's) $2,343

Late 19th century Eastlake folio stand. (Lots Road Galleries) $1,152

A Regency rosewood double-sided music stand, the sides with candle sconces, 48in. high. (Christie's) $3,344

An open-sided music stand, possibly by Stickley Bros., circa 1907, 39in. high. (Robt. W. Skinner Inc.) $400

A maple black painted and decorated candlestand, New England, circa 1775-1800, 26in. high. (Christie's) $660

STOOLS

A Federal carved mahogany window seat, attributed to the shop of Duncan Phyfe, N.Y., 1810-20, 40in. wide. (Christie's) $26,400

Late Regency rosewood framed window seat with swept rail ends, 42in. wide. (Lots Road Galleries) $648

An early Victorian stool on cabriole legs, 26in. wide. (Woolley & Wallis) $437

A mahogany stool with padded octangular drop-in seat, on cabriole legs, 21in. wide. (Christie's) $1,478

A George II mahogany foot-stool, the upholstered seat on cabriole legs, 22in. wide. (Christie's) $1,320

A Napoleon III giltwood stool, designed by A. M. E. Fournier, 29½in. diam. (Christie's) $3,960

An Edwardian mahogany framed stool with floral tapestry covered pad seat, 23in. wide. (Anderson & Garland) $464

A giltwood stool with square seat covered in patterned velvet, 24½in. sq. (Christie's) $1,178

A George I red walnut stool with a slip-in seat and shaped apron, on cabriole legs. (Phillips) $4,828

A cream painted and parcel gilt stool, the oval seat upholstered in a pale blue and white cotton, 33½in. wide. (Christie's) $3,124

One of a pair of mid 19th century giltwood tabourets, covered in pink silk with gold stencilled dots, 21in. diam. (Christie's) $3,030

A Louis Philippe giltwood stool in the manner of A. M. E. Fournier, with square crimson velvet seat, 21¼in. wide. (Christie's) $4,785

A George III beechwood stool with concave-fronted rectangular seat covered in close-nailed crimson velvet, 20½in. wide. (Christie's) $1,573

An oak stool on solid notched ends, circa 1600, 20¼in. wide. (Christie's) $1,179

A Biedermeier mahogany tabouret with padded seat, stamped G. Jacob with a fleur-de-lys, 24in. wide. (Christie's) $2,030

A George II walnut and parcel gilt stool on cabriole legs, 24½in. wide. (Christie's) $14,734

One of a pair of oak stools, each with a squab, Italian or Spanish, 23½in. wide. (Christie's) $937

A walnut stool, the drop-in seat with gros and petit point needlework, 22in. wide. (Christie's) $826

STOOLS

A George III mahogany window seat, the seat and arms upholstered in pale pink floral damask, 30in. wide. (Christie's) $930

Gustav Stickley spindle-sided footstool, circa 1907, no. 395, 15in. high. (Robt. W. Skinner Inc.) $150

A George III mahogany window seat with serpentine seat covered in gold damask, 37in. wide. (Christie's) $13,183

One of a pair of mahogany stools, the seats with petit point needlework sprays on a camel- colored ground, the . cabriole legs carved with clasps and claw-and-ball feet. (Christie's) $5,582

Late 17th century oak coffin stool, initialled WC, 18½in. wide. (Christie's) $2,044

A Spanish brass and wrought-iron faldistorio, partly 17th century. (Christie's) $3,436

A Regency parcel gilt and simulated rosewood X-framed stool, the seat with a squab cushion covered in striped silk, 35in. wide. (Christie's) $3,146

A Louis Philippe giltwood stool, in the manner of A. M. E. Fournier, with deep buttoned red velvet seat, 20in. diam. (Christie's) $2,552

A Liberty & Co. walnut 'Thebes' stool, the square seat strung with brown hide. (Christie's) $1,267

SUITES

Part of a seven-piece Renaissance Revival walnut and burl veneer parlor set, consisting of sofa, 73in. long, two armchairs and four side chairs, America, circa 1860. (Robt. W. Skinner Inc.) $2,300

A mid 19th century suite of giltwood seat furniture, comprising: a settee and four open arm elbow chairs on fluted and turned legs. (Parsons, Welch & Cowell) $12,525

A 19th century suite of Louis XV-style giltwood seat furniture, comprising a canape and four fauteuils, upholstered in 19th century Aubusson tapestry. (Robt. W. Skinner Inc.)
$2,600

FURNITURE

Part of a mid 19th century Spanish giltwood suite of furniture comprising: a settee with cartouche-shaped back and serpentine seat covered in close-nailed brown leather, painted with flowers on a trellis ground and four side chairs, the settee 85in. wide. (Christie's) $4,375

Part of a four-piece Harden & Co. livingroom set, comprising: settee, rocker and two armchairs, settee 54in. wide, circa 1910. (Robt. W. Skinner Inc.) $1,800

Part of a suite of giltwood seat furniture of Louis XV design comprising: four fauteuils and a canape, each upholstered in floral Aubusson tapestry. (Christie's) $9,130

CARD & TEA TABLES

A Federal mahogany card table, the top with canted corners, N.Y., 1800-20, 35in. wide. (Christie's) $2,200

A Chippendale carved mahogany card table, Phila., 1765-85, 36in. wide. (Christie's) $8,800

A Federal inlaid mahogany card table with hinged, shaped top, Mass., 1790-1810, 37in. wide. (Christie's) $6,600

An early Georgian mahogany tea table with D-shaped folding top, 30in. wide. (Christie's) $2,326

A Federal inlaid mahogany card table with D-shaped top, E. Mass., 1790-1810, 35½in. wide. (Christie's) $2,860

A William and Mary black and gold japanned card table decorated with chinoiserie, 30in. wide. (Christie's) $6,979

A mahogany and burr walnut tea table with folding semi-circular top, 34in. wide. (Christie's) $781

George III style mahogany galleried tea table on three carved ogee legs, England, 27½in. wide. (Robt. W. Skinner Inc.) $1,000

A Federal mahogany inlaid card table with hinged top, Mass., 1810-25, 36in. wide. (Christie's) $1,650

CARD & TEA TABLES

A Federal inlaid cherrywood card table with hinged D-shaped top, 1800-10, 35¾in. wide. (Christie's) $9,350

Queen Anne painted tiger maple tea table, probably Rhode Island, circa 1760, 34in. long. (Robt. W. Skinner Inc.) $40,000

Early 19th century gilt metal mounted mahogany card table with D-shaped folding top, 42¾in. wide. (Christie's) $1,874

A Regency brass inlaid rosewood card table, 35½in. wide. (Christie's) $3,412

One of a pair of mid Victorian walnut and marquetry card tables, 34in. wide. (Christie's) $8,751

An 18th century mahogany card table, top with needlework inset, Boston. (Robt. W. Skinner Inc.) $8,250

A mahogany card table, the baize-lined eared top with candle sconces and guineawells, 35in. wide. (Christie's) $3,828

Late 18th century Louis XVI brass bound mahogany demilune card table, 42½in. diam., open. (Robt. W. Skinner Inc.) $500

A Federal inlaid mahogany circular card table, with hinged D-shaped top, Massa., 1790-1810, 36in. wide. (Christie's) $7,700

One of a pair of William IV rosewood card tables, each with fold-over top, 36in. wide. (Christie's) $1,661

A Chippendale tilt-top mahogany tea table, Mass., 1760-80, 32in. diam. (Christie's) $4,400

A classical carved mahogany card table, N.Y., 1815-25, 36¼in. wide. (Christie's) $1,760

A Queen Anne mahogany porringer-top tea table, Rhode Island, 1740-70, 33in. wide. (Christie's) $19,800

A George III mahogany card table, the baize-lined eared top with one frieze drawer, 34in. wide. (Christie's) $3,509

A George III carved mahogany card table, the baize-lined hinged top with egg and dart edge, the hinges engraved G. Tibats, 91cm. long. (Phillips) $1,950

One of a pair of Regency rosewood card tables, banded with maple, 36in. wide. (Christie's) $3,190

A Chippendale walnut circular tilt-top tea table, Phila., 1760-85, 33¾in. diam. (Christie's) $8,800

A late Federal carved mahogany card table, New York, 1815-25, 36in. wide. (Christie's) $990

CARD & TEA TABLES

A George III mahogany tea table with eared folding top and frieze drawer, 34in. wide. (Christie's) $2,674

Mid 18th century George III walnut 'Isle of Man' tilt-top tea table, 31¾in. diam. (Christie's) $4,620

A Regency mahogany card table inlaid with ebonized lines, the canted, folding top enclosing a well, 35¾in. wide. (Christie's) $1,861

An early George III mahogany card table on cabriole legs, 35½in. wide. (Christie's) $17,061

A George II walnut and mahogany tea table with later semi-circular folding top enclosing a well, 30½in. wide. (Christie's) $1,735

Classical Revival carved mahogany card table, circa 1810, 25¾in. wide. (Robt. W. Skinner Inc.) $550

A Federal inlaid mahogany card table, with hinged top, Massa., 1790-1810, 34¾in. wide. (Christie's) $6,050

A Chippendale mahogany tilt-top tea table, probably Newport, Rhode Island, 1760-80, 30¾in. diam. (Christie's) $1,100

A Chippendale mahogany tilt-top tea table, Mass., 1770-85, top 30.1/3 x 30in. (Christie's) $28,600

CENTER TABLES

A mid Victorian gilt metal mounted amboyna and marquetry center table, 42¼in. wide. (Christie's) $3,366

A William IV walnut center table with octagonal specimen marble top bordered with black limestone, stamped Eastmure, 45in. wide. (Christie's) $43,428

A German walnut center table on shackled slave legs, 51in. wide. (Christie's) $4,712

A George III sycamore center table with waved crossbanded top centered by an amboyna oval, edged with chequered stringing, on cabriole legs, 23¾in. wide. (Christie's) $3,030

An early Victorian walnut center table in the manner of Baldock, 35½in. diam. (Christie's) $4,375

A Renaissance Revival walnut center table, with variegated red and white marble insert, circa 1860, 36in. wide. (Robt. W. Skinner Inc.) $550

A mid Victorian mahogany and marquetry center table, 58in. wide. (Christie's) $4,375

An early Victorian ebonized and parcel gilt center table with Italian scagliola top, 36¼in. diam. (Christie's) $9,306

A gilt and green japanned center table on cabriole legs, possibly German, 41in. wide. (Christie's) $2,811

CENTER TABLES

A Dutch oyster-veneered walnut and marquetry center table, the top 17th century, 45½in. wide. (Christie's) $4,061

Renaissance Revival inlaid walnut center table, circa 1870, 42¼in. wide. (Robt. W. Skinner Inc.) $1,600

An ormolu center table in the style of Weisweiler, with inset marble top, 38in. wide. (Christie's) $7,656

A Napoleon III ormolu and purple quartz center table, twice stamped Monbro, 32in. wide. (Christie's) $15,152

An ormolu mounted tulipwood and ebony center table with inset breccia marble top, 28.5in. wide. (Christie's) $4,785

A Scandinavian cream painted and parcel gilt center table with tray top inset with twelve Dutch Delft tiles, 24in. wide. (Christie's) $781

A Victorian pollard oak and painted center table, the top on a naturalistic bullrush pedestal, 28¾in. diam. (Christie's) $15,730

A George II mahogany center table with rounded rectangular tray top, 30¼in. wide. (Christie's) $1,101

A Regency rosewood, satinwood, mahogany and amboyna center table, 26in. diam. (Christie's) $1,817

CONSOLE TABLES

A Regency serpentine gilt console table with green marble top, 44in. wide. (Morphets) $2,160

A Regency simulated rosewood and parcel gilt console in the manner of Thos. Hope, 89cm. wide. (Phillips) $9,230

One of a pair of giltwood console tables in the manner of Thos. Johnson, 49¾in. wide. (Christie's) $20,163

A giltwood console table with verde antico marble top, circa 1830, 28¾in. wide. (Christie's) $2,516

Pair of early 19th century Danish parcel gilt and cream painted pier glasses and console tables, 28¼in. wide, 109½in. high. (Christie's) $7,040

Late 18th century George III mahogany inlaid console table, 42in. wide. (Christie's) $2,640

A Classical Revival brass inlaid mahogany console table, 36in. wide. (Robt. W. Skinner Inc.) $1,300

A 19th century giltwood and gesso serpentine fronted console table. (Parsons, Welch & Cowell) $800

A George II pine console table with molded white and gray marble top, 48½in. wide. (Christie's) $50,204

CONSOLE TABLES

One of a pair of mahogany console tables with D-shaped tops, 58in. wide. (Christie's) $2,974

An 18th century giltwood console table, 52¼in. wide. (Christie's) $5,428

A George III pine console table with later D-shaped mahogany top, 59in. wide. (Christie's) $2,148

A George III satinwood and marquetry half-round pier table surmounted by a gray-viened white marble top, 92cm. wide. (Phillips) $2,250

A Venetian parcel gilt and ebonized console table with eared serpentine white marble top supported by a blackamoor, 31in. wide. (Christie's) $4,785

Classical Revival mahogany and mahogany veneer pier table with white marble top, possibly New York, circa 1825, 36½in. wide. (Robt. W. Skinner Inc.) $1,300

Late 18th century Italian parcel gilt and black painted console table with inset jasper top, 29½in. wide. (Christie's) $4,061

An 18th century Italian carved giltwood console table with a serpentine sienna marble top, 1.46m. long. (Phillips) $1,650

An Empire mahogany and gilt metal mounted console table, 44in. wide. (Christie's) $2,019

DINING TABLES

A George III oval snap-top breakfast table, 4ft.10in. long. (Woolley & Wallis) $1,317

A William IV rosewood veneered circular snap-top breakfast table, 4ft. diam. (Woolley & Wallis) $1,267

A Regency satinwood and mahogany breakfast table inlaid with ebonized lines, 57¼in. wide. (Christie's) $5,505

A mahogany drum table with circular red leather lined top, 42in. diam. (Christie's) $3,932

Gustav Stickley hexagonal top library table, circa 1904, no. 625, 48in. diam. (Robt. W. Skinner Inc.) $5,700

A rosewood and brass inlaid breakfast table in the Regency taste, 1.24m. diam. (Phillips) $4,500

A Regency mahogany breakfast table with circular tip-up top, 50½in. diam.(Christie's) $3,412

A George III satinwood and inlaid breakfast table, cross-banded in tulipwood, with oval snap top, 1.23m. (Phillips) $12,070

A George III mahogany breakfast table, the cross-banded top with satinwood banding, 54¾in. wide. (Christie's) $3,139

DINING TABLES

A Regency mahogany break-
fast table with tip-up top,
53in. long. (Christie's)
$1,249

A Regency circular maho-
gany and brass inlaid
breakfast or dining table.
(Parsons, Welch & Cowell)
$1,585

A Regency mahogany break-
fast table on ring-turned
baluster shaft, branded W. &
C. Wilkinson, 59½in. diam.
(Christie's) $12,760

Round oak pedestal base
dining table, signed with
metal tag, circa 1908, 54in.
diam. (Robt. W. Skinner
Inc.) $1,400

A George III mahogany
library table with circular
gilt tooled leather-lined top,
46in. diam. (Christie's)
$4,625

A 19th century mahogany
ebony strung and brass
mounted drum top library
table, 1.01m. diam.
(Phillips) $3,456

A mahogany drum top library
table, the top with tooled
leather inset, the drawers
stamped A. Blain, Liverpool,
47in. diam. (Parsons, Welch &
Cowell) $2,464

An early Victorian mahogany
veneered circular snap-top
breakfast table, 4ft.7in. diam.
(Woolley & Wallis)
$1,180

An early Victorian mahogany
drum table, the circular top
lined in tooled brown leather,
53in. diam. (Christie's)
$1,224

DINING TABLES

A Regency rosewood brass inlaid center table with circular tip-up top, 48½in. diam. (Christie's) $8,065

Mid Victorian oak dining table carved in Elizabethan style, extending with six leaves to 17ft.8in. (Lots Road Galleries) $1,920

A mid Victorian burr walnut breakfast table with quarter veneered inlaid marquetry tilt-top, 60in. diam. (Christie's) $3,586

A George III mahogany library table with leather lined circular top, 39in. diam. (Christie's) $5,977

A Georgian mahogany circular snap-top dining table, 5ft.2in. diam. (Prudential Fine Art) $8,640

A Victorian coromandel ebonized and parcel gilt loo table, 48in. diam. (Christie's) $1,208

A Regency mahogany breakfast table with oval tip-up top, 60in. wide. (Christie's) $3,460

A Renaissance Revival walnut and burl veneer dining table, the base separates to accommodate nine leaves, circa 1860. (Robt. W. Skinner Inc.) $2,000

A mahogany breakfast table with crossbanded circular top, 58in. diam. (Christie's) $1,848

DINING TABLES

A George III mahogany breakfast table with tip-up top, 60in. wide. (Christie's) $3,511

An early Victorian mahogany dining table, extending to 93in., including two extra leaves. (Christie's) $2,103

A Regency satinwood breakfast table, the top crossbanded with rosewood, 53¼in. wide. (Christie's) $15,708

A George IV rosewood dining table on pedestal with tripod base, 4ft. diam. (Worsfolds) $1,001

A 19th century Celonise ebony center table with peacock octagonal tilt-top, 39in. wide. (Christie's) $5,280

A late George III mahogany library table with leather lined oval top and six frieze drawers, 49in. wide. (Christie's) $14,058

George III mahogany two pedestal dining table, circa 1800, 123in. long. (Robt. W. Skinner Inc.) $3,300

A George IV mahogany breakfast table, the tilt top on a quadripartite turned support, 56in. wide. (Christie's) $847

A George IV mahogany twin pedestal 'D' end dining table, including an extra leaf, 1.89 x 1.19m. extended. (Phillips) $7,344

A Queen Anne carved and inlaid walnut dressing table, New Hampshire, circa 1735-60, 36in. wide. (Christie's) $88,000

A late Chippendale mahogany dressing table with tripartite top, probably Rhode Island, 1780-1800, 31.1/8in. wide. (Christie's) $7,700

Late 18th century Italian kingwood, marquetry and painted dressing table, 45¼in. wide. (Christie's) $2,811

A Liberty oak dressing table with adjustable mirror, 132.6cm. wide with flaps extended. (Christie's) $660

A George III mahogany breakfront dressing table, the divided top with three tambour shutters, 62½in. wide. (Christie's) $1,663

A Peter Waals walnut dressing table with rectangular cheval mirror, 116.4cm. wide. (Christie's) $841

A Chippendale carved walnut dressing table, Phila., 1765-85, 36in. wide. (Christie's) $253,000

Mid 19th century carved walnut marble top shaving stand, America, 58¼in. high. (Robt. W. Skinner Inc.) $1,200

Queen Anne tiger maple dressing table, circa 1760, 28½in. wide. (Robt. W. Skinner Inc.) $4,000

DRESSING TABLES

A George III mahogany veneered dressing table, the drawers with original brass plate paterae embossed handles, 3ft.2in. wide. (Woolley & Wallis) $2,574

A Regency mahogany dressing table with three drawers and an arched kneehole frieze, 3ft.3in. wide. (Woolley & Wallis) $1,912

A George III rectangular mahogany kneehole dressing table, 49 x 32½in. high. (Anderson & Garland) $2,160

Part of an Edwardian satinwood bedroom suite, the dressing table 51in. wide, 10 pieces. (Christie's) $2,015

Late 18th century Scandinavian mahogany and parquetry dressing table, 33½in. wide. (Christie's) $3,124

An Art Nouveau mahogany and inlaid dressing table with cartouche-shaped bevelled swing-frame mirror, 122cm. wide. (Phillips) $748

A George III tulipwood bonheur-du-jour with leather lined writing slide, 30in. wide. (Christie's) $4,032

Late 18th century George III mahogany dressing table, the hinged top opens to reveal a fitted interior, 24in. wide. (Robt. W. Skinner Inc.) $950

A Sheraton period mahogany tulipwood crossbanded and chequerstrung serpentine front enclosed dressing table, 75cm. wide. (Phillips) $2,880

DROP-LEAF TABLES

Mid 18th century George III mahogany drop-leaf table, 36in. wide. (Christie's) $1,760

Painted pine drop-leaf harvest table, New England, circa 1800, 41½in. wide, open, 84¾in. long. (Robt. W. Skinner Inc.) $2,100

A Louis XVI provincial walnut dining table on six turned tapering legs, 42¾in. wide. (Christie's) $2,343

An Empire cherry and bird's-eye maple drop-leaf table, New England, circa 1825, 74in. long, open. (Robt. W. Skinner Inc.) $1,200

Chippendale walnut drop-leaf table, circa 1780, 38½in. wide. (Robt. W. Skinner Inc.) $700

A George III mahogany oval twin-flap top dining table, 4ft.11in. x 5ft.4in. (Woolley & Wallis) $4,147

A Federal tiger maple dining table with shaped leaves, New England, circa 1820, 49½in. long, open. (Robt. W. Skinner Inc.) $1,900

Late Federal rosewood veneer, gilt and brass inlaid breakfast table, attributed to Charles-Honore Lannuier, N.Y., circa 1815, 46in. long, extended. (Christie's) $71,500

Queen Anne tiger maple drop-leaf table, New England, circa 1780, 16¾in. wide (closed). (Robt. W. Skinner Inc.) $1,500

DROP-LEAF TABLES

A George III mahogany single drop-leaf occasional table, with a rectangular hinged top, 84 x 64cm. extended. (Phillips) $1,275

A Queen Anne walnut drop-leaf dining table, the cabriole legs with peaked knees, New England, circa 1740-70, top 51½ x 46½in. (Christie's) $9,900

A Federal mahogany dining table with four swing legs, Boston, 1810-25, 62½in. long. (Christie's) $4,950

A Federal mahogany breakfast table with D-shaped leaves, 1800-15, 45in. wide, open. (Christie's) $3,080

A Spanish walnut drop-leaf table, 32½in. wide. (Christie's) $1,874

A Federal inlaid mahogany breakfast table, circa 1790-1810, 39¼in. wide. (Christie's) $6,600

An Empire cherry dining table, possibly New York, circa 1825, 45½in. wide. (Robt. W. Skinner Inc.) $600

Federal mahogany dining table, the large drop-leaves with rounded and molded edge, N.Y., circa 1800, 65in. wide, open. (Robt. W. Skinner Inc.) $8,000

A Chippendale mahogany drop-leaf dining table, Townsend School, 1760-80, 43in. deep. (Christie's) $28,600

GATELEG TABLES

A Charles II oak gateleg table with oval twin-flap top, some later supports and later bun feet, 71½in. wide, open. (Christie's) $5,742

An oak and grained elm gateleg table with oval twin-flap top and one frieze drawer, mid 17th century, 68in. wide, open. (Christie's) $6,198

A mid Georgian red walnut gateleg table with oval twin-flap top on scroll headed cabriole legs, 57in. wide, open. (Christie's) $4,404

An oak gateleg table with oval twin-flap top, 17th century, 56½in. long. (Christie's) $1,683

A George II mahogany gateleg side table, the top with one flap, 26½in. wide. (Christie's) $2,478

Mid 17th century small oak gateleg table with oval twin-flap top, possibly Dutch, 32¼in. wide, open. (Christie's) $2,956

A late 17th century oak oval twin-flap top gateleg table, the friezes with a drawer each end, 4ft.6in. x 5ft. (Woolley & Wallis) $4,342

Yewwood topped gateleg dining table, oval, on turned and knopped supports, 4ft.1½in. x 3ft.6in. (Hobbs & Chambers) $2,184

GATELEG TABLES

An oak gateleg dining table with oval twin-flap top, part 17th century, 80in. long. (Christie's) $1,600

A Jacobean oak oval top gateleg table, two drawers, carried on double baluster legs, 57in. wide. (Christie's) $2,880

A mid Georgian mahogany gateleg table with oval twin-flap top, on club legs and pad feet, 56in. wide, open. (Christie's) $3,146

An oak gateleg dining table, the planked oval folding top with two frieze drawers, extending to 63in., basically late 17th century. (Christie's) $1,667

George II mahogany gateleg table, England, circa 1750, 57½in. long. (Robt. W. Skinner Inc.) $1,600

A 17th century oak gateleg table, the oval twin-flap above an end drawer, 38½in. long. (Christie's) $800

Late 17th century oak gateleg table with oval twin-flap top and frieze drawer, possibly Dutch, 49½in. wide. (Christie's)
                $3,141

Late 17th century William and Mary gateleg table, England, 60¼in. long, extended. (Robt. W. Skinner Inc.) $650

A mahogany dining table of early Georgian style in two sections, each drop-leaf section with twin-flap rectangular top, 96in. long. (Christie's) $13,175

A George IV mahogany extending dining table, the top with two drop leaves on seven turned and ribbed tapering legs, 132in. long extended. (Christie's) $4,719

A Federal three-part mahogany dining table on square tapering legs with stringing, American, 1790-1810, 154¾in. long. (Christie's) $12,100

William and Mary walnut tavern table, the top with breadboard ends, Pennsylvania, circa 1740, 71½in. long. (Robt. W. Skinner Inc.) $3,900

A Regency mahogany and ebony strung D-end dining table in three sections, center section with reconstruction, 1.87 x 1.22m. extended. (Phillips) $5,184

A George III mahogany bow-ended sectional dining table, 4ft.5in. x 7ft.2in. (Woolley & Wallis) $4,032

One of a pair of George III giltwood side tables designed by Robt. Adam and made by S. Alken, 65½in. long. (Christie's) $403,260

A Regency mahogany drop-leaf table on turned tapering ribbed legs, 70½in. long. (Christie's) $4,963

LARGE TABLES

Large Queen Anne style mahogany oval drop-leaf table, 83¼in. long. (Robt. W. Skinner Inc.) $2,600

Early 20th century mahogany library table with leather inset top, by Waring & Gillows, 8ft. x 4ft. (Peter Wilson) $1,128

A Regency mahogany twin pedestal dining table, on ring turned column and quadruped hipped splayed legs, 2.41 x 1.33m. overall. (Phillips) $5,184

A George III mahogany serpentine serving table with fluted frieze, 103in. long. (Christie's) $13,370

A William IV oak extending dining table, with three leaves, 53¼in. wide, 99½in. long. (Christie's) $4,342

A George III yewwood serpentine serving table with eared top and fluted frieze flanked and divided by roundels, 83½in. long. (Christie's) $11,797

A George III oval snap-top dining table with a reeded edge, 4ft.1in. x 5ft.8in. (Woolley & Wallis) $4,896

A Georgian D-ended mahogany dining table, the friezes with rosewood bands, 8ft.8in. long. (Parsons, Welch & Cowell) $1,540

A mahogany three-pillar dining table, the rounded rectangular top with a reeded edge, 150in. long, including two leaves. (Christie's) $2,416

A Wiener Werkstatte black stained limed oak table designed by J. Hoffmann, 224.7cm. long. (Christie's) $10,281

A George III Irish mahogany drop-leaf dining table of 'Hunt' or 'Wake' type, 2.75 x 1.36m. (Phillips) $22,720

A George III mahogany D-end dining table in three sections, the center with two flaps above a plain frieze on square tapering legs, 106in. (Christie's) $3,190

A George III style mahogany three-pillar dining table with D-ended top, 140in. x 46in. (Christie's) $3,775

A George III mahogany side table of Adam design, 60in. wide. (Dreweatts) $5,800

An oak draw-leaf table on baluster turned legs joined by box stretcher, basically 17th century, 72in. wide, extended. (Christie's) $1,573

An early Victorian figured mahogany extending dining table, the oval ends with five extra leaves, stamped Cope & Collinson, 12ft.4in. long, extended. (Woolley & Wallis) $4,433

LARGE TABLES

A mid Victorian burr walnut dining table on fluted and turned twin-column supports and scrolled feet, 96in. long. (Christie's) $2,988

An early 19th century D-ended mahogany dining table. (Parsons, Welch & Cowell) $3,020

A George III giltwood side table with D-shaped white marble top, 62¼in. wide. (Christie's) $15,510

A Regency rosewood veneered platform base extending dining table, the splayed legs with brass sabots on castors, 4ft.2in. x 8ft.4in. extended. (Woolley & Wallis) $3,289

A late George III mahogany twin-pedestal dining table, 105½ x 48in., including three extra leaves. (Christie's) $7,755

One of a pair of George III mahogany serpentine serving tables, 67in. wide. (Christie's) $17,303

A Regency ormolu mounted mahogany breakfront serving table, 81in. wide. (Christie's) $13,370

A George III mahogany dining table with wide darker mahogany borders, fully extended 122in. (Graves Son & Pilcher) $2,642

OCCASIONAL TABLES

One of a pair of parcel gilt and rosewood tripod tables with leather lined tops, 16¼in. diam. (Christie's) $2,988

A mahogany circular snap-top galleried occasional table, 32in. diam. (Woolley & Wallis) $1,872

A 19th century carved rose-wood, brass embellished and inlaid marble top occasional table. (Phillips) $3,124

A Regency ormolu mounted mahogany and bronze gueridon in the manner of Thos. Hope, 21¼in. diam., 32¼in. high. (Christie's) $49,632

A brushed steel and chromium-plated table, the design attributed to Ringo Starr, 121.5cm. wide, 66cm. high. (Christie's) $314

An ormolu gueridon in the manner of Weisweiler with pink granite top, stamped P. Sormani, Paris, 19¾in. diam. (Christie's) $20,196

A George III satinwood tripod table, the tip-up top crossbanded with tulipwood, 21½in. wide. (Christie's) $13,959

A Chippendale period maho-gany snap-top table, 34½in. diam. (Parsons, Welch & Cowell) $1,232

An early Victorian black and gilt japanned papier-mache pedestal table, 24in. wide. (Christie's) $7,078

OCCASIONAL TABLES

A George III mahogany tripod table with scalloped circular tip-up top, 25½in. diam. (Christie's) $4,342

A George III satinwood, sycamore and marquetry tripod table with circular tip-up top, 29½in. diam. (Christie's) $5,505

A George II mahogany tripod table with circular piecrust top, 18in. diam. (Christie's) $1,318

A Regency penwork and ebonized table, the octangular top with a temple in a land-scape, 18½in. wide. (Christie's) $2,831

A George III mahogany tripod table with octagonal tilt-top, 47in. wide. (Christie's) $3,460

A Victorian walnut occasional table, labelled Plucknett & Steevens, Cabinet Makers & Upholsterers, Warwick & Leamington, 28in. high. (Christie's) $1,178

Early 19th century rosewood tripod table, the top centered by a glazed panel enclosing a Viennese porcelain plate, 13in. sq. (Christie's) $7,735

A Georgian mahogany tripod table. (Lots Road Galleries) $573

An early Victorian oak occasional table with cross-banded circular top, 21.5in. diam. (Christie's) $1,473

OCCASIONAL TABLES

One of a pair of ebonized tripod tables with concave-sided rectangular eared tops, on bobbin-turned shafts and scrolling legs with brass bun feet, 17½in. wide.(Christie's) $3,030

A Regency mahogany table with rectangular top and ring-turned tapering legs, 24in. wide. (Christie's) $660

A rosewood occasional table with rectangular specimen marble top and ripple-molded edge, 18in. wide. (Christie's) $2,073

An Italian specimen marble low table on gilt metal ring-turned ribbed tapering legs, 30¾in. diam. (Christie's) $5,582

A mahogany tripod table, the octagonal top centered by a fan roundel with pierced fluted gallery, 27in. wide. (Christie's) $1,404

William and Mary oval top painted tavern table, New England, circa 1740, 29in. wide. (Robt. W. Skinner Inc.) $6,750

An Emile Galle fruitwood and marquetry table a deux plateaux, 52.5cm. wide. (Christie's) $858

A laminated beechwood two-tier low circular table designed by Gerald Summers for The Makers of Simple Furniture, 73.3cm. diam. (Christie's) $2,478

A Majorelle marquetry beech occasional table, the trefoil top inlaid in tulip and rosewood, 74.8cm. high. (Phillips) $748

OCCASIONAL TABLES

One of a pair of rosewood occasional tables, edged with brass, 16½in. wide. (Christie's) $8,772

Country Chippendale maple table, New England, circa 1780, 26in. wide. (Robt. W. Skinner Inc.) $1,900

A late 18th century Russian mahogany, tulipwood cross-banded and ormolu mounted oval occasional table, 50cm. long. (Phillips) $2,100

An early Victorian ebony and marquetry octagonal library table by Edward Holmes Baldock, banded with kingwood, 58in. wide. (Christie's) $11,165

Chippendale mahogany serpentine top tip table, Mass., circa 1780, 32½in. diam. (Robt. W. Skinner Inc.) $2,000

Early 19th century Chinese Export black and gold lacquer tripod table, 45¼in. diam. (Christie's) $9,251

A George II mahogany tripod table with circular tray top, 9¾in. diam. (Christie's) $1,116

A John Penn Chippendale carved mahogany slab-top table, with gray and white inset marble top, 44¾in. wide, 1765-1775. (Christie's) $605,000

A Regency rosewood drum table inlaid with boxwood lines, with circular green leather lined top, 24in. wide. (Christie's) $8,530

OCCASIONAL TABLES

A mahogany tric-trac table of Louis XVI style, the leather lined reversible tray top with ebony and fruitwood chess players, 44½in. wide. (Christie's) $2,871

A Chippendale cherrywood tilt-top stand, Mass., 1780-1800, 28in. high, 18¼in. wide. (Christie's) $1,760

A Chippendale cherrywood side table, probably Conn., 1760-90, 34in. wide. (Christie's) $880

A late 18th/early 19th century Chinese coromandel and lacquer occasional table, 47cm. sq. (Phillips) $1,207

An Art Deco coffee table, circular parquetry top on four scrolling wrought iron legs, 79.6cm. diam. (Christie's) $660

Country Federal maple and mahogany veneer tray table, with original red translucent stain finish, circa 1820, 28in. high. (Robt. W. Skinner Inc.) $8,000

A mahogany tripod table, the circular tilting top with scalloped edge, 25in. diam. (Christie's) $924

L. & J. G. Stickley oak server with open plate rack, circa 1912, no. 750, 48in. wide. (Robt. W. Skinner Inc.) $500

A late Victorian mahogany specimen marble occasional table, 21in. wide. (Christie's) $2,831

OCCASIONAL TABLES

A George II mahogany tripod table with hexagonal tip-up top, 26½in. wide.(Christie's) $3,102

Gustav Stickley cut-corner library table, 1902-04, 48in. wide. (Robt. W. Skinner Inc.) $750

A nest of three satinwood quartetto tables, the tops crossbanded with rosewood and with ebonized low galleries, one 19in., one 14½in. (Christie's) $4,342

A George III mahogany urn table with square rosewood banded top, 11½in. sq. (Christie's) $1,730

A Chippendale period carved mahogany half round side table of Director design, 1.29m. wide. (Phillips) $5,760

A black lacquer and simulated bamboo two-tier occasional table, 23¼in. wide. (Christie's) $1,771

A set of four mahogany quartetto tables with twin-turned spreading trestle ends, 11½in. to 18in. (Christie's) $2,171

A Georgian mahogany snap-top table, on turned column and tripod, 2ft.11in. diam. (Hobbs & Chambers) $257

A mahogany occasional table with circular galleried top and fluted frieze, 23¼in. diam. (Christie's) $471

A George III mahogany Pembroke table with twin-flap top and pierced fretwork frieze, 41½in, wide, open. (Christie's) $18,612

Federal cherry Pembroke table with drop-leaf top, New England, circa 1790, 36in. wide. (Robt. W. Skinner Inc.) $900

An 18th century mahogany Pembroke table with cross-banded serpentine twin-flap top, 32¾in. wide, open. (Christie's) $2,326

A George III mahogany and marquetry Pembroke table, the oval top inlaid with a musical trophy, 38in. wide, open. (Christie's) $1,861

A small Regency mahogany Pembroke table, the top crossbanded with satinwood, on baluster shaft and quadripartite legs, 34in. wide. (Christie's) $1,321

A George III mahogany and satinwood Pembroke table, 38in. wide. (Christie's) $6,204

A George III mahogany Pembroke table, the oval twin-flap top crossbanded in satinwood, 36½in. wide, open. (Christie's) $2,481

A Federal inlaid mahogany Pembroke table, the oval top with two drop-leaves, 1795-1825, 29½in. wide. (Christie's) $2,200

A George III mahogany Pembroke table crossbanded with rosewood, 37in. wide, open. (Christie's) $4,653

PEMBROKE TABLES

An early George III maho-
gany Pembroke table with
serpentine twin-flap top,
34in. wide, open.
(Christie's) $1,735

A Chippendale mahogany
Pembroke table, Rhode
Island, 1760-90, 42½in.
wide. (Christie's)
$1,650

A Regency mahogany
Pembroke table with rose-
wood banded twin-flap top,
37¼in. wide. (Christie's)
$471

A George III mahogany
Pembroke table, the top
crossbanded with tulipwood,
35½in. wide. (Christie's)
$2,233

A 19th century satinwood
and decorated Pembroke
table, 99 x 80cm. extended.
(Phillips) $5,680

A George III mahogany
Pembroke table, the oval
twin-flap top crossbanded
in satinwood, 36½in. wide,
open. (Christie's)
$2,313

A George III inlaid maho-
gany oval Pembroke table,
92 x 74cm. extended.
(Phillips) $6,248

A Federal inlaid mahogany
Pembroke table, the oval top
with two drop leaves, 1790-
1810, 39¼in. wide, open.
(Christie's) $8,800

A painted satinwood Pembroke
table, the oval twin-flap top
crossbanded with rosewood,
36in. wide, open. (Christie's)
$6,606

FURNITURE

A laburnum and walnut side
table with associated oyster-
veneered top, basically late
17th century, 35¾in. wide.
(Christie's) $5,020

A maple side table, the design
attributed to Ico Parasi, with
plate glass top, 128.1cm. wide.
(Christie's) $2,217

An early 18th century walnut
side table inlaid with feather
banding, 38¼in. wide.
(Christie's) $786

A late Victorian cast iron
side table with associated
specimen marble top on
scrolling foliate trestle-ends,
43in. wide. (Christie's)
$3,932

An early Georgian walnut
side table on cabriole legs
and pad feet, 27½in. wide.
(Christie's) $2,148

Classical Revival pier table,
possibly Boston, circa 1830,
minus marble top, 39in. wide.
(Robt. W. Skinner Inc.)
$1,600

A Regency black painted and
gilded side table in the Brighton
Pavilion taste, 38in. wide.
(Christie's) $6,813

A Regency mahogany side
table on ring-turned tapering
legs, 22in. wide. (Christie's)
$393

A William and Mary oak side
table banded with walnut
and inlaid with boxwood
lines, 25¾in. wide.
(Christie's) $1,982

SIDE TABLES

An Anglo-Dutch walnut
side table with three
drawers in the shaped frieze,
on cabriole legs and hoof
feet, 30½in. wide.
(Christie's) $3,139

A Charles X mahogany side
table with red-veined black
marble top. (Christie's)
$4,686

A Dutch walnut and floral
marquetry side table of
serpentine outlines, 30½in.
wide. (Christie's)
$3,124

A Regency amboyna and
yewwood side table with
two frieze drawers,
35½in. wide. (Christie's)
$2,313

A George III sycamore and
marquetry side table, the
top inlaid with a parrot on
a branch, 22in. wide.
(Christie's) $3,190

A George III mahogany side
table with rounded rectangular top and two frieze
drawers, 32in. wide.
(Christie's) $1,258

A Dutch walnut and floral
marquetry side table,
33¾in. wide. (Christie's)
$2,811

An early Georgian walnut
side table with crossbanded
quartered rectangular top
and three drawers, 25in.
wide. (Christie's)
$1,652

An early Georgian walnut
side table, the top with
later carved border, 30in.
wide. (Christie's)
$1,569

A George III rosewood and marquetry side table in the manner of Pierre Langlois, 50½in. wide. (Christie's) $13,183

A George III Irish carved mahogany folding top table, 1.17m. wide. (Phillips) $5,040

A late George III mahogany bowfront side table, 29½in. wide. (Christie's) $830

A George I mahogany side table on lapetted turned spreading legs and pad feet, 30in. wide. (Christie's) $2,016

A George III mahogany side table with rectangular molded top, 36in. wide. (Chrstie's) $707

One of a pair of Queen Anne gilt gesso side tables on cabriole legs and foliate pad feet, 29in. wide. (Christie's) $46,530

A George III mahogany side table with serpentine top, 34¾in. wide. (Christie's) $2,636

A giltwood side table with rectangular eared verde antico marble top, 40¼in. wide. (Christie's) $11,797

An Irish walnut side table with serpentine marble top, basically mid 18th century, 41½in. wide. (Christie's) $5,273

A Regency rosewood side table with one drop-leaf, 52in. wide. (Christie's) $3,102

A George III mahogany serving table, the top outlined with boxwood, 63in. wide.(Christie's) $3,190

A George III mahogany and giltwood pier table, 45in. wide. (Christie's) $10,857

A George III mahogany and cream painted serving table with three-quarter brass gallery, 66in. wide. (Christie's) $7,444

A George III painted satinwood small side table, the top with a low gallery, 20½in. wide. (Christie's) $7,755

A George I walnut side table with four drawers around an arched kneehole, 32in. wide. (Christie's) $15,510

One of a pair of early George III giltwood side tables each with a serpentine eared Portor marble top, 48in. wide. (Christie's) $58,938

A 19th century Anglo-Indian carved hardwood side table, 52in. wide. (Parsons, Welch & Cowell) $708

An early George III mahogany side table with later rectangular serpentine marble top, 51in. wide. (Christie's) $7,931

SOFA TABLES

A satinwood sofa table with rounded rectangular twin-flap top, on trestle ends and splayed feet, 56in. wide, open. (Christie's) $1,036

A Regency rosewood sofa table, the top with rope-twist brass border, 58in. wide, open. (Christie's) $2,871

A George III satinwood sofa table banded with partidge-wood and inlaid with ebonized lines, 58½in. wide, open. (Christie's) $24,816

A mid 19th century satinwood and inlaid sofa table with a hinged top crossbanded in kingwood, 1.41m. x 64cm. (Phillips) $2,130

A George III mahogany sofa table, the twin-flap top crossbanded with rosewood, 54in. wide, open. (Christie's) $2,831

A sofa table veneered and decorated as satinwood and painted with a design of flowers and ribbon border, 5ft. long, extended. (Lots Road Galleries) $1,650

A George III mahogany sofa table with twin-flap cross-banded top above two frieze drawers, 57½in. wide, open. (Christie's) $3,987

A Regency brass inlaid roswood sofa table with twin-flap top and ebonized border, 61¼in. wide, open. (Christie's) $10,224

A George III mahogany sofa table crossbanded with rose-wood and inlaid with box-wood lines, 59in. wide, open. (Christie's) $4,032

SOFA TABLES

A Regency mahogany sofa
table with twin-flap top and
reeded edge, 58¾in. wide,
open. (Christie's)
$9,306

A Regency rosewood and
brass inlaid sofa table,
stamped T. Sharples,
Liverpool, 1.66m. x 69cm.
(Phillips) $6,624

A Regency mahogany sofa
table with twin-flap top
and reeded edge, 57¼in. wide.
(Christie's) $2,202

An Empire ormolu mounted
mahogany sofa table, possibly
Sweden, circa 1815, 39¼in.
wide. (Robt. W. Skinner Inc.)
$1,600

A William IV rosewood sofa
table, stamped T. & A. Blain,
Liverpool, 58in. wide.
(Christie's) $4,785

Regency rosewood sofa
table, 58in. wide, open.
(Worsfolds)
$6,468

A Regency mahogany and
ebony strung sofa table, the
hinged top crossbanded in
satinwood and rosewood,
1.48m. x 71cm. (Phillips)
$2,448

A Regency rosewood sofa
table with twin-flap top and
three frieze drawers, 73in.
wide. (Christie's)
$7,444

A Regency mahogany sofa
table with twin-flap top above
two frieze drawers, 52in. wide.
(Christie's) $3,567

WORKBOXES & GAMES TABLES

A George III satinwood work table with a fitted frieze drawer and slide hung with a pleated green silk work basket, 19¼in. wide. (Christie's) $1,355

A Regency padoukwood games table, the satinwood banded twin-flap top with reversible center section, 43in. wide, open. (Christie's) $13,183

A Federal walnut and maple work table, New England, 1815-25, 20in. wide. (Christie's) $990

A late Federal mahogany work table, New York, 1815-25, 23in. wide. (Christie's) $3,300

A Victorian walnut and parcel gilt etched pedestal games table with inset octagonal specimen marble top, 33in. wide. (Christie's) $3,460

A Federal mahogany work table, the drawer fitted with compartments, Penn., 1810-20, 18¾in. wide. (Christie's) $3,300

A Victorian papier-mache games table, the revolving top inlaid for chess in mother-of-pearl, stamped Jennens & Bettridge, 67cm. wide. (Phillips) $3,692

Regency rosewood games table with tooled red leather top and fitted backgammon drawer. (Lots Road Galleries) $3,410

A George III Scottish black and gold lacquer work table, stamped Bruce & Burns, Edin., 18½in. wide. (Christie's) $991

WORKBOXES & GAMES TABLES

Early 19th century Shaker pine and maple work table, probably New England, 36in. high. (Robt. W. Skinner Inc.) $2,000

A Chinese Export lacquer games table, the top with reversible lift-out center enclosing chess squares and a backgammon board, circa 1820, 35½in. wide. (Christie's) $2,974

A Regency satinwood games and work table with lift-out top crossbanded with rosewood and inlaid on the reverse with a chessboard, 20in. wide. (Christie's) $4,404

A George IV rosewood sewing table with velvet-lined swivelling hinged top, with pleated olive simulated-silk basket, 21in. wide. (Christie's) $957

Federal cherry inlaid work table, New Jersey, circa 1815, 27in. high. (Robt. W. Skinner Inc.) $1,600

A Victorian figured walnut games/sewing table with serpentine front and ends, 23in. wide. (Peter Wilson) $1,057

A mid Victorian black, gilt and mother-of-pearl japanned papier-mache pedestal work table, 18½in. wide.(Christie's) $943

An early 19th century Chinese Export lacquer games table with twin-flap top, 39in. wide, open. (Christie's) $1,551

A mid Victorian black, gilt and mother-of-pearl japanned papier-mache pedestal table, 24½in. wide. (Christie's) $1,258

WORKBOXES & GAMES TABLES

An Empire mahogany and mahogany veneer work table, circa 1830, 20½in. wide. (Robt. W. Skinner Inc.) $225

A Jaipur marble games table, top inlaid with polychrome marbles, including lapis lazuli and colored quartz, 25½in. sq. (Christie's) $3,146

A Regency penwork games table, on spirally-turned shaped ebonized shaft, 21½in. wide. (Christie's) $2,044

Late 18th century Anglo-Indian ivory work table with oval hinged top, Vizagapatam, 24¼in. wide. (Christie's)$26,367

A classical mahogany work table with hinged top enclosing a compartmented interior, New York, 1815-25, 27in. wide. (Christie's) $12,100

A George III mahogany work table inlaid with boxwood stringing, 17¾in. wide. (Christie's) $1,651

A Regency ormolu mounted rosewood work table with pierced galleried hinged top, 16¼in. wide. (Christie's) $1,730

A George III mahogany work table, the top with adjustable slide to the back filled with sky blue moire silk, 25½in. wide. (Christie's) $4,653

A mid Victorian black, gilt and mother-of-pearl japanned papier-mache games table, 19¾in. diam. (Christie's) $1,101

WORKBOXES & GAMES TABLES

A George III satinwood work table, the kidney-shaped quartered top crossbanded with rosewood, 32½in. wide. (Christie's) $13,183

A Regency mahogany games table inlaid with ebonized lines and with reversible center section, 42½in. high. (Christie's) $15,510

A William IV burr elm work table, the folding top with rosewood banded borders, 33½in. wide. (Christie's) $1,386

A George III satinwood work table with twin-flap octangular top crossbanded with rosewood, 21¼in. wide. (Christie's) $8,065

Early 20th century Regency brass and ebony inlaid work table, England, 23½in. wide. (Robt. W. Skinner Inc.) $1,300

A 19th century walnut and fruitwood pictorial marquetry games table, 25in. diam. (Christie's) $2,016

A Regency beechwood and oak work table with crossbanded, twin-flap rounded top, 25½in. wide. (Christie's) $797

An early 19th century Chinese Export black lacquer work table, the top enclosing a fitted interior, 26in. wide. (Christie's) $1,036

A George III tulipwood work table of tricoteure form, 23¼in. wide. (Christie's) $7,755

WRITING TABLES & DESKS

A Regency ormolu mounted
rosewood writing table in
the manner of John McLean,
42¼in. wide. (Christie's)
$55,836

Federal mahogany and mahogany veneer desk, possibly
New York, circa 1820, 50½in.
wide. (Robt. W. Skinner Inc.)
$600

A Robert Thompson 'Mouse-
man' oak writing desk, signed
with a carved mouse, 182.5cm.
wide. (Christie's) $554

A Federal inlaid mahogany
writing desk, with hinged
lid, 1790-1810, 29.7/8in.
wide. (Christie's)
$1,650

A Victorian walnut roll-top
desk, Winneberger, Penn.,
circa 1890, 40½in. wide.
(Robt. W. Skinner Inc.)
$1,100

A George III mahogany
writing table with leather
lined, kidney-shaped top,
40in. wide. (Christie's)
$3,102

Mid 18th century George III
mahogany writing table,
44in. wide. (Christie's)
$6,600

A Dutch walnut and floral
marquetry bureau de dame
of serpentine outline, 35in.
wide. (Christie's)
$3,436

A Regency maple and rose-
wood marquetry library
table, on standard end
supports, 1.30m. (Phillips)
$8,064

WRITING TABLES & DESKS

A Regency mahogany writing table with green leather lined top, the ends with brass balustrade galleries, 42in. wide. (Christie's) $2,202

A Regency ormolu mounted mahogany and ebonized Carlton House desk with Bramah locks, 57in. wide. (Christie's)
$93,060

A George III mahogany veneered rectangular writing table with inset gilt tooled green leather top, 3ft.3in. long. (Woolley & Wallis)
$1,550

A Louis XV/XVI transitional period parquetry, marquetry and ormolu decorated bureau a cylindre veneered in tulipwood, kingwood and purpleheart, 1.44m. wide. (Phillips) $10,650

A lady's oak desk with fall-front, circa 1890, 28½in. wide. (Robt. W. Skinner Inc.)
$500

A mid Victorian ormolu mounted walnut and tulip-wood writing table with leather lined top, 43in. wide. (Christie's) $8,530

A walnut bureau-on-stand with baize-lined sloping flap enclosing a fitted interior, 21in. wide. (Christie's) $1,239

A Regency mahogany writing table with leather lined top, the panelled frieze with five drawers, 54¾in. wide. (Christie's) $5,033

A George III satinwood writing table with leather lined easel top and slide, 23½in. wide. (Christie's)
$7,755

WRITING TABLES & DESKS

A Louis XIV marquetry bureau mazarin, the top with brass edge, 1.17m. wide. (Phillips) $18,000

A Heal's oak writing desk, designed by Ambrose Heal, 152.3cm. wide. (Christie's) $3,801

A 19th century scarlet tortoiseshell and brass marquetry bureau mazarin in the manner of Boulle, 1.22m. wide. (Phillips) $5,680

A Federal inlaid mahogany writing desk, 1790-1810, 29in. wide. (Christie's) $2,860

A rococo walnut marquetry lady's desk, bombe and serpentine case with fall-front, Italy, 31in. wide. (Robt. W. Skinner Inc.) $1,400

A mid Victorian ormolu mounted rosewood and satinwood writing table, on cabriole legs, 32½in. wide. (Christie's) $2,233

A Regency pollard oak and parcel gilt writing table, the top centered by a hinged easel, 31in. wide. (Christie's) $2,791

Late 19th century Wooton's Patent desk of walnut and burr walnut, 39½in. wide. (Christie's) $6,380

A George III satinwood cylinder desk with tambour shutter enclosing a fitted interior, 39¼in. wide. (Christie's) $40,326

WRITING TABLES & DESKS

A Spanish walnut writing table with hinged top, basically 17th century, 51in. wide. (Christie's) $10,934

A George III mahogany architect's desk with rectangular sloping double-flap top, 54in. wide. (Christie's) $3,509

An early Victorian rosewood library writing table with inset gilt tooled red leather top, 64in. long. (Christie's) $3,460

Louis XV walnut and parquetry bureau a pente on cabriole legs, 36in. wide. (Robt. W. Skinner Inc.) $1,200

A Japanese red and black lacquer cylinder pedestal desk, inlaid with mother-of-pearl and inset with gold lacquer panels, 1.04. wide. (Phillips) $6,900

Late 18th century Louis XVI walnut veneered bureau plat, 43in. wide. (Robt. W. Skinner Inc.) $1,100

Late 19th century lady's rosewood veneered cylinder bureau with inlaid marquetry sprays of flowers and stringing, 32in. wide. (Woolley & Wallis) $1,144

A Victorian walnut and ebonized kidney-shaped writing table, by Gillow & Co., 6555, 45½in. wide. (Christie's) $1,015

A George III mahogany cylinder bureau with tambour shutter enclosing a fitted interior, 21in. wide. (Christie's) $6,380

TRUNKS & COFFERS

A late 17th century brass mounted kingwood coffre fort, the interior with a well, two drawers and two compartments, 11½in. wide. (Christie's) $1,015

An early Victorian oak coffer, the panels 16th century, 65in. wide. (Christie's) $4,712

A Chippendale walnut blanket chest, Penn., probably 1782, 54½in. wide. (Christie's) $1,870

William and Mary child's blanket chest, New England, circa 1740, 28in. wide. (Robt. W. Skinner Inc.) $5,500

A Louis Vuitton cabin trunk covered in brown hide secured by brass pins and mounted with brass lock plate, 114cm. wide. (Christie's) $1,404

Late 18th century painted pine blanket chest on straight bracket feet, Penn., 33¼in. wide. (Christie's) $3,850

A Chippendale painted pine blanket chest, attributed to the Himmelberger Shop, circa 1790, 51in. wide. (Christie's) $11,000

Late 18th century elm chest with panelled front and plank top, 52in. long. (Peter Wilson) $282

TRUNKS & COFFERS

Late 16th century Momoyama period small coffer with hinged domed cover, 28.5 x 17 x 13cm. (Christie's) $781

An Italian walnut cassone with hinged top, 17th century and later, 67½in. wide. (Christie's) $2,499

An iron-bound round topped coffer chest, inscribed 'Clara Angela from Men Anno 1744 21 January'. (Worsfolds) $604

Mid 18th century black and gold lacquer coffer, mounted with shaped and engraved gilt brass angles and lock-plate, 56in. wide. (Christie's) $15,510

A 17th century oak coffer with molded hinged top and panel front, 61cm. wide. (Phillips) $3,168

Painted pine dower chest, the molded lift lid above dovetailed case with deep well above three drawers, Penn., dated 1829, 47in. wide. (Robt. W. Skinner Inc.) $850

An Italian walnut cassone, partly 17th century, 80in. wide. (Christie's) $6,248

A Chinese Export black and gold lacquer coffer decorated with foliage and with hinged lid, 36in. wide. (Christie's) $1,321

TRUNKS & COFFERS

Pine and white cedar board chest, the lift top with snipe hinges, probably Mass., circa 1700, 51in. wide. (Robt. W. Skinner Inc.)
$2,700

Items of vintage leather luggage, including two trunks, hat box, picnic case and others. (Lots Road Galleries) $400

A George III mahogany chest with hinged lid, .52½in. wide. (Christie's) $1,320

A Momoyama period black lacquer domed chest in hiramakie and takamakie and inlaid in shell, circa 1600, 52cm. wide. (Christie's)
$3,124

Late 17th century Flemish leather covered coffer banded with pierced metal strapwork, 43½in. wide. (Christie's) $2,288

A large rectangular roironuri chest decorated in gold and brown hiramakie with mon, engraved gilt kanagu, late Edo period, 120 x 61 x 74cm. (Christie's) $3,498

Early 18th century oak chest with panelled top enclosing an interior fitted with a well and two small drawers, 55½in. wide. (Christie's) $1,771

A putty painted pine blanket box, New England, late 18th century, 47in. wide. (Robt. W. Skinner Inc.) $1,700

WARDROBES & ARMOIRES

A bachelor's mahogany wardrobe, the doors opening to reveal four sliding trays, 52in. wide. (Outhwaite & Litherland) $1,334

A 17th century Flemish rosewood and ebony armoire with massive bun feet, 91in. wide. (Christie's) $3,436

A Dutch fruitwood armoire with a pair of shaped panelled doors, 76in. wide, 96in. high. (Christie's) $7,040

A Louis XV provincial oak armoire on scrolled feet, 57½in. wide. (Christie's) $2,288

A 17th century Dutch walnut and ebony armoire, 76in. wide. (Christie's) $1,874

Mid 18th century French provincial oak armoire with molded foliate cornice, 64in. wide, 88in. high. (Christie's) $6,688

Late 18th century George III inlaid mahogany linen press on bracket feet, 47½in. wide. (Christie's) $4,950

An 18th century French provincial oak armoire, 6ft. 2in. wide. (Capes, Dunn & Co.) $1,522

Mid 18th century French provincial oak armoire, 62in. wide, 89in. high. (Christie's) $3,168

WARDROBES & ARMOIRES

A George III gentleman's mahogany wardrobe with gilt brass cast swag handles, 4ft.2in. wide. (Woolley & Wallis) $1,268

A William and Mary gumwood kas in two sections, New York, 1725-55, 54in. wide. (Christie's) $4,180

A Regency mahogany clothes press, the panelled doors enclosing four slides and two drawers, 56½in. wide. (Christie's) $3,828

A 17th century Flemish oak press in two parts, 53½in. wide. (Christie's) $3,748

An 18th century Dutch walnut armoire, the bombe lower part fitted with three drawers, 1.83m. wide. (Phillips) $3,124

Gustav Stickley two-door wardrobe, panelled doors opening to pull-out shelves, 1904, 33in. wide. (Robt. W. Skinner Inc.) $1,500

George III pine linen press, the drawers with replaced brass bail handles, England, circa 1800, 46in. wide. (Robt. W. Skinner Inc.) $1,500

An 18th century gumwood kas, in three sections, Long Island, N.Y., 74½in. wide. (Christie's) $6,600

Late 18th century French provincial oak armoire on squat cabriole legs, 59¾in. wide. (Christie's) $3,748

WARDROBES & ARMOIRES

A French provincial fruitwood armoire on squat cabriole legs, 61in. wide. (Christie's) $2,343

A George III mahogany clothes press on bracket feet, 50in. wide, 71in. high. (Christie's) $1,487

A George III satinwood clothes press, the sides cross-banded with rosewood, 51½in. wide, 77¼in. high.(Christie's) $21,714

A Louis XV cherrywood armoire with molded chamfered cornice, 56in. wide. (Christie's) $5,935

A Regency mahogany breakfront wardrobe, 102in. wide. (Christie's) $6,292

George III mahogany linen press, the panelled doors enclosing sliding trays, 4ft. x 7ft.6in. high. (Hobbs & Chambers) $1,258

An 18th century South German figured and burr walnut armoire, 74in. wide. (Christie's)$20,306

An 18th century German walnut veneered and marquetry armoire, 78in. wide. (Robt. W. Skinner Inc.) $15,500

A George III mahogany clothes press with a pair of shaped panelled doors enclosing slides, 47in. wide. (Christie's) $2,148

A late George III inlaid mahogany corner washstand, 38½in. high, 22in. wide. (Christie's) $1,540

A Regency period faded mahogany veneered toilet stand, 21in. wide. (Woolley & Wallis) $334

A George III Sheraton design gentleman's washstand, 28in. wide. (Locke & England) $1,224

A George III mahogany toilet stand inlaid with satinwood bands and geometric boxwood lines, 24¼in. wide. (Christie's) $620

A Classical Revival mahogany washstand, probably Boston, circa 1815, 17½in. diam. (Robt. W. Skinner Inc.) $16,500

Shaker pine, tiger maple and butternut washstand, 20¼in. wide. (Robt. W. Skinner Inc.) $10,000

A George III Sheraton design mahogany serpentine front washstand, 17½in. wide. (Lalonde Fine Art) $571

A mahogany washstand with small shelf, two drawers and pot shelf, 26 x 18 x 29in. high. (County Group) $273

A Regency oval two-tier washstand, the top tier with open center 24½in. wide. (Christie's) $1,293

WHATNOTS

One of a pair of George IV rosewood whatnots with bead-and-reel- molded tops, 53½in. high. (Christie's) $7,975

A snuff and gold lacquer etagere, the two shelves with pierced strapwork galleries, 28½in. long. (Christie's) $2,956

Napoleon II ebonized and marquetry three-tier whatnot, 18¼in. wide. (Robt. W. Skinner Inc.) $475

Regency rosewood whatnot, oblong, the three tiers with three-quarter spindle galleries, 1ft.2in. wide. (Hobbs & Chambers) $1,221

A George IV mahogany serving whatnot, the three-quarter galleried tiers joined by baluster supports, 40½in. wide. (Christie's) $1,240

A Regency mahogany two-tier whatnot with easel top and ribbed supports, 21in. wide. (Christie's) $3,102

A Regency brass three-tier whatnot with rosewood shelves, 15 x 28in. high. (Dreweatts) $4,437

A gilt metal mounted mahogany etagere with two tiers crossbanded with satinwood and centered by a shell medallion, 23½in. wide. (Christie's) $1,415

Victorian figured walnut whatnot, three tier, on scroll feet, 2ft.5in. wide. (Hobbs & Chambers) $571

WINE COOLERS

A George III brass bound mahogany cellarette with a lead lined interior, 18½in. wide. (Christie's) $7,022

A Regency mahogany sarcophagus wine cooler with detachable divided tin liner, 33in. wide. (Christie's) $1,735

A George III mahogany cellarette with hinged lid enclosing a divided interior, 16¾in. wide. (Christie's) $1,551

A Federal inlaid walnut cellarette on stand, 1790-1810, 42½in. high, 18½in. wide. (Christie's) $2,640

A Regency mahogany wine cooler with lead lined interior, formerly with a lid, 39in. wide. (Christie's) $5,667

A George III mahogany and satinwood molded octagonal cellarette on contemporary stand, 46cm. high. (Phillips) $2,400

A Regency mahogany and parcel gilt wine cooler with hinged lid enclosing a tin liner, 26¼in. wide. (Christie's) $2,202

A George III mahogany wine cooler, the lined oval body banded in brass, 28in. wide. (Christie's) $4,228

A William IV mahogany sarcophagus-shaped wine cooler with lead lined interior, 27½in. wide. (Christie's) $1,328

WINE COOLERS

A Regency mahogany sarcophagus shaped wine cooler with lead lined interior, on paw feet, 29½in. wide. (Christie's) $3,800

A Regency mahogany and inlaid cellarette of boat design, with triple hinged top, 1.02m. wide. (Phillips) $6,532

A late Regency mahogany sarcophagus-shaped wine cooler with lid enclosing a lead lined interior, 29½in. wide. (Christie's) $1,887

A Regency mahogany cellarette with hinged octagonal top and tin lined interior, 22in. wide. (Christie's) $1,069

A Regency mahogany wine cooler with bronze lion-mask ring handles, on paw feet, 17in. wide. (Christie's) $1,036

A George III mahogany wine cooler with octagonal hinged lid enclosing a metal liner, 19½in. wide. (Christie's) $4,653

A large Regency mahogany and ebonized wine cooler in the manner of Gillows, with a lead lined divided interior, 33in. wide. (Christie's) $4,963

A George III brass bound mahogany hexagonal cellarette, 28in. high, 17in. wide. (Christie's) $4,400

A George III brass bound mahogany wine cooler with arched brass carrying handle and lead lined interior, 13in. wide. (Christie's) $10,081

BEAKERS

Mid 18th century Central European 'milchglas' armorial flared beaker, 14.5cm. high. (Christie's) $1,082

A 17th/18th century Venetian 'Calcedonia' bell-shaped beaker of blue, green and brown marbleized glass, 9cm. high. (Christie's) $665

A Bohemian blue overlay engraved beaker perhaps by A. Pfeiffer, Karlsbad, circa 1840, 13cm. high. (Christie's) $811

A Bohemian 'Zwischensilberglas' beaker, circa 1730, 9cm. high. (Christie's) $2,376

Four Lobmeyr beakers, the bowls fluted, enamelled with cartouches portraying ladies and gentlemen in 18th century costume, 4in. high. (Christie's) $400

A Bohemian portrait beaker, the bowl engraved in the manner of Biemann, circa 1840, 13cm. high. (Christie's) $1,984

A Bohemian 'Zwischengoldglas' and polychrome beaker, circa 1735, 10cm. high. (Christie's) $2,851

One of a pair of Lobmeyr beakers, decorated with Arabic script in blue and red on a gilt ground, 4in. high. (Christie's) $319

A Bohemian 'Zwischengoldglas' flared beaker, by Johann Mildner, 1790, 10.5cm. high. (Christie's) $1,584

BOTTLES

A late Victorian cut glass square cologne bottle with a silver openwork mount by William Comyns, 5½in. high. (Christie's) $600

Three Vistosi tall bottle vases, designed by Peter Pelzel, circa 1960, 43.5cm., 41cm. and 34cm. (Christie's) $2,112

A 19th century overlaid cranberry glass scent bottle and stopper decorated with a painted oval portrait of a lady, 5¾in. high. (Dacre, Son & Hartley) $193

An oil or vinegar bottle with a beaded stopper, 15cm. high, and a finger bowl, 12cm. (Phillips) $277

A set of three Bristol green spirit bottles and stoppers, with cut shoulders and canted corners, gilt with Rum, Shrub and Brandy, 20cm. high. (Lawrence Fine Art) $672

A German silver gilt mounted ruby glass pilgrim bottle, by Tobias Baur, Augsburg, circa 1690, 12¼in. high. (Christie's) $36,179

Mid 17th century Netherlands turquoise serving bottle with gilt metal domed cover, chain and collar attachment, 18.5cm. high. (Christie's) $4,510

A Lalique clear and frosted glass bottle and stopper, the cylindrical body molded with thorny branches, 4¼in. high. (Christie's) $550

Mid 17th century Netherlands turquoise serving bottle, the globular body with kick-in base, 19.5cm. high. (Christie's) $3,968

407

BOWLS

Saint-Vincent, a Lalique amber plafonnier, the circular bowl in clear and satin-finished glass molded with bands of scrolling fruit laden vines, 34.6cm. wide. (Christie's) $792

Probably mid 19th century cut glass barber's bowl, 26.5cm. diam. (Christie's) $165

A Dale Chihuly basket set, composed of a blown glass bowl with four other free blown 'squashed' bowl shapes, 37.9cm. diam. of large bowl. (Christie's) $4,296

An Irish cut glass oval fruit bowl with alternate prismatic-cut turnover rim, circa 1800, 32.5cm. wide. (Christie's) $1,188

An Irish cut glass circular fruit bowl, circa 1800, 25cm. diam. (Christie's) $601

A Burmese satin finished toothpick holder, Boston & Sandwich Glass Co., Mass., circa 1885, 1.7/8in. high. (Robt. W. Skinner Inc.) $200

A Lalique bowl, clear and pale green glass, 9.5cm. high. (Christie's) $165

An amethyst glass bowl and cover, the design attributed to Josef Hoffmann, 12.5cm. high. (Christie's) $1,573

A Dale Chihuly basket set, composed of a large blown glass bowl with four other free blown 'squashed' bowl shapes, 1980, 37cm. diam. of large bowl. (Christie's) $4,957

BOWLS

A Tiffany 'Favrile' bowl, the gold and violet iridescent glass wheel engraved with maple leaves, 30cm. wide. (Christie's) $1,101

A Galle enamelled bowl, boat-shaped with frilly rim, engraved Galle signature incorporating mushroom, 29cm. wide. (Christie's) $1,742

A Lalique bowl, jade green opalescent glass molded with budgerigars, 24cm. diam. (Christie's) $3,643

Late 19th century two-part cut glass punch bowl, America, 14½in. high, 14¾in. diam. (Robt. W. Skinner Inc.) $900

Early 18th century engraved 'Goldrubinglas' bowl and cover, Bohemia, 15cm. high. (Christie's) $1,425

A Daum bowl, the white, green and red mottled glass acid-etched with primroses and foliage, 13.9cm. high. (Christie's) $865

A Venetian enamelled shallow bowl, decorated in iron-red, white and blue, circa 1500, 16cm. high. (Christie's) $1,900

A Daum acid-etched cameo bowl, the clear glass etched with poppies heightened with gilt decoration, 25cm. wide. (Christie's) $707

Glossy Burmese bowl, star shaped form with fluted, ruffled rim, circa 1890, 2¼in. high. (Robt. W. Skinner Inc.) $200

BOWLS

A Christopher Williams dust bowl, engraved The Glasshouse 1986, 30.5cm. diam. (Christie's) $706

'Jardiniere Acanthus', a Lalique canoe-shaped bowl in clear and satin finished glass, 45.4cm. long. (Christie's) $693

A Lalique plafonnier, the hemispherical bowl of yellow frosted glass molded with peaches and leaves, 38cm wide. (Christie's)
$1,108

A Diana Hobson pate-de-verre bowl form, 1986. (Christie's) $2,356

An Irish cut glass punch bowl in the form of an urn, circa 1800, 32cm. high. (Christie's) $950

'Limbo for Three', a David Prytherch sculpture bowl form, 1986, 38cm. high. (Christie's) $5,049

One of a pair of white overlay ruby flash bowls, 9in. diam. (Christie's)
$504

A Jacobite two-handled glass bowl with rose and thistle engraved emblems, 9in. high. (Prudential Fine Art)
$756

A Steven Newell bowl with decoration of Adam and Eve, 1986, 23.5cm. high. (Christie's) $3,702

CANDLESTICKS

Pair of 20th century Colred cut glass candlesticks, European, 14¼in. high. (Robt. W. Skinner Inc.) $500

A Tiffany 'Favrile' glass candlestick in iridescent gold, 4½in. high. (Du Mouchelles) $300

Two of a set of four dwarf candlesticks, each with an alternative pink or clear glass shade decorated with flowers and foliage, 9.5in. high. (Christie's) $240

Pair of 19th century opalene crystal candlesticks, 15½in. high. (Du Mouchelles) $800

A cut glass candlestick with cylindrical nozzle, circa 1800, 25cm. high. (Christie's) $285

A pair of ormolu and cut glass candlesticks with petal nozzles. 12½in. high. (Christie's) $1,416

A faceted taperstick, the slender diamond-cut column with base knob supporting a cylindrical fluted nozzle, circa 1780, 16.5cm. high. (Christie's) $411

Pair of early 20th century Dominick & Haff sterling silver and cut glass candlesticks, threaded into Classical Revival bases, 13½in. high. (Robt. W. Skinner Inc.) $1,200

Mid 18th century molded pedestal stemmed candlestick, 25.5cm. high. (Christie's) $871

DECANTERS

One of a pair of George III decanters with bull's eye lozenge stoppers, late 18th century. (Woolley & Wallis) $543

A James Powell decanter, clear glass, with pear-shaped stopper, 32cm. high. (Christie's) $201

Early 20th century kew blas decanter, Union Glass Co., Mass, 13½in. high. (Robt. W. Skinner Inc.) $250

An English Jeroboam decanter, the reverse engraved March 8th 1791, 38cm. high. (Phillips) $1,925

An Orrefors decanter and stopper, by Nils Landberg. (Christie's) $2,516

One of a pair of early 19th century dark emerald green cut glass decanters and stoppers of slender club shape, 30.5cm. high. (Christie's) $792

A Netherlands blue-tinted decanter, the metal mounted cork stopper secured by a chain, 25cm. high. (Phillips) $2,772

One of a pair of cylindrical decanters and shaped spiral stoppers, 10½in. high. (Christie's) $81

A Bohemian engraved and cut decanter, circa 1730, 27.5cm. high. (Christie's) $475

DISHES

A Lalique frosted gray green glass boat-shaped dish, 18in. long. (Dacre, Son & Hartley) $586

Lalique amber glass shell duck ashtray, 2¾in. high. (Reeds Rains) $186

A Lalique glass circular dish, the sides and center decorated with molded daisy stems, 13¼in. wide. (Dacre, Son & Hartley) $326

Mid 18th century molded pedestal stemmed sweetmeat glass, 16.5cm. high. (Christie's) $601

A large Lalique circular, blue opalescent dish, molded on the underside with carp among bubbles, 35cm. diam. (Christie's) $1,188

A Liberty pewter and Clutha glass dish on stand, designed by A. Knox, 6½in. high. (Christie's) $589

An 18th century cut glass turnover fruit dish, 9in. high. (Prudential Fine Art) $705

An Irish cut center dish, the bowl of canoe shape, circa 1800, 35cm. wide. (Christie's) $1,984

Mid 16th century Venetian bucket or aspersory with rope twist loop handle, 18.5cm. diam. (Christie's) $1,584

DRINKING SETS

Bohemian gold decorated cobalt blue glass punch set, late 19th century, 9½in. high. (Robt. W. Skinner Inc.) $900

A Victorian liqueur set with crimped heart-shaped tray, by Heath & Middleston, Birmingham, 1891, the liqueur bottle 8¼in. high, 12.75oz. free. (Christie's) $480

Part of an Art Deco liqueur set, consisting of an engraved glass decanter and stopper, the semi-circular body black, 8¼in. high, and five glasses en suite, 3½in. high, and another three decanters and seven glasses similar. (Christie's) $924

A Japanese cocktail set decorated in high relief with iris, circa 1900. (Phillips)
$1,640

A Schott & Gen 'Jena er Glas' clear glass tea-set, designed by Wm. Wagenfeld, teapot, cover and filter, 11cm. high. (Phillips) $316

FLASKS

'Rosace Figurines', a Lalique
frosted glass circular scent
flask and stopper, 11cm.
high. (Phillips) $668

A 17th century spirit flask
(Tonnelet) of barrel shape,
Low Countries or France,
11.5cm. wide. (Christie's)
$631

A Nuremburg metal mounted
engraved serving bottle, circa
1700, 27.5cm. high.
(Christie's) $1,267

A 17th/18th century South
German pewter mounted
spirit flask, 15.5cm. high.
(Christie's) $3,066

Mid 18th century Venetian
enamelled small scent flask
from the atelier of O. Brussa,
11cm. high. (Christie's)
$2,525

A Netherlands diamond
engraved, pewter mounted,
green tinted serving bottle,
inscribed B. Boers, Warmont,
12 April 1690, 25cm. high.
(Christie's) $3,960

An 18th century Central
European enamelled pewter
mounted rectangular spirit
flask, 20cm. high.
(Christie's) $541

A 17th century Bohemian
enamelled small pewter
mounted blue flask, 8cm.
high. (Christie's)
$4,118

A 16th century Bohemian
enamelled flask, the body
painted in colors, 16.5cm.
high, together with another
15cm. high, 1595. (Christie's)
$1,533

GOBLETS

An incised twist goblet of
emerald green tint, circa
1760, 14cm. high.
(Christie's) $760

A Bohemian engraved and
stained ruby goblet, circa
1860, 23cm. high.
(Christie's) $792

One of a set of six large
Vedar goblets with cylindrical
stems and hemispherical bowls,
8in. high. (Christie's)
$1,510

Early 18th century German
engraved double bowled
goblet, 18.5cm. high.
(Christie's) $665

A Netherlands or Rhenish
roemer, the egg-shaped bowl
and hollow stem applied
with irregular prunts,
15.5cm. high. (Phillips)
$246

A semi-polychrome enamelled
opaque twist goblet with ogee
bowl, circa 1775, 17.5cm.
high. (Christie's) $2,217

A N. Bohemian (Haida)
engraved amber flash goblet
and cover, perhaps by F.
Egermann Jnr., circa 1845,
44.5cm. high. (Christie's)
$4,118

A Wiener Werkstatte glass
goblet, the design attributed
to Dagobert Peche, 8.4cm.
high. (Phillips) $316

A 17th century Facon-De-
Venise serpent stemmed
goblet, Venice or Netherlands,
31cm. high. (Christie's)
$2,534

GOBLETS

Late 17th century Netherlands diamond engraved goblet, 14.5cm. high. (Christie's) $2,217

A Bohemian dated green and enamelled goblet and cover, the fluted bowl decorated in silver, 1841, 25.5cm. high. (Christie's) $1,584

A Bohemian engraved ruby and clear glass goblet in the manner of Karl Pfohl, circa 1855, 22cm. high. (Christie's) $1,029

A James Powell flower-form goblet, milky vaseline-colored glass, 30.5cm. high. (Christie's) $1,404

One of a pair of champagne coupes, by Hans Christiansen, 17cm. high. (Christie's) $1,575

Late 17th century Facon-De-Venise diamond engraved serpent stemmed goblet, 18cm. high. (Christie's) $871

A Silesian mercantile goblet and cover perhaps for the Dutch market, circa 1745, 27cm. high. (Christie's) $6,652

One of a set of six Tiffany 'Favrile' champagne coupes, 15cm. high. (Christie's) $2,359

A Potsdam armorial goblet and cover, circa 1720, 41cm. high. (Christie's) $1,029

JUGS

Glossy Burmese molded
cream pitcher, Boston &
Sandwich Glass Co., 1885,
3¼in. high. (Robt. W.
Skinner Inc.) $350

Smith Bros. enamel decorated
creamer, Mass., circa 1890,
3.3/8in. high. (Robt. W.
Skinner Inc.) $150

A cut glass tapering claret
jug with domed hinged
cover, 8¾in. high.
(Christie's) $166

A Bohemian dated enamelled
jug with applied loop handle
1601, 15cm. high. (Christie's)
$2,851

An oviform water jug with
applied scroll handle, 6½in.
high. (Christie's) $53

A 16th/17th century Spanish
serving vessel of green tint,
25.5cm. high. (Christie's)
$475

Crown Milano enamel decorated cream pitcher, Mt.
Washington Glass Co., circa
1893, 4¼in. high. (Robt. W.
Skinner Inc.) $450

A Victorian silver mounted
cut glass claret jug, by Hirons,
Plante & Co., Birmingham,
1866, 12in. high.
(Christie's) $1,584

A Victorian plain bellied glass
claret jug, by M. G., London,
1883, 7¼in. high. (Christie's)
$576

Wheeling peach blow drape pattern pitcher, Hobbs, Brockunier & Co., circa 1886, 4½in. high. (Robt. W. Skinner Inc.) $325

An enamelled glass jug with stopper, by Galle, decorated with enamelled hearts and a dwarf playing a violin, 20cm. high. (Christie's) $633

A Victorian silver mounted dimple glass claret jug, London, 1894, 6¾in. high. (Christie's) $269

Late Victorian cut glass claret jug, by John Round, Sheffield, 1898, 10in. high. (Woolley & Wallis) $633

An oviform wrythen-molded cream jug, 3½in. high, and another with globular body. (Christie's) $89

A 17th/18th century Spanish amethyst jug, 22.5cm. high. (Christie's) $316

Threaded art glass pitcher, tinted in cranberry and amber, circa 1890, 8½in. high. (Robt. W. Skinner Inc.) $225

A diamond quilted satin glass creamer, probably England, circa 1880, 3¾in. high. (Robt. W. Skinner Inc.) $250

An amberina miniature cream pitcher, New England Glass Co., Mass., circa 1880, 2½in. high. (Robt. W. Skinner Inc.) $225

MISCELLANEOUS

A Lalique plafonnier, the circular bowl in clear and satin finished glass molded with bands of fan motifs, 37.4cm. diam. (Christie's) $1,569

A Lalique frosted glass figure on bronze base, Suzanne, 23cm. high without base. (Christie's) $6,019

A Lalique press-papier in clear and satin-finished glass molded as a reclining Indian sacred bull, 5.2cm. high. (Christie's) $712

Early 19th century glass and ormolu table centerpiece of eight pieces. (Hobbs & Chambers) $633

One of a pair of early 20th century prairie school-style leaded glass windows, 58in. high, 18in. wide. (Robt. W. Skinner Inc.) $375

Two plate glass Royal Warrant Holder's display signs, bearing the coat of arms of H.M. Queen Alexandra, 18½ x 18in. (Christie's) $393

'Cote d'Azur Pullman Express' a Lalique figure, the clear satin finished glass molded as a naked maiden, 16.8cm. high. (Christie's) $4,404

A large Daum cameo glass hanging lampshade of shallow domed form, 46cm. diam., signed. (Phillips) $3,024

A 19th century Continental soda glass lace maker's lamp, of baluster form, 22cm. high. (Phillips) $293

A Colin Reid cast glass sculptural form, 37cm. high. (Christie's) $3,366

Pair of 19th century cut glass lustres, 11½in. high. (Du Mouchelles) $700

A cut glass cruet in the form of an open tourer motor car, 9in. long. (Christie's) $147

A Salviati glass sculpture designed by Livio Seguso, 1960, 61.5cm. high. (Christie's) $629

A 19th century Chinese painting on glass with a group of richly clad children playing with flowers, one with a model goldfish, 28½in. wide. (Christie's) $991

One of two early 20th century prairie school-style leaded glass windows, 20½ x 53½in., and five smaller, 18 x 18¾in. (Robt. W. Skinner Inc.) $1,100

One of a set of six wine glass coolers. (Worsfolds) $107

A late 19th century leaded stained and colored glass window, signed W. J. McPherson, Tremont St., Boston, Mass. (Robt. W. Skinner Inc.) $800

A cameo glass urn, inscribed Le Verre Francais, 11½in. high. (Christie's) $767

A Kaziun poinsettia paperweight, Mass., 2¼in. diam.
(Robt. W. Skinner Inc.)
$1,600

A St. Louis colored ground
pom-pom weight, set on a
pink cushion with swirling
white threads, 6.9cm. diam.
(Christie's) $1,267

A St. Louis signed and dated
concentric millefiori mushroom weight, 8cm. diam.
(Christie's) $4,118

A St. Louis faceted upright
bouquet weight, 5.8cm.
diam. (Christie's)
$269

A Baccarat snake weight,
the pink reptile with green
spine markings, 7.9cm. diam.
(Christie's) $4,752

A Kaziun Morning Glory
paperweight, Mass., 2.1/16in.
diam. (Robt. W. Skinner Inc.)
$1,000

A St. Louis fuchsia weight,
the flower resting on a cushion
of white spiral latticinio thread,
8cm. diam. (Christie's)
$2,851

A Clichy initialled 'barber's
pole' concentric millefiori
weight, 6.8cm. diam.
(Christie's) $1,584

Mid 19th century Sandwich
cherry paperweight, probably
by Nicholas Lutz, 2.15/16in.
diam. (Robt. W. Skinner Inc.)
$700

PAPERWEIGHTS

A Clichy swirl weight with alternate pink and white staves radiating from a central red, white and green cane, 5.5cm. diam. (Christie's) $760

A Clichy pink-ground patterned millefiori weight, 8.3cm. diam. (Christie's) $950

A Kaziun pansy paperweight, Mass., signed with gold K on bottom, 2.1/8in. diam. (Robt. W. Skinner Inc.) $750

A Baccarat blue and white flower weight on a star-cut base, 6.7cm. diam. (Christie's) $554

A Kaziun snake paperweight, Mass., 1940's, signed with gold K on bottom, 2.5/16in. diam. (Robt. W. Skinner Inc.) $1,200

A Baccarat garlanded butterfly weight, the insect with purple body, blue eyes and marbleized wings, 8cm. diam. (Christie's) $2,217

A Clichy 'Sodden Snow' ground concentric spaced millefiori weight, 9cm. diam. (Christie's) $348

A St. Louis blue dahlia weight on a cushion of white spiral latticinio thread, 7.7cm. diam. (Christie's) $918

A Baccarat mushroom weight on a star-cut base, 8cm. diam. (Christie's) $792

A St. Louis three-dimensional
fuschia weight, 7cm. diam.
(Christie's) $1,584

A Baccarat 'thousand-
petalled' rose weight, 7cm.
diam. (Christie's)
$3,484

A Kaziun pedestal rose,
Mass., signed with gold K
on bottom, 2in. high. (Robt.
W. Skinner Inc.) $500

A Baccarat close millefiori
mushroom weight on a
star-cut base, 8cm. diam.
(Christie's) $475

A St. Louis faceted upright
bouquet weight, 6.5cm.
diam. (Christie's)
$1,346

A Clichy blue-ground
patterned millefiori weight
on a translucent cobalt blue
ground, 8cm. diam.
(Christie's) $633

A Baccarat yellow and red
flower weight, 6.5cm.
diam. (Christie's)
$2,217

A Baccarat dated scattered
millefiori weight, 7.7cm.
diam. (Christie's)
$1,029

A Baccarat double-clematis
weight on a star-cut base,
6.5cm. diam. (Christie's)
$633

SCENT BOTTLES

Jade glass ovoid perfume flask and stopper, the molded body decorated with fish, 7in. high. (Peter Wilson) $331

A Spode globular table scent bottle and stopper, circa 1820, 8.5cm. high. (Christie's) $406

An Apsley Pellatt emerald green cut glass scent bottle and stopper, circa 1825, 14cm. high. (Christie's) $316

A large Victorian porcelain scent bottle of circular shape, by Sampson Mordan, 1885, 5.8cm. diam. (Phillips) $256

A London or South Staffordshire scent bottle molded as The Tyrolean Dancers, circa 1770, 3½in. high. (Christie's) $1,859

An Orrefors perfume bottle and stopper, designed by E. Hald, engraved H 193 24 B9, 15cm. high. (Christie's) $633

Mid 18th century Venetian lattimo scent bottle of flattened tear-drop form, 10cm. high. (Christie's) $475

Galle cameo glass perfume bottle and mushroom stopper, 4½in. wide, 3¾in. high. (Capes, Dunn & Co.) $739

A Galle flask-shaped scent bottle, the neck with a gilt band, rim chip, 12.5cm. high. (Christie's) $570

TUMBLERS

A plated amberina tumbler, New Bedford Glass Co., Mass., circa 1886, 3¾in. high. (Robt. W. Skinner Inc.) $850

Late 16th century enamelled armorial 'Stangenglas', S. German or Hall, 26cm. high. (Christie's) $1,900

A Bohemian engraved cylindrical tumbler, circa 1825, 10cm. high. (Christie's) $760

A Bohemian 'Zwischengoldglas' flared tumbler, circa 1730, 9cm. high. (Christie's) $950

A tumbler, 9cm. high, together with a pair of cylindrical mugs with loop handles, 6cm. high. '(Phillips) $308

A Bohemian cut glass coin tumbler, circa 1830, 12.5cm. high. (Christie's) $538

Green opaque art glass tumbler, New England Glass Co., Mass., 1887, 3.7/8in. high. (Robt. W. Skinner Inc.) $450

A German enamelled 'Stangenglas' for Augustus Sudoflen, Saxony or Bohemia, 1658, 23cm. high. (Christie's) $3,960

A plated amberina tumbler, New Bedford Glass Co., Mass., circa 1886, 3¾in. high. (Robt. W. Skinner Inc.) $1,000

A Viennese transparent enamelled topographical 'ranftbecher' attributed to Anton Kothgasser, circa 1830, 12cm. high. (Christie's) $7,128

A German 'Reichsadler' humpen of greenish-gray tint, Bohemia, dated 1601, 28.5cm. high. (Christie's) $12,672

A Viennese transparent enamelled 'ranftbecher', the body painted with three playing-cards from a Tarot pack, circa 1830, 11cm. high. (Christie's) $7,603

A peachblow agata tumbler, New England Glass Co., Mass., circa 1887, 3.5/8in. high. (Robt. W. Skinner Inc.) $475

A Viennese gold-ground enamelled 'ranftbecher', attributed to Anton Kothgasser, circa 1830, 11cm. high. (Christie's) $6,652

A German enamelled 'Reichsadler' humpen of greenish metal, dated 1678, Bohemia, 28cm. high. (Christie's) $2,851

A Viennese transparent enamelled topographical tumbler, attributed to G. Samuel Mohn, 1815-20, 9cm. high. (Christie's) $3,484

Late 16th century enamelled armorial 'Stangenglas', S. German or Hall, 27.5cm. high. (Christie's) $1,900

A N. Bohemian transparent enamelled armorial tumbler, circa 1835, 12cm. high. (Christie's) $1,900

A Galle cameo glass vase of
flared cylindrical shape,
31.5cm. high, signed with
sinuous cameo 'Galle'.
(Phillips) $4,032

'Camargue', a Lalique frosted
glass vase, molded with
horses in amber stained
cartouches, 28.5cm. high.
(Christie's) $4,561

A Le Verre Francais overlay
and acid etched vase, the
white and amber mottled
glass decorated with amethyst
stylized tulips, 39.5cm. high.
(Christie's) $314

A Sabino blue opalescent
glass elongated vase, 29.2cm.
high. (Christie's) $393

An 18th century Spanish
four-handled vase of transparent greenish tint, 22cm.
high, and another, 21cm.
high. (Christie's)
$285

Lalique smoky-gray flared
vase, cobweb design in
relief, 9½in. high. (Capes,
Dunn & Co.)
$1,595

A Vallerysthal enamelled
and acid etched vase,
24.9cm. high. (Christie's)
$629

Early 20th century cut glass
flower center, America,
9.1/8in. high. (Robt. W.
Skinner Inc.) $800

An artistic Galle 'verrerie
parlante' vase, engraved
Galle expos 1900, 41.5cm.
high. (Christie's)
$75,504

VASES

A tall Le Verre Francais over-lay acid etched vase, the milky-white and yellow mottled glass overlaid with mottled green, brown and orange glass, 48cm. high. (Christie's) $629

A Lalique baluster vase, the clear satin finished glass molded with bands of roses with blue staining, 23.6cm. high. (Christie's) $660

A Galle double overlay carved and acid etched land-scape vase, the yellow glass overlaid with amethyst trees, 32cm. high. (Christie's) $3,932

'Chamois', an amber Lalique vase, the green stained clear and satin finished glass molded with stylized antelopes, 12cm. high. (Christie's) $1,101

A French glass vase of elliptical section, 24.5cm. high, stamped with poincon and maker's mark JM in lozenge. (Phillips) $547

A Russian cameo glass vase, the milky-white martele glass overlaid with amber stylized leaves, 17cm. high. (Christie's) $1,179

A Galle carved and acid-etched vase, the amber glass overlaid with green oak leaves and acorns, 40cm. high. (Christie's) $1,415

'Soucis', a Lalique blue opalescent glass vase in clear and satin finished glass, 17.2cm. high. (Christie's) $826

A Nuutajarvi Notsjo vase, designed by Gunnel Nyman, 38.8cm. high. (Christie's) $503

A Galle acid etched and
enamelled soli-fleur glass
vase, the cylindrical body
with ribbed and splayed
base, 31.6cm. high.
(Christie's) $1,487

A Galle cameo vase with
carved and acid etched decoration of a lakeside scene,
the yellow glass overlaid
with brown, 26.5cm. high.
(Christie's) $2,478

A tall Galle double overlay
landscape vase, the matt pale
white ground overlaid in
brown, green and amber
polished glass with daffodils,
41.8cm. high. (Christie's)
$2,478

A vase attributed to Barovier,
of flattened urn shape,
29.1cm. high. (Christie's)
$1,569

An Aureliano Toso vase of
asymmetric double-gourd
shape, clear glass with thin
white latticinio stripes,
27.4cm. high. (Christie's)
$2,217

A Galle blowout vase with
flowering clematis in shaded
purple on a yellow ground,
25.5cm. high. (Christie's)
$5,287

A Daum cameo vase, the
matt yellow, amethyst and
green ground overlaid in
shaded claret-colored glass,
26.3cm. high. (Christie's)
$4,626

A Daum enamelled and acid
etched vase of rounded cube
form, enamelled in white,
black and gray, with black-
birds in winter landscape,
15.2cm. diam. (Christie's)
$2,534

A tall Daum cameo vase with
bulbous neck, with Cross of
Lorraine, 50.2cm. high.
(Christie's) $1,652

VASES

A Daum cameo vase of tall cylindrical shape with slightly everted rim and compressed globular base, 29.1cm. high. (Christie's) $4,461

A green Lalique vase, Epicea, with molded overall decoration of palm fronds, 23.5cm. high. (Christie's) $3,484

A Galle acid etched and enamelled vase with cylindrical body and spreading base, 34.9cm. high. (Christie's) $991

A Schneider vase, the mottled orange, yellow and blue glass blown through a wrought-iron mount, 29.3cm. high. (Christie's) $428

'Fountainebleu', a Lalique blue glass vase, the body molded with fruit-laden trailing vines, 17.4cm. high. (Christie's) $1,487

A Venini 'vetro a file' vase. the russet colored glass internally decorated with gray veining inlaid with purple rafia. (Christie's) $1,074

A Galle triple cameo fire-polished vase, waisted and flaring cylindrical shape, 49.1cm. high. (Christie's) $3,304

A handkerchief vase, attributed to Venini, cased glass with alternating vertical stripes in yellow and purple latticinio, 14.7cm. high. (Christie's) $578

A Tiffany Jack-in-the-Pulpit vase, deep purple and gold iridescent glass, 33cm. high. (Christie's) $3,139

VASES

A Daum vase with cameo-cut and enamel painted winter landscape on acid treated matt pale amber ground, 25cm. high. (Christie's) $1,504

A Barovier patchwork vase, clear and amber-colored glass outlined in a darker amber, 18cm. high. (Christie's) $2,534

A Galle double overlay carved and acid etched vase, the light green glass overlaid with ferns in shades of green and light brown, 41cm. high. (Christie's) $2,376

A Lalique blue opalescent vase, Ceylan, the satin-finished glass molded with band of budgerigars, 24.2cm. high. (Christie's) $1,742

A Galle vase, pale amber-colored glass with gold foil inclusions overlaid with white and blue, 18.5cm. high. (Christie's) $3,168

An Orrefors vase, wheel-engraved in neo-classical style, etched signature Orrefors 1930 S Gate 238 E.W., 17.5cm. high. (Christie's) $601

A Galle marqueterie-sur-verre vase of cylindrical shape, engraved Galle etude, circa 1895, 19.5cm. high. (Christie's) $15,840

A small Daum carved and acid etched vase of boat shape, engraved signature Daum Nancy with the Cross of Lorraine, 10.5cm. high. (Christie's) $3,801

A Daum internally decorated engraved and applied glass vase of slender shouldered form and bulbous flaring neck, 35cm. high. (Christie's) $79,200

VASES

A Galle internally decorated vase, the amber-colored glass decorated with dark red streaks, engraved Cristallerie de Galle, 20cm. high. (Christie's) $3,168

A D'Argental cameo bowl with trefoil rim, overlaid in claret-coloured glass with water-lily and lily-pad on a pond against a pale amber ground, 16cm. diam. (Christie's) $950

A Galle carved and fire-polished vase, the glass shading from purple to milky white and amber with silver foil inclusions, 32.5cm. high. (Christie's) $9,504

A Galle etched and double overlay glass vase, the aquamarine glass overlaid in white and brown and etched with penguins, 20.3cm. high. (Christie's) $17,424

A Galle double overlay martele carved and acid etched vase of goblet shape, 15.5cm. high. (Christie's) $12,672

A Cenedese vase, milky glass partly overlaid with white, the decoration and rim in deep amethyst-colored glass, 34cm. high. (Christie's) $1,188

'Roses de France', a Galle internally decorated, applied martele and overlay glass vase of pear shape, 19.2cm. high. (Christie's) $76,032

A Lalique amber oviform vase, Gros Scarabees, engraved signature R. Lalique, France, No. 892, 29.4cm. high. (Christie's) $9,504

A clear glass vase, the cylindrical shape pulled out on one side to form two oval prunts, engraved Vistosi 1970, 28.5cm. high (Christie's) $1,029

VASES

A tall Galle double overlay landscape baluster vase with everted rim and circular base, 45.9cm. high. (Christie's) $6,606

A Muller carved vase, the clear and satin finished glass deeply carved with a reclining tiger, 18.5cm. high. (Christie's) $597

A Gabriel Argy-Rousseau tall pate-de-verre vase, 26cm. high. (Christie's)
$7,078

Royal Flemish enamel decorated glass vase, Mt. Washington Glass Co., circa 1885, 6.7/8in. high. (Robt. W. Skinner Inc.) $1,100

A Loetz iridescent glass vase, the silvery-purple and green glass with tall tapering neck, 35.8cm. high. (Christie's) $1,258

A Galle double overlay carved blowout vase, the amber glass overlaid with fruiting vines, 27.5cm. high. (Christie's)
$7,078

A tall Legras acid etched vase, the milky-white and blue glass with trapped air inclusions, 41cm. high. (Christie's)
$629

An Orrefors vase, designed by Ingeborg Lunam, shaped like a giant bubble, 40cm. high. (Christie's) $786

A Loetz vase, the textured clear glass with gold iridescence on an amber ground, 20cm. high. (Christie's) $220

A Galle cameo vase, the matt amber ground overlaid in shaded claret-colored glass, 45.5cm. high. (Christie's) $5,033

'Palissy', a Lalique green tinted vase, the satin finished glass molded with snail shells, 15.8cm. high. (Christie's) $251

A G. Argy-Rousseau pate-de-verre vase, numbered 16485, 26.5cm. high. (Christie's) $7,550

A Galle cameo glass moon-shaped vase, 7in. high. (Reeds Rains) $1,440

One of a pair of Moser vases, the clear and amethyst tinted glass carved and engraved with flowers, 26.5cm. high. (Christie's) $471

Burmese satin finish enamel decorated vase, Mt. Washington Glass Co., Mass., circa 1890, 4¾in. high. (Robt. W. Skinner Inc.) $325

A Galle carved acid etched and fire-polished vase, 23.5cm. high. (Christie's) $2,831

'Gui', a Lalique vase, the clear satin finished glass with turquoise staining molded with branches of mistletoe, 17.2cm. high. (Christie's) $220

Late 17th/early 18th century Facon-De-Venise filigree vase, 20.5cm. high. (Christie's) $823

WINE GLASSES

One of a pair of ogee shaped wine glasses, 5¼in. high. (Christie's) $191

An opaque twist wine glass, the ogee bowl on double series stem and plain foot, 6¼in. high. (Christie's) $627

A facet stem wine glass of Jacobite significance, 5¾in. high. (Christie's) $152

Late 17th century Bohemian Facon De Venise wine goblet, 16.5cm. high. (Phillips) $800

A molded pedestal stemmed champagne glass with ogee bowl, circa 1750, 16cm. high. (Christie's) $475

An air-twist wine glass, 5¼in. high, and another 6in. high. (Christie's) $196

A cut cased wine glass, by E. Bakalowits, Vienna, 8in. high, circa 1908. (Giles Haywood) $1,440

An engraved opaque twist cordial glass, the funnel bowl with stylized hatched and foliate border, circa 1765, 16.5cm. high. (Christie's) $443

A mercury twist cordial glass of Jacobite significance and drawn trumpet shape, circa 1750, 17cm. high. (Christie's) $506

WINE GLASSES

An opaque twist wine glass with ogee bowl, 5¼in. high, and another of similar type. (Christie's) $251

A wine glass, the opaque twist stem with a pair of six-ply spiral bands outside lace twist, 13.5cm. high. (Phillips) $492

An opaque twist wine glass, the ogee bowl with hammered flute to the lower part on double series stem, 6¼in. high. (Christie's) $233

An armorial wine glass of drawn trumpet shape, circa 1740, 18cm. high. (Christie's) $2,217

A dark green tinted wine glass with ribbed cup-shaped bowl, circa 1765, 12.5cm. high. (Christie's)$950

An opaque twist deceptive cordial glass, the ogee bowl on a double-series stem and conical foot, circa 1765, 17.5cm. high. (Christie's) $1,504

The 'Breadalbane' Amen glass, the bowl engraved in diamond point, 1745-50, 20cm. high. (Christie's) $41,184

One of a set of five ogee shaped drinking glasses, 6in. high. (Christie's) $590

Mid 18th century mercury twist Jacobite cordial glass with bucket bowl, 17cm. high. (Christie's) $871

A Continental jewelled gold
and enamel snuff box,
unmarked, 3.1/8in. long.
(Christie's)
$49,572

Late 19th century Australian
gold inkstand formed as a
possum climbing over a tree
trunk, unmarked, 12in. long
overall, 41oz. (Christie's)
$14,045

A French gold mounted
marquetry snuff box by
Alexandre Leferre, Paris,
circa 1840, 3¼in. long.
(Christie's)
$13,219

An early 19th century Swiss
gold musical fob seal, maker's
initials JJ.H. (Christie's)
$1,652

A gold and enamel mounted
nephrite vinaigrette, probably 19th century, 3¼in.
high. (Christie's) $1,321

A George II small shaped
oblong gold patch box
with mirrored interior,
circa 1740, 2in. long.
(Christie's) $991

An Omar Ramsden 9kt. beaten
gold cigarette case with cut
steel relief decoration, gold
mark for 1922, 11.3 x 8.8cm.
(Christie's) $950

A two-color gold and
amethyst table seal, the
citrine matrix with crest
and initials, circa 1830,
2¾in. high. (Christie's)
$1,900

A Louis XVI vari-colored
gold automaton musical
snuff box, the lady tight-
rope walker on the cover
dances to the music, circa
1780, 3.1/8in. long.
(Christie's)
$99,144

GOLD

A Louis XV rectangular gold and mother-of-pearl snuff box, the panels engraved in the manner of J. B. Oudry, Paris, 1745/6, 3¼in. long. (Christie's) $14,871

A gold fob seal, the cornelian base inscribed 'Registrar of Colonial Slaves', circa 1820, small chip. (Christie's) $693

An oblong gold mounted Cairngorm snuff box, circa 1820, possibly Scottish, in slip case, 2¾in. long. (Christie's) $5,618

18kt. gold purse, 'Buccellate', Italy, with diamond set thumbpiece, 131gr. (Robt. W. Skinner Inc.) $1,700

A 19th century large shaped oblong gold vinaigrette, the lid set with malachite, 1.7/8in. long. (Christie's) $1,074

A 19th century miniature gold mounted mother-of-pearl bureau, in fitted case, 5.1/8in. high. (Christie's) $4,957

A Swiss oval gold and enamel snuff box, by J. Georges Remond & Compagnie, the painting on cover by Adam f., circa 1790-1800, 3½in. long. (Christie's) $9,914

A George III small enamelled gold scent bottle, in fitted leather case, circa 1775, 2in. high. (Christie's) $3,139

A gold mounted agate scent bottle case, containing two 18th century scent bottles, the case 19th century, 2¾in. high. (Christie's) $2,974

A small gold and enamel mounted two-handled jasper cup with pierced scroll handles, circa 1625, with later French control mark, 3½in. diam. (Christie's)$5,977

A gold, turquoise and diamond lady's mesh evening purse, 10.5cm. across, stamped 9kt., import marks for London 1905. (Phillips) $604

A George III oval gold snuff box, by Elias Russell, London, 1777, 2.7/8in. long. (Christie's) $10,224

A gold and enamel musical watch key, the music played on single comb. (Christie's) $2,044

A circular gold mounted micro-mosaic box, 2.7/8in. diam. (Christie's) $14,045

A gold mounted bloodstone table seal, the stem formed as a hand, 1830, 3.5/8in. high. (Christie's) $1,982

A gold mounted amethystine quartz snuff box, modelled as the head of a gryphon, 2.1/8in. long. (Christie's) $5,505

A George II gold mounted etui, circa 1750, 3¾in. high. (Christie's) $3,139

An Irish circular gold Freedom Box, by Abraham Tuppy, Dublin, 1780, 2½in. diam. (Christie's) $5,033

A Swiss shallow octagonal gold and enamel snuff box, by Francois Joanin, with Russian control marks, Geneva, circa 1820, 3½in. long. (Christie's) $4,719

An archaic gold crescent-shaped ornament, Sino-Siberian/Warring States, 21.6cm. wide. (Christie's) $34,606

A Swiss octagonal gold and enamel snuff box, circa 1820, with incuse maker's initials H?, in fitted case, 3in. long. (Christie's) $3,460

A 19th century Swiss gold musical seal with chased foliage handle. (Christie's) $1,573

An archaic gold arch-shaped ornament with repousse decoration, Warring States, 6.5cm. wide. (Christie's) $2,831

A 17th century gold bar, salvaged from the Santa Margarita, 9in. long, 824.5 grams. (Christie's) $10,740

A George III oblong engine turned gold snuff box, by A. J. Strachan, London, 1808, 18kt., 3¼in. long. (Christie's) $7,865

Three gold stone set keys formed respectively as the head of a hound, fox and unicorn. (Christie's) $943

A George I oblong gold snuff box, circa 1715, 3.1/8in. long. (Christie's) $22,022

HATS

A top hat of brown felt, with black ribbon, by A. Giessen, Delft, circa 1870. (Christie's) $688

A boy's cap of black moleskin with peak of patent leather, circa 1845. (Christie's) $114

A top hat of black beaver, with black silk ribbon, 7in. high, circa 1840. (Christie's) $360

A mourning bonnet of black crepe, circa 1830. (Christie's) $163

A top hat of gray beaver, possibly 1829, labelled M. Strieken, 8in. high. (Christie's) $1,065

A bonnet of black satin trimmed with a large bow and rouleaux, circa 1830. (Christie's) $360

A top hat of gray beaver with narrow ribbon of cream ribbed silk, 5½in. high, circa 1830. (Christie's) $426

A pearl gray bowler hat, made in Italy by Borsalino for Cecil, 112 rue de Richelieu, circa 1800, together with two others and a bowler. (Christie's) $65

A top hat of gray beaver, 7½in. high, circa 1830. (Christie's) $426

A 17th century rhinoceros horn libation cup, 16cm. wide. (Christie's) $876

A 16th/17th century rhinoceros horn libation cup, 16cm. wide. (Christie's) $3,460

A 17th century rhinoceros horn libation cup carved as a half-open hibiscus flower, 14.7cm. wide. (Christie's) $2,044

A 17th century rhinoceros horn libation cup, the handle pierced and carved as groups of chilong, 17cm. wide. (Christie's) $8,651

Part of a set of twelve Victorian silver mounted horn beakers, maker's initials H.W.D., London, 1877, together with a horn claret jug, 11½in. high. (Christie's) $1,346

A 17th/18th century rhinoceros horn libation cup with pierced pine handle, 13cm. wide. (Christie's) $4,089

A 17th century rhinoceros horn libation cup, 18.5cm. diam., wood stand. (Christie's) $3,146

A 17th/18th century rhinoceros horn libation cup, showing a scene from 'The Romance of the Western Chamber', 13cm. wide. (Christie's) $1,299

A 17th/18th century rhinoceros horn libation cup with pierced pine-trunk handle, 16.7cm. wide. (Christie's) $4,404

INROS

Late 18th century four-case
inro, fundame compartments,
signed Jokasai, with red agate
ojime attached. (Christie's)
$4,719

A 19th century bamboo
Kodansu inro, signed Toyo
and Kao, with a bone ojime
attached. (Christie's)
$2,516

A 19th century five-case
inro, signed Yoyusai, and
Kao. (Christie's)
$4,719

Early 19th century four-
case Nashiji inro, unsigned.
(Christie's) $503

Late 19th century boxwood
three-case inro formed as a
terrapin, signed Chuichi.
(Christie's) $3,146

A 19th century four-case
Roiro inro with fundame
compartments, signed Koma
Kyuhaku saku. (Christie's)
$4,719

A 19th century five-case
Roiro inro, fundame com-
partments, with an attached
coral ojime. (Christie's)
$2,359

Early 19th century three-case
inro decorated in hiramakie,
kirikane and heidatsu with a
mountainous landscape.
(Christie's) $2,359

A 19th century four-case
Kinji inro, signed Kakosai,
with a spherical Kinji ojime.
(Christie's) $4,719

An 18th/19th century five-case Somada inro with compartments in nashiji, unsigned. (Christie's) $2,359

A 19th century small Roiro two-case inro of fluted fan-shaped form, unsigned. (Christie's) $755

A 19th century four-case inro with a spherical red glass ojime and a manju netsuke. (Christie's) $6,292

Early 19th century five-case Fundame inro, signed Hirose Nagaharu. (Christie's) $786

Early 19th century four-case inro, signed Toju, with a soft metal mokume ojime attached. (Christie's) $4,719

A 19th century five-case Kinji inro, signed Kakosai Shozan, with red tsubo seal and attached agate ojime. (Christie's) $4,404

A 19th century five-case inro, signed Kajikawa saku, with an ojime and a wood manju netsuke. (Christie's) $6,292

A seven-case inro with gyobu nashiji compartments, unsigned, with coral ojime attached. (Christie's) $2,359

A 19th century three-case Kamakura-Bori inro with a glass ojime and a manju netsuke. (Christie's) $4,719

A 17th/18th century three-case Samegawa-Togidashi inro, unsigned, with a spherical shell ojime attached. (Christie's) $865

Early 19th century four-case kinji inro, nashiji interiors, signed Shokosai. (Christie's) $1,718

A 19th century four-case Roiro inro, signed with two red lacquer seals Shiomi Masanari, and with a glass ojime. (Christie's) $3,932

A four-case kinji inro, signed Kakosai Teimin, with hardstone ojime and ivory manju netsuke, signed Shibayama. (Christie's) $1,483

A 19th century three-case inro with nashiji compartments, unsigned. (Christie's) $1,101

Late 18th/early 19th century five-case roironuri inro, signed Kajikawa saku. (Christie's) $1,327

Early 19th century four-case kinji inro decorated in gold, red and black hiramakie and takamakie, signed Kajikawa. (Christie's) $1,483

A 19th century three-case Roiro inro, signed Jokasai, with a coral ojime attached. (Christie's) $5,505

Late 19th century three-case yoroigata inro, modelled as an o-yoroi set up on an armor box. (Christie's) $7,497

A mid 19th century brass astronomical refracting telescope, signed Carpenter & Westley, London, 95cm. long. (Phillips) $2,635

A large brass equatorial Universal dial, Indian, possibly Jaipur, probably 19th century, 29in. long. (Christie's) $1,760

A 19th century lacquered brass astronomical refracting telescope, signed Baker, London, 79cm. long. (Phillips) $744

An early 19th century brass single draw monocular, signed Berge, London late Ramsden, with ivory body tube, 10cm. long, in case. (Phillips) $124

A lacquered brass precision balance, the beam stamped To Weigh/To Grain, No. 5962, with electrical attachments in a glazed mahogany case, 14¾in. wide. (Christie's) $278

Pajot's midwifery forceps, signed Charriere a Paris, late 19th century, 34cm. long. (Christie's) $286

An early 19th century pocket drawing instrument set, in silver mounted shagreen case, 13cm. long. (Phillips) $310

A Regency mahogany new terrestrial globe, signed by Cruchley, 20in. diam., 47in. high. (Christie's) $7,444

An early 18th century ivory and brass folding 12in. rule, together with an 8in. boxwood rule and a shaped 3in. rule. (Phillips) $108

An early 19th century brass astronomical refracting achromatic telescope, signed Dollond, London, 107cm. long. (Phillips) $2,790

A late 18th century brass ellipsograph, signed J. & W. Watkins, London, in T-shaped mahogany case. (Phillips)　$728

A 19th century anodized brass Troughton & Simms double frame sextant, the index arm with 8in. radius. (Phillips)　$806

A mid 19th century 12in. celestial globe, with printed coloured and varnished paper gauze, Wyld Globe of the Heavens .. published by James Wyld, Charing Cross East 1869. (Phillips)　$1,007

Early 19th century Nuremburg microscope, the base impressed I M, 33cm. high. (Christie's)　$880

A 16th/17th century Italian ship's drycard compass, 11cm. diam. (Phillips)　$6,200

A 19th century brass three-draw monocular, signed Dollond, with ivory body tube, 10.5cm. long, in case. (Phillips)　$248

A brass Brewster's law apparatus to produce polarized light, signed Deleuil a Paris, circa 1850, 30.5cm. high. (Christie's)　$825

A late 18th century lacquered brass Ramsden theodolite, 29cm. high. (Phillips)　$1,007

A 19th century lacquered brass four prism spectroscope, signed John Browning, 32cm. high, in mahogany case. (Phillips) $1,550

A late 19th century 14in. Betts's Portable Terrestrial Globe, by George Philip & Son Ltd. (Phillips) $279

A brass graphometer with case, signed Martin au Temple a Paris, circa 1760, 28cm. diam. (Christie's) $1,760

A mid 19th century miniature terrestrial globe, by Malby & Co., 1½in. diam. (Phillips) $341

Probably 19th century large brass drum microscope, 36cm. high. (Christie's) $220

An American celestial globe on stand, signed Wilson's New Thirteen Inch Celestial globe, by C. Lancaster, N.Y., 1845, 13in. diam. (Christie's) $825

An early 19th century 3in. pocket globe, 'A Correct Globe with the New Discoveries', contained in a simulated fishskin covered case. (Phillips) $1,085

A brass 5in. Gregorian reflecting telescope, signed W. & S. Jones, circa 1810, length of body tube 78.5cm. (Christie's) $1,650

A 19th century gilt brass nocturnal, probably French, 95mm. diam. (Christie's) $880

One of a pair of Regency terrestrial and celestial globes, dated March 1816, 24in. diam., 43in. high.(Christie's) $21,714

An early marine chronometer by John Arnold & Son, with 4½in. circular silvered dial, in mahogany box. (Phillips) $11,600

An early 19th century lacquered brass Culpeper-type compound monocular microscope, signed F. Day, 41cm. high. (Phillips) $1,162

A lacquered brass compound monocular microscope, by Powell & Lealand, 1901, 49cm. high, in case. (Phillips) $4,650

An ivory diptych dial, with the thrush trademark of Hans Troschel, Nuremburg, dated 1649, 4¼in. long. (Christie's) $2,420

An orrery on turned mahogany stand with three scroll feet, French, circa 1810, 53cm. high. (Christie's) $2,420

An 18th century boxwood nocturnal, probably English, 8¼in. long. (Christie's) $1,980

A hydraulic tourniquet on octagonal mahogany base, circa 1830, 54cm. high. (Christie's) $605

A mid 19th century lacquered brass compound monocular microscope, signed Dollond, 38cm. wide. (Phillips) $1,860

Thomas' forceps, with ebony grips, circa 1860, 29.5cm. long. (Christie's) $132

A small 18th century silver perpetual calendar, one volvelle engraved with days of the week, the other with hours of the day and months, 2.5cm. wide. (Phillips) $248

A Malby's 1858 terrestrial globe on a mahogany tripod stand with turned shaft, 40½in. high. (Christie's) $2,711

An ivory diptych magnetic Azimuth dial, signed Fait par Charles Bloud a Dieppe, late 17th century, 70mm. long. (Christie's) $990

Early 19th century French papier-mache ptolemaic armillary sphere, 18½in. high. (Christie's) $2,420

Late 19th century 'Easter Egg' globe, made in Germany for the English market, 14cm. long. (Phillips) $341

An 18th century brass Butterfield dial, signed, 7.8cm. long. (Christie's) $462

An American lacquered brass monocular microscope, signed E. H. & F. H. Tighe, Detroit, circa 1885, length of tube 5in. (Christie's) $605

A brass air pump with bell jar, probably English, circa 1790, 43cm. long including handle. (Christie's) $880

Pair of cast iron armorial andirons with scrolled feet, 19in. high. (Christie's) $440

One of a pair of cast iron hall trees, America, circa 1875, 75in. high. (Robt. W. Skinner Inc.) $700

Early 20th century Art Deco cast and wrought iron parcel gilt pier table, France, 53in. wide. (Robt. W. Skinner Inc.) $950

A set of three polished steel fire-irons with baluster pommels, 36in. long. (Christie's) $1,144

A George III steel and brass basket grate with serpentine front, 32½in. wide. (Christie's) $3,635

Mid 19th century cast iron interior plant stand, America, 43in. high. (Robt. W. Skinner Inc.) $1,900

A molded zinc polychrome tobacconist figure, Wm. Demuth, N.Y., circa 1890, 67½in. high without base. (Robt. W. Skinner Inc.) $11,000

Pair of Federal bell metal andirons, probably New York, 1800-10, 25in. high. (Christie's) $770

A wrought-iron candelabrum with triangular shaped top applied with five pricket candle sconces, 62¼in. high. (Christie's) $369

Victorian polished steel coal scuttle with a lifting flap and shovel. (Lots Road Galleries) $144

A George III polished steel basket grate with railed basket, 33¼in. wide. (Christie's) $5,893

Mid 19th century blackened steel basket grate, 22¼in. wide. (Christie's) $1,570

An iron mounted oak Alms box, the hinged lid with chained loop handle above coin slot, 25cm. high. (Phillips) $748

A George III steel basket grate, 26¾in. wide, 33½in. high. (Christie's) $3,678

An early iron bound oak octagonal Alms box, 12.5cm. high. (Phillips) $374

One of a pair of cast iron foliate andirons, attributed to E. Gimson, circa 1905, 22¼in. high. (Robt. W. Skinner Inc.) $5,500

A fully articulated russet iron model of a crayfish, (ebi), signed Miochin, Edo period, 26cm. long. (Christie's) $1,562

An American 19th century painted iron trade sign, 40in. high, 15in. wide. (Christie's) $2,640

Late 19th century ivory okimono of a seated musician, signed Kyoga, 14.9cm. high. (Christie's) $1,249

Late 19th century sectional ivory carving of four bears, 26.5cm. long. (Christie's) $2,811

One of two late 19th century ivory tusk vases, signed by Kikugawa Jorinsai Masamitsu, one 34cm., the other 31cm. high. (Christie's) $2,499

A Tokyo School ivory group of an old fisherman with a boy on his back and another crouching at his feet, signed Gyokusui, Meiji period, 24cm. high. (Christie's) $3,436

A 19th century French or German ivory group of a medieval woodsman and a court jester, 20cm. high. (Christie's) $7,537

Late 19th century ivory carving of an old woman holding a boy on her back, signed Kozan, 13.8cm. high. (Christie's) $235

Late 19th century ivory group of a farmer with his wife and son, 18cm. wide. (Christie's) $2,655

Late 19th century ivory box and cover carved as Benkei seated on top of the great bell of Miidera, signed Takayuki, 24cm. high. (Christie's) $1,015

Late 19th century sectional ivory okimono of Daikoku, signed Gyokuyu, 13.8cm. high. (Christie's) $624

IVORY

Late 19th century sectional ivory okimono of three apes playing with a biwa, signed Masaaki, 13.5cm. long. (Christie's) $755

Late 19th century English silver mounted ivory tusk box with hinged cover and scroll feet, the mounts London, 1902, 23.8cm. long. (Christie's) $2,343

Late 19th century sectional ivory carving of a drummer, signed Munehisa, 19.5cm. high. (Christie's) $1,562

Late 19th century ivory okimono of a Chinese girl holding a boy up to her chest, another boy standing at her side riding a hobby horse, 11cm. high. (Christie's) $440

Late 19th century ivory okimono of a group of five Kendo fighters in a melee, signed Ikkosai, 8.2cm. high. (Christie's) $1,337

Late 19th century ivory group of a farmer with two small boys. signed Wasui, 21.5cm. high. (Christie's) $1,124

A 19th century French carved ivory tankard, in the Baroque style, 26cm. high.(Christie's) $3,702

A Japanese 19th century carved ivory okimono, 6.3/8in. high. (Robt. W. Skinner Inc.) $850

'Girl with Hoop', an ivory figure carved after a model by F. Preiss, 17.5cm. high. (Christie's) $1,404

IVORY

An early 19th century barley-corn chess set in natural and black stained ivory, king 9.5cm., pawn 4.3cm., in contemporary penwork box. (Phillips) $832

An ivory carving of a scholar reading a manuscript, signed Seiraku, Meiji period, 21cm. high. (Christie's) $624

A mid 19th century Jaques Staunton ivory chess set, stained red and natural, king 10cm., pawn 4.8cm., in carton pierre box. (Phillips) $5,440

An ivory figure of a girl, 'Invocation', carved from a model by D. Chiparus, 24.5cm. high. (Phillips) $1,584

Late 19th century stained ivory okimono style netsuke of Kintoki astride a carp, signed Meisai. (Christie's) $390

A Tokyo School ivory carving of a standing girl, signed Meido, Meiji period, 24.4cm. high. (Christie's) $937

An English pattern chess set, natural and black stained, the white king signed G. Merrifield, Maker, circa 1825, king 8cm., pawn 4cm. (Phillips) $2,720

Late 19th century ivory carving of a fisherman, signed Kyoshu, 24.4cm. high. (Christie's) $781

A Jaques In Statu Quo travelling chess set of large size, the bone pegged pieces approx. 2cm., in sycamore folding board. (Phillips) $576

IVORY

A Lund ivory and red stained chess set, the white king signed Lund, Maker, king 10.5cm. high, pawn 4.2cm., in original fitted leather box. (Phillips) $4,000

A Tokyo School ivory carving of a falconer, signed Korin, Meiji period, 27.5cm. high. (Christie's) $2,343

An ivory 'Washington' chess set, stained red and natural, king 8.5cm., pawn 3.8cm., circa 1880, in tortoiseshell veneered box. (Phillips) $1,312

A Tokyo School ivory carving of an old man reading a book, signed Masaaki, Meiji period, 23.1cm. high. (Christie's) $1,874

An ivory carving of a kneeling girl, a small boy seated by her side, signed Yoshimas, Meiji period, 12.3cm. high. (Christie's) $786

One of a pair of late 19th century ivory tusk vases, one signed Sasada Kanemitsu, 46.2cm. high. (Christie's) $3,436

An early ivory rectangular plaque, Yuan/Ming Dynasty, 9cm. wide. (Christie's) $2,044

Late 19th century ivory okimono style netsuke, signed Zenraku. (Christie's) $624

A Tibetan ivory ritual phallus, possibly 16th century, 23cm. long, and a wood casket, 12.5 x 25cm. (Phillips) $690

A 16th/early 17th century late Ming small flecked grayish-celadon jade model of a recumbent buffalo, 16.5cm. wide, box. (Christie's) $8,651

A pale celadon and white flecked jade bowl, Qing Dynasty, 20.6cm. wide. (Christie's) $943

A brown and gray flecked jade carving of a recumbent horse, Song Dynasty, 5.6cm. wide, wood stand. (Christie's) $346

An archaic black and cream jade cylinder, cong, 3rd/2nd Millenium B.C., 11.2cm. sq. (Christie's) $15,730

An archaic mottled celadon and brown jade blade, Shang/ W. Zhou Dynasty, 17cm. wide. (Christie's) $1,101

A mottled spinach and celadon jade table screen, late Qing Dynasty, 30cm. wide, wood stand. (Christie's) $1,101

A string of thirteen neolithic white calcified jade circular pendant discs, 3rd Millenium B.C., 4 to 3.5cm. diam. (Christie's) $1,730

A brown and celadon jade square cylinder, cong, E. Han Dynasty, 5.7cm. wide, wood stand, fitted box. (Christie's) $550

A jade phoenix rhyton, Yuan Dynasty or earlier, 12.8cm. wide. (Christie's) $1,101

A yellowish-green and gray jade carving of a recumbent horse, possibly Ming Dynasty, 11cm. long. (Christie's) $1,573

An 18th century pale celadon and russet jade gourd-shaped brushwasher, 24.5cm. wide. (Christie's) $4,404

A small russet and caramel jade crouching dog, Song Dynasty, 6.3cm. wide, box, wood stand. (Christie's) $5,662

Pair of dark green jade figures of hawks, Qing Dynasty, 22.5cm. high. (Christie's) $786

An 18th/early 19th century pale celadon jade figure of Guanyin. (Christie's) $2,359

One of a pair of green and grey jade Buddhistic lions, carved as censers with detachable heads, 23cm. high. (Christie's) $2,988

An 18th century pale celadon jade group of a scholar and his attendant looking up at a crane, 12.8cm. high, wood stand. (Christie's) $1,022

A string of twelve neolithic calcified jade discs, from 2.5 to 1.5cm. diam., and an axe-shaped pendant, 2.5cm. long, all 3rd Millenium B.C. (Christie's) $1,337

An apple-green jade pendant of triangular form carved with two boys, 3.5cm. high. (Christie's) $2,044

Three-stone ring with a total of 3¼ct. claw set in white metal. (Peter Wilson) $2,961

Sapphire and diamond ear-clips, 'Yard', the oval sapphires weighing approx. 5kt. (Robt. W. Skinner Inc.) $5,000

Gold stickpin, set with a large realistically rendered gold 'fly'. (Robt. W. Skinner Inc.) $250

Art Deco diamond bow pin, pave-set with 105 diamonds weighing approx. 3.00kt. and highlighted by calibre cut onyx. (Robt. W. Skinner Inc.) $3,600

A gold, diamond and plique-a-jour pendant fashioned as a seagull in flight, 7.5cm. wide, probably French. (Phillips) $576

A Theodor Fahrner enamelled bar brooch, the ends set with coral beads, 5.2cm. long, stamped TF monogram and indistinct 925. (Phillips) $360

An Arts & Crafts brooch, possibly Birmingham Guild of Handicrafts, 4cm. diam. (Phillips) $108

A George Hunt enamelled and gemset locket pendant of oval shape, inside is a lock of hair, 8.5cm. long. (Phillips) $1,008

An enamelled and garnet set 'Gothic' brooch, based on a design by A. W. N. Pugin, 4.5cm. across. (Phillips) $504

One of a pair of 18kt. gold earrings, composed of fluted hoops, 29.6gm. (Robt. W. Skinner Inc.) $400

A gold mounted diamond set trembleuse feather brooch, converting to an aigrette, in fitted case. (Woolley & Wallis) $4,023

An enamelled 'wasp' pendant, holding a baroque pearl, 4.5cm. wide, stamped 900 and Depose, probably Austrian. (Phillips) $345

JEWELRY

A Tiffany & Co. two-color gold, sapphire and moonstone oval brooch, 3.3cm. across. (Phillips) $1,008

A sunray brooch, centering an opal with diamond set cluster and rays, gold set, in Goldsmiths & Silversmiths case. (Woolley & Wallis) $1,490

A Kerr gilded Art Nouveau brooch, 6.5cm. across, stamped with maker's mark, Sterling and 1702. (Phillips) $432

A German 'Egyptianesque' plique-a-jour brooch, formed as a scarab, 11cm. wide. (Phillips) $547

A Liberty & Co. gold sapphire and moonstone pendant, probably designed by A. Gaskin, 5cm. long, 15ct. (Phillips) $547

Antique gold and diamond brooch, French hallmarks, designed as a French poodle. (Robt. W. Skinner Inc.) $1,000

Enamelled diamond ring on an 18kt. gold band, English hallmark. (Robt. W. Skinner Inc.) $800

A silver brooch, stamped Georg Jensen 300 and with London import marks for 1965. (Christie's) $117

14kt. gold and diamond ring, the center oval gold plaque with tiny raised 'fly' encircled in a frame of diamonds. (Robt. W. Skinner Inc.) $850

Cultured pearl and diamond necklace, 'Cartier', a double strand of 86, 9mm. pearls, the diamonds weighing approx. 2.20kt. (Robt. W. Skinner Inc.) $7,000

Art Deco emerald and diamond ring, diamonds weighing a total of approx. 2kt. (Robt. W. Skinner Inc.) $1,100

An Unger Brothers Art Nouveau brooch, 5.5cm. across, stamped 925 Sterling fine. (Phillips) $360

An Arts & Crafts ring with an oval cabochon of green turquoise. (Phillips) $100

An Arts & Crafts pendant, 7cm. long, engraved 1936, with chain. (Phillips) $244

A Van Cleef and Arpels gold and sapphire 'Serti Invisible' ring, stamped with French gold poincon, numbered 16995. (Phillips) $8,352

A pearl, emerald and enamelled pendant, 5.7cm. long. (Phillips) $432

A Liberty & Co. diamond and aquamarine negligee necklace, 39cm. long. (Phillips) $2,088

Art Deco platinum and diamond necklace, diamonds approx. 7.25kt. (Robt. W. Skinner Inc.) $660

An Art Nouveau necklace, 38cm. long, stamped H & S and 333. (Phillips) $216

A gold and moonstone pendant, 4cm. long. (Phillips) $273

A gold, enamel, plique-a-jour and diamond Art Nouveau necklace. (Phillips) $460

A Murrle Bennett gold pendant locket, 5.5cm. long, 15kt. (Phillips) $288

An Art Nouveau trefoil shaped silver and green enamel pendant. (Reeds Rains) $139

A diamond and pearl set Art Nouveau pendant, 3.5cm. long. (Phillips) $417

A 14kt. yellow gold ring set with a diamond weighing approx. .50kt. (Robt. W. Skinner Inc.) $250

Arts & Crafts necklace, a heart shaped pendant suspended from a gold chain, hallmarked. (Robt. W. Skinner Inc.) $500

A diamond and peridot necklace, chain 37,5cm. long, in fitted case for Shepheard & Co. (Phillips) $748

A Gaskin Arts & Crafts pendant with central amethyst, having seed pearl and fresh-water pearl drop, 4cm. wide. (Phillips) $576

Platinum, diamond and ruby earrings, the diamond cap supports a 9mm. cultured pearl. (Robt. W. Skinner Inc.) $1,800

An Art Nouveau pin/ pendant, profile of a young girl on a plique-a-jour ground. (Robt. W. Skinner Inc.) $1,000

A Theodor Fahrner Art Deco bracelet, 19cm. long. (Phillips) $1,440

A George Hunt 'Medusa' brooch, 6cm. long, maker's mark in sheild, inscribed 'Medusa' on reverse. (Phillips) $1,440

An apple-green jade pendant, 5cm. high, wood stand. (Christie's) $2,988

Victorian gold earrings. (Robt. W. Skinner Inc.) $275

A 14kt. yellow gold ring, mounting pave-set with 18 diamonds and 5 rubies. (Robt. W. Skinner Inc.) $475

Early 20th century plique-a-jour necklace and earrings. (Robt. W. Skinner Inc.) $325

Bi-color gold and ruby ear-clips, circa 1940, each a blossom with a cluster of rubies. (Robt. W. Skinner Inc.) $225

A Jean Despres Art Deco ring fashioned in carved ivory with inner silver colored band, set with a turquoise. (Phillips) $2,232

A German horn comb, sur-mounted by panels of green plique-a-jour enamels amid tendrils set with marcasites, 8.5cm. wide. (Phillips) $136

14kt. white gold bar set with two diamonds, each weigh-ing approx. 1kt. and high-lighted by 7 small diamonds. (Robt. W. Skinner Inc.) $2,500

A Murrle Bennett gold and amethyst brooch, 3.2cm. wide, stamped with monogram and 9kt. (Phillips) $172

Art Deco platinum and diamond jabot pin. (Robt. W. Skinner Inc.) $1,900

A Wiener Werkstatte button brooch designed by Josef Hoffmann, circular with molded decoration of a robin. (Christie's) $743

Victorian gold and diamond pin, a fleur-de-lys pave-set with turquoise beads and diamonds. (Robt. W. Skinner Inc.) $175

Gold and citrine brooch, an oval brooch set with over-lapping gold leaves high-lighted with four cultured pearls. (Robt. W. Skinner Inc.) $300

An Arts & Crafts pendant, attributed to Sibyl Dunlop, with a teardrop plaque of Labradorite, 5.5cm. long. (Phillips) $403

Gold and ruby earclips and pin, 'Tiffany & Co.', designed as a leaf. (Robt. W. Skinner Inc.) $650

An Arts & Crafts pendant, in the manner of Omar Ramsden, set with three oval almondine garnet cabochons, 6cm. (Phillips) $230

Antique rose-cut diamond earrings. (Robt. W. Skinner Inc.) $800

A plique-a-jour brooch, formed as a locust, 10.6cm. long, stamped with maker's mark and 900, probably Austrian. (Phillips) $691

Diamond earclips, designed as a diamond plume with a cultured pearl at the base, 18kt. white gold. (Robt. W. Skinner Inc.) $850

An 18kt. gold brooch, designed as two textured gold leaves, 13.3gm. (Robt. W. Skinner Inc.) $150

Art Deco 14kt. gold, pearl and enamel pin, designed as a sailfish. (Robt. W. Skinner Inc.) $300

A Victorian gold pendant set with cabochon tear-drop garnets in a petal mount with central old cut diamond. (Reeds Rains) $434

A French gold, pearl and plique-a-jour circular pendant, 2cm. diam., inscribed F. Vernon. (Phillips) $216

An enamelled brooch, after a design by Henri Matisse, 6cm. wide, possibly produced in the U.S.A. (Phillips) $172

French gilt metal and enamel peacock feather buckle, circa 1900. (Reeds Rains) $279

An Art Nouveau sapphire and diamond ring in a scrolled gold mount. (Robt. W. Skinner Inc.)$160

Diamond earrings, each a cluster of diamonds in platinum top yellow gold, total weight of diamonds approx. 1.6kt. (Robt. W. Skinner Inc.) $750

An Austrian silver gilt, enamel and plique-a-jour dragonfly spring clip brooch, circa 1885. (Reeds Rains) $350

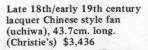

An early 19th century
Japanese black and gold
lacquer jardiniere, 20½in.
diam. (Christie's)
$2,674

Late 18th/early 19th century
lacquer Chinese style fan
(uchiwa), 43.7cm. long.
(Christie's) $3,436

A Chinese 18th century cinna-
bar lacquer box of 5in. circular
lobed form. (Parsons, Welch &
Cowell) $217

A red lacquer altar vase
carved with eight Buddhist
emblems, Qianlong seal
mark and of the period,
24.5cm. high. (Christie's)
$865

A Gyobu silver rimmed tebako
decorated in gold takamakie
with flowering peonies, circa
1800, 27.5 x 22.5 x 16.5cm.
(Christie's) $6,996

An 18th century Export lacquer medallion, 12.6cm. high.
(Christie's) $1,049

Late 17th century Export
lacquer cabinet, 74cm. high,
with a fitted 18th century
English japanned wood stand,
80cm. high. (Christie's)
$6,121

A set of three mid Victorian
black and gilt japanned papier-
mache oval trays, the largest
31in. wide. (Christie's)
$1,861

A 19th century Chinese lacquered panel, 33 x 25in.
(Dreweatts) $1,680

A Chinese red, black and brown lacquer box and cover, 12¾in. diam., the base incised with a Qianlong six-character mark. (Christie's) $475

A Korean inlaid black lacquer hinged rectangular box and cover, 17th/18th century, 21.8cm. wide. (Christie's) $2,381

An 18th century Chinese 4½in. circular red lacquer box. (Parsons, Welch & Cowell) $73

A 16th century inlaid black lacquer four-tiered box and cover, 27cm. high. (Christie's) $1,142

A 19th century silver rimmed fundame tebako, fitted wood box, 24.2 x 19.1 x 12cm. (Christie's) $11,368

A red and yellow lacquer six-tiered square box and cover, Ming Dynasty, 28.2cm. high. (Christie's) $2,381

Early 19th century Chinese Export lacquer picnic box, 15in. wide. (Christie's) $708

A black and gold lacquer tray decorated with chinoiserie figures in a landscape, 30in. wide. (Christie's) $2,675

One of a pair of 19th century Japanese lacquer picnic baskets, 52cm. high. (Phillips) $1,453

A Daum cameo table lamp with wrought-iron, three-branch neck mount, 44.1cm. high. (Christie's) $8,712

An Art Nouveau table lamp, beaten brass inset with colored glass, on oval wooden base, 49cm. high. (Christie's) $660

A Tiffany three-light table lamp, shade 40.6cm. diam., 61.5cm. high. (Christie's) $11,566

A German Art Nouveau silvered pewter nautilus shell desk lamp, stamped M H 20, 27cm. high. (Christie's) $2,692

A Galle cameo glass table lamp with domed shade and baluster base, 60cm. high. (Christie's) $11,566

Gustav Stickley oak table lamp with wicker shade, circa 1910, 22in. high, 18in. diam. (Robt. W. Skinner Inc.) $1,100

A Tiffany Studios 'lotus' leaded glass and bronze table lamp, 62.5cm. high. (Christie's) $15,048

Rudolph, a robot light fitting, designed by Frank Clewett, 149cm. high. (Christie's) $3,484

Bronze table lamp with green swirl glass and calcite shade, probably Steuben, circa 1910, 14in. high. (Robt. W. Skinner Inc.) $750

A Tiffany three-light table lamp, the bronze base bun-shaped on four ball feet, 41cm. diam. of shade, 63.5cm. high. (Christie's) $11,566

One of a pair of Tiffany Studios three-light, lily-gold favrile glass and bronze table lamps, 33.2cm. high. (Christie's) $6,336

A Daum overlaid and acid-etched table lamp with wrought-iron mount, 60cm. high. (Christie's) $11,088

A Tiffany Studios bronze and glass filigree table lamp, 42.5cm. high. (Christie's) $3,643

A Daum enamelled and acid etched cameo table lamp with three-cornered bulbous domed shade, 45.3cm. high. (Christie's) $9,583

A German Art Nouveau silvered pewter nautilus shell desk lamp, 29.7cm. high. (Christie's) $3,326

Hampshire pottery lamp with leaded shade, circa 1910, 19½in. high, 16in. diam. (Robt. W. Skinner Inc.) $750

A 1950s solid rosewood table lamp, 45.5cm. high. (Christie's) $2,809

Art pottery lamp with pierced copper and slag glass shade, circa 1905, 14½in. high. (Robt. W. Skinner Inc.) $600

LAMPS

A mid 19th century gilt metal lampe bouillotte with green and gilt tole shade, 23½in. high. (Christie's) $11,723

Early 20th century Hampshire pottery lamp with leaded Handel shade, 21in. high, 16in. diam. (Robt. W. Skinner Inc.) $700

Roycroft hammered copper and mica lamp, E. Aurora, N.Y., circa 1910, no. 903, 14¾in. high. (Robt. W. Skinner Inc.) $1,300

A patinated metal table lamp, marked 'Benedict United States', circa 1915, 26in. high. (Robt. W. Skinner Inc.) $225

An Art Nouveau bronze figural lamp, cast from a model by E. Druout, the young woman personifying music, 34in. high. (Christie's) $2,310

A Stilnova painted metal lamp, by Gaetano Scolari, Italy, circa 1959, 67cm. high. (Phillips) $174

A brass and rosewood lamp table, fitted for electricity with fringed pleated cream silk shade piped in red, 58in. high. (Christie's) $1,573

A Tiffany Studios stained glass dragonfly lamp/pendant, 25.5cm. wide, chain for suspension. (Phillips) $720

A Continental porcelain oil lamp base in the form of a white owl with glass eyes, 17½in. high. (Dreweatts) $754

LAMPS

A Daum cameo glass table lamp with conical shade, 51cm. high, signed. (Phillips) $4,320

An Art Nouveau bronze and leaded glass shade on bronze base, 22½in. high. (Christie's) $1,078

A Charles X gilt metal lampe bouillotte with spreading circular tole shade and ostrich feather finial, 32in. high. (Christie's) $2,967

Early 20th century Tiffany bronze table lamp with leaded shade, 22in. high. (Robt. W. Skinner Inc.) $2,500

An Italian glass and chromed standard lamp by Barovier and Toso, 180cm. high. (Phillips) $792

Early 20th century leaded cased glass lantern in vintage pattern, 13¼in. high, 9in. wide. (Robt. W. Skinner Inc.) $450

A Galle cameo glass table lamp with domed shade of amber tone, 57cm. high, signed. (Phillips) $8,352

Grueby pottery two-color lamp base, Boston, circa 1905, bronze foot signed Gorham Co., 18in. high. (Robt. W. Skinner Inc.) $11,750 £8,217

A Galle glass table lamp with domed shade, 52cm. high, signed in fine linear manner on shade and on base 'Galle' (Phillips) $5,472

LAMPS

A brass table lamp, the pierced and scrolled base with three urn-turned candle-cups and scrolled thumbpiece, 21½in. high. (Christie's) $385

One of a pair of gilt metal and turquoise porcelain twin-branch wall lights, fitted for electricity, 11in. high. (Christie's) $393

A Tiffany Studios 'Pansy' leaded glass and bronze table lamp, 54cm. high. (Christie's) $7,865

A tall Galle cameo table lamp, the domed shade and stem overlaid with claret-colored glass, 63.5cm. high. (Christie's) $12,584

A Lalique table lamp, the clear satin finished glass with amber staining, 27.1cm. high. (Christie's) $3,775

A Gabriel Argy-Rousseau pate-de-verre and wrought-iron veilleuse, the gray, blue and dark blue mottled glass molded with stylized leaves, 25.5cm. high. (Christie's) $3,146

One of a pair of giltwood single-branch wall appliques with frosted glass flambeaux, 21in. high. (Christie's) $503

A brass and tole painted table lamp, 20in. high. (Christie's) $330

A 19th century dark blue tinted lacemaker's lamp, 27cm. high. (Christie's) $554

A brass table lamp, the turned standard with three scrolled arms, 24in. high. (Christie's) $770

A Tiffany Studios 'Dragonfly' leaded glass and gilt bronze table lamp, 46.7cm. high. (Christie's) $24,381

A Daum Nancy acid etched glass table lamp, France, circa 1900, 14in. high. (Robt. W. Skinner Inc.) $2,000

An Andre Delatte cameo table lamp with metal neck mount, 52.5cm. high. (Christie's) $2,359

An Almaric Walter pate-de-verre and wrought-iron lamp, the amber glass plaque molded with a blue and amber mottled peacock, 27cm. high. (Christie's) $3,146

Early 20th century pairpoint reverse painted table lamp, New Bedford, base signed and numbered 3011, 22¾in. high. (Robt. W. Skinner Inc.) $1,500

A brass and glass ship's lantern, with a plaque inscribed 'Samuel Hall/Ship Chandler/East Boston', mounted as a lamp, 15in. high. (Christie's) $440

A Gabriel Argy-Rousseau pate-de-verre and wrought-iron veilleuse, 17.5cm. high. (Christie's) $4,404

A Regency brass frame hall lantern with six glass panels, one a door, 26in. high. (Woolley & Wallis) $1,887

A 19th century French marble statue of a girl possibly representing Winter, by E. Carlier, 86cm. high. (Christie's) $2,356

An early 19th century English marble group of a King Charles spaniel watching a cat, by Joseph Gott, 26in. high. (Christie's) $3,460

A mid 19th century English marble statue of Sabrina, the base signed Holme Cardwell Fecit Roma 1856, 101cm. high, 60cm. diam. (Christie's) $20,735

One of a pair of carved white marble standing lions, 24½in. high. (Robt. W. Skinner Inc.) $3,300

A late 19th century Italian marble statuette of a maiden looking at her reflection in a pool, by E. Brunelleschi, 79cm. high. (Christie's) $3,509

A Roman marble torso of a male, 1st-2nd century A.D. (Phillips) $1,425

A white marble Buddhist stele formed as Buddha, Tang Dynasty or earlier, 31cm. high. (Christie's) $4,089

Pair of 19th century Italian marble busts representing Spring and Autumn, by A. Bottinelli, 77.5 and 70cm. high.(Christie's) $8,772

A 19th century sculptured marble cat, America, 8¾in. high. (Robt. W. Skinner Inc.) $700

MARBLE

Late 19th century Austrian marble figure of Diana, by Victor Tilgner, 1896, 127cm. high. (Christie's) $84,150

An 18th century English marble group of two lions fighting, 15 x 19¾in. (Christie's) $3,775

A 19th century white marble group of two Greco-Roman wrestlers, 20in. high, on a dark green marble pedestal, 4ft. high. (Capes, Dunn & Co.) $1,160

A French 19th century marble group of Venus with Cupid asleep in her lap, by Albert E. C. Belleuse, 56 x 58cm. (Christie's) $25,245

Pair of early 19th century Italian marble statues of Hercules and Omphale, 68cm. high. (Christie's) $1,093

A late 19th century Italian colored marble bust of Beatrice, 45cm. high. (Christie's) $3,190

An early 20th century Italian marble bust of a classical woman in a headdress, by Clerici, 40cm. high. (Christie's) $841

An agate and specimen marble chessboard with wide borders, the squares with lapis lazuli, malachite and other hardstones and marbles, 14in. sq. (Christie's) $589

One of a pair of 19th century ormolu and marble urns and covers, the ovoid bodies with twin bacchante handles, 37cm. high. (Phillips) $3,168

MINIATURES

An American, 19th century, miniature painted bannister-back armchair, 9½in. high. (Christie's) $495

A 19th century miniature grain painted bowfront chest-of-drawers, American or English, 12in. high. (Christie's) $1,210

A 19th century, American, miniature classical maple fiddleback chair, 10¾in. high, 8¼in. wide. (Christie's) $550

Mid 18th century miniature Chippendale cherrywood chest-of-drawers, 7¾in. high. (Christie's) $1,540

An American, 18th century, miniature Queen Anne maple and pine slant-front desk, with a cherrywood mirror, the desk 11in. high. (Christie's) $3,520

Late 19th century miniature Chippendale walnut slant-front desk, American, 7¼in. high. (Christie's) $1,650

Late 18th century miniature George III mahogany side table, English, 6in. high. (Christie's) $330

Late 18th century miniature Chippendale mahogany chest-on-chest, English, 16¾in. high. (Christie's) $1,870

An American, 19th century, miniature Federal mahogany four-post bedstead with canopy, 15½in. high. (Christie's) $330

MINIATURES

A 19th century miniature green painted pine blanket chest, American, 9½in. high. (Christie's) $330

Early 19th century miniature Federal mahogany oxbow chest-of-drawers, New England, 7¼in. high. (Christie's) $4,400

Early 19th century miniature Federal mahogany tilt-top tea table, American, 9in. high. (Christie's) $990

A 19th century miniature Federal mahogany picture mirror, American, 9½in. high. (Christie's) $1,210

A 17th century miniature oak coffer of panelled construction, probably French, 35 x 21 x 23cm. (Phillips) $1,008

Late 18th/early 19th century miniature Continental painted tall clock case, 17in. high. (Christie's) $550

A miniature Chippendale mahogany desk and bookcase, Rhode Island, 1760-80, 16in. high. (Christie's) $2,090

Two 19th century miniature painted side chairs, American, 9¾in. and 8¼in. high. (Christie's) $528

A Dutch mahogany and oak miniature clothes press, 21in. wide, 33in. high. (Christie's) $3,168

One of a pair of German silvered wood girandoles, each with a cartouche-shaped plate, 32 x 19in. (Christie's) $2,499

A 19th century Chinese Export lacquer swing-frame toilet mirror with cartouche-shaped plate, 69cm. high. (Phillips) $750

A giltwood mirror with later waved rectangular plate, regilded, 53 x 24in. (Christie's) $2,171

A grained and parcel gilt mirror with shaped rectangular plate, 53 x 42in. (Christie's) $2,637

An early George III giltwood mirror with later circular plate, 42½ x 32¼in. (Christie's) $15,510

An Italian giltwood mirror with later plate, the frame 17th century, 84 x 68in. (Christie's) $5,467

A George I burr walnut and parcel gilt mirror, 49½ x 23in. (Christie's) $10,081

A Regency giltwood convex mirror with circular plate in ebonized slip, 48 x 43½in. (Christie's) $13,183

Mid 19th century large giltwood pier glass with rectangular plate, 103 x 66in. (Christie's) $2,326

An early George III giltwood mirror with later plate, 33½ x 21¼in. (Christie's) $8,530

A Regency satinwood large toilet mirror with oval swing frame, lacking plate, 25½in. wide. (Christie's) $495

One of a pair of giltwood mirrors in the rococo style with cartouche-shaped plates, 35 x 21in. (Christie's) $1,022

A giltwood mirror with rectangular plate in shaped frame, 45½ x 35½in. (Christie's) $4,998

A Chippendale carved gilt-wood oval marginal wall mirror with contemporary plate and bird crestings, 1.06m. high. (Phillips) $7,200

A George II silver gilt dressing table mirror, by Edward Feline, 1750, 23¾in. high, 62oz. (Christie's) $25,168

A giltwood mirror with later arched shaped bevelled plate with mirrored slip, 54 x 33in. (Christie's) $2,343

A Lalique hand mirror, 'Deux Chevres', 16.20cm. diam., in original fitted case. (Phillips) $1,152

One of a pair of Regency giltwood pier glasses with rectangular plates in leaf molded frames, 98 x 52½in. (Christie's) $13,959

A George III inlaid mahogany cheval glass, 59in. high, 24in. wide. (Christie's) $2,420

A Regency period circular carved giltwood frame convex mirror, 33in. x 3ft. 8in. (Woolley & Wallis) $1,152

A Queen Anne mahogany shaving mirror, American or English, 1730-60, 24in. high. (Christie's) $1,320

An early Georgian walnut mirror with later bevelled rectangular plate and gilt slip, 38¼ x 21½in. (Christie's) $2,073

A late Federal mahogany dressing glass, Penn., 1810-20, 29½in. wide. (Christie's) $825

Late 18th century neo-classical cream painted and parcel gilt mirror, 59½ x 20½in. (Christie's) $7,029

A Federal mahogany looking glass, bears label 'Wells M. Gaylord, no. 59, Genesee St., Utica', circa 1820, 39in. high. (Robt. W. Skinner Inc.) $350

A Renaissance Revival walnut and burl veneer hall tree, circa 1870, 100in. high. (Robt. W. Skinner Inc.) $1,700

Late 18th century Chippendale mahogany mirror, 32½in. high, 18¼in. wide. (Christie's) $3,520

A 19th century carved ivory
and walnut dressing mirror,
Europe, 23in. high. (Robt.
W. Skinner Inc.)$950

A Regency giltwood convex
mirror with ebonized ribbed
surround, 41 x 24in.
(Christie's) $2,988

An early George III gilt metal
automaton toilet mirror, by
James Cox, with musical and
mechanical base, 11½in. wide.
(Christie's) $89,958

A George II gilt and gesso
wall mirror with a broken
pediment and cartouche
cresting, 1.20m. x 63cm.
(Phillips) $5,112

A William III giltwood mirror
with later oval plate, 74½ x
46in. (Christie's)
$7,550

A Dieppe ivory mirror with
rectangular arched bevelled
plate, 60¼ x 34in.
(Christie's) $9,372

A Continental mirror with
chamfered blue glass border,
44 x 20¼in. (Christie's)
$2,186

A George II mahogany toilet
mirror, the base with three
drawers on ogee bracket feet,
17in. wide. (Christie's)
$1,861

A German dressing table
mirror of shaped outline, by
Johann Christoph Berns,
Magdeburg, circa 1755,
24¼in. high. (Christie's)
$9,123

A George II walnut and parcel gilt mirror, 52 x 26½in. (Christie's) $21,714

A Regency carved giltwood and gesso convex girandole, 1.03m. x 59cm. (Phillips) $3,168

Queen Anne walnut mirror, original glass and backing, probably England, circa 1750, 24in. high. (Robt. W. Skinner Inc.) $425

A George III giltwood mirror with later oval plate in a tied, out-scrolled rush frame, 39 x 26½in. (Christie's) $6,940

A Dutch marquetry toilet mirror, the solid cylinder enclosing a fitted interior, 21½in. wide. (Christie's) $3,190

A dressing glass by Howard & Co., N.Y., 1884, 33in. high, 30in. wide. (Christie's)$17,600

One of a pair of giltwood mirrors of George III style with oval plates and urn crestings, 38½ x 18in. (Christie's) $2,791

A George II giltwood over-mantel with later rectangular bevelled plate, 79 x 76½in. (Christie's) $17,303

A George III giltwood mirror with later oval plate, 21½ x 32½in. (Christie's) $3,635

A Queen Anne giltwood mirror with shaped divided partly bevelled plate, 69 x 44in. (Christie's) $46,530

Early 19th century Federal giltwood mirror surmounted by gold leaf eagle, 44in. high. (Robt. W. Skinner Inc.) $1,700

One of a pair of mid 18th century carved giltwood girandoles, probably France, 14½in. wide, sconces missing. (Robt. W. Skinner Inc.) $700

A WMF silvered pewter table mirror, stamped marks WMF, 70g., 34.9cm. high. (Christie's) $1,425

Early 18th century Italian lead framed mirror, 60½ x 28in. (Christie's) $11,715

Mid 18th century Italian giltwood mirror with later shaped plate and molded foliate slip, 59 x 42in. (Christie's) $1,562

A George III giltwood mirror with later oval plate, 45¼ x 23¾in. (Christie's) $3,257

A Charles II giltwood mirror with later bevelled plate, 43 x 33in. (Christie's) $1,754

An Adam carved giltwood oval wall mirror with anthemion cresting, 1.62m. x 76cm. overall. (Phillips) $5,184

MISCELLANEOUS

A Regency scarlet and gold papier-mache tray with everted gallery, 30in. wide. (Christie's) $660

A lead figure of a child holding a scallop shell bowl, 40in. high. (Heathcote Ball & Co.) $1,874

A Regency mahogany cheese coaster, 17in. wide. (Christie's) $480

One of a pair of rock crystal and gilt metal pricket candlesticks, mid 19th century, 11in. high. (Christie's) $3,436

A chromium plated automatic traffic warner, inscribed Auto Signal Pat. 375944, 42in. long. (Christie's) $186

A pair of fireside companions painted with a boy and a girl in 18th century costume, 42in. and 45in. high. (Christie's) $4,347

A Dunhill white metal and enamelled watch lighter, 4.5cm. high. (Christie's) $717

One of a pair of Chinese hardstone flowering trees in lacquer jardinieres, 16½in. high. (Christie's) $702

A French circular medallion enclosing black ink prints on silk on both sides, circa 1795, 3.1/8in. diam. (Christie's) $597

One of a pair of gilt metal six-branch candelabra of Louis XVI style, stamped AB on the bases, 20½in. high. (Christie's) $1,754

Cast zinc St. Bernard dog figure, probably Mass., circa 1880, 45in. wide. (Robt. W. Skinner Inc.) $2,600

One of a group of six circular gilt metal knobs with short stems and threaded fitments, circa 1780, each 2¾in. diam. (Christie's) $707

A Dunhill electroplated table lighter, stamped Made in England, patent no. 143752, 9cm. high. (Christie's) $179

A Shaker splint sewing basket, probably Enfield, Connecticut, 19th century, 15½in. diam. (Christie's) $880

An Art Deco white metal minaudiere, shaped as a guitar, 16cm. long. (Christie's) $717

One of a pair of metal mounted flambe stoneware vases, designed by Otto Eckmann, 52.2cm. high. (Christie's) $1,730

A faience ushabti fired green and mottled black with crisp impressed inscription, 11.5cm. high, and two others, all late Dynastic Period. (Phillips) $260

An American 19th century arrangement of various wax fruits on a wooden pedestal base, under a glass dome, 21in. high. (Robt. W. Skinner Inc.) $475

A builder's model of the single screw cargo ship M.V. 'Deerwood' of London, built 1955 by Wm. Pickersgill & Sons Ltd., for Wm. France, Fenwick & Co. Ltd., 12½ x 53in. (Christie's) $1,530

A display model of the motor tanker 'London Glory', built by Messrs. Sir James Laing & Sons Ltd., Sunderland for London & Overseas Freighters Ltd. Yard No. 793, 1952 and modelled for the builders by I. R. Amis Ltd. London, 7 x 31in. (Christie's) $1,071

An exhibition standard 1:72 scale planked and fully rigged model of the French frigate 'La Venus' of circa 1782, built by P. M. di Gragnano, Naples, 31 x 44in. (Christie's) $6,885

A 1:100 scale model of the Le Havre Pilot Boat 'Henriette', pennant No. H2, of 1866, built by M. Deveral, Folkestone, 8 x 8in. (Christie's) $336

A 1:60 scale model of the late 18th century French Ceremonial Galley 'Reale de France', built by J. Cherrill, Weybridge, 25 x 42in. (Christie's) $1,377

.A 1:100 scale model of the three masted auxiliary schooner 'Cruz del Sur' built by W. M. Wilson, Silloth, 12 x 17½in. (Christie's) $306

MODEL SHIPS

A 1/8in.:1ft. scale builder's model of the single screw steam newsprint carrier 'Sarah Bowater' of London, built 1955 by Denny Bros., Dumbarton for the Bowater Paper Corporation Ltd., 12 x 52in. (Christie's) $3,060

An exhibition standard ¾in.:1ft. scale model of the steam yacht 'Turbinia', as developed to 1895 'and modelled by A. Broad, Bromley, 18½ x 77in. (Christie's) $1,989

A 1:100 scale model of a Trouville trawler of circa 1866, built by M. Deveral, Folkestone, 6 x 6½in. (Christie's) $336

Late 19th century possibly builder's model of the fully rigged model of a yawl believed to be the 'Constance' of 1885, built for C. W. Prescott-Westcar by A. Payne & Sons, Southampton and designed by Dixon Kemp, 28 x 35¾in. (Christie's) $6,120

A finely carved 'Dieppe' ivory model three masted man-of-war with spars and rigging, full suit of carved ivory sails, mounted on wood with two ship's boats, 7 x 9in. (Christie's) $994

An exhibition standard 1:75 scale fully planked and rigged model of the French 60 gun man-of-war 'Le Protecteur' of circa 1760, built by P. M. di Gragnano, Naples, 31 x 38in. (Christie's) $7,650

A builder's mirror backed half model of the
schooner rigged steam yacht 'Rona', built for
A. H. E. Wood Esq., by David and William
Henderson & Co., 1893/4 to the order of
Thomas and Campbell, designed by G. L.
Watson & Co., 10 x 71 in. (Christie's)
$5,508

A builder's 3/16 in.:1 ft. scale model of H.M.S.
'Transport Ferry No. 3016', built for the
Royal Navy by R. & W. Hawthorn, Leslie &
Co. Ltd., Hebburn-on-Tyne, 1945, 16 x 63½ in.
(Christie's) $4,590

A 20th century carved and painted model of
the paddle steamer 'City of Key West',
American, in wooden and glass case, 38 in. long.
(Christie's) $1,210

A well detailed live steam, spirit fired, radio
controlled, fully planked and framed model of
the Barry Pilot Cutter 'Chimaera' of circa 1918,
built by Marvon Models, Doncaster, 24½ x 47 in.
(Christie's) $1,530

A carved and painted model of the 'Royal Ark',
by J. R. Whittemore, on a molded wooden
base, 43 in. long. (Christie's) $1,980

Late 19th century carved and painted model of
the 'William Tapscot', in a glass and mahogany
case, 38 in. long. (Christie's) $1,540

A carved and painted model of ocean liner
'Liberte', executed for the Companie Generale
Transatlantique, circa 1950, in wooden and
plexi-glass case, 54 in. long. (Christie's)
$6,050

A builder's mirror back half model of a single
screw cabin motor cruiser built by John I.
Thorneycroft & Co. Ltd., London, 6 x 26 in.
(Christie's) $1,989

A Voltamp gauge 2 trolley No. 2123, 0-4-4-0, circa 1913. (Christie's) $3,080

No. 5 thin rim locomotive lettered 'B & O R.R.', circa 1907. (Christie's) $2,090

A gauge 1 Bing locomotive 4-4-0 with 6-wheel tender, circa 1915. (Christie's) $1,430

Carette green locomotive, 2-2-0, 4-wheel tender, alcohol burner, together with an olive 4-wheel baggage car, circa 1905. (Christie's) $935

A 'Washington Special', No. 385E locomotive with tender and cars, circa 1934. (Christie's) $1,980

A late 19th century 3¾in. gauge spirit fired brass model of the Great Northern Railway Stirling 2-4-0 locomotive and tender No. 152, built by H. J. Wood, London, 10¼ x 35in. (Christie's) $1,836

A 5in. gauge model of the Great Western Railway 57XX Class 0-6-0 pannier tank locomotive No. 5702, built by C. G. Balding, Bideford, 13½ x 34in. (Christie's) $2,448

A 7¼in. gauge model of the North Eastern Railway Class G5 0-4-4 side tank locomotive No. 505, built by D. W. Horsfall, Northowram, 20½ x 52½in. (Christie's) $3,060

Set No. 1771RW, gauge 0 No. 1681 Hudson type locomotive 2-6-4, 8-wheel 1936 version tender and three pullmans, American Flyer Lines. (Christie's) $660

A 7mm. finescale two rail electric model of the London and North Eastern Railway Class B12 4-6-0 locomotive and tender No. 8523, built by K. J. Leeming and painted by A. Brackenborough, 3½ x 16½in. (Christie's) $1,836

A 7¼in. gauge model of the Great Western Railway Armstrong Class 4-4-0 locomotive and tender No. 8 'Gooch', built by T. Childs, Churchill, 20¼ x 88in. (Christie's)
$10,710

An exhibition standard 5in. gauge model of the Great Western Railway River Class 2-4-0 loco-motive and tender No. 69 'Avon' as running in 1906, built from builder's drawings and photo-graphs by R. W. Gale, Newport, 14¼ x 53¼in. (Christie's) $11,475

A well engineered 3½in. gauge model of the Great Western Railway County class 4-6-0 loco-motive and tender No. 1022 'County of Northampton', 10 x 47in. (Christie's)
$2,295

A 3½in. gauge model of the British Railways Class 7 4-6-2 locomotive and tender No. 70013 'Oliver Cromwell, built by H. C. Luckhurst, Oxley, 10¼ x 52½in. (Christie's)
$3,060

A 5in. gauge model of the London Midland and Scottish Railway Class 2F 0-6-0 side tank locomotive No. 11270, 13 x 27½in. (Christie's) $2,907

A 7¼in. gauge model of the London Midland and Scottish Railway Class 2F 0-6-0 side tank locomotive No. 11270, built by C. Ottaway, Chippenham, 18½ x 41in. (Christie's)
$6,885

A 3½in. gauge model of the Southern Railway 0-4-2 side tank locomotive No. 2036, built to the designs of Juliet by M. Darlow, 1972 — 10 x 21in. (Christie's) $688

A Hornby gauge 0 (3-rail) electric model of the No. 1 LNER 0-4-0 special locomotive and tender, original paintwork, (loco in original box). (Christie's) $403

A well engineered 2½in. gauge model of the London Midland and Scottish Railway 4-4-0 locomotive and tender No. 1000, built to the designs of Eagle by G. Ward, 8 x 31in. (Christie's) $612

An exhibition standard 5in. gauge model of the Great Northern Railway Stirling Single 4-2-2 locomotive and tender No. 53, built from works drawings and photographs by J: S. Richardson, Halifax, 14 x 56in. (Christie's) $7,650

A finely detailed 7mm. finescale two rail electric model of the Deutches Bundesbahn 144 Bo Bo class electric outline locomotive No. E44070 built by Hego Modellbahn for the Nuremburg Toy Fair, 1976, 4 x 13½in. (Christie's) $765

A mid 19th century live steam spirit fired 4¾in. gauge brass model of the 2-2-2 locomotive and tender 'Express', built by Steven's Model Dockyard, 11¾ x 30in. (Christie's) $3,213

A fine Marklin gauge 1 clockwork model of the LB & SCR 4-4-2 'Atlantic' tank locomotive No. 22, in original paintwork, with lamps, circa 1920 (1 loose bogie). (Christie's) $2,880

A gauge 1 (3-rail) electric model of the G.N.R. 0-4-0 side tank locomotive No. 112, in original paintwork by Bing for Bassett-Lowke (lacks 3 buffers). (Christie's) $374

An exhibition standard 5in. gauge model of the Great Western Railway Armstrong Class 4-4-0 locomotive and tender No. 14, 'Charles Saunders', built by P. J. Rich, Rhiwderin, 14 x 62in. (Christie's) $15,606

A fine contemporary late 19th century 3¼in. gauge brass and steel spirit fired model 4-2-0 locomotive and tender, built by H. J. Wood, London, 8½ x 21½in. (Christie's) $994

A 3in. scale model of a single cylinder two speed, four shaft Clayton & Shuttleworth traction engine, built by K. Prout, 31 x 56in. (Christie's) $4,284

A model Stuart triple expansion vertical reversing marine engine built by G. B. Houghton, Rochester, 7 x 8¾in. (Christie's) $994

An exhibition standard 3in. scale model of the Savage horse-drawn Electric Light Engine No. 357, built by C. J. Goulding, Newport, 27 x 47in. (Christie's) $4,284

An early 19th century model of a single cylinder table engine, possibly by Murdock, 15½ x 10in. (Christie's) $1,377

A well engineered 2in. scale model of an Aveling and Porter twin crank compound two speed, four shaft Road Roller, 19½ x 35in. (Christie's) $3,987

Late 19th century model of the three cylinder compound vertical surface condensing mill engine 'Asia', 16¼ x 13¼in. (Christie's) $2,907

A well presented approx. 1:20 scale model of the Weatherhill Pit Winding Engine of 1833, built by W. K. Walsam, Hayes, 19 x 14½in. (Christie's) $918

A 1:20 scale brass model of the Fenton, Murray & Wood 6 N.H.P. underlever beam engine of 1806 built by G. L. Dimelow, Ashton-under-Lyne, 9¾ x 9¼in. (Christie's) $918

An unusual model of a steam driven 19th century twin bore Deep Well Engine House and Pump, built by R. J. Sare, Northleach, 16½ x 18½in. (Christie's) $306

An exhibition standard 2in. scale model of a Burrell 5 N.H.P. double crank compound three shaft, two speed Showman's Road Locomotive, 20 x 30½in. (Christie's) $8,415

An ingenious and well presented model steam driven Stone Sawing Plant, built by R. J. Sare, Northleach, 13½ x 24½in. (Christie's) $489

A finely engineered model twin cylinder compound undertype stationary steam engine built to the designs of A. H. Greenly, by P. C. Kidner, London, 14½ x 24½in. (Christie's) $2,295

A contemporary early 19th century brass and wrought iron single cylinder six pillar beam engine, built by Chadburn Bros., Sheffield, 19 x 19¼in. (Christie's) $3,060

An approx. 4in. scale Foden type twin cylinder overtype two speed steam lorry, built by A. Groves, Watford, 1937 and restored by M. Williams at the British Engineerium, Hove, 1983, 36½ x 88in. (Christie's) $7,650

A well presented model single cylinder vertical reversing stationary engine, built from Clarkson castings, 17½ x 9¾in. (Christie's) $1,071

An exhibition standard model of the three cylinder compound surface condensing vertical reversing marine engine, fitted to S.S. 'Servia', and modelled by T. Lowe, 1907, 14½ x 12½in. (Christie's) $6,120

A sturdily constructed 2in. scale model of a Fowler twin crank compound three speed, four shaft road locomotive built by S. W. Brown, Newbury, 23 x 37in. (Christie's) $3,672

An early 19th century small full size single cylinder six pillar beam engine, 31 x 34in. (Christie's) $1,377

Two frogs cast iron mechanical bank, J. & E. Stevens, Co., Pat. 1882, 8¾in. long. (Robt. W. Skinner Inc.) $625

Owl cast iron mechanical bank, J. & E. Stevens, Co., pat. 1880, 7.5/8in. high. (Robt. W. Skinner Inc.) $200

'Bad Accident' cast iron mechanical bank, J. & E. Stevens, Co., 1891-1911, 10.3/8in. long. (Robt. W. Skinner Inc.)$1,100

'Bull Dog Bank' cast iron mechanical bank, J. & E. Stevens, Co., pat. 1880, 7½in. high. (Robt. W. Skinner Inc.) $500

William Tell cast iron mechanical bank, J. & E. Stevens, Co., pat. 1896, 10.5/8in. long. (Robt. W. Skinner Inc.) $600

Lion and Monkeys cast iron mechanical bank, Kyser & Rex Co., Pat. 1883, 10in. long. (Robt. W. Skinner Inc.) $400

'World's Fair' cast iron mechanical bank, J. & E. Stevens, Co., pat. 1893, 8¼in. long. (Robt. W. Skinner Inc.) $600

'Jolly Nigger' metal money bank. (Hobbs & Chambers) $97

'Chief Big Moon' cast iron mechanical bank, J. & E. Stevens, Co., pat. 1899, 10in. long. (Robt. W. Skinner Inc.) $1,200

Early 19th century micro-mosaic plaque, depicting the Temple of Vesta at Tivoli, 2½in. long. (Christie's) $1,200

Early 19th century circular Roman micro-mosaic decorated with a duck and duckling, the box 3in. diam. (Christie's) $1,573

A Roman rectangular micro-mosaic panel decorated with a bull-baiting scene, circa 1800, 3in. long. (Christie's) $4,404

Early 19th century circular Roman micro-mosaic decorated in the style of Rafaelli with a finch, the box 3in. diam. (Christie's) $1,730

A 19th century Roman micro-mosaic panel decorated in bright colors with a bunch of flowers, approx. 8in. long. (Christie's) $5,505

A circular tortoiseshell snuff box with detachable cover, the mosaic circa 1820, 2¾in. diam. (Christie's) $1,487

A Roman micro-mosaic panel decorated with Pliny's Doves of Venus, circa 1840, 2.5/8in. long. (Christie's) $1,337

A circular Roman micro-mosaic of a pannier brimming with flowers, circa 1830, the box 2¾in. diam. (Christie's) $2,674

A 19th century Roman rectangular mosaic panel, decorated with a view of the Piazza del Popolo in Rome, 2¾in. long. (Christie's) $1,573

MOTORING ITEMS

Victorie (Spirit of the Wind), a Lalique glass female head car mascot, 10¼in. long. (Christie's) $2,480

A chromium plated and enamelled Aero-Club Brooklands badge, 3¾in. high. (Onslow's) $686

'Perche', a Lalique car mascot in clear and satin finished glass, molded as a fish, 9.5cm. high. (Christie's) $1,022

An 18kt. gold key-ring modelled as a Rolls-Royce radiator, 3in. overall. (Christie's) $294

The Romance of a Record Breaker, by F. G. Crosby, signed and dated 1911, watercolor — 11 x 11in. (Christie's) $4,030

A rosewood and ivory toucan radiator cap, inscribed Howett, London, 5in. high. (Christie's) $248

'Sanglier', a Lalique car mascot in clear and satin finished glass, molded as a boar, 6.5cm. high. (Christie's) $1,022

Le Rire, special 13 July number, 1901 for the Paris-Berlin automobile race, brochure. (Christie's) $116

'Tete de Coq', a Lalique car mascot, in clear and satin finished glass, 18cm. high. (Christie's) $2,044

MOTORING ITEMS

A brass Lucas King of the Road oil sidelight, stamped no. 630, 10½in. high. (Onslow's) $114

A silver gilt and enamelled dashboard St. Christopher, Birmingham, 1922, 2¼in. long. (Christie's) $77

A brass figure of a stylized eagle perched on a decorative base, 8in. high. (Christie's) $100

'Falcon', a Lalique car mascot in clear and satin finished glass, 15.5cm. high. (Christie's) $2,674

Racing Cars, by R. Brone, signed and dated 1969, 38½ x 39in. (Christie's)$155

A silver plated R.A.C. badge, hollow, stamped B1631, 7in. high. (Onslow's) $357

A brass Lucas King of the Road oil light, stamped no. 435, 12in. high. (Onslow's) $114

A chromium plated and enamelled B.A.R.C. Brooklands badge, stamped 1367, 3¾in. high. (Onslow's) $572

A brass car mascot of Minerva, inscribed 'Minerva P. de Soete', 6in. high. (Christie's) $403

A chromium plated car mascot figure of 'Puss in Boots', 6in. high. (Christie's) $465

'Pharaoh', a Red-Ashay, car mascot in clear and satin finished glass, 11.5cm. high. (Christie's) $1,321

A Lalique glass car mascot, modelled as the head of a cockerel, 8½in. high. (Parsons, Welch & Cowell) $2,310

'Saint-Christopher', a Lalique car mascot in clear and satin finished glass, with Breves Galleries Knightsbridge metal radiator mount, 22.5cm. high. (Christie's) $314

Two of twenty-one R.A.C.I. dashboard plaques, late 1920's early 1930's, approx. 3 x 2in. (Christie's) $1,085

A Lalique car mascot in clear and satin-finished glass, molded as a falcon, 16.5cm. high. (Christie's) $2,217

A nickel plated brass stylized tyre with seated speed god inside, inscribed Coffin, 6in. high. (Christie's) $620

A motoring picnic hamper, four settings, marked Coracle, 22½in. long. (Christie's) $1,085

'Archer', a Lalique car mascot in clear and satin finished glass, 12cm. high. (Christie's) $2,044

MOTORING ITEMS

A brass stylized car mascot bust of Minerva, inscribed P. de Soete, 5½in. high. (Christie's) $589

A Lalique greyhound car mascot. (Woolley & Wallis) $4,185

A nickel plated car mascot of a polar bear standing on a stylized rock plinth, 4½in. high. (Christie's) $100

A Rolls-Royce Spirit of Ecstasy car mascot, indistinctly marked Trade Mark Reg., Reg. U.S. Pat. Off., 5¾in. high. (Christie's) $248

Olympia, Motor Show, Oct. 12 1933, color lithograph poster. after A. E. Marty, 10 x 12½in. (Christie's) $248

A brass Lucas King of the Road oil sidelight, stamped no. 724, 12½in. high. (Onslow's) $178

A chromium plated bronze car mascot, Farman Icarus, inscribed Colin George, Made in France, circa 1922, 6in. high. (Christie's) $496

A Lalique car mascot, Longchamps, in clear and satin-finished glass, 13cm. high. (Christie's) $12,672

'Grand Libellule', a Lalique car mascot in clear and satin finished glass, 21cm. high. (Christie's) $5,783

An Edison Home phonograph, Model A No. H104435, with B reproducer, crane 42in. long, and 25 cylinders. (Christie's) $693

An interchangeable cylinder mandolin musical box on table with six eight-air cylinders, 47in. wide overall, the cylinders 11in. (Christie's) $6,160

A Mandoline Expressive Zither musical box by P.V.F. playing twelve airs, 28in. wide, the cylinder 17¼in. long. (Christie's) $2,310

A key-wind forte piano musical box, by Nicole Freres, No. 39788, playing twelve airs, 22in. wide, the cylinder 13 x 3⅛in. diam. (Christie's) $2,618

An HMV Automatic Model 1 gramophone No. 570 with 5a soundbox, 42in. wide, circa 1929. (Christie's) $539

Late 19th century rosewood veneer and ebonized wood cylinder music box on stand, F. Conchon, Manufacturer, Switzerland, 39½in. wide. (Robt. W. Skinner Inc.) $3,700

A G. & T. single-spring Monarch gramophone with Morning Glory horn, 24in. diam., circa 1903-04. (Christie's) $492

An interchangeable cylinder music box on stand, by B. A. Bremond, circa 1875, cylinder 13in. long, table 35½in. long. (Christie's) $2,420

A Gramophone Co. mahogany Junior Monarch ('Doric') with single-spring motor, the horn 21½in. diam., circa 1908. (Christie's) $1,001

An HMV Model V mahogany horn gramophone with single-spring motor, Exhibition soundbox and fluted mahogany horn, circa 1914. (Christie's) $1,232

A hidden drum, bells and castagnette musical box playing six airs, 20½in. wide, the cylinder 13in. (Christie's) $1,386

A horn Pathephone with chequer-strung oak case, horn 22in. diam., (Christie's) $924

Walnut cased polyphon coin-operated, wind-up gramophone with key, winder and nine discs. (Lots Road Galleries) $1,836

A clockwork barrel-organ, by Flight & Robson, 66½in. wide, the barrels 35 x 8in. diam., and a discus electric suction unit. (Christie's) $8,470

An Edison Fireside phonograph, Model A No. 31916, now with Diamond B reproducer, Model R and Model K reproducers with adapter ring. (Christie's) $646

An Edison Triumph phonograph, Model A No. 45259, in 'New Style' green oak case, with 14in. witch's hat horn. (Christie's) $770

A G. & T. double-spring Monarch in oak case, the oak horn 18in. diam., the gramophone circa 1906. (Christie's) $1,232

A musical box, by Baker-Troll, playing eight airs accompanied by drum, castanet and six-engraved bells, 23½in. wide. (Christie's) $3,080

A violoncello, by Ch. J. B. Collin-Mezin, dated 1884, length of back 29.7/8in. (Christie's) $7,865

A violin, by Dante and Alfredo Guastalla, 1929, length of back 14.1/8in. (Phillips) $2,926

A violin, by Giovanni Battista Gaibisso, 1922, length of back 14.1/16in. (Christie's) $4,147

A violin, by Jean M. Remy, Paris, circa 1810, length of back 14¼in., with two bows in case. (Phillips) $1,267

A viola, by Bruno Barbieri, maker's label Liutaio in Mantova Anno 1974, length of back 15½in. (Christie's) $3,003

An Italian violin, by F. Ruggieri, length of back 14in. (Christie's) $60,192

A violin, by Paul Bailly, circa 1890, length of back 14.1/16in., with a bow in case. (Phillips) $1,872

An Italian violin, by Pietro Guarneri of Mantua, 1707, length of back 14in. (Christie's) $126,720

An Italian viola, attributed to G. & L. Bisiach, 1932, length of back 16.3/8in. (Christie's) $8,712

A viola da gamba, labelled Joachim Tielke/in Hamburg/An 1685, length of back 26in. (Christie's) $47,520

A violin, by Nicolas Aine in Mirecourt, circa 1800, length of back 14¼in. (Phillips) $1,800

An Austrian viola d'amore, by M. I. Stadlmann, length of back 14.13/16in. (Christie's) $1,267

A violin, by Etienne Vatelot 1946, length of back 14.1/16in. (Phillips) $1,617

A French violin, by Pierre Silvestre, Lyon 1850, length of back 14.1/8in. (Christie's) $15,048

A Neapolitan violin, by a member of the Gagliano family, circa 1780-1810, length of back 14.1/16in. (Phillips) $10,472

A violin, by T. Earle Hesketh in Manchester, dated 1929, length of back, 13.7/8in. (Christie's) $1,315

A viola, circa 1870, of the Honore Derazey School, length of back 16.1/16in. (Christie's) $3,146

A violin, by Enrico Veronesi, 1931, length of back 14.1/16in. (Christie's) $2,431

A violin, by Carlo Storioni, 1895, length of back, 14¼in. (Phillips) $893

A violin, by Leon Mougenot Gauche, maker's label dated 1927, length of back 14.1/8in. (Christie's) $1,716

A violin, probably the work of George Wulme Hudson, circa 1920, length of back 14¼in. (Christie's) $1,108

A violin, by A. Kloz, dated 1789, length of back 13.7/8in. (Christie's) $4,147

An Italian violin, unlabelled, circa 1780, length of back, 13.15/16in. (Christie's) $3,801

A violin, by Job Ardern, bearing the label 'born 1826, died 1912', length of back 14.1/8in. (Phillips) $585

A viola, by Jean Baptiste Colin, length of back 15.13/16in., with bow. (Phillips) $1,617

An English violoncello, Panormo School, circa 1820, length of back 28.15/16in. (Christie's) $7,920

A violin, by Pierre Silvestre of Lyons, circa 1850, length of back 14.3/16in. (Christie's) $9,295

A viola of the Meurot School, Paris, circa 1910, length of back 15.5/8in., in a hide case. (Phillips) $1,440

A viola, by Giovanni Battista Gaibisso, 1915, length of back 16.7/16in. (Phillips) $2,926

An Italian violin, by C. F. Landolfi, 1750, length of back 13.7/8in. (Christie's) $38,016

A viola, by William Ebsworth Hill, 1849, length of back 16.3/8in. (Phillips) $10,472

A viola, by Alfred Vincent, London, 1930, length of back 17.1/8in. (Phillips) $2,772

An Italian violin,
by Fratelli Melegari,
1903, length of back
14.1/8in. (Christie's)
$3,168

A violin, by Joannes
C. Leidolf, 1748,
length of back
14.1/8in., with two
bows in case.
(Phillips)
$1,180

A composite Italian
violin, length of
back 14.1/8in.
(Christie's)
$38,016

A violin, by T. Earle
Hesketh, dated 1931,
length of back
14.1/16in., with a
nickel mounted bow.
(Christie's)
$1,716

A violin, by Laurence
Cocker, bearing maker's
label in Derby dated
1964, length of back
14in. (Phillips)
$708

An English viola,
circa 1800, labelled
Amati, length of
back 15.5/16in.
(Christie's)
$2,851

A violin, by Giuseppe
Lucci, maker's label
Da Bagnacavallo Fece
in Roma 1978, length
of back 14.1/16in.
(Christie's)
$3,432

A violin, by Thos.
Perry, 1785, length
of back 13.7/8in.
(Phillips)
$2,310

An Austrian violin, by A. F. Mayr, Salzburg An 1726, length of back 13.15/16in. (Christie's) $4,435

A violin, by Alexandre Delanoy in Bordeaux, dated 1879, length of back 14.1/8in. (Christie's) $2,431

An English violin, by Clifford A. Hoing, 1934, length of back 14in. (Christie's) $2,059

A violoncello, by L. M. Gauche, in Mirecourt, label dated 1912, length of back 30.1/8in. (Christie's) $6,006

A violin, by Dr. N. Aine, circa 1830, length of back 14.1/16in. (Christie's) $2,216

An Italian violin, by Giovanni B. Gabrielli, length of back 13.7/8in. (Christie's) $22,176

Early 19th century Italian violoncello, length of back 29.1/8in. (Christie's) $6,019

A viola of the Claude Pierray, Paris School, circa 1740, length of back 16.7/16in. (Christie's) $12,584

A 19th century boxwood
netsuke of a Sennin, signed
Toyomasa. (Christie's)
$2,967

Mid/late 19th century ivory
netsuke of a Samurai seated
next to a kneeling hunter,
signed Ichijusai Seizan.
(Christie's) $702

Late 18th century triangular
ivory netsuke of Gama
Sennin, unsigned. (Christie's)
$1,093

Mid 19th century stained
boxwood netsuke of a rat
with a chestnut beneath one
paw, signed Ikkan. (Christie's)
$6,560

Mid 19th century ivory
manju netsuke decorated
with a herdboy astride an
ox, signed Kosai.(Christie's)
$781

Late 19th century ivory
netsuke of a Noh dancer in
the role of a Shojo, and
another. (Christie's)
$343

Early 19th century wood
netsuke of a seated monkey
cradling one of its offspring,
signed Mitsuhide, Kyoto
School. (Christie's)
$1,093

Early 19th century ivory
netsuke of one of the Three
Heroes of Han, Gentoku,
inscribed Tametaka, and
another of a priest. (Christie's)
$781

A 19th century ivory netsuke
of a rat on a pumpkin, signed
Toshinobu. (Christie's)
$1,483

A 19th century ivory netsuke of a Shoki, the Demon Queller. (Christie's) $702

Early 19th century boxwood netsuke of Okame, signed Kokei, Tsu School. (Christie's) $1,093

A 19th century ivory netsuke of Ashinaga and Tenaga. (Christie's) $749

Mid 19th century wood netsuke of Raijin, the God of Thunder, signed Tomokazu. (Christie's) $5,467

Mid 19th century ivory netsuke of a South Sea islander seated inside a lotus leaf, signed Hakusen. (Christie's) $1,483

A 19th century wood netsuke of a fieldmouse curled into a ball, signed Masanao, Yamada School. (Christie's) $2,499

An ivory netsuke of a group of five playful rats, signed Kaigyokudo. (Christie's) $4,061

Mid 19th century ivory netsuke, signed Toun (Ikkosai), Edo School. (Christie's) $1,405

A 19th century ivory netsuke of three Samurai in full armor in a melee, unsigned. (Christie's) $393

A 19th century boxwood
netsuke of a smiling karako
astride a hobby horse,
unsigned. (Christie's)
$503

Early 19th century boxwood
netsuke of a snake passing
through a pumpkin, signed
Tadayoshi or Tadatoshi,
Nagoya School. (Christie's)
$943

A 19th century red lacquer
netsuke modelled as a double
gourd, with silver ring attachment for suspension.
(Christie's) $298

An 18th century ivory seal
netsuke carved as a groom
asleep next to a recumbent
horse. (Christie's)
$550

Early 19th century wood
netsuke of a toad, signed
Shigetada. (Christie's)
$550

A wood netsuke of ten Noh
and Kyogen masks, including
Hiottoku, Hannya, Okame
and a fox, unsigned, circa
1800. (Christie's) $456

Late 19th century wood
okimono of an ape seated on
a carapace of a turtle, signed
Shinpuken Masakatsu,
8.5cm. high. (Christie's)
$2,831

A 19th century bronze
kagamibuta netsuke decorated in nikubori and takabori
with 'Gentoku's ride', ivory
bowl. (Christie's)
$707

A 19th century ivory and
buffalo horn netsuke of
Okame in a parody of
Daruma during his nine year
meditation. (Christie's)
$511

A 19th century lacquer, ivory, shell and pressed horn netsuke of a performing Noh actor wearing a Sambaso dancer's outfit, unsigned. (Christie's) $550

A 19th century wood netsuke of a lotus pod with ten moveable seeds, the stalk forming the himotoshi, unsigned. (Christie's) $393

Late 18th century ivory netsuke of a man running and holding one hand up to his chin. (Christie's) $471

Late 18th century wood netsuke of a crouching ape, unsigned. (Christie's) $393

Mid 19th century ivory netsuke of a crouching karako, signed Kosai, Edo School. (Christie's) $629

An ivory netsuke of three mice on a partly eaten mushroom, unsigned. (Christie's) $1,573

A wood netsuke of a cockerel seated on a drum, signed Hori Yasumoto, circa 1800. (Christie's) $660

A 19th century circular lacquered wood manju-type netsuke decorated in hiramakie and takamakie. (Christie's) $550

A 19th century boxwood netsuke of a Noh mask of Okina, unsigned. (Christie's) $314

Mid 19th century ivory netsuke of a crouching karako, signed Gyokuyosai. (Christie's) $550

Early 19th century ivory netsuke of a fish, its eyes inlaid in dark polished horn, unsigned. (Christie's)
$1,337

A 19th century silvered metal kagamibuta netsuke with gilt and copper detail and ivory bowl. (Christie's) $534

A 19th century ivory netsuke of a large snake gripping a toad in its tail and baring its fangs, signed Sako. (Christie's) $2,202

An ivory netsuke of triangular section carved with a tiger among bamboo and rocks, circa 1800. (Christie's)
$440

A 19th century gold, silver, red and black lacquered wood netsuke of a dog, unsigned. (Christie's)
$440

Mid 19th century wood netsuke of an oni and a skeleton crouching on a lotus, signed Hojitsu, Edo School. (Christie's) $1,258

A 19th century bronze kagamibuta netsuke with ivory bowl. (Christie's)
$440

A 19th century ivory netsuke of the demon Soshiki kneeling on clouds, signed Masatomo. (Christie's)
$629

19th century natural double walnut netsuke with attached ojime, signed Kozan. (Christie's) $503

Late 18th century ivory netsuke of a recumbent ox, signed Tomotada, Kyoto School, probably pupil's work. (Christie's) $597

Late 18th century ivory netsuke of a seated dog , unsigned, Kyoto School. (Christie's) $629

A 19th century wood netsuke of a chestnut, one side inlaid with an ivory maggot, unsigned. (Christie's) $346

Mid 19th century marine ivory okimono-style netsuke of Ashinaga and Tenaga, signed Mitsuchika. (Christie's) $550

A small stained ivory okimono of the 'Disappointed Rat Catcher', signed Juzan, Meiji period, 5.8cm. long. (Christie's) $440

Late 18th century ivory netsuke of a seated karashishi, in the style of Karaku, Kyoto School. (Christie's) $550

A 19th century silver manju netsuke decorated in niku-bori, kebori, takabori and gold and shakudo hirazogan. (Christie's) $1,101

A 19th century wood netsuke of three boys, their eyes inlaid in dark horn, metal ring attachment, unsigned. (Christie's) $283

Mexico: 1916 Tesoreria General del Estado for Merida, Yucatan 2 pesos front and back proofs on card printed by the Parsons Trading Co. of New York. (Phillips) $104

Canada: 1914 Banque d'Hochelaga $10 color trial in black and blue with four cancellation holes. (Phillips) $166

Mozambique: 1909 1,000 escudos overprint on 20 libras. (Phillips) $391

Bank of Ireland: £5, 1916. (Phillips) $181

Royal Bank: £1, 1872. (Phillips) $464

Part of a set of 1902 Keeling & Cocos Islands 1/10, ¼. ½, 1, 2 and 5 rupees.(Phillips) $362

Germany: 1960 5-1,000 Deutsche mark Specimen set. (Phillips) $551

National Bank: £10, 1920 small size (150 x 90mm.) (Phillips) $217

Channel Islands, Guernsey: £1, 1 September 1917. (Phillips) $3,190

Uruguay: 1865 El Banco Navia 1 doblon unissued and with crayoned 'X' across lower half. (Phillips) $224

Portugal: 1910 10 milreis. (Phillips) $104

Columbia: 1883 El Banco Americano 100 pesos unissued and perforated 'Specimen C. Skipper & East'. (Phillips) $333

Mozambique: 1921 1, 2½, 5, 10, 20 and 50 escudos Specimen notes. (Phillips) $580

Portugal: 1910 50 milreis. (Phillips) $159

Italy: 1947–62, 500, 1,000, 5,000 and 10,000 lire Specimens. (Phillips) $203

French West Africa: 1942, 1,000 francs. (Phillips) $152

A mid Victorian black and gilt japanned papier-mache tray of waved and shaped rectangular form, 23¾ x 31in. (Christie's) $2,055

A mid Victorian black and gilt japanned papier-mache writing-slope with hinged flap, 12in. wide. (Christie's) $503

An 19th century oval papier mache tray, centrally decorated after Morland, 30in. wide. (Dreweatts) $1,276

An early Victorian black and gilt japanned papier-mache card box with lifting lid, 11¼in. wide. (Christie's) $550

One of a pair of early Victorian papier-mache fans, both signed Jennens and Betteridge, with ring turned stained beech handles, 17½in. high. (Christie's) $414

A 19th century papier-mache tray with shaped edge and a design of flowers by Evans. (Lots Road Galleries) $417

A mid Victorian black, gilt and mother-of-pearl japanned papier-mache table-bureau, 14¾in. wide. (Christie's) $1,258

A Regency scarlet and gilt japanned papier-mache tray, with impressed mark 'Clay King St/Covt. Garden', 20¼in. wide. (Christie's) $8,995

One of a pair of mid Victorian black, gold japanned papier-mache spill vases, 8in. wide. (Christie's) $471

A National Benzole Mixture, diamond with Mercury head petrol pump globe. (Onslow's) $214

Cleveland Super Discol petrol pump globe. (Onslow's) $148

Esso petrol pump globe. (Onslow's) $100

A post war B.P. shield petrol pump globe. (Onslow's) $300

A Redline Super, pre war petrol pump globe. (Onslow's) $185

Shell petrol pump bowl. (Onslow's) $143

A Shell, first design, pre war glass petrol pump globe. (Onslow's) $300

Pratts petrol pump bowl, pre-war. (Onslow's) $171

A Pratts post war glass petrol pump globe. (Onslow's) $429

A covered sugar bowl, by
Hiram Yale & Co., 1822-31,
6in. high. (Christie's)
$330

Pair of mid 19th century
fluid lamps, each with a
brass double wick holder,
6½in. high. (Christie's)
$154

A globular shaped teapot, by
Israel Trask, Mass., circa 1813-
56, 7½in. high. (Christie's)
$198

A beaker, by Rufus Dunham,
1837-60, marked with
Montgomery touch, 3.3/8in.
high. (Christie's) $77

A circular pewter basin with
single reed brim, marked on
base with 'Love' touch,
Laughlin 868, Phila., circa
1750-1800, 8in. diam.
(Christie's) $418

A mug on molded flaring
base with double scroll
handle, by T. Boardman &
Co., N.Y., 1822-25, marked
with Laughlin touch 432,
4½in. high. (Christie's)
$495

A cylindrical tankard, by
F. Bassett, N.Y., marked on
interior with Laughlin touch
468, 7in. high. (Christie's)
$8,800

A circular salt, the rim and
footrim with a beaded
molding, attributed to Wm.
Will, Phila., 1764-98, 2¼in.
high. (Christie's)$660

A small tapering, cylindrical
pitcher, by Wm. Savage,
circa 1838, 4½in. high.
(Christie's) $275

An oval shaped teapot with a domed oval cover, American, 1790-1810, 7½in. high. (Christie's)　$660

A pewter chamber pot, stamped with crown and other marks. (Lots Road Galleries)　$115

A covered sugar bowl, by G. Richardson, Rhode Island, 1830-45, 5in. high. (Christie's) $2,200

A small covered pitcher, by Simpson & Benham, N.Y., 1845-47, 6¼in. high. (Christie's) $220

A coffee pot of baluster shape with a hinged lid, by Daniel Curtiss, 1822-40, 11in. high. (Christie's) $242

A mug with double scroll handle, by Boardman & Hart, N.Y., 1827-50, 4½in. high. (Christie's) $495

A mug with S-scroll handle with a shell grip, by Robt. Bonynge, circa 1750-64, marked with Laughlin touch 292, 4¾in. high. (Christie's) $6,050

Pair of mid 19th century candlesticks, American, 9¾in. high, together with a modern pair, 7in. high. (Christie's) $286

A circular porringer, by S. Hamlin, marked with Laughlin touch 337, 5.5/8in. diam. (Christie's) $550

A coffee pot of shaped baluster form, by Luther Boardman, Mass., 1834-37, 11in. high. (Christie's) $220

A cylindrical humidor, with a domed and molded lid with an acorn finial, 6¾in. high. (Christie's) $242

A coffee pot of pyriform shape, by Roswell Gleason, Mass., 1821-71, 10¾in. high. (Christie's) $88

A vase-shaped pitcher, by George Richardson, 1828-45, marked with Jacobs touch 237, 7in. high. (Christie's) $308

A plate, by Frederick Bassett, N.Y., 1761-80 and 1785-99, marked with Montgomery touch, 8.3/8in. diam. (Christie's) $165

A globular teapot, by Chas. Yale, Conn., 1817-35, 8in. high. (Christie's) $132

A circular porringer with beaded brim and dolphin handle, by S. Danforth, marked with Laughlin touch 401, 5.5/8in. diam. (Christie's) $2,860

A covered pitcher of baluster form, by Thos. D. and S. Boardman, 1830-50, marked with Laughlin touch 435, 10in. high. (Christie's) $330

A flask with a threaded cap, by James Weekes, N.Y., 1820-43, marked with Laughlin touch, 7in. high. (Christie's) $495

A lighthouse coffee pot, by G. Richardson, Boston, 1818-28, 10½in. high. (Christie's) $330

A ship's hanging fluid lamp, by H. Yale and S. Curtis, N.Y., 1858-67, marked with Montgomery touch, 5in. high. (Christie's) $715

A coffee pot of baluster form, by Leonard, Reed & Barton, Mass., 1835-40, 12¾in. high. (Christie's) $308

A small pitcher, by Boardman & Hart, N.Y., 1830-50, marked with Laughlin touch 437, 4in. high. (Christie's) $220

A circular pewter plate, by J. C. Heyne, P.A., circa 1756-80, marked with initial and Jacobs touch 169, 6.3/8in. diam. (Christie's) $5,720

A pitcher of baluster form, by Daniel Curtiss, 1822-40, marked with Laughlin touch 523, 7¾in. high. (Christie's) $715

A pewter flagon with a domed lid, by Boardman & Co., N.Y., circa 1825-30, 12.1/8in. high.(Christie's) $1,760

A teapot of pyriform, by Luther or Thomas D. Boardman, circa 1840, 7¼in. high. (Christie's) $550

A porringer, by Thos. D. and S. Boardman, CT., 1810-30, the handle marked with Laughlin touch 428, 4in. diam. (Christie's) $286

A globular shaped teapot with a domed lid, by Roswell Gleason, Mass., 1830-40, with Jacobs touch 147, 7½in. high. (Christie's) $132

Late 18th century porringer, New England, 4½in. diam. (Christie's) $264

A globular teapot, by Thomas D. and Sherman Boardman, marked with Laughlin touch 428, 7½in. high. (Christie's) $198

A WMF pewter mounted engraved green glass decanter of flaring form, 9½in. high, stamped marks. (Christie's) $196

A Kayserzinn pewter teaset, the tray 18in. wide, all with stamped marks. (Christie's) $286

Late 18th century porringer with dolphin handle, New London or Hartford, 5½in. diam. (Christie's) $1,210

A porringer, the Old English handle marked with Laughlin touch 399, by S. Bamforth, 1795-1816, 5in. diam. (Christie's) $1,210

A beaker with two incised mid-bands on a single beaded base, by T. Boardman & Co., N.Y., 1822-25, marked with Laughlin touch 425, 3in. high. (Christie's) $176

A compressed globular shaped teapot, by H. B. Ward & Co., 1849 and later, 9in. high. (Christie's) $132

A teapot, by Wm. Will, Phila., 1764-98, marked on inside with Laughlin touches 538 and 539, 6¼in. high. (Christie's) $24,200

A porringer with flowered handle, by Gershom Jones, 1774-1809, with Laughlin touch 341, 5in. diam. (Christie's) $418

A teapot with a domed lid, a disc finial and an S-scroll spout, by G. Richardson, 1818-28, marked with Laughlin touch 310, 6¼in. high. (Christie's) $308

Late 18th/early 19th century beaker, American, 3in. high. (Christie's) $88

A 16th century German pewter sauce plate, the reverse with wheel touchmark (of Mainz), 19.2cm. diam. (Phillips) $576

A circular pewter salt, attributed to Wm. Will, Phila., 1764-98, 2¼in. high. (Christie's) $660

A circular plate, by F. Bassett, N.Y., 1761-80 and 1785-99, marked with Laughlin touches 467 and 464a, 9in. diam. (Christie's) $308

A vase-shaped pitcher with a flaring rim, by Rufus Dunham, Maine, 1837-61, 6½in. high. (Christie's) $385

A beaker, by Boardman & Hart, N.Y., 1828-53, 3.1/8in. high. (Christie's) $110

A lighthouse coffee pot, by Wm. Calder, Rhode Island, 1817-56, marked with Laughlin touch 350, 11¾in. high. (Christie's) $220

A porringer with everted brim and curved sides, probably by R. Lee, 1795-1816, 4½in. diam. (Christie's) $198

A coffee pot of tapering, cylindrical form, by Israel Trask, Mass., circa 1825-35, marked with Jacobs touch 262, 11½in. high. (Christie's) $418

A circular plate, by Thos. Danforth II or III, marked with Montgomery touch, 9½in. diam. (Christie's) $990

A WMF electroplated center-piece, modelled in full relief with a Middle Eastern lady, 19½in. high. (Christie's) $483

A pewter basin, marked on the interior with two eagle touches and the 'Richmond Warranted' touch, by Thos. Danforth, Virginia, circa 1807-12, 11.7/8in. diam.(Christie's) $2,640

A tapering, cylindrical flagon, by Boardman & Co., N.Y., 1825-27, marked 'X' and a Laughlin touch 431, 8in. high. (Christie's) $1,870

A tapering cylindrical mug, by Frederick Bassett, N.Y., 1761-80, marked with Montgomery touch, 4½in. high. (Christie's) $935

A tankard, by Thos. D. & Sherman Boardman, marked with Laughlin touch 428, 8in. high. (Christie's) $5,280

PEWTER

A coffee pot of baluster form, by Roswell Gleason, 1830-40, 11½in. high. (Christie's) $352

A porringer by Wm. Calder, 1817-56, flowered handle marked with Laughlin touch 350, 4¼in. diam. (Christie's) $550

A flagon with a low domed lid, attributed to Henry Will, Albany, 1775-83, 11¾in. high. (Christie's) $16,500

A circular pewter plate, Phila., marked on base with 'Love' touch, Laughlin 868, circa 1750-1800, 7¾in. diam. (Christie's) $242

A WMF pewter mounted green glass decanter of flaring form on four leaf molded feet, 15in. high. (Christie's) $453

A pewter circular plate, marked on base with 'Love' touch, Laughlin 868, Phila., circa 1750-1800, 8½in. diam. (Christie's) $286

A lighthouse coffee pot, by Israel Trask, Mass., 1813-56, 12¼in. high. (Christie's) $605

A tapering cylindrical mug, by Henry Will, N.Y., 1761-76, marked with Laughlin touch 491, 6¼in. high. (Christie's) $1,760

A cylindrical flagon, by Boardman & Co., N.Y., 1825-27, marked with Montgomery touch, 12½in. high. (Christie's) $2,420

A footed, vase-shaped pitcher, by Hiram Yale & Co., 1822-31, 13½in. high. (Christie's) $495

A circular porringer, by S. Hamlin, 1771-1801, handle marked with Laughlin touch 334, 4.1/8in. diam. (Christie's) $495

Late 19th century tankard of pyriform, with a low domed lid, probably English, 8in. high. (Christie's) $495

A tapering cylindrical tankard, by Wm. J. Ellsworth, N.Y., 1767-98, 9½in. high. (Christie's) $3,300

A Loetz pewter mounted two-handled iridescent glass vase, 8¾in. high. (Christie's) $483

A flagon with stepped domed lid, by Boardman & Co., N.Y., 1825-27, marked 'XX' and Laughlin touch 431, 12½in. high. (Christie's) $2,640

A ship's hanging lamp, by Yale & Curtis, N.Y., 1858-67, 7.7/8in. high. (Christie's) $550

An 18th century European basin, 13in. diam. (Christie's) $275

One of a pair of Art Nouveau silvered pewter vases, each cast Flora, with copper liners, 41.5cm. high. (Christie's) $1,346

A tapering cylindrical tankard, possibly by Parks Boyd, 7.5/8in. high. (Christie's) $4,180

Late 18th century porringer, with beaded brim and Penn. tab handle, 5.3/8in. diam. (Christie's) $110

A coffee pot of baluster form, marked 'I. Curtiss', circa 1818-25, marked with Laughlin touch 452, 10½in. high. (Christie's)
$220

A flagon with a domed lid and scrolling thumbpiece, by Boardman & Co., N.Y., 1825-27, marked with Montgomery touch, 11.1/8in. high. (Christie's) $550

A Liberty & Co. 'Tudric' pewter box and cover, designed by Archibald Knox, 11.9cm. high. (Christie's) $380

A tankard with S scroll handle, by Parks Boyd, Phila., 1795-1819, marked with Laughlin touch 546, 7½in. high. (Christie's)
$2,090

One of a set of mid 19th century American chalices, 8in. high. (Christie's) $550

A plate with smooth brim, by Nathaniel Austin, 1763-1807, marked with Laughlin touch 301, 8¾in. diam. (Christie's) $88

One of a pair of fluid lamps, by Joshua B. and Henry H. G. Graves, circa 1850, 9in. high. (Christie's) $880

PHOTOGRAPHS

Garibaldi, by Gustave Le Gray, albumen print, oval 10 x 7¾in., date 1860. (Christie's) $169

'The Everton Toffee Shop', ambrotype, approx. 8 x 9½in., photographer's label 'Lee, Portrait Rooms, Liverpool' and date April 1855. (Christie's) $105

Male nude, by R. Mapplethorpe, gelatin silver print, image size, 13¾ x 13¾in., dated '78. (Christie's) $775

'Fox Talbot', by John Moffat, carbon print, 17 x 12½in. (Christie's) $1,057

'Top Withens, West Riding, Yorkshire, 1944', by B. Brandt, gelatin silver print, 13½ x 11¼in., printed 1970's. (Christie's) $846

'Miners returning to daylight, South Wales', by B. Brandt, gelatin silver print, 16 x 12in., 1930's. (Christie's) $634

'Souvenir de St. Petersbourg', by Wm. Carrick and J. Dazario, album of 86 photographs, albumen prints, sizes from 3¾ x 2¼in. to 8½ x 10½in., 1870's. (Christie's) $634

Military group portrait, daguerreotype, approx. 4 x 5in., gilt matt, folding morocco case, circa 1850. (Christie's) $705

A Dexo Hoffman black and white gelatin silver print of Marilyn Monroe and Sir Lawrence Olivier, 1958. (Christie's) $382

PHOTOGRAPHS

Innes of Cowie family photographs, collection of 14 albums and a book-form case of cabinet cards, over 700 photographs, 1850-1920's. (Christie's) $1,339

Street Scene with Wine Shop, waxed paper negative, 6.7/8 x 8¾in., and an albumen positive print, 1850's. (Christie's) $775

Paris, after the Commune, 1871, by Franck and Liebert, fifteen albumen prints, majority 9¾ x 7¾in., 1871. (Christie's) $423

'Man Ray et Ses Amis', portfolio with essay by T. Baum, 4to, Paris: Filipacchi, n.d. (Christie's) $267

'Memorials of Bonnie Bonaly', by D. O. Hill and R. Adamson, album of twenty-seven calotypes. (Christie's) $23,970

Portraits from S. Europe, The Middle East and Russia, an album of 112 cartes-de-visite and 12 cabinet portraits, 1860's. (Christie's)$987

Japanese landscape, Samurai Warriors and military life, by F. Beato, F. C. Gould and others, an album of ninety-nine photographs, circa 1864. (Christie's) $19,740

Lady brushing her hair, by Oscar Gustave Rejlander, albumen print, 10 x 8in., circa 1860. (Christie's) $197

Japanese portraits, landscape and flower studies, two albums, each with fifty hand-tinted albumen prints, approx. 7½ x 9¾in., late 19th century. (Christie's) $535

'The Kiss of Peace', by J. M. Cameron, albumen print, 9 x 7in., 1869. (Christie's) $634

Farm Interior, by J. Whistler, salt print, 8½ x 10in, 1855-65. (Christie's) $1,692

Lt. James Lacey Reynolds and others, four quarter-plate daguerreotypes, late 1840's and early 1850's. (Christie's) $634

'Japanese Costumes', by F. Beato, Baron Von Stillfried and K. Kimbei, album of eighty-five albumen prints, 1870's. (Christie's) $1,692

South Pacific Islands, by J. W. Lindt, an album of twenty-four photographs, albumen prints, 6 x 8in., 1880's. (Christie's) $987

Royal portraits, Mr. Baldwin, Sir T. Lipton and others, by C. Van Dyk, H. Cecil and W. & D. Downey, collection of 39 portraits, gelatin silver prints and 3 carbon prints, 1929. (Christie's) $253

The snake collection, by F. Downer, album of 32 cabinet . cards, 1890's. (Christie's) $648

''The Old Country Houses of the Old Glasgow Gentry', by Thos. Annan, 4to, 1870. (Christie's) $564

'Mrs. Ewen Hay Cameron', by J. M. Cameron, albumen print, 13 x 10¼in., 1869. (Christie's) $493

PHOTOGRAPHS

'Old Closes and Streets', by Thos. Annan, a series of photogravures 1868-99 (Christie's) $493

The Scott Monument, by D. O. Hill and R. Adamson, calotype, 11½ x 14¾in., 1845. (Christie's) $1,057

'Salle des Statues, Vatican', by Charles Soulier, albumen print, 9¾ x 7½in., late 1860's. (Christie's) $141

Lord and Lady Canning family album, by Capt. J. Constantine Stanley, an album containing 117 albumen prints, dated 1858-61. (Christie's) $12,690

'Japan', by ?Baron Von Still-fried, album of twenty-nine hand-tinted albumen prints, 5½ x 4 to 10¼ x 8¼in., 1870's. (Christie's) $916

'The People of India', a series of photographic illustrations of the Races and Tribes of Hindu-stan, 1872 and 1875. (Christie's) $493

Still life and wall study, by R. Mayne, two gelatin silver prints, 8¾ x 7¼in. and 10½ x 9¼in., 1950's. (Christie's) $169

'Nude, March 1952', by B. Brandt, gelatin silver print, 16 x 12in. (Christie's) $987

'Old Closes and Streets of Glasgow', by T. Annan, 31 albumen prints, folio, 1868. (Christie's) $21,150

A George III mahogany square piano with ivory keyboard, enamel plaque inscribed 'Longman, Clementi & Comp'y, London, New Patent', 5ft.5in. wide. (Woolley & Wallis) $936

A Classical Revival mahogany inlaid pianoforte, Boston, circa 1825, 72½in. long. (Robt. W. Skinner Inc.) $3,400

A Carillon of twenty-five hemispherical metal bells (glockenspiel), by H. Godden, circa 1810, overall height with stand 55in. (Phillips) $835

A double-manual harpsichord, by Jacob Kirckman, 1761, 91½ x 37in. (Christie's) $123,200

A portable table harmonium in an oak case, by Metzler & Co., circa 1845, 23¼in. wide. (Phillips) $384

An English single manual harpsichord, by Jacob Kirckman, in a mahogany case, 87 x 37in. (Christie's) $24,564

An English spinet, by Charles Haward, in a walnut case, circa 1685, 58½in. wide. (Christie's) $24,640

A spinet shaped pianoforte by John C. Hancock, 1779, in a crossbanded mahogany case with figured walnut interior. (Christie's) $16,720

An English grand pianoforte, by John Broadwood, in mahogany case with sycamore interior on trestle stand, 88 x 38in. (Christie's) $5,702

A single manual harpsichord, by Jacob and Abraham Kirckman, London, 1784, 3ft.1in. wide. (Phillips) $15,030

An English spinet in a crossbanded mahogany case, circa 1740, 74in. wide, on later stand. (Christie's) $4,576

A W. Menzel Secessionist piano, the mahogany case with elaborate brass mounts, circa 1900, 148.1cm. wide. (Christie's) $1,029

A Meerschaum figural pipe, in the form of a Victorian lady's head, amber stem, bowl 3¼in. long, in leather case. (Robt. W. Skinner Inc.) $400

A Meerschaum trick rider pipe, blossom bowl with lady on ground near running horse, 4.3/8in. long, in leather case. (Robt. W. Skinner Inc.) $375

A Meerschaum figural pipe, in the form of Turkish man's head wearing tasseled fez, bowl 3¼in. long. (Robt. W. Skinner Inc.) $350

Eastern Plains/Wester Woodlands wood and stone pipe, 23¾in. long. (Robt. W. Skinner Inc.) $880

Late 19th century Meerschaum pipe, carved with a lion's head, 7½in. long. (Robt. W. Skinner Inc.) $400

An Imperial German Hussar Reservists porcelain pipe, overall length 44in. (Wallis & Wallis) $83

A Meerschaum figural pipe, bowl in the form of tree trunk with rearing horse startled by a snake, bowl 4¾in. long, in leather case. (Robt. W. Skinner Inc.) $750

A Meerschaum figural pipe, conch shell bowl with lady and two dolphins, bowl 4.1/8in. long, and another. (Robt. W. Skinner Inc.) $475

A Staffordshire pottery curled pipe painted with blue and yellow dashes. (Christie's) $400

PLASTER

A plaster bust of George II, his hair dressed with laurels. (Christie's) $707

A Richard Garbe green-tinted plaster figure of a naked seated maiden, 1928, 104cm. high. (Christie's) $1,074

Pair of painted plaster bookends, each modelled as a bowl of fruit, 8¾in. high. (Christie's) $277

A Richard Garbe plaster figure of a naked maiden, 1912, 99cm. high. (Christie's) $660

An English plaster panel, in oak frame carved 'Speed with the light-foot winds to run', 42.2 x 37.7cm. (Christie's) $168

A plaster instructional torso colored and numbered and arranged so as to dismantle for display purposes, 33in. high. (Christie's) $918

A colored plaster instructional torso, showing muscular construction and some internal organs, 33in. high. (Christie's) $94

A Richard Garbe plaster figure of a naked kneeling maiden with streaming hair and flowing drapery, 102cm. high. (Christie's) $1,239

A Richard Garbe buff tinted plaster group of a seated fawn with a figure gazing up at him, 1924, 76.5cm. high. (Christie's) $495

A gentleman, by Jean E. P. M. Delacluze, on card, gilt metal frame, oval, 5.1/8in. high. (Christie's) $471

A lady, possibly Angelica Kauffman, by Richard Cosway, gold frame, silver mount with diamond border, oval, 1¾in. high. (Christie's) $1,573

George, 3rd Earl of Egremont, by Thomas Day, signed and dated 1785, gold colored frame, oval, 1¾in. high. (Christie's) $1,022

Catharine Inglis, aged 31, by George Engleheart, gold frame, oval, 1¾in. high. (Christie's) $2,202

William Freeman, by Christian Frederick Zincke, enamel, gilt metal frame, oval, 1.7/8in. high. (Christie's) $1,022

A lady in decollete white dress, by Jean-Francois-Marie Huet-Villiers, gilt metal frame, oval, 2.7/8in. high. (Christie's) $550

Louis XIV wearing the sash of the Order of the St. Esprit, by Jean Petitot, enamel, gilt metal frame, oval, 1½in. high. (Christie's) $2,988

Maria Theresa, by Le Sage, signed, gilt metal frame, 3in. diam. (Christie's) $660

An officer in scarlet uniform with white facings and gold lace, black turned wood frame, oval, 3in. high. (Christie's) $503

A lady in decollete brown dress, by Susan Penelope Rosse, on vellum, gilt metal frame with spiral cresting, oval, 1.7/8in. high. (Christie's) $1,573

A miniature of Gurmin, George Adolph Barras, by Rodolphe Bel (Bell), on card, signed and dated 1820, oval, 4¾in. high. (Christie's) $1,258

A lady in black dress, by Jacques J. G. Vidal, signed and dated 1859, oval, 2¾in. high. (Christie's) $629

A lady nearly full face in white dress and fichu, by John Barry, oval, 2in. high. (Christie's) $578

Major Edward John Lake, aged 13, by Herman, signed and dated 1836, 2.5/8in. high. (Christie's) $1,022

Catherine Blount (Mrs. Freeman), Circle of Charles Boit, enamel, gilt metal frame, oval, 1.7/8in. high. (Christie's) $786

A gentleman in blue coat, by Andrew Robertson, turned wood frame, oval, 2.7/8in. high. (Christie's) $597

Lettice Knollys, The Countess of Essex, English School, circa 1720, on card, 1.7/8in. diam. (Christie's) $1,074

A gentleman, by Samuel Shelley, signed on the reverse, gold frame, oval, 2¼in. high. (Christie's) $550

Col. Montalba in scarlet uniform of the second Horse Guards, by John Smart, signed and dated 1771, oval, 1½in. high. (Christie's) $4,293

A lady full face in decollete white dress, by Louis Lie Perin-Salbreux, signed, 2½in. diam. (Christie's) $1,404

A gentleman with gray hair and blue eyes, wearing a black coat, by Raphael Peale, circa 1795, 2.3/8in. high. (Christie's) $1,980

A lady facing right in white dress with lace border, by Le Chevalier De Chateaubourg, oval, 2¾in. high. (Christie's) $330

A gentleman in blue coat with black collar, white waistcoat and cravat, by S. Shelley, oval, 2¾in. high. (Christie's) $462

A lady with white turban, brown hair and gray dress, attributed to Henry Inman, circa 1820, 2½in. high. (Christie's) $1,320

Perhaps Mr. Vavasour facing right in blue coat, by George Engleheart, signed with cursive E, oval, 3.1/8in. high. (Christie's) $1,453

A gentleman with his son and daughter, attributed to Michael M. Daffinger, oval, 1¼in. high. (Christie's) $1,023

A gentleman in ochre-colored coat, by Noah Seeman, enamel, signed on the reverse N. Seeman and dated 1723, oval, 2in. high. (Christie's) $1,156

Robert Parry Nesbet, M.P., by John C. D. Engleheart, oval, 3¼in. high. (Christie's) $1,982

A lady seated before a harp, in mauve dress edged with lace, Continental School, 2½in. diam. (Christie's) $1,618

A Sea Captain with cropped gray hair and brown eyes, American, circa 1800, 2½in. high. (Christie's) $605

Mrs. Wm. Few, (Catharine Witter), by John Ramage, 1787, in a gold locket frame with half pearls, 1½in. high. (Christie's) $4,520

A gentleman facing left in blue coat with gold buttons, white waistcoat and tied cravat, by N. Plimer, oval, 2¾in. high. (Christie's) $413

A girl facing three-quarters to left in white muslin dress, by Andrew Plimer, oval, 3.1/8in. high. (Christie's) $1,321

A nobleman facing left in black doublet and lace ruff, by Isaac Oliver, on card, signed with monogram, oval, 2in. high. (Christie's) $1,569

A lady resting her elbow and head on the edge of a blue sofa, by Jeremiah Meyer, oval, 2¼in. high. (Christie's) $1,404

Gustav IV Adolph, King of Sweden, by Jacob Axel Gillberg, oval, 1¼in. high. (Christie's) $578

A lady nearly full face in white dress, black hat with bow, coral bead necklace, by G. Engleheart, signed and dated 1805 on the reverse, oval, 3¼in. high. (Christie's) $2,974

A gentleman in dark brown coat, by Abraham Seaman, enamel, signed on the reverse AB Seaman, oval, 1¾in. high. (Christie's) $957

A lady facing right in white dress sewn with ropes of pearls, by John Smart, signed with initials and dated 1786, oval, 1.7/8in. high. (Christie's) $8,262

A portrait miniature of a gentleman, American, circa 1790, 1¾in. high. (Christie's) $550

William Young wearing a black coat with black waistcoat, by James Peale, 1807, 2.7/8in. high. (Christie's) $5,500

A gentleman with long gray hair, attributed to Wm. Verstille, circa 1790, oval, 1¾in. high. (Christie's) $715

Edward Shaw, bust length, facing right, by Wm. Verstille, circa 1790, oval, 1.7/8in. high. (Christie's) $1,320

A lady in white dress and turban headgear, by George Engleheart, oval, 3in. high. (Christie's) $1,453

A gentleman wearing a dark purple coat and yellow waistcoat, by James Peale, 1791, 2½in. high. (Christie's) $7,150

A girl in white muslin dress with lace border, yellow sash and coral bead necklace, by Andrew Plimer, oval, 3.1/8in. high. (Christie's) $2,974

A gentleman in crimson coat, lace cravat and powdered wig, by C. F. Zincke, enamel, oval, 1.7/8in. high. (Christie's) $1,074

Matilda Few, wearing a white dress with shirred lace collar, shoulders and bust, by N. Rogers, circa 1820, 2.7/8in. high. (Christie's) $3,080

Lt.-Col. Benjamin Tallmadge, wearing Continental Army uniform, by John Ramage, circa 1785, 1.7/8in. high. (Christie's) $4,400

A gentleman, facing left, the reverse with locket of hair shaped as a feather, American, circa 1815, 2.7/8in. high. (Christie's) $605

Thomas Witter with a fringe of gray hair, by John Ramage, circa 1780, 1¾in. high. (Christie's) $1,100

Samuel Foote wearing a black coat, against a shaded green field, American, circa 1800, 2¾in. high. (Christie's) $990

A miniature of Mrs. Sturm, by Richard Cosway, signed and dated 1795 on reverse, oval, 3½in. high. (Christie's) $4,626

A nobleman in brown coat with gold frogging, by C. F. Zincke, enamel, oval, 1.7/8in. high. (Christie's) $991

L.N.E.R. Fraserburgh, Glorious Sands, Bathing, Golf, Tennis, by H. G. Gawthorn. (Onslow's) $418

Shillingford Bridge, Oxfordshire, See Britain First On Shell, No. 282, by D. Adams, 30 x 45in. (Onslow's) $248

Anchor Line Glasgow & New York via Londonderry, by K. Shoesmith. (Onslow's) $527

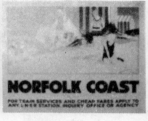

L.N.E.R. Harrogate, by Frank Newbould. (Onslow's) $336

Your Cue for Summer Sunshine, by Shep. S.R., quad royal, 40 x 50in. (Onslow's) $345

L.N.E.R. The Norfolk Coast, by Picking. (Onslow's) $640

The Glasgow Herald £650 Golf Tournament at Gleneagles Open to the World's Players May 1920, 40 x 30in., and another. (Onslow's) $93

L.N.E.R. Scarborough, by Austin Cooper, 1932. (Onslow's) $573

Maurice Denis: 'La Depeche — Grand Format', a chromolithographic poster, 145.5 x 100cm. (Phillips) $100

Rio de Janeiro by Royal Mail to South America, by K. Shoesmith. (Onslow's) $384

S.R. Winter in the Southern Sunshine and Warmth of Bournemouth City Gaiety Amid Rural Surroundings, by H. G. Gawthorn, 1939. (Onslow's) $434

L.M.S. Travel to Ireland By The Stranraer-Larne Route, by N. Wilkinson. (Onslow's) $279

L.M.S. Southport, by Fortunio Matania, quad royal, 40 x 50in. (Onslow's) $720

L.N.E.R. Felixstowe, by Tom Purvis. (Onslow's) $713

L.M.S. Llandudno, by Chas. Pears, quad royal 40 x 50in. (Onslow's) $129

Cunard, Europe America Berengaria, by Odin Rosenvinge. (Onslow's) $775

Caledonian Railway, Gleneagles For Golf 'In The Very He'rt o' Scotland', by Fred Taylor. (Onslow's) $511

P.S.N.C. to South America, by K. Shoesmith. (Onslow's) $308

Pierre Bonnard: Le Menu,
lithograph, circa 1925, on
Chine, signed in pencil,
309 x 273mm. (Christie's)
$1,093

Sheep, Plate VI from Sheep
Album, by Henry Moore,
etching with drypoint, 1972,
on Rives, 188 x 253mm.
(Christie's) $2,534

Three Heads of Women, by
Rembrandt Harmensz. van
Rijn, etching, 143 x 96mm.
(Christie's) $2,376

Slippery Steps, by Sir William
Russell Flint, drypoint printed
in brown, 1929, on J. Whatman
wove paper, watermark 1831,
238 x 173mm. (Christie's)
$601

El Lissitzky: Mani Leib, Ingle
Zingle Chwat, Kultur-Lige,
Warsaw, 1922, zincographs,
title page plus ten pages of text
and illustrations, 138 x 109mm.
(Christie's) $2,030

The Holy Family with the
Butterfly, by Albrecht Durer,
engraving, 237 x 165mm.
(Christie's) $2,851

David Hockney: Gregory,
etching printed in colors,
1974, 688 x 545mm.
(Christie's) $2,655

Hokusai, oban yoko-e, from the series
Fugaku Sanjurokkei, Sunshu Ejiri,
signed Zen Hokusai Iitsu hitsu, 25.4 x
38.5cm. (Christie's) $2,851

The vision of St. Francis,
etching by F. Barocci,
534 x 323mm.
(Christie's) $712

David Hockney: Godetia, etching, 1973, on Arches, signed and dated, 433 x 292mm. (Christie's) $4,998

Hokusai, oban yoko-e, from the series Fugaku Sanjurokkei, Sunshu Ejiri, signed Zen Hokusai Iitsu hitsu, 24.1 x 36.6cm. (Christie's) $3,168

Gerald Leslie Brockhurst, Le Beguin, etching, signed in pencil, 13.8 x 11cm. (Phillips) $158

Utamaro, oban tate-e, a bust portrait of the courtesan Hanaoogi, published by Omiya Gonkuro, 37.7 x 25cm. (Christie's) $3,168

Henri Matisse: Marie-Jose en Robe jaune, aquatint printed in five colors, 1950, on Arches, 537 x 417mm. (Christie's) $43,736

Hokusai, oban tate-e, from the series Shokoku Takimeguri, 37.2 x 25.5cm. (Christie's) $8,712

The Great War: Building Ships, by Sir M. Bone, 668 x 550mm. (Christie's) $443

St. Anthony, by Albrecht Durer, engraving, 99 x 142mm. (Christie's) $3,009

Henri de Toulouse-Lautrec: Mme. Marcelle Lender en Buste, de Trois Quarts, lithograph, 1898. (Christie's) $11,715

El Lissitzky: Beat the Whites with the Red Wedge, lithograph printed in red and black, 1919, on tan wove paper, 460 x 557mm. (Christie's) $29,678

An engraving of two galleys and a man of war, after Pieter Brueghel, the Elder, 248 x 278mm. (Christie's) $2,296

Winifred Austen, Budgerigars, aquatint printed in colors, signed and titled in pencil, 21 x 27cm. (Phillips) $230

Michael Chijarev: The Progress of the Five Year Plan, offset lithograph printed in black, red, blue and yellow, 1929, on wove paper, 681 x 1018mm. (Christie's) $562

Christ Healing the Sick, by Rembrandt Harmensz. van Rijn, etching with drypoint and engraving, third state (of four), 278 x 398mm. (Christie's) $4,118

Marc Chagall: Le Jugement de Chloe, from Daphnis et Chloe, lithograph printed in colors, 1961, on Arches, signed in pencil, 427 x 641mm. (Christie's) $39,050

A hand-colored lithograph on paper, 'Arguing The Point', by Nathaniel Currier, N.Y., 1855. (Robt. W. Skinner Inc.) $1,000

Georges Braque: Oiseau bleu et jaune, lithograph printed in colors, 1960, on Japon nacre, signed in pencil, 330 x 515mm. (Christie's)
$5,935

Paul Cezanne: Les Baigneurs, lithograph printed in colors, circa 1898, on laid paper, 419 x 528mm. (Christie's) $28,116

Max Beckmann: Der Morgen, drypoint, 1923, on cream wove paper, signed in pencil, 258 x 308mm. (Christie's) $2,343

Homenatge a Joan Prats, by Joan Miro, lithograph printed in colors, 1971, on Guarro wove paper, from the set of fifteen, numbered 40/75 (full edition 113), 545 x 753mm. (Christie's) $1,742

Currier and Ives: 'Winter Morning — Feeding The Chickens', circa 1863, hand-colored lithograph. (Robt. W. Skinner Inc.)
$4,400

PRINTS

Felix the Cat, one of nine original animated celluloids including The Pink Panther, Inspector Clouseau and others. (Christie's) $76

Pablo Picasso: Tete de jeune Fille, lithograph, 1949, on Arches, second (final) state, signed in pencil, 397 x 298mm. (Christie's) $15,620

Walter Richard Sickert: The Hanging Gardens, etching, published by Ernest Brown & Phillipi, 1928, 17.6 x 11cm. (Phillips) $187

Eishi, oban tate-e, from the set Ukiyo Genji Hakkei, print published by Nishimuraya Yohachi. (Christie's) $2,059

Edvard Munch: Das kranke Madchen, drypoint, 1894, on stiff wove paper, fifth state of six, 384 x 289mm. (Christie's) $13,277

Hiroshige, oban tate-e, from the series Meisho Edo Hyakkei, Ohashi, Atake no Yudachi, 37.4 x 25.3cm. (Christie's) $12,672

Kathe Kollwitz: Arbeiterfrau mit Schlafenden Jungen, lithograph, 1927, on stiff wove paper, signed in pencil, 393 x 336mm. (Christie's) $5,467

Eine Liebe, by Max Klinger, etchings, 1887, on wove paper, title and set of ten plates, from the fourth (final) edition, 695 x 534mm. (Christie's) $1,425

Tsuguji Foujita: Le Chat, etching with aquatint and roulette printed in colors, circa 1925, on Chine applique, 378 x 290mm. (Christie's) $8,591

PRINTS

Kasimir Malevich: Patriotic Poster against the Germans, lithograph printed in colors, 1914-15, on wove paper, 516 x 340mm. (Christie's) $4,061

One of two original hand paintings on celluloid, from the Walt Disney film Snow White and the Seven Dwarfs, 6½ x 9½in. (Christie's) $994

The Great War: Britain's Efforts and Ideals, Making Soldiers, by Sir F. Brangwyn, lithographs, 1917, set of six, five signed, 455 x 357mm. and smaller. (Christie's) $1,108

Henri de Toulouse-Lautrec: Le Jockey, lithograph printed in colors, 1899, on Chine, second (final) state, 514 x 361mm. (Christie's) $28,116

Rue de Seine, by David Hockney, etching, 1971, on J. Green, moldmade wove paper, signed and dated '72, 537 x 434mm. (Christie's) $7,603

Kunisada, oban tate-e, an okubi-e of the actor Onoe Matsusuke II as the carpenter Rokusaburo, 37.1 x 25.6cm. (Christie's) $91,008

Jacques Villon' Autre Temps, 1830, drypoint with aquatint printed in colors, 1904, on wove paper, 445 x 353mm. (Christie's) $10,934

The Great War: Britain's Efforts and Ideals, Making Sailors, by Sir F. Brangwyn, lithographs, circa 1917, set of six, 670 x 545mm. (Christie's) $396

Henri de Toulouse-Lautrec: Mme. Marcelle Lender, en Buste, 1898, 249 x 215mm. (Christie's) $11,715

Mid 19th century pieced and applique cotton quilt, American, 103½in. long, 100in. wide. (Christie's) $2,420

An undyed linen coverlet, the whole embroidered in colored wools with crewel work, 2.26 x 2.12m. (Phillips) $369

A 19th century pieced and quilted cotton coverlet, American, 87½in. long, 71½in. wide. (Christie's) $1,430

Mid 19th century appliqued quilt, the field divided into squares with a variation of the 'Rose of Sharon' pattern, 92 x 104in. (Robt. W. Skinner Inc.) $650

Political patchwork quilt, American, circa 1844, 88 x 88in. (Robt. W. Skinner Inc.) $1,200

Mid 19th century American pieced and appliqued quilted coverlet, worked in a Rose of Sharon variation pattern, 94 x 94in. (Christie's) $1,320

QUILTS

Patchwork coverlet, variant of 'The Star of
Bethlehem' pattern, possibly by Mrs. George
R. Newton, America, circa 1856, 118in. sq.
(Robt. W. Skinner Inc.) $3,200

A mosaic patchwork cover composed of plain
and patterned silks and velvets, E. F. Slade,
March 2nd 1864, 80 x 84in. (Christie's)
$237

Mid 19th century American pieced and appliqued quilted coverlet, 88 x 87in. (Christie's)
$715

Mid 19th century applique and stuffed cotton
quilt, American, 77½in. long, 74in. wide.
(Christie's) $1,760

Pieced Star of Bethlehem quilt, New England,
circa 1850, 90 x 92in. (Robt. W. Skinner Inc.)
$900

Mid 19th century pieced and appliqued quilt
top, probably Penn., 88 x 88in. (Christie's)
$2,420

Dire Straits, a presentation 'Platinum' disc, 'Brothers In Arms', the album mounted above a reduction of the L.P. cover and a plaque. (Christie's) $489

A set of hand 'Reindeer' bells, with red wooden handle used by John Lennon for the recording of 'Happy Christmas (War Is Over)', 1972, 12in. long.(Christie's) $1,377

A promotional postcard for the release of The Move album, 'Flowers In The Rain', circa 1967. (Christie's) $306

A 1966-69 Vox Mando 12 String Guitar in sunburst, serial no. 74309. (Christie's) $306

George Harrison, the original artist's proof for an un-issued album cover, 'Somewhere in England', Dark Horse Records, 1981, 18½ x 26in. (Christie's) $994

An early 1960's Hofner Violin (Beatle) Bass in sunburst with added Hofner style knobs, serial no. 1019. (Christie's) $382

One of four polychrome Richard Avedon psychedelic posters of The Beatles, produced for the Daily Express, circa 1967, each 27½ x 19½in., together with another of the four Beatles, 15½ x 40½in. (Christie's) $428

A 1976 Portative Organ by N. P. Mander Ltd., custom made for David Palmer of Jethro Tull, used on tour between 1976-80 and on the album 'Songs From The Wood'. (Christie's) $1,530

A Corgi 'Yellow Submarine' toy, the die cast scale model with two opening hatches revealing figures of The Beatles, circa 1967, 5in. long, in original box. (Christie's) $183

'Old Wrecked Car — Portugal', circa 1977, a silk screen print of a color photograph taken by Linda McCartney, no. 5 of a limited edition of 150, 18¾ x 13in. (Christie's) $382

'Our First Four', a cardboard presentation folder containing the first four 45 r.p.m. records produced by Apple Records Ltd., 13½ x 9½in. (Christie's) $336

George Benson, a presentation 'Platinum' disc, 'Breezin', the album mounted above a reduction of the L.P. cover, and a plaque. (Christie's) $275

A limited edition resin bronze G.R.P. bust of Jimi Hendrix, circa 1985, by J. Somerville, no. 5 of an edition of 20, 24in. high. (Christie's) $459

John Lennon, a self portrait with Yoko Ono in black felt-tip pen, autographed by John and Yoko beside each appropriate caricature, 7½ x 10½in., 1969. (Christie's) $1,836

A Mark Smith Custom electric guitar, the body and sides in mahogany with a two-piece bird's-eye maple top. (Christie's) $765

Original etching and aquatint of 'The King', by David Oxtoby, signed by the artist, 27 x 21½in. (Christie's) $382

A quantity of autograph material from Pink Floyd, The Who, Marvin Gaye and 'Auf Wiedersehen Pet'. (Christie's) $306

A 1960's Fender Tremolux amplifier and 2 x 10in. speaker cabinet in light colored Tolex vinyl, used on the set of the Paul McCartney Film, 'Give My Regards to Broad Street'. (Christie's) $734

Dire Straits, a presentation 'Platinum' disc, 'Brothers In Arms', the album mounted with a 'platinum' cassette above a reduction of the album cover. (Christie's) $612

A copy of the Marriage Certificate of John Winston Lennon and Yoko Ono Cox, contracted at the Registrar's Office, in the City and Garrison of Gibraltar, by Governor's Special Licence, on 20th March, 1969. (Christie's) $4,590

A colored screen print portrait of Mick Jagger, by Andy Warhol, number 176 of 250 copies, 44 x 29in., 1975. (Christie's) $841

The Beatles, 'Help', Parlophone 33⅓ r.p.m., mono, 1965, signed on the cover by each of The Beatles, and inscribed 'All the Best, George Harrison'. (Christie's) $1,836

Jimi Hendrix, one of four unpublished black and white photographs taken at The Round House, Chalk Farm, London, in Feb. 1967, 14 x 9in. (Christie's) $581

The Beatles, Peter le Vasseur, 'Illustration for the Beatles Song "In My Life" ', dated 1969, oil on board, 8½ x 8½in. (Christie's) $994

Pete Townshend's pound note suit worn in 'Tommy', circa 1975, with label 'Bermans & Nathans'. (Christie's) $2,754

The Beatles, a signed menu for the Supper Party following Royal World Premiere "Help!". (Christie's) $642

One of three Dezo Hoffman portrait photographs of The Rolling Stones, 8 x 12in., 9 x 12in. and 12 x 9½in. (Christie's) $168

An Armenian Caucasian rug, dated 1916, 4ft.9in. x 8ft. (Robt. W. Skinner Inc.) $3,200

A Shirvan long rug, 10ft.8in. x 4ft.9in. (Christie's) $6,600

A Lesghi rug, the sable field with three medallions, enclosed by a main ivory serrated leaf and calyx border, 1.52m. x 99cm. (Phillips) $1,704

A Kashan carpet, the ivory ground covered by three concentric medallions, 12ft.2in. x 8ft.8in. (Christie's) $9,350

A Bidjar rug, the red field with indigo radiating medallion and design of arabesque scrolling stems, 2.08 x 1.08m. (Phillips) $1,349

Late 19th century Gendje rug, the ivory, blue and gold diagonal stripes of botehs and palmettes, 5ft.9in. x 4ft.4in. (Robt. W. Skinner Inc.) $2,400

Kazak prayer rug, dated 1311 (1894), ivory mihrab bordered in blue-green, 4ft.5in. x 3ft.7in. (Robt. W. Skinner Inc.) $800

A 17th century Ushak rug, W. Anatolia, 5ft. x 3ft.3in. (Robt. W. Skinner Inc.) $27,000

Mid 19th century Bergama rug, W. Anatolia. (Robt. W. Skinner Inc.) $2,000

An Uzbek Bochara suzani, the linen ground embroidered in colored silks, 2.46 x 1.46m. (Phillips) $755

A Qum rug, the ivory field with an overall pattern of cusped flowerheads, boteh and medallions, 6ft.9in. x 4ft.4in. (Christie's) $1,435

A Sarouk rug, the ivory field with rows of boteh enclosed by a main sable stylized flowerhead border, 1.95 x 1.19m. (Phillips) $1,368

A Kashan silk rug of prayer design, 2.10 x 1.25m. (Phillips) $4,032

A Tabriz silk prayer rug, the pistachio mihrab with a hanging bowl of flowers. (Phillips) $2,304

One of two India Drugget scatter rugs, designed by Gustav Stickley, circa 1910, 38in. wide. (Robt. W. Skinner Inc.) $650

A hand-knotted woollen rug, the design possibly by A. Knox, with Celtic motif in pink and blue on a white ground, 153.5 x 86cm. (Christie's) $527

A 19th century Aubusson tapestry rug with plum field, 1.84 x 1.87m. (Phillips) $5,472

Late 19th/early 20th century Kuba rug, Eastern Caucasus, 4ft.7in. x 3ft.3in. (Robt. W. Skinner Inc.) $2,400

A mid 19th century Rescht cover, the red ground with yellow, green and blue insertions with ivory silk embroidery, 2.20 x 1.44m. (Phillips) $634

Late 19th century Baluch rug, (sides and ends rebound), 3ft.10in. x 7ft. (Robt. W. Skinner Inc.) $625

A 19th century Spanish Aubusson part metal thread Entre Fenetre, 3.26 x 1.88m. (Phillips) $3,600

A 'Savonnene' carpet, the ivory trellis field enclosed by a gray foliate meander border, 4.50 x 3.20m. (Phillips) $5,760

A Ziegler carpet, the mustard field with a central lozenge-shaped terracotta pendant medallion, 3.42 x 3.36m. (Phillips) $7,800

An Isfahan carpet, the ivory field with scrolling palmettes and flowering vine, 10ft.2in. x 6ft.8in. (Christie's) $3,987

India Drugget area carpet, Nile pattern, circa 1910, 9ft.10in. x 7ft.8½in. (Robt. W. Skinner Inc.) $475

An Agra carpet, the wine field with an all over design, 4.5 x 3.6m. (Phillips) $6,048

Late 19th/early 20th century Sennah mat, 3ft.7in. x 1ft. 9in. (Robt. W. Skinner Inc.) $200

Early 20th century Chinese rug, 3ft.1in. x 4ft.10in. (Robt. W. Skinner Inc.) $1,100

Late 19th/early 20th century Kazak rug, the red field with central blue stepped hexagon, 5ft.3in. x 6ft. 5in. (Robt. W. Skinner Inc.) $3,100

Late 19th/early 20th century Feraghan rug, C.Persia, 7ft.3in. x 4ft.8in. (Robt. W. Skinner Inc.) $4,200

Late 19th century Shirvan rug with an ivory 'wine cup' main border, 5ft.8in. x 3ft. 8in. (Robt. W. Skinner Inc.) $3,400

Early 20th century Heriz carpet, the brick-red field with dark blue and blue-green central medallion, 8ft.9in. x 11ft. (Robt. W. Skinner Inc.) $2,000

Late 19th century Serapi carpet, the rust-red field with dark blue lobed medallions, 8ft.2in. x 12ft. 6in. (Robt. W. Skinner Inc.) $7,500

Late 19th century Kuba rug, the electric blue field with all-over geometric floral grid, 5ft.3in. x 4ft. (Robt. W. Skinner Inc.) $4,500

Early 19th century 'pin-wheel' Kazak rug, 5ft.8in. x 7ft.5in. (Robt. W. Skinner Inc.) $4,300

Mid 19th century Kazak rug, the abrashed yellow green to blue green field with four hooked hexagons, 4ft.9in. x 6ft.8in. (Robt. W. Skinner Inc.) $6,500

Late 19th/early 20th century
Kazak rug, 8ft.2in. x 5ft.9in.
(Robt. W. Skinner Inc.)
$4,000

Mid 19th century Bordjalou
Kazak rug, 5ft. x 6ft.7in.
(Robt. W. Skinner Inc.)
$5,100

Late 19th/early 20th century
Kazak rug, 4ft.7in. x 6ft.5in.
(Robt. W. Skinner Inc.)
$3,100

Late 19th century Kazak
rug, 4ft.8in. x 7ft.10in.
(Robt. W. Skinner Inc.)
$1,800

Late 19th century Konagend
rug, E. Caucasus, the lattice
of ivory stylized floral designs
on a dark blue field, 4ft.5in.
x 3ft.8in. (Robt. W. Skinner
Inc.) $2,700

Early 19th century Ghiordes
prayer rug, 4ft. x 5ft.6in.
(Robt. W. Skinner Inc.)
$3,900

Mid 19th century Kuba rug,
E. Caucasus, the red field
woven in a trellis of red, blue,
black and ivory diamonds,
3ft.7in. x 4ft.6in. (Robt. W.
Skinner Inc.) $900

Early 20th century Kashan carpet
with an all-over trellis of flower
filled cartouches, 10ft.2in. x 15ft.
8in. (Robt. W. Skinner Inc.)
$8,000

A Chi-Chi rug, the indigo
field with stepped hooked
medallions, 1.85 x 1.29m.
(Phillips) $2,272

Late 19th century Kazak rug, the red field with three blue and green medallions, 4ft.4in. x 3ft.5in. (Robt. W. Skinner Inc.) $1,100

Mid 19th century Kazak rug, S.W. Caucasus, 3ft.11in. x 5ft.8in. (Robt. W. Skinner Inc.) $3,600

An Indian Dhurry, the ivory field with lozenge design and stylized flowering plants, 2.08 x 1.18m. (Phillips) $2,448

Late 19th/early 20th century cloud-band Kazak long rug, 8ft.8in. x 4ft.1in. (Robt. W. Skinner Inc.) $1,800

A 19th century E. Turkestan Kashgar silk mat, 3ft.1in. x 3ft.2in. (Robt. W. Skinner Inc.) $2,900

Late 19th century Ersari Chuval with all-over mina khani pattern, 5ft.3in. x 3ft. (Robt. W. Skinner Inc.) $350

Late 19th century Chi-Chi rug, the blue field with all-over pattern of geometrical shapes, 3ft.10in. x 5ft.4in. (Robt. W. Skinner Inc.) $300

Late 19th century Lesghi star E. Caucasian rug, 2ft.8in. x 3ft.7in. (Robt. W. Skinner Inc.) $700

Late 19th century Afshar rug, S.W. Persia, the yellow green field with all-over grid of small red flowerheads and blue boteh motifs, 4ft.2in. x 5ft.2in. (Robt. W. Skinner Inc.) $4,500

RUGS

A 19th century E. Caucasian long rug, 4ft.5in. x 8ft.6in. (Robt. W. Skinner Inc.) $2,400

Cotton Disney characters scatter rug, 1950's, 45 x 59in. (Robt. W. Skinner Inc.) $35

Mid 19th century Kuba rug, the abrashed blue field filled with ivory and abrashed green shield-like palmettes, 3ft.7in. x 6ft. (Robt. W. Skinner Inc.) $3,800

A 19th century Chinese carpet, embossed phoenix figures on an ivory-taupe field, 8ft.9in. x 11ft.5in. (Robt. W. Skinner Inc.) $3,100

A Kashan silk rug, the ivory field with a crimson cartouche pendant medallion, 2.06 x 1.24m. (Phillips) $1,872

An Afshar rug, the field with yellow, indigo and plum-red columns of stylized plants, 4ft.9in. x 3ft.8in. (Christie's) $2,481

A shield Kazak rug with tomato-red field, 7ft.9in. x 5ft.11in. (Christie's) $3,190

Late 19th century Malayer rug, the ivory field woven in a design of offset palmettes on leafy vines, 4ft.4in. x 6ft. 4in. (Robt. W. Skinner Inc.) $2,400

Late 19th century East Caucasian rug, the dark blue field with two saw-tooth edged medallions, 4ft. x 5ft. 8in. (Robt. W. Skinner Inc.) $950

SAMPLERS

Needlework sampler, silk yarns worked on ivory linen ground fabric, by 'Harriatt Shoveller, 1799', England, 12½ x 17in. (Robt. W. Skinner Inc.) $1,600

Framed needlework pictorial sampler, inscribed 'Harroit Hoyle, Aged 21, 1834', 24 x 24in. (Robt. W. Skinner Inc.) $2,200

Needlework spot sampler, Germany, 1759, vivid polychrome silk yarns on natural linen fabric, 12 x 21½in. (Robt. W. Skinner Inc.) $2,500

Needlework sampler, 'Sally Butman her work in the 11th year of her age, 1801', Marblehead, Mass., 10.3/8 x 12½in. (Robt. W. Skinner Inc.) $15,000

Needlework sampler, England, dated 1826, silk yarns in a variety of stitches on natural linen ground, 13 x 15½in. (Robt. W. Skinner Inc.) $700

A needlework picture, by Mary Fentun, dated 1789, 21¼ x 16½in. (Christie's) $2,860

An early 19th century needlework sampler by S. Parker, aged 14 years 1817, 37 x 32cm. (Phillips) $862

An early 19th century needlework sampler, by Elizabeth Campling, aged 12 years, the linen ground embroidered in silks, 31.5 x 34.5cm. (Phillips) $338

A nicely worked needlework sampler, by Sarah Iesson, the linen ground embroidered in silks, 33 x 21cm. (Phillips) $708

Late 18th century needlework sampler, worked in silk yarns of gold, light blue, red, brown, ivory and black on natural linen, 7 x 10½in. (Robt. W. Skinner Inc.) $3,300

A needlework sampler worked in silk yarns on natural colored linen, 'Susannah Cadmore, 1805', 12½ x 13¼in. (Robt. W. Skinner Inc.) $500

An early 19th century needlework sampler, inscribed 'Rachel Fowler's work finished May 29, 1837', 40 x 32cm. (Phillips) $739

Late 18th century Spanish needlework sampler with silk embroidered stylized floral and geometric designs, 15½ x 18½in. (Robt. W. Skinner Inc.) $300

A needlework family record, silk yarns in shades of blue, green, pale peach, ivory and black on natural linen ground fabric, 18¼ x 14½in. (Robt. W. Skinner Inc.) $900

A needlwork sampler, by 'Sarah Pell, Febrery 21, 1830', wool yarns on white wool fabric, 12½ x 16in. (Robt. W. Skinner Inc.) $850

An early 19th century needlework sampler by Elizabeth Bushby, March 6, aged 10 years, 1822, 45 x 42cm. (Phillips) $523

Framed needlework pictorial verse sampler, by Eliza. A. Machett, New York, March 22, 1828, 16½ x 16in. (Robt. W. Skinner Inc.) $500

Needlework sampler, by 'Elizabeth Tonnecliff, her work done in 1791', silk yarns, 16 x 20¼in. (Robt. W. Skinner Inc.) $8,700

A mid 17th century needle-work sampler in drawnthread, cutwork and needlepoint stitches, 75 x 22.5cm. (Phillips) $1,155

An 18th century silk embroidered sampler, Europe, 20 x 35in. (Robt. W. Skinner Inc.) $7,500

A 17th century needlework sampler, probably by Mary Tratt of Boston, 7½ x 22¾in. (Robt. W. Skinner Inc.) $2,500

A framed pictorial needle-work sampler, inscribed 'Celia(?) Procter Montrose 1833', England, 16 x 20in. (Robt. W. Skinner Inc.) $425

A late 17th century needle-work sampler, embroidered in silks, 36 x 14cm. (Phillips) $446

A framed pictorial needlework sampler, inscribed 'Mary Jagger 1807', England, 17¼ x 19½in. (Robt. W. Skinner Inc.) $275

Late 19th century Bidjar sampler, N.W. Persia, 3ft. 10in. x 4ft.11in. (Robt. W. Skinner Inc.) $4,500

A framed needlework verse sampler, 'Rebecca Miers', New England, circa 1830, 22 x 21in. (Robt. W. Skinner Inc.) $700

Needlework sampler, England, 'Margaret Smith, aged 12 AD 1848', worked in heavy wool yarns, 17 x 18in. (Robt. W. Skinner Inc.) $600

SHARE CERTIFICATES

Liverpool Music Hall 1798. Share No. 261, on vellum. (Phillips) $522

Canterbury Navigation and Sandwich Harbour 1826, one £20 share, tear top right. (Phillips) $181

Keller-Dorian Colorfilm Corpn. $20 share certificates 1932, 4 examples, also Fox Film Corpn. 1931-3 warrants, 4 examples. (Phillips) $188

Poyais: Pouaisian 3% Consolidated Stock 1827, £250 Bond, hand signed by Gregor MacGregor. (Phillips) $362

South Africa: The Great Kruger Gold Mining Co. Ltd. 1889, 100 x £1 shares. (Phillips) $406

Republic of China (Pacific Loan) 1937, U.S. $1,000 bond. (Phillips) $435

British Motor Coupe Company 1900, 10 x £1/$5 shares. (Phillips) $58

Australia: Western Australian Co. Settlement of Australind 1841, with 'Duplicate Original', Town Order certificate for ¼ acre. (Phillips) $493

The Company of Proprietors of the Herefordshire and Gloucester Canal Navigation 1793, £100 share certificate, on vellum. (Phillips) $377

BASKETS

SILVER

A George III Irish oval
bread basket on rim foot,
by Joseph Jackson,
Dublin, 1786, 14¾in.
long, 26oz. (Christie's)
$2,988

An Unger Brothers basket,
24cm. across, stamped with
monogram and Sterling 925
Fine, numbered 02616.
(Phillips) $460

A shaped oval swing-handled
cake basket with applied
foliate border, Sheffield,
1914, 12in., 23oz.
(Christie's) $438

A George III shaped oval
bread basket, by Sarah
Buttall, 1770, 14in. long,
37oz. (Christie's)
$4,604

A George III small sugar
basket, by Charles Hougham,
1790, 8cm. high, 4oz.
(Phillips) $459

A George II Irish shaped
oval bread basket, by Geo.
Hill, Dublin, 1760, 15in.
long, 72oz. (Christie's)
$23,595

A George I circular bread
basket, by Thomas Farren,
1725, date letter struck
twice, 12¾in. diam., 94oz.
(Christie's)
$111,540

A George II oval cake basket,
by John Jacob, 1742, 36cm.
wide, 63oz. (Phillips)
$18,960

A Victorian silver gilt basket,
by Barnard & Co., 1846,
6¼in. diam., 13oz.3dwt.
(Christie's) $1,301

566

BEAKERS

A Latvian tapering cylindrical beaker and cover, by C. Dey, Riga, circa 1740, 10½in. high, 23oz. (Christie's) $2,478

A late 17th century Continental covered beaker, maker's mark EA conjoined, perhaps for Everhard Alffen of Cologne, circa 1680, 14.5cm. high, 8oz. (Phillips) $1,215

A Hungarian parcel gilt slightly tapering cylindrical beaker, by Johannes (Hans) Retsch, Brasso, circa 1630, 5¼in. high, 3oz.12dwt. (Christie's) $5,348

A German parcel gilt beaker on three ball feet, by Gerdt Eimbke (Eimeke) III, circa 1690, 5in. high, 8oz. (Christie's) $2,809

A small beaker designed by Jean Puiforcat, 4.8cm. high, silver colored metal. (Phillips) $259

A William and Mary plain beaker, pricked with initials AL.IM, by James Daniel, Norwich, 1689, 3½in. high, 3oz.3dwt. (Christie's) $3,146

One of two George III interlocking beakers, each pair forming a barrel, by C. Aldridge and H. Green, 1778, overall height of a barrel 5¼in., 16oz.18dwt. (Christie's) $3,304

One of a pair of silver beakers, by John Taylor and H. Hinsdale, N.Y., 1804-30, 3½in. high, 9oz. (Christie's) $770

A Swedish parcel gilt trumpet shaped beaker, by P. Eneroth, Stockholm, 1776, 8¾in. high, 14oz.5dwt. (Christie's) $1,156

A Connell two-handled bowl, designed by Kate Harris, with bottle-green glass liner, London hallmarks for 1904, 39.1cm. diam., 22oz.15dwt. without liner. (Christie's) $1,425

A presentation punch bowl, by Tiffany & Co., N.Y., 1890-91, 9in. high, 15¾in. diam., 101oz. (Christie's) $24,200

A 17th century Dutch oval brandy bowl, by Hindrick Muntinck, Groningen, 1661. 6.5oz. (Phillips) $1,029

A covered silver sugar bowl, by Edmund Milne, Phila., circa 1785, 7¼in. high, 11oz. (Christie's) $3,850

An Omar Ramsden silver punch bowl with everted rim, London hallmarks for 1931, 23.6cm. wide, 65oz.14dwt. (Christie's) $6,732

A George III Scottish swing-handled, boat-shaped sugar bowl, by John Leslie, Aberdeen, circa 1785, 9.5cm. high, 10.5oz. (Phillips) $750

A sugar bowl, the cover with a green stone finial, by Tiffany & Co., N.Y., 1877-91, 3¼in. high, gross weight 13oz. (Christie's) $10,450

A Scottish silver bowl, designed by D. Carleton Smythe, 48.5cm. across, bearing Glasgow hallmarks for 1905. (Phillips) $547

A George II circular punch bowl on molded foot, Dublin, probably 1754, town mark and Hibernia only, 9¼in. diam., 34oz. (Christie's) $3,146

An Art Nouveau Continental white metal bowl in the style of J. Hofman, 14in. across. (Christie's) $716

William III style Victorian punch bowl, by Walker & Hall, Sheffield, 1898. (Reeds Rains) $1,108

An Omar Ramsden silver gilt bowl, London hallmarks for 1935, 46.2cm. wide. (Christie's) $13,370

A George II Channel Islands circular sugar bowl and cover, by G. Henry, Guernsey, circa 1740, 4in. diam., 6oz.10dwt. (Christie's) $7,436

An Unger Brothers silver bowl of flower form, 15.4cm. diam., stamped maker's monogram, Sterling 925 Fine, 0850 (3oz.). (Phillips) $145

A late Victorian spiral fluted bowl, by James Dixon & Sons, Sheffield, 1893, 9¼in., 22.75oz. (Christie's) $589

A centerpiece bowl with a scalloped rim, the sides fluted, by Simeon Coley, N.Y., circa 1768, 8.7/8in. diam., 21oz. 10dwt. (Christie's) $28,600

A Victorian boat-shaped sugar bowl, makers Messrs. Barnard, London, 1883, 5in. high, 8oz., and a matching sugar spoon, London, 1882. (Hobbs & Chambers) $228

A German shaped circular bowl, the ground decorated with a pastoral scene, 9in. diam. (Christie's) $440

BOXES

A Dutch plain shaped octagonal casket, by J. Logerat, The Hague, 1728, 5¼in. long, 14oz.16dwt. (Christie's) $8,592

A smoker's set, comprising a two-handled tray, a cigar box, four ashtrays and a matchbox holder, by Asprey & Co. Ltd., 1937, 1938 and 1943, tray 17¼in. long, wt. excluding cigar box 103oz. (Christie's) $6,606

A Swiss silver gilt and enamel singing bird box, the movement stamped C. Bruguier a Geneve, 9.5cm. wide. (Phillips) $7,250

A George II square sugar box, together with two tea caddies, by Thos. Heming, 1747, 60oz. (Christie's) $11,566

A Charles II oval silver gilt tobacco box with detachable cover, maker's mark W H only, circa 1675, 4in. long, 5oz.10dwt. (Christie's) $1,573

A Guild of Handicraft silver and enamel box and cover, London hallmarks for 1901, 10cm. diam., 6oz.5dwt. gross weight. (Christie's) $665

A 19th century Swiss oblong silver gilt and enamel singing bird box, by Chas. Bruguier, 3.7/8in. long. (Christie's) $4,957

A Victorian biscuit box, in the form of a book, 21cm. long, circa 1870. (Phillips) $429

A George II silver gilt shaped oblong toilet box, by Ayme Videau, 1755, the cover, unmarked, 6¾in. long, 36oz. (Christie's) $4,131

CANDELABRA

One of a pair of French six-light candelabra, by J. Chaumet, Paris, 1918, 24½in. high, 471oz. (Christie's) $22,000

Pair of Louis XVI four-light candelabra, by Antoine Boullier, Paris, 1787, with the charge of Henri Clavel and export discharge mark, 26in. high, 269oz. (Christie's) $99,000

One of a set of four Italian six-light candelabra, Rome, mid 19th century, maker's mark CV in oval, 19¼in. high, 526oz. (Christie's) $57,200

One of a pair of silver gilt two-light candelabra, the branches bearing marks for Wm. Elliot, London, 1812, bases unmarked, 16¼in. high, 179oz. (Christie's) $33,000

A two-branch candelabrum, designed by Soren Georg Jensen, 17.7cm. high, 26oz.10dwt. (Christie's) $2,044

A Russian Hanukah lamp, 1879, assaymaster OC, possibly Minsk, struck with the name L. Zammer and town mark a crescent between mullets, 21¼in. high, weight of branches 30oz. (Christie's) $3,146

Pair of Spanish four-light candelabra, by Juan de San Fauri, Madrid, 1762, with the warden's mark of Melun, 19¾in. high, 180oz. (Christie's) $88,000

A Victorian three-light candelabrum/centerpiece, by W. & G. Sissons, Sheffield, 1865, 24¾in. high, 165oz. (Christie's) $4,719

Pair of French four-light candelabra, by Puiforcat, Paris, circa 1900, 17¼in. high, 210oz. (Christie's) $8,250

CANDLESTICKS

One of a pair of Continental candlesticks, probably German, maker's mark possibly FO, 10in. high, 24oz. (Christie's) $2,809

Pair of George III cast candlesticks, by Ebenezer Coker, 1768, 25.5cm. high, 34oz. (Phillips) $1,950

One of a pair of German silver gilt candlesticks, by F. Proll, Cassel, circa 1840, 10in. high, 36oz. (Christie's) $6,600

One of a set of four Dutch silver candlesticks, by P. Kersbergen, The Hague, 1772, 10in. high, 95oz. (Christie's) $34,606

A pair of plated candlesticks of circular baluster form, 13in. high. (Parsons, Welch & Cowell) $154

One of a pair of German candlesticks, Allenstein, circa 1750, maker's mark I.C. over S, 7¼in. high. (Christie's) $3,304

One of a set of four German cast candlesticks, probably by J. W. Voigt, Osnabruck, circa 1740, 8½in. high, 69oz. (Christie's) $33,048

A pair of Louis XV candlesticks, by Etienne Pollet, Paris, 1743, 10.1/8in. high, 52oz. (Christie's) $5,500

One of a pair of George III Corinthian candlesticks, by Ebenezer Coker, 1762, 35cm. high. (Phillips) $2,850

CANDLESTICKS

One of a pair of William IV cast silver gilt candlesticks, by Paul Storr, 1835, 23cm. high, 31.5oz. (Phillips) $18,000

An Art Nouveau silver 'counter-balanced' candlestick, 16.5cm. high, marked KK, London, 1905. (Phillips) $288

One of a pair of William and Mary candlesticks, 1693, maker's mark B in script, crown above, 7½in. high, 38oz. (Christie's) $18,176

One of four Louis XV/XVI candlesticks, by Joseph-Theodore Vancombert, Paris, two 1771, and two 1775, 10.5/8in. high, 81oz. (Christie's) $13,200

A pair of stylized silver and green onyx candlesticks, probably made by Dixon & Sons for Hyams, 22cm. high, London marks for 1907. (Phillips) $892

One of a pair of 18th century German candlesticks, by Johann Balthasar Heggenauer, Augsburg, 1783/85, 23.5cm. high, 28oz. (Phillips) $1,650

One of a pair of German table candlesticks, by C. Lieberkuhn II, Berlin, circa 1735, 8in. high, 31oz. (Christie's) $11,011

Pair of silver gilt candlesticks, French or English, circa 1680, 8in. high, 37oz. (Christie's) $52,800

One of a pair of George III candlesticks, by Wm. Holmes, 1780, 11½in. high, 43oz. (Christie's) $3,932

CANDLESTICKS

SILVER

Pair of WMF Art Nouveau silver colored metal candlesticks, 11in. high. (Reeds Rains) $465

One of a pair of Georg Jensen candlesticks, designed by S. Bernadotte, 6cm. high, 8oz.16dwt. (Christie's) $871

Pair of late 18th century Corinthian column Paktong candlesticks, 11in. high. (Woolley & Wallis) $906

A pair of neo-Gothic candlesticks with cluster columns, circa 1770, 30cm. high. (Phillips) $285

One of a pair of George II candlesticks, by Wm. Cafe, London, 1759, 11¾in. high, 57oz.10dwt. (Christie's) $7,700

A pair of candlesticks, American, each with a removable bobeche above a vasiform candlecup, circa 1841, 7¾in. high, 19oz. (Christie's) $1,210

Pair of George II plain candlesticks, with spool-shaped sockets and detachable nozzles, by J. Cafe, 1742, 8in. high, 33oz. (Christie's) $3,775

One of a pair of Louis XVI silver gilt candlesticks, by E. Moreau, Paris, 1776, 10.5/8in. high, 38oz.10dwt. (Christie's) $6,600

Pair of early George III Doric column candlesticks, by E. Coker, London, 1764, 12in. high. (Woolley & Wallis) $1,221

SILVER

A caster, the domed pierced
cover with pinecone finial,
by Zachariah Brigden, Boston,
1770-85, 5¼in. high, 3oz.
(Christie's) $2,200

Three George I plain pear-shaped
casters, by Samuel Welder 1716
and 1717, 6¼in. and 7¼in. high,
18oz.5dwt. (Christie's)
$4,427

One of a pair of German
silver gilt casters, by B. F.
Behrens, Hanover, date
letter I, circa 1755, 8¾in.
high, 29oz. (Christie's)
$22,000

A caster of baluster form,
by John Edwards, Boston,
circa 1745, 5½in. high., 3oz.
(Christie's) $3,520

A set of three late 17th century
West Country casters, by Gabriel
Felling of Bruton Co., Somerset,
circa 1690, 28oz. (Phillips)
$45,760

A Belgian octagonal pear-
shaped caster, Brussels, 1730-
33, maker's mark AL, 7½in.
high, 9oz.18dwt.(Christie's)
$3,445

A Belgian caster, by Peter Alio,
Jnr., Brussels, 1737-40, 7¼in.
high, 7oz.10dwt. (Christie's)
$4,180

A set of three Queen Anne silver
gilt casters, by Charles Adam,
1703, 8in. and 6½in. high, 22oz.
(Christie's) $18,590

A George II large plain
vase-shaped caster, by
Samuel Wood, 1753,
8¾in. high, 21oz.
(Christie's)
$2,359

CENTERPIECES

An Art Nouveau centerpiece of open boat shape, 57.5cm. long, silver colored metal, possibly Austrian or German. (Phillips) $2,304

A George III Irish epergne, by Thomas Jones, Dublin, 1789, 17½in. high, 180oz. (Christie's) $28,314

A George II epergne, by Paul de Lamerie, the waiters 1736, the centerpiece 1737, 14¼in. high, 301oz. (Christie's) $1,101,100

Early 20th century French silver gilt centerpiece, Paris, maker's mark AD, bird between, 10¾in. high, 134oz. (Christie's) $6,600

A Victorian centerpiece, by Messrs. Barnard, 1844, 64cm. high, weight excluding glass bowl 327oz. (Phillips) $12,000

A William IV six-branch centerpiece, by Benjamin Smith, 1836, 25¼in. high, 421oz. (Christie's) $10,626

A George III openwork epergne, by Francis Butty and Nicholas Dumee, 1769, 19in. high, 117oz. (Christie's) $8,651

Late 19th century Viennese silver gilt and enamel centerpiece, in glazed showcase, 25½in. high overall. (Christie's) $69,400

A George III epergne, by Thos. Pitts, 1770, 51cm. high, 156oz. (Phillips) $12,155

An Art Nouveau oil chamberstick with leaf-capped loop
handle, 14.25cm. diam.
(Phillips) $492

One of a pair of Victorian
fluted shaped circular chamber
candlesticks, by Robinson,
Edkins & Aston, Birmingham,
1840, 6¼in. high, 24.25oz.
(Christie's) $1,280

A Victorian silver gilt small
chamber candlestick in the
manner of Paul de Lamerie,
by S.W., London, 1841, 11cm.
diam. (Christie's) $400

A George IV chamberstick
with conical snuffer, T.B.,
London, 1822, and a matching chamberstick, London,
1832, each 5½in. diam.,
total weight 22oz. (Christie's)
$1,496

Pair of George III circular
chamber candlesticks, by
T. Hannam and J. Crouch,
London, 1801, 20oz.
(Heathcote Ball & Co.)
$4,401

A George III chamber candlestick with detachable nozzle
and conical snuffer, by E.
Coker, London, 1771, 5¾in.
high, 7.75oz. (Christie's)
$760

An early Victorian chamber
candlestick, by Joseph and
John Angell, London, 1837,
6½in. high, 8.75oz.
(Christie's) $506

Small Georgian silver chamber
candlestick with snuffer,
Sheffield, 1809. (Lawrence
Butler & Co.) $290

A Victorian gadrooned
circular chamber candlestick
in the 18th century taste,
R.S., London, 1870, 7¾in.
high, 7.75oz. (Christie's)
$352

CHOCOLATE POTS

A Queen Anne plain tapering cylindrical chocolate pot, by Gabriel Sleath, 1711, 9¾in. high, gross 27oz. (Christie's) $6,292

Late 18th century French silver chocolate pot, 8in. high, 23 troy oz. including wooden handle. (Robt. W. Skinner Inc.) $2,400

An early George III pear-shaped chocolate pot with hinged cover, maker's mark W.C., London, 1763, 9¾in. high, 18oz. all in. (Lalonde Fine Art) $768

An early 18th century silver chocolate pot, by Wm. Fawdery, London, 12oz. (Robt. W. Skinner Inc.) $500

Georgian silver chocolate pot with ebony handle, London, 1816. (Lawrence Butler & Co.) $382

A Queen Anne plain tapering cylindrical chocolate pot, by Edmund Pearce, 1705, 10½in. high, gross 22oz. (Christie's) $5,662

A Queen Anne plain tapering cylindrical chocolate pot, by Jonah Clifton, 1710, 9¾in. high, gross 20oz. (Christie's) $7,078

A silver baluster shaped chocolate pot, by Samuel Kirk & Son Co., Baltimore, 1903-07, 10¼in. high, gross wt. 25oz. (Christie's) $1,430

A Queen Anne plain tapering cylindrical chocolate pot, by William Pearson, 1711, 24cm. high, 25oz. (Phillips) $9,840

SILVER

CIGARETTE BOXES

A Georg Jensen white metal cigarette box, stamped GJ 925S and inscription 6 Oktober 1933, 10¾in. wide. (Christie's) $1,718

A Continental oblong wood lined cigarette box decorated in the Art Deco style, 6¼in. long, engraved dated 1938. (Christie's) $652

A rectangular cigarette box, designed by Jorgen Jensen, Dessin JJ, Georg Jensen 857 A, 16cm. wide, 13oz.15dwt. (Christie's) $943

CIGARETTE CASES

A Wiener Werkstatte cigarette case, the design attributed to Carl Otto Czeschka, 8.5cm. wide, silver colored metal. (Phillips) $936

An Edwardian gilt lined rounded oblong quadruple cheroot case, J.G., Birmingham, 1905, 5in. high. (Christie's) $170

A Continental cigarette case, cover enamelled with a nude lying on the edge of the shore, with English import marks for 1906. (Phillips) $528

A Portuguese enamel cigarette case, the cover depicting a bare-breasted Classical girl, circa 1900. (Phillips) $573

A Victorian cheroot case, by Yapp & Woodward, Birmingham, 1854, 12.7cm. high, 4.75oz. (Phillips) $271

Late 19th century Austrian enamel cigarette case, the cover enamelled with an Ancient Egyptian scene, circa 1895. (Phillips) $906

CLARET JUGS

A Victorian slender vase-shaped claret jug, by Elkington & Co., 12¾in. high. (Christie's)
$221

•A Hukin & Heath silver mounted claret jug with ebony handle, designed by Christopher Dresser, London hallmarks for 1880, 22.5cm. high. (Christie's)
$1,504

A Victorian pear-shaped claret jug, W.H., London, 1868, 13in. high, 23.25oz. (Christie's) $988

A Victorian silver gilt mounted glass claret jug, by E. J. and W. Barnard, 1872, 12¼in. high. (Christie's)
$2,516

A Victorian parcel gilt claret jug formed as a bird, by George Fox, 1877, (patched), 8¼in. high, 22oz. (Christie's) $3,470

A William IV and Victorian silver mounted ruby glass claret jug, by C. Reily and G. Storer, 1836, 12in. high. (Christie's) $8,855

A Victorian silver mounted glass claret jug, by Elkington & Co., Birmingham, 1878, 10½in. high. (Reeds Rains)
$1,512

A French silver gilt mounted tapering cylindrical clear glass claret jug, by Charles-Nicholas Odiot, Paris, circa 1860, 11in. high. (Christie's)
$3,470

A Victorian silver mounted clear glass claret jug, by Wm. Hutton & Sons Ltd., 1894, 13¾in. high. (Christie's)
$2,044

COASTERS

One of a pair of William IV circular decanter stands, makers Howard, Battie & Hawkesworth, Sheffield, 1832, 10oz. (Woolley & Wallis) $1,639

A set of six Wiener Werkstatte circular wine glass coasters, designed by J. Hoffman and K. Moser, 5.5cm. diam., silver colored metal. (Phillips) $1,296

One of a pair of George III circular decanter stands, by John Roberts & Co., Sheffield, 1806/10. (Woolley & Wallis) $1,152

A Hutton & Sons silver wine bottle coaster, 16.80cm. high, total weight 19oz., maker's marks for Sheffield, 1905. (Phillips) $374

A wine coaster, stamped marks 925.S Georg Jensen & Wendel A/S 289A, 9.5cm. high, 14oz.10dwt. (Christie's) $1,415

Georgian mahogany and brass bound bottle coaster. (Lots Road Galleries) $214

One of a pair of George III wine coasters, London, 1795, maker Michael Plummer, 4¾in. diam. (Hobbs & Chambers) $1,644

Pair of Regency molded circular wine coasters, by S. C. Younge & Co., Sheffield, 1820, 6¼in. diam. (Christie's) $1,500

A Liberty & Co. silver and enamel wine coaster, Birmingham hallmarks for 1905, 9.5cm. diam., 2oz.14dwt. gross wt. (Christie's) $706

COFFEE POTS

A Queen Anne plain taper-
ing cylindrical coffee pot,
by Richard Raine, 1712,
9.5/8in. high, gross 24oz.
(Christie's) $5,820

A Victorian silver coffee pot,
London, 1898, 27¼oz.
(Parsons, Welch & Cowell)
$392

A William III plain tapering
cylindrical coffee pot, by
John Martin Stockar, 1701,
8.7/8in. high, gross 17oz.
12dwt. (Christie's)
$2,516

A Queen Anne plain tapering
cylindrical coffee pot, by
Anthony Nelme, 1713, 8¾in.
high, gross 22oz. (Christie's)
$4,089

A George III silver coffee pot,
London 1817, makers S. Royes
and J. E. Dix, 9in. high, 28oz.
(Parsons, Welch & Cowell)
$508

A George I cylindrical
coffee pot engraved with
a coat-of-arms, by John
Edwards II, 1726, 9in.
high, gross 25oz.
(Christie's)
$2,988

A George III plain pear-
shaped coffee pot, by
Robt. Peat, Newcastle,
1778, 11in. high, 30oz.
gross. (Christie's)
$2,831

A George IV coffee pot on
circular foot, 8in. high,
London, 1824, 26oz. (Hobbs
& Chambers) $572

A Liberty silver coffee pot,
designed by A. Knox,
Birmingham, hallmarks for
1906, 21.6cm. high.
(Christie's) $673

COFFEE POTS

A Belgian coffee pot, Tournai, 1771, maker's mark NH below a sunburst, 15½in. high, gross weight 36oz. (Christie's) $8,250

A William IV fluted pear-shaped coffee pot, by Paul Storr, 1836, the finial by J. S. Hunt, 8¼in. high, 26oz. (Christie's) $2,123

A George II pear-shaped coffee pot, by Isaac Cookson, Newcastle, 1737, 10in. high, gross 30oz. (Christie's) $2,359

A George II pear-shaped coffee pot, by Samuel Courtauld, 1753, 10½in. high, 40oz. (Christie's) $33,033

A Victorian silver coffee pot with ivory finial, Sheffield 1874, maker's mark J.H., 20oz. (Parsons, Welch & Cowell) $477

Early 20th century repousse decorated sterling silver coffee pot, Gorham Mfg. Co., 12.7/8in. high, approx. 26 troy oz. (Robt. W. Skinner Inc.) $1,100

A George III plain pear-shaped coffee pot, by Hester Bateman, 1781, 32cm. high, 27.5oz. (Phillips) $5,056

A Victorian silver coffee pot, London, 1897, 25¼oz. (Parsons, Welch & Cowell) $422

A Queen Anne plain tapering cylindrical coffee pot, by John Rand, 1707, 9½in. high, gross 18oz.18dwt. (Christie's) $4,404

CREAM JUGS

A cream pitcher, by Albert Coles, N.Y., circa 1869, 6¼in. high, 6oz. (Christie's) $330

A Victorian cream jug, by Messrs. Garrard, London, 1884. (Reeds Rains) $244

A cream pitcher, marked 'ID', probably Phila., 1790-1810, 6¾in. high, 5oz. (Christie's) $1,045

A cream pitcher, helmet-shaped, by Henry J. Pepper, Delaware, 1813-26, 5¾in. high, 7oz. (Christie's) $605

A cream pitcher with a scalloped rim and scroll handle, by Z. Brigden, Boston, 1770-85, 4.7/8in. high, 3oz. (Christie's) $2,200

A Continental fluted pear-shape milk jug with an elaborate scroll handle, 6½in. high. (Christie's) $136

A cream pitcher, pyriform, by Philip Syng, Jnr., Phila., 1750-80, 4in. high, 3oz. (Christie's) $6,600

A George III inverted pear-shaped cream jug, probably by R. and D. Hennell, London, 1766, 4¼in. high. (Christie's) $168

A silver pyriform cream pitcher, by Samuel Minott, Boston, circa 1750-60, 4¼in. high, 3oz. (Christie's) $1,980

A Victorian egg cruet, the
basket 23cm. wide, with six
egg cups, 7cm. high, by
Robt. Hennell, 1851, and
six spoons, by F. Higgins,
35oz. (Phillips) $1,501

A George III two-handled boat-
shaped cruet stand, by Robert
Hennell, 1781, the bottle
mounts by Wm. Abdy II, 1798,
13in. long, 14oz.11dwt.
(Christie's) $1,730

A Victorian six-cup egg
cruet, by Henry Wilkinson &
Co., Sheffield, 1846, 6in.
high, 20.75oz. (Christie's)
$356

A Hukin & Heath electro-
plated cruet set, attributed
to Dr. C. Dresser, 4¾in. high.
(Christie's) $67

A George III Irish Warwick
cruet, the base engraved 'In
all 49oz.9 pwts', 9½in. high,
48oz. (Christie's)
$4,089

An early George III cinquefoil Warwick cruet on shell
and scroll feet, by J. Delmester,
London, 1763, 9¾in. high,
23.5oz. (Christie's) $657

A Hukin & Heath silver condiment set designed by Dr. C.
Dresser, London hallmarks for
1881, 14.2cm. high. (Christie's)
$1,598

A China Trade egg cruet
on four ball feet, by
Khecheong, probably
Canton, circa 1860, 10½in.
high, 39oz. (Christie's)
$1,101

Victorian cruet, oblong with
central scrolled handle,
London, 1852, 18½oz.
(Hobbs & Chambers)
$524

CUPS

A French silver gilt and enamel vase-shaped cup and cover, circa 1830, both cover and body with guarantee mark 1819-38, 9¾in. high, gross 24oz. (Christie's) $1,415

A handled cup, with an S-scroll handle, by Thos. Coverly, Rhode Island, 1730-60, 2½in. high, 2oz. (Christie's) $2,860

A Victorian silver gilt two-handled vase-shaped cup and cover, by John S. Hunt, 1949, 28¾in. high, 88oz. (Christie's) $3,775

Judaica: An 18th century German silver gilt Kiddush cup, Augsburg, 1763/5, 13cm. high, 3.75oz. (Phillips) $4,131

One of a pair of George III Irish two-handled cups, maker's mark WH, Dublin, circa 1760, 29oz. (Phillips) $1,401

An Austro-Hungarian stirrup cup modelled as a kitten's head, circa 1870, 7.4cm. high, 4.25oz. (Phillips) $906

A German parcel gilt cup and associated cover, Nuremberg, circa 1620, maker's mark IF, 9¼in. high, 6oz.3dwt. (Christie's) $1,415

A William IV two-handled cup, by Paul Storr, 1835, the foot stamped Storr & Mortimer, 10½in. high, 109oz. (Christie's) $14,943

A late Victorian neo-classical style two-handled trophy cup, by Charles S. Harris, London, 1899, 15in. high, 81oz. (Woolley & Wallis) $789

CUPS

A 19th century French racing trophy cup, the lower part of the foot electroplate, circa 1870, 38cm. high, weighable silver 115oz. (Phillips) $2,574.

A George III Scottish gilt lined cup, W. & P. Cunningham, Edinburgh, 1791, 9¼in. high, 21.75oz. (Christie's) $290

A George III silver gilt two-handled cup and cover, by Philip Rundell, 1818, the cover 1819, 13in. high, 94oz. (Christie's) $3,460

A silver gilt two-handled 'Trafalgar Vase', by B. Smith, 1807, the finial by C. Gordon, circa 1835, 15¾in. high, 104oz. (Christie's) $4,719

A spout cup, by Edward Winslow, Boston, circa 1710-20, 3¼in. high, 4oz. (Christie's) $19,800

An Indian Colonial two-handled campana-shaped cup and cover, by Pittar & Co., Calcutta, circa 1838, 10½in. high, 45oz. (Christie's) $1,101

A replica of the Broderers Cup, circa 1830, maker's mark only JB perhaps for John Beauchamp, cf. Grimwade No. 1785, 16in. high, 61oz. (Christie's) $3,146

A Regency silver gilt two-handled campana shaped cup, by W. & P. Cunningham, Edin., 1818, 10¼in. high. (Reeds Rains) $504

A Victorian campana shaped cup on a floral foot, maker's initials probably I.S., London, 1864, 7in. high, 10oz. (Christie's) $330

One of a pair of second-course dishes, bearing probably spurious marks, D crowned possibly from Riom, 1781-85, maker's mark SWB, 13½in. diam., 68oz. (Christie's) $1,320

A George III shaped oblong entree dish, cover and handle, by Paul Storr, 1809, 16½in. wide overall, 68oz. (Christie's) $4,957

A Louis XVI second-course dish, by Jacques-Charles Mongenot, Paris, 1788, with the charge and discharge of Henri Clavel, 15in. diam., 44oz. (Christie's) $3,300

One of a pair of George III silver gilt kidney shaped vegetable dishes, by B. Smith, 1807, 11¾in. long, 66oz. (Christie's) $15,697

One of ten Louis XV dinner plates, by various makers, 10.1/8in. diam., 184oz. (Christie's) $4,400

One of a pair of German meat dishes, by Johann C. Otersen, 1784-91, 18in. long, 119oz. (Christie's) $11,000

One of a pair of French second-course dishes, by J. Chaumet, Paris, circa 1918, 14in. diam., 136oz. (Christie's) $8,800

A set of four German second-course dishes, by Franz A. H. Nubell, circa 1820, 12¼in. diam., 154oz. (Christie's) $26,400

One of a pair of shaped circular silver gilt dishes, circa 1700, maker's mark only WH between rosettes and pellets, 15in. diam., 65oz. (Christie's) $5,948

DISHES

One of a set of six Queen Anne soup plates, by Philip Rollos I, London, 1706, 9.7/8in. diam., 108oz. (Christie's)
$55,000

One of four George III shaped oblong entree dishes and covers, by Paul Storr, 1814, each on hot-water stands by Matthew Boulton, 11in. long, 281oz. (Christie's)
$28,314

A Louis XV second-course dish, Paris, 1771, 12¾in. diam., 34oz. (Christie's)
$1,760

One of a pair of Louis XV entree dishes, Paris, 1773, maker's mark apparently that of Jean-Francois Genu, 11in. long, 41oz. (Christie's)
$5,500

An Arts & Crafts fluted circular cake stand on a rising foot, J.S.B., London, 1915, 12¼in. high, 26.75oz. (Christie's) $506

A 17th century German silver gilt shaped oval dish, by Hans Mehrer, Augsburg, circa 1660, 46.5cm. long, 31.5oz. (Phillips) $6,000

A Louis XVI dish, by Jacques Debrie, Paris, 1777, decagonal, 11.3/8in. diam., 22oz. (Christie's) $4,400

A set of twelve Spanish dinner plates, by Larranaga, San Sebastian, mid 18th century, 9½in. diam., 185oz. (Christie's) $13,200

A George II circular strawberry dish, by Paul Crespin, 1735, 9½in. diam., 19oz. 5dwt. (Christie's)
$4,296

One of a pair of George III
shaped circular vegetable
dishes, by J. Parker and E.
Wakelin, 1768, 11in. diam.,
43oz. (Christie's)
$5,948

A Louis XVI large second-
course dish, by Jacques-
Charles Mongenot, Paris,
1788, with the charge of
Henri Clavel, 18in. diam.,
101oz. (Christie's)
$9,350

One of a set of six Austrian
dinner plates, by Ferdinand
Ebenwimer, 1776, 9.7/8in.
diam., 98oz. (Christie's)
$5,500

A Louis XV second-course
dish, by A. Pinel, Rodez,
circa 1750, 14¼in. diam.,
51oz. (Christie's)
$6,600

One of a pair of German silver
gilt second-course dishes, by
G. Menzel, 1717-18, 12¾in.
diam., the covers by C. Winter,
1729-30, 11.3/8in. diam.,
163oz. (Christie's)
$192,500

One of a pair of George II
fluted dishes, by B. Godfrey,
London, 1735, 8.3/8in. diam.,
25oz. (Christie's)
$15,400

Eighteen German dinner
plates, by Joachim C. Neuss,
seven 1801 and eleven 1804,
10in. diam., 345oz.
(Christie's) $26,400

One of a pair of silver
covered vegetable dishes,
by Tiffany & Co., N.Y.,
1947-55, 5in. high, 11in.
wide, 92oz.10dwt.
(Christie's) $2,860

A set of twelve George III
silver gilt dinner plates, by
John Wakelin and Wm.
Taylor, London, six 1787
and six 1788, 9¼in. diam.,
181oz. (Christie's)
$26,400

DISHES

A Louis XV basin, by Gilles Degage, Nantes, 1766, 12in. diam., 30oz. (Christie's) $1,760

A Louis XVI second-course dish, Paris, 1782, maker's mark illegible, 13in. diam., 27oz. (Christie's) $880

One of three George IV second-course dishes, by Philip Rundell, London, 1822, 11.7/8in. diam., 87oz. (Christie's) $8,250

One of a set of four George II fluted dishes, by B. Godfrey, London, 1732, 8.3/8in. diam., 52oz. (Christie's) $39,600

One of a set of four Russian silver gilt second-course dishes and covers, the covers by J. W. Feurbach, 1766, 12.5/8in. diam. of dishes, 391oz. (Christie's) $41,800

One of a pair of Louis XV silver gilt dinner plates, by Nicolas Outrebon, Paris, 1738, 10in. diam., 50oz. 10dwt. (Christie's) $4,400

Part of a set of thirty-six German silver gilt dinner plates, by Johann H. Fromm, 1821-41, 9in. diam., 375oz. (Christie's) $30,800

One of a set of four George III entree dishes, covers and handles, by Paul Storr, 1812, 12in. long, 236oz. (Christie's) $15,697

Twelve Austrian dinner plates, seven 1761, and five 1763, maker's mark IS, 9¾in. diam., 203oz. (Christie's) $9,900

DISHES

One of a pair of George III oval two-handled entree dishes and covers, by A. Fogelberg, 1772, 11in. long, gross 55oz. (Christie's) $2,988

One of four George III cushion shaped entree dishes, covers and handles, by J. Angell, 1818, one handle by R. Gainsford, 1820, 12in. long, 272oz.   (Christie's) $6,279

One of a pair of Georgian entree dishes and covers, one London, 1767, maker's mark IW, the other by J. Bridge, 1825, 14.1/8in. long, 101oz. (Christie's) $6,050

One of twelve George III shaped circular dinner plates, by George Methuen, 1752, 9½in. diam., 174oz. (Christie's) $6,940

A pair of Victorian oval plated entree dishes, 12in. long. (Parsons, Welch & Cowell) $246

One of three George II second-course dishes, by P. Archambo I and Peter Meure, London, 1753, 11.7/8in. diam., 79oz. (Christie's) $8,250

One of six German dinner plates, 1784-91, five with maker's mark IFF, and one by J. P. Crutzenberg, 9½in. diam., 76oz. (Christie's) $7,700

One of a pair of French fish platters, by J. Chaumet, Paris, circa 1918, 27½in. long, 255oz. (Christie's) $18,700

One of six German dinner plates, four by the widow of J. C. Lieberkuhn, circa 1740, and two by A. Fickert, late 19th century, 9.5/8in. diam., 107oz. (Christie's) $6,050

EWERS

An Austro-Hungarian wine
ewer, 1821, 41in. high.
(Christie's) $1,496

A Victorian baluster wine
ewer, by Elkington & Co.,
Ltd., Birmingham, 1893,
12¼in. high, 54oz.
(Christie's) $2,602

An American ovoid wine
ewer, by Samuel Kirk,
Baltimore, circa 1830,
16¼in. high, 48oz.
(Christie's) $3,160

A presentation ewer, by
Baldwin Gardiner, N.Y., circa
1835, 13½in. high, 45oz.
10dwt. (Christie's)
$1,100

A ewer, by John Kitts, Louis-
ville, 1838-76, 12¼in. high,
17oz. (Christie's)
$2,640

A George II helmet shaped
ewer, by David Willaume II,
1742, 10½in. high, 53oz.
(Christie's)
$69,400

A vase-shaped silver ewer, by
Thos. Fletcher, Phila., circa
1838, 13¼in. high, 39oz.
(Christie's) $1,320

A large covered ewer, bearing
spurious marks for Charles-
Cesar Haudry, Paris, 1745,
11in. high, 55oz. (Christie's)
$13,200

A pitcher, by Adolf Himmel,
New Orleans, circa 1854-61,
11in. high, 25oz. (Christie's)
$1,650

FLATWARE

A James I apostle spoon surmounted by the gilt figure of St. Paul, 1604, maker's mark a crescent enclosing a W, probably for Wm. Cawdell. (Christie's) $1,288

A Dutch spoon, the stem of tapering diagonal section, Harlem 1644, maker's mark perhaps that of Dirck Dircksz. (Christie's) $1,321

Part of a German silver gilt dessert service, by Abraham Warnberger IV, Augsburg; 1781-89, eleven pieces by C.-H. Constant, Berlin, 1788-1802, 36 pieces, 29oz.10dwt. (Christie's) $3,300

Two of three Louis XV basting spoons, by Nicolas Collier, Paris, 1768, with the charge and discharge of Julien Alaterre, 12½in. long, 17oz.10dwt. (Christie's) $3,080

Part of a Louis XV silver gilt dessert service, by the Widow of Jean-Frederic Fritz, Strasbourg, 1773, one spoon and two knives Vienna, 1790, 150oz., 54 pieces. (Christie's) $8,250

Part of a set of eighteen Louis XV silver gilt dessert spoons and eighteen dessert forks, by Johann Heinrich Oertel, Strasbourg, circa 1773, 75oz. (Christie's) $9,900

Part of a set of twelve George II fiddle and shell pattern dessert forks and six matching dessert spoons, by Paul de Lamerie, circa 1740, 27oz. (Christie's) $20,449

Part of a Louis XVI silver gilt dessert service, by Jean-Louis Kirstein, Strasbourg, 1778, 98oz., 54 pieces. (Christie's) $15,400

FLATWARE

A 16th century French spoon, the stem of tapering diamond section, with cone finial, marked with a crowned date letter? said by Emery to be circa 1450. (Christie's) $826

Part of a set of six Bow polychrome knives and forks, the pistol-grip handles enamelled in Chinese style, circa 1750, the handles 7.5 and 7cm. (Phillips) $1,047

Four of twelve Dutch silver gilt table knives and twelve dessert knives, Amsterdam, circa 1750, maker's mark I.B. (Christie's) $2,860

Part of a Mappin & Webb silver table service, 'Rosalind', designed by Eric Clements, London, hallmarks for 1963, in teak canteen, 153oz. 8dwt. gross weight. (Christie's) $7,435

Part of a Louis XV silver gilt dessert service by the workshop of Jean-Louis Imlin III, Stras., the knives 1770, the forks and spoons 1769, 69oz., 36 pieces. (Christie's) $7,700

Part of a Louis XVI silver gilt dessert service, the twelve dessert spoons and twelve dessert forks by J.-E. Langlois, Paris, 1782, the twelve dessert knives, Paris, 1779, 36 pieces. (Christie's) $17,600

Part of a set of twelve Louis XVI table spoons and ten table forks, by N. Collier, Paris, 1776, together with two other table forks, 71oz., 24 pieces. (Christie's) $3,300

Part of a Louis XVI silver gilt dessert service, by Johann-Heinrich Oertel, Strasbourg, 1778, 1779, etc., fiddle, thread and shell pattern, 119oz., 54 pieces. (Christie's)
$13,200

Part of a Georg Jensen 75-piece 'Pyramid' pattern table service, designed by Harald Nielsen, 1926, stamped marks, 132oz.6dwt. gross weight. (Christie's) $8,712

Part of a German silver gilt dessert service, by Phillip Jacob Jager I, Augsburg, 1732-33, 146oz., 66 pieces. (Christie's) $19,800

Two of twenty-one Dutch table knives and twelve dessert knives, nine Maastricht, circa 1760, maker's mark on some FH crowned, the rest Amsterdam, maker's mark on some IB. (Christie's) $1,320

Part of a set of French porcelain-handled table silver, by Puiforcat, Paris, circa 1900, the handles Chantilly, 18th century, 54 pieces. (Christie's) $3,080

Part of a 138-piece Elizabethan pattern composite table service, 1846, 1864, 1883 etc., some modern, weight without table and cheese knives 250oz. (Christie's) $8,651

A 19th century canteen dinner service, flatware by Henin et Vivier, dishes by Puiforcat, Paris, circa 1870, weighable silver 341.5oz., 156 pieces. (Phillips) $6,864

FLATWARE

Part of an early 20th century plated table service, probably Bolivian, the shaped stems with laurel leaf terminals, 221 pieces. (Christie's) $1,430

Part of a Louis XVI silver gilt dessert service, by Jean-Etienne Langlois, Paris, 1786, with the charge and discharge of Henri Clavel, 70 pieces, 130oz. (Christie's) $7,700

Part of a composite silver gilt dessert service, the majority by C.-S. Mahler, Paris, 1824-38, the rest by P.-F. Queille, post 1838, the fruit knives by A. Touron, 1819-38, 49 pieces. (Christie's) $4,840

Part of a set of twelve Louis XV silver gilt teaspoons, by Claude-Pierre Deville, Paris, 1769 and 1773, 13oz. (Christie's) $10,450

Part of a set of twenty-seven Louis XV table-spoons and twenty-seven table forks, by Nicolas Collier, Paris, 1768, fiddle, thread and shell pattern, 156oz. (Christie's) $7,700

Part of a Louis XV silver gilt dessert service, by Edme-Pierre Balzac, Paris, 1768/69, the reeded fiddle pattern, together with a silver table fork, circa 1777, 69oz., 37 pieces. (Christie's) $11,000

FLATWARE

A soup ladle, Persian pattern, by Tiffany &
Co., N.Y., 1872—circa 1875, 12¾in. long,
overall, 7oz.10dwt. (Christie's) $385

A soup ladle, wave edge pattern, with a
spirally-fluted oval bowl, by Tiffany & Co.,
N.Y., 1884-91, 10¾in. long, 5oz.10dwt.
(Christie's) $418

A pair of late 18th century tongs, marked 'IE',
English or American, 5½in. long, 1oz.
(Christie's) $550

Stilton scoop with ivory handle and
silver mount, marked Sheffield 1935.
(Peter Wilson) $84

Part of a French silver gilt dessert service, by
Francois-Daniel Imlin, Strasbourg, Warden's
mark a five, for 1785 or 1796, fiddle and
thread pattern, 37 pieces, 115oz. (Christie's)
$9,900

Part of a set of twelve Louis XV/Louis XVI
tablespoons and twelve table forks, by
Antoine Chaye, Paris, 1752, fiddle and thread
pattern, 68oz. (Christie's) $1,760

Part of a Louis XV silver gilt dessert service,
Strasbourg, 1770 and 1771, thread and shell
pattern, 78oz., 52 pieces. (Christie's)
$18,700

Part of a Louis XV silver gilt dessert service,
fiddle, thread and shell pattern, 70oz., 36
pieces. (Christie's) $7,700

Two of twelve Louis XV dessert knives and
six cheese knives, by Jean-Pierre Chezelle,
Paris, 1766, weight of dessert knives 30oz.
(Christie's) $8,800

Three of thirty-six, possibly late 18th century,
Dutch table knives, eighteen cheese knives and
twelve fruit knives, 66 pieces. (Christie's)
$9,900

FLATWARE

A French 'Puritan' spoon, with notched top to the stem, engraved with initials FH, Paris 1621, maker's mark perhaps HR. (Christie's) $1,404

A Dutch spoon with curved stem of diamond section and hoof finial, by E. Loesinck, Groningen 1656, together with another. (Christie's) $1,404

A soup ladle with a circular bowl, by James Kendall, Delaware, 1795-1808, 11¾in. long, 5oz.10dwt. (Christie's) $825

Early 17th century French three-pronged table fork with lobed top, by C. Ferrand, maker's mark perhaps CP for Chas. Payen. (Christie's) $3,139

Part of a Louis XV agate-handled dessert service, by Eloy Guerin, Paris, 1740, 24 pieces. (Christie's) $15,400

Five of twelve George III stag-hunt pattern table forks, by Paul Storr, 1816, 43oz. (Christie's) $1,487

Part of an assembled flatware service, King's pattern, by R. & W. Wilson, Philadelphia, 1825-46, 175oz. excluding knives. (Christie's) $3,080

Part of a service of fruiting vine design, also a pair of pierced and engraved fish carvers with bone handles, 1906, weighable silver 22oz., 68 pieces. (Phillips) $1,573

A Louis XV sugar sifter, Paris, 1744-50 and a silver gilt example, Paris, 1738-44, 8¼in. and 8.5/8in. long, 7oz. (Christie's) $935

Part of a set of seventeen silver gilt dessert-spoons and seventeen dessert forks, all with Belgian surcharge mark of 1814-1832, 61oz. (Christie's) $2,750

FRAMES

An Art Nouveau silver picture frame, 35cm. high, marked WN and for Chester 1903. (Phillips) $518

A Wm. Hutton & Sons Arts & Crafts silver picture frame, London hallmarks for 1903, 20cm. high. (Christie's) $2,272

A Wm. Hutton & Sons Arts & Crafts silver picture frame, London hallmarks for 1903, 20cm. high. (Christie's) $2,187

An Edwardian Art Nouveau silver and enamel photograph frame, Wm. Hutton & Sons Ltd., London, 1904, 10.25in. high, also an Elkington & Co. vase, Birmingham, 1906. (Reeds Rains) $1,162

A Liberty & Co. silver and enamelled picture frame, 19 x 14.50cm., with Art Nouveau hinged support, hallmarked L. & Co., Birmingham, 1899. (Phillips) $2,664

An Art Nouveau photograph frame, maker's marks W.N. and Chester hallmarks for 1903, 31cm. high. (Christie's) $3,048

A late Victorian oblong photograph frame, Birmingham, 1895, 8½in. high. (Christie's) $273

An Art Nouveau silver picture frame, 28cm. high, marked SB, Birmingham, 1903. (Phillips) $374

A late Victorian oblong photograph frame, by Wm. Comyns, London, 1904, 6¾in. high. (Christie's) $230

600

GOBLETS

One of two Edwardian
silver gilt goblets, by
Edward Barnard & Sons
Ltd., 1902 and 1903,
10¼in. high, 46oz.
(Christie's)
$1,415

Early 19th century Spanish
Colonial silver gilt chalice,
8½in. high, 12oz. (Christie's)
$1,870

A China Trade goblet, by
Leeching, probably Hong
Kong, circa 1870, 7½in.
high, 8oz.14dwt.
(Christie's) $707

One of a pair of George III
gilt lined goblets, London,
1770. (Christie's) $880

One of a pair of George III
plain goblets, by John
Wakelin and Wm. Taylor,
1779, 6in. high, 15oz.
(Christie's) $2,359

An Omar Ramsden beaten
silver goblet, the foot with
inscription MCMXXI, 5in.
high, London hallmarks for
1920. (Christie's)
$271

A German silver gilt goblet,
by Johann Cristoph Treffler,
Augsburg, early 18th century,
4½in. high, 3oz.5dwt.
(Christie's) $7,064

Late 18th century goblet
on trumpet foot, circa
1790. (Phillips)
$150

An early 19th century Mexican
silver gilt chalice, maker's mark
possibly that of Jose M.
Martinez, 9¼in. high, 22oz.
(Christie's) $2,200

INKSTANDS

A George III inkstand, by Samuel and George Whitford, London, 1804, 9in. long, 17.75oz. free. (Christie's) $960

A late Victorian oblong inkstand, by Wm. Comyns, London, 1895, 12¼in. long, 16oz. (Christie's) $950

An early Victorian shaped oblong inkstand, by R.F.A., Birmingham, 1838, 11½in. long, 20.75oz. (Christie's) $2,288

A Victorian shell-shaped inkstand, by Elkington & Co., 1851, 9¾in. long. (Christie's) $1,022

A rectangular inkstand, fitted with a candleholder, by John and Thomas Settle, Sheffield, 1817, 15oz. (Christie's) $3,300

A Victorian rococo silver gilt shaped oval inkstand on bun feet, by G. Fox, London, 1875, 10in. long, 9.25oz. free. (Christie's) $1,108

A George III inkstand, by Samuel and George Whitford, London, 1804, 10in. long, 29oz. weighable silver. (Christie's) $2,420

An Australian plate mounted emu egg inkstand, 11in. wide, circa 1870. (Abridge Auctions) $680

A George III silver gilt shaped circular inkpot and cover, by B. Smith II and B. Smith, Jnr., 1817, 6in. high, 32oz. (Christie's) $4,647

A George II oblong inkstand, by Edward Wakelin, 1751, 13½in. long, 59oz. (Christie's) $11,511

A late Victorian circular tortoise-shell inkstand with plated rococo scroll mounts, on bun feet, London, 1899, 5¼in. (Christie's) $385

An oblong gallery inkstand on bracket feet, 8in. long, 13.25oz. free. (Christie's) $401

INKSTANDS

A William IV inkstand on shell and foliate feet, by Joseph and John Angell, London, 1836, 8in. long, 10oz. (Christie's) $924

An Edwardian oblong inkstand in the Regency taste, W.K., London, 1910, 8½in. long, 17oz. free. (Christie's) $1,095

An Edwardian novelty inkstand in the form of an ear of maize, maker I.S.B., London, 1907, 9in. long, 9oz. (Woolley & Wallis) $1,280

A George II shaped rectangular inkstand, by John Jacob, 1752, 11in. long, 43oz. (Christie's) $13,013

An 18th century style beaded oblong inkstand on ball feet, 8in. long. (Christie's) $144

A Dutch 19th century beaded oblong gallery inkstand on bracket feet, 6in. long, 13oz. (Christie's) $320

Victorian gilt metal inkwell modelled as a parakeet on a branch, the head hinged to reveal a space for the well. (Lots Road Galleries) $214

A Victorian Scottish inkwell, by Aitchison of Edinburgh, 1885, inkwell 15cm. high. (Phillips) $1,296

Plated inkwell in the form of a Zulu warrior, 10in. high. (Worsfolds) $217

An Edward VII inkstand, by J. B. Carrington, 1903, 29cm. wide, weighable silver 40oz. (Phillips) $2,054

A George II shaped rectangular inkstand, by Paul de Lamerie, 1730, Britannia Standard, 8¾in. long, 24oz. (Christie's) $23,595

A Victorian inkstand, by Chas. Thomas and G. Fox, 24cm. diam., 1852, 27oz. (Phillips) $1,716

A George III beaded vase-shaped hot water jug by J. B. Stephenson, London, circa 1775, 11¼in. high, 23oz. gross. (Christie's) $618

A pitcher of baluster form, with a curved spout and S-scroll handle, by Jones, Ball & Poor, Boston, circa 1852, 11¼in. high, 29oz.(Christie's) $1,100

An urn-shaped pitcher, by Charters, Cann & Dunn, N.Y., circa 1850, 8½in. high, 12oz. (Christie's) $264

A silver gilt mounted tiger-ware jug with mermaid thumbpiece, 7½in. high. (Christie's) $4,250

A vase-shaped pitcher, American, with unidentified eagle touch mark, circa 1825-35, 12in. high, 35oz. (Christie's) $1,430

A 19th century American 'ivy chased' jug, by Tiffany & Co., circa 1870, 23cm. high, 27.5oz. (Phillips) $3,003

A silver vase-shaped pitcher, with double scroll handle, by Samuel Kirk & Son, 1846-61, or 1880-90, 10in. high, 25oz. (Christie's) $1,100

A Louis XVI hot milk jug, by Nicolas Canet, Paris, 1785, 6¼in. high, 9oz.10dwt. (Christie's) $1,760

A George I covered jug, maker Paul de Lamerie, Britannia Standard, London, 1724, 7in. high, 16oz. (Hobbs & Chambers) $600

JUGS

A George III vase-shaped hot water jug, by Emick Romer, 1776, 12in. high, gross 30oz. (Christie's) $5,205

A Louis XVI hot milk jug, Paris, 1780, maker's mark indistinct, 5¼in. high, gross weight 6oz. (Christie's) $1,650

A Louis XVI hot water jug, by Louis Clery, Paris, 1789, with the charge and discharge of Jean-Francois Kalandrin, 9¾in. high, gross weight 20oz. (Christie's) $1,320

A vase-shaped ewer, by Wm. Forbes for Ball, Black & Co., N.Y., 1851-circa 1860, 16½in. high, 46oz. (Christie's) $1,100

A pitcher of baluster form with an open handle, by Gorham Manuf. Co., 1897, 8¾in. high, gross weight 31oz. (Christie's) $1,980

A small pitcher, designed by J. Rohde, stamped marks JR Georg Jensen GJ 295 432A, circa 1928, 22.7cm. high, 17oz. (Christie's) $1,494

An Elkington & Co. electro-plated jug designed by Dr. C. Dresser, 19.3cm. high. (Christie's) $1,982

One of a matched pair of plain vase-shaped hot water jugs, 9in. high, 20.75oz. gross. (Christie's) $390

A milk pot on three scroll legs with pad feet, by T. Stoutenburgh, N.Y., circa 1735, 4¾in. high, 7oz.10dwt. (Christie's) $4,400

Mid 19th century Australian silver mounted emu's egg table ornament on a wood plinth, by Wm. Edwards, 11½in. high. (Christie's) $5,977

A Charles Boynton silver toast-rack of oval, almost boat shape, 9.5cm. high, 5.5oz., marked CB for London 1936. (Phillips) $504

Mid 17th century German silver gilt mounted canister, unmarked, 6½in. high. (Christie's) $4,719

A parcel gilt toothpick-holder formed as the figure of Neptune standing before a shell, Oporto, circa 1850, 7in. high, 10oz. 6dwt. (Christie's) $943

A set of three Tiffany & Co. spirit flasks, the flattened rectangular bodies with screwed hinged covers, 20.6cm. high. (Christie's) $2,059

A George III argyll, by H. Bateman, 1775, 18cm. high, 10oz. (Phillips) $3,003

A silver mounted coconut cup, by Peter and Anne Bateman, 1792, 4¾in. high. (Christie's) $786

A Victorian cylindrical commemorative urn, formed as the Choragic monument of Lysicrates in Athens, 1888, 8in. high, 50oz. (Christie's) $1,101

Late 19th century silver mounted cut glass beehive honeypot, unmarked, 8¾in. high. (Christie's) $8,262

MISCELLANEOUS

SILVER

A silver menu holder, with a caption 'Give me a Bite', 10cm. wide, 1.25oz., marked H. & A, Birmingham, 1901. (Phillips) $136

A Continental model knight in Gothic style armor, import marks, 13¼in. long. (Christie's) $3,146

A small silver mounted prayer-book, the interior printed in German and with date 1652, 3in. long. (Christie's) $1,337

A Dunhill architect's lighter, silver metal formed as a 12in. box ruler surmounted by a lighter with wheel and flint mechanism. (Christie's) $871

A Charles II shaving jug, dish and soap box, the jug circa 1677, the dish 1682, the soap box circa 1680, 52oz. (Christie's) $38,005

A 19th century Portuguese toothpick-holder formed as a female figure supporting a bowl with two doves, 7¾in. high, 7oz.6dwt. (Christie's) $393

A toastrack, the base in the form of 'The Man in the Moon', the handle as a cast owl, 17cm. wide, 5cm. high, circa 1900. (Phillips) $371

A Victorian plated spoon warmer, in the form of a ship's buoy, 21cm. long, circa 1870. (Phillips) $200

A Dutch silver plated jardiniere with rope twist rim, on paw feet, 20½in. wide. (Christie's) $4,404

'Zeppelin' a white metal cigarette and match holder, 22.8cm. long. (Christie's) $267

Late 19th century Viennese silver gilt and enamel coach and horses, maker's initials F.W., 10½in. long. (Christie's) $1,817

MG Magic Midget George Eyston's Record Breaking Car, modelled as a silver petrol lighter, Birmingham, 1931, 7½in. long. (Onslow's) $1,573

An ivory and silver cigar holder on six flattened ball feet, by Tiffany & Co., N.Y., 1881, 6½in. high. (Christie's) $5,280

A George III honey skep and stand, by Paul Storr, 1799, with clear glass liner, 4¼in. high, 10oz.11dwt. (Christie's) $12,641

A George IV fireman's arm badge, by R. Emes and E. Barnard, 1823, 6in. high, 9oz.5dwt. (Christie's) $2,479

A George III plain vase-shaped argyll, by Wm. Elliott, 1818, 8½in. high, gross 25oz. (Christie's) $3,718

A WMF plated corkholder, each cork surmounted by a sculptural figure, 15.5cm. high. (Christie's) $896

A late 19th century Russian vodka set, maker's mark IIN (Cyrillics), St. Petersburg, circa 1890, 7oz. (Phillips) $1,072

MUGS

A gilt lined christening mug with loop handle, 3¾in. high, and another 3¾in. high. (Christie's) $158

A 19th century Indian Colonial gilt lined baluster mug, Hamilton & Co., Calcutta, 6¼in. high, 13oz. (Christie's) $403

A Victorian beaded tapering christening mug, London, 1865, 4in. high. (Christie's) $330

An early George III baluster mug, by T. Whipham and C. Wright, London, 1760, 8.5oz. (Woolley & Wallis) $752

A small mug, barrel-shaped, with a reeded rim and foot-rim, by Thadeus Keeler, N.Y., circa 1805-13, 2oz. (Christie's) $440

A George I mug with scroll handle, by George Wickes, London, 1726, 8.9oz. (Woolley & Wallis) $662

A silver applied enamelled copper mug, by Gorham Manuf. Co., Providence, 1881, 6½in. high. (Christie's) $1,650

An 18th century Channel Islands mug on collet foot, 8.75cm. high, by Philippe Le Vavasseur dit Durell, circa 1745, 5oz. (Phillips) $514

A Victorian christening mug with loop handle, W. E., London, 1878, 4½in. high. (Christie's) $248

MUSTARDS

A Victorian melon fluted
pear-shaped mustard pot, by
Joseph Angell, London, 1859,
4¼in. high. (Christie's)
$118

A Regency cauldron mustard
pot on floral and scrolling
foliate feet, London, 1816,
5in. high, 9oz. free. (Christie's)
$285

A George IV gilt lined
mustard pot, by Pearce &
Burrows, London, 1825,
4½in. high. (Christie's)
$174

A 17th century Continental
silver gilt mustard pot of
inverted bell shape, circa
1680, 16cm. high, 7.5oz.
(Phillips) $800

A Liberty & Co. three-piece
silver condiment set, Birmingham hallmarks for
1899, pepper-pot 5.5cm.
high. (Christie's)$589

A Victorian mustard pot,
by W. H., London, 1841.
(Christie's) $422

A Victorian circular mustard
pot, with blue glass liner, by
G. R., London, 1855.
(Christie's) $440

A Victorian medieval-style
baluster mustard pot and
matching castor, by John
Hardman & Co., Birmingham,
1869, 13.75oz. (Christie's)
$918

A Victorian hexagonal
mustard pot, with blue glass
liner, London, 1843.
(Christie's) $387

PORRINGERS

A Commonwealth two-handled porringer, by Gilbert Shepherd, 1658, 2½in. high, 4oz.14dwt. (Christie's) $2,516

A silver Guild of Handicrafts single handled porringer with attributed design to C. R. Ashbee, 7in. long, London hallmarks for 1903. (Christie's) $785

A Charles II two-handled porringer, 1679, maker's mark IR, between rosettes, probably for John Ruslen, 3¼in. high, 4oz.17dwt. (Christie's) $2,202

A circular silver porringer, by Daniel Russell, Rhode Island, circa 1740-71, 7¾in. long, overall, 8oz. (Christie's) $1,870

A William and Mary two-handled porringer and cover, by J. Jackson, 1690, 7¾in. high, 28oz. (Christie's) $4,957

A porringer with a pierced keyhole handle, marked 'Davis', early 19th century, 5½in. diam., 8oz. (Christie's) $1,540

A Charles II two-handled porringer and cover, 1663, maker's mark AC or CA in monogram, 7¼in. high, 32oz. (Christie's) $10,224

An early 18th century porringer, possibly by Wm. Gibson, London, circa 1705, 7¾in., 13.25oz. (Christie's) $673

A Charles II two-handled porringer, engraved 'Little Canfield Church', 1675, 2¾in. high, 4oz.2dwt. (Christie's) $1,179

SALTS & PEPPERS

One of a pair of German silver gilt trencher salts, by Paul Solanier, Augsburg, apparently 1710-12, 1¾in. long, 8oz.10dwt. (Christie's) $2,860

A condiment set comprising two salt cellars, two mustard pots, two pepperettes and two spoons, in a fitted case. (Christie's) $387

One of a pair of oval salts, by Bigelow Bros. & Kennard, Boston, circa 1860, 2¾in. high, 4½in. long, 7oz. (Christie's) $385

Two of a set of four 18th century Americal oval salts on pedestal bases, by Lewis Fueter, N.Y., circa 1785, 13.75oz. (Phillips) $2,700

A set of four George II salt cellars, by Paul de Lamerie, London, 1733, scratch weight 32oz.19dwt. (Heathcote Ball & Co.) $4,890

A pair of Edwardian novelty peppers, the articulated bodies with porcelain heads, 13.5cm. long, 1905. (Phillips) $1,859

One of four George II silver gilt salt cellars, two by Anne Tanqueray, London, 1732, and two by D. Willaume II, 1753, 3½in. diam., 20oz. (Christie's) $3,850

Two of a set of four Victorian cast salts, fashioned as shells supported by stylized dolphins, 8cm. wide, circa 1860. (Phillips) $829

A Louis XV covered double salt cellar and two single examples, by J. T. Van Cauwenbergh, Paris, 1771 and 1773, the double 6in. long. (Christie's) $3,080

SALTS & PEPPERS

A Victorian novelty cruet in the form of three acorns, C. F., Sheffield, 1876, 4in. high. (Christie's) $131

Two of a set of four George III silver gilt two-handled boat-shaped salt cellars, by William Pitts, 1783, 5½in. wide., 30oz. (Christie's) $7,807

One of three William and Mary circular trencher salts, 1814, maker's mark IL.WA, 12oz.18dwt. (Christie's) $2,044

A pair of Regency gadrooned and gilt lined cauldron salt cellars, by R. Garrard, London, 1808, 4in., 24.25oz. (Christie's) $1,937

Four Victorian salt cellars each formed as a standing peasant figure, by R. Garrard, 1863, 1865 and 1866, 62oz. (Christie's) $20,449

Pair of Russian salt boxes with shaped back plates and stud feet, gilt lined, Moscow, 1876, 5in. high. (Christie's) $1,007

One of a set of four George III silver gilt octagonal salt cellar stands, by Robert and Samuel Hennell, 1805, 5¼in. long, 28oz. (Christie's) $4,626

A set of four George II silver gilt salt cellars, by George Wickes, London, 1754, 3.1/8in. diam., 31oz. (Christie's) $14,300

One of a pair of George II/ III salts, by David Hennell I, 1760, 7cm. diam., and J. Pasley, Dublin, 1770, and a pair of Russian salt spoons, 1861, 10oz. (Phillips) $379

SAUCEBOATS

One of a pair of George III two-handled double-lipped sauceboats, by Thos. Heming, 1761, 38oz. (Christie's) $5,783

A sauceboat, oval, with a scalloped rim and double scroll handle, by John Coburn, Boston, circa 1750, 8½in. long, 14oz. (Christie's) $18,700

One of a pair of George III sauceboats, by Thos. Heming, 1760, 21cm. long, 32oz. (Phillips) $3,318

One of a matching pair of George III sauceboats, by D. Smith and R. Sharp, 1760/62, 22cm. long, 27oz. (Phillips) $2,054

One of a pair of 19th century French hallmarked silver rococo serving boats, 10½in. long, approx. 54 troy oz. (Robt. W. Skinner Inc.) $2,700

One of a pair of Belgian double-lipped sauceboats, Mons, 1778, maker's mark CL crowned, 7¼in. long, 19oz.10dwt. (Christie's) $5,500

One of a pair of late Victorian cast shell-shape sauceboats, by Charles S. Harris, London, 1897. (Woolley & Wallis) $685

One of a pair of silver gilt sauceboats and stands in the style of D. Willaume II, 1965, together with a pair of ladles, 66oz. (Christie's) $2,478

One of a pair of George III plain oval sauceboats, by Wm. Skeen, 1763, 5¾in. high, 35oz. (Christie's) $4,275

One of a pair of George II sauceboats, by Edward Wakelin, 1749, 9¼in. long, 38oz. (Christie's) $2,974

An Austro-Hungarian 19th century gilt lined double-lipped sauceboat on an oval stand, 9¾in. wide, 23.25oz. (Christie's) $404

One of a pair of George II Irish shaped oval sauceboats, by J. Hamilton, Dublin, circa 1745, 33oz. (Christie's) $3,304

SNUFF BOXES

A George IV oblong snuff box, the cover engraved with the Nassau Balloon rising over Norwich, by T. Shaw, Birmingham, 1824, 7.9cm. long. (Phillips) $724

An engraved snuff box, oval, with channel-molded and rope-molded sides, by B. Schaats, N.Y., circa 1720, 2.1/16in. wide, 2oz. (Christie's) $17,600

A George III oblong engine turned gold snuff box, by A. J. Strachan, London, 1815, 18ct., 3½in. long. (Christie's) $4,404

An early 19th century oval French snuff box, Paris, 8.9cm. long. (Phillips) $428

An English hallmarked silver and horn presentation snuff mull, Sheffield, 1901-02, by Walker & Hall, 20½in. wide. (Robt. W. Skinner Inc.) $1,300

A George II cartouche-shaped silver snuff box, circa 1740, unmarked, 3in. long. (Christie's) $1,156

A Louis XV cartouche-shaped silver gilt snuff box, Paris, with the decharge of Julien Berthe (1750-56), 3in. long. (Christie's) $1,505

A 19th century small silver snuff box modelled as a skull with articulated jaw, 1.5/8in. long. (Christie's) $755

A George IV silver gilt oblong table snuff box with double hinged cover, by Thos. Edwards, 1820, 3¾in. long, 9oz.4dwt. (Christie's) $1,258

A Victorian oblong engine-turned snuff box, inscribed 'Coronation 1841 the Derby Winner', by F. Clarke, Birmingham, 1841, 8.3cm. long. (Phillips) $459

An 18th century Scottish silver mounted mother-of-pearl and lignum vitae oval snuff mull, 2¼in. high. (Christie's) $1,144

A William IV oblong table snuff box with hinged cover, by Chas. Reily and George Storer, 1835, 4in. long, 10oz.12dwt. (Christie's) $943

A Charles II lidded tankard,
by Dorothy Grant, London,
1681, 20oz. (Woolley & Wallis)
$6,400

A 19th century German
silver mounted ivory tankard
of a battle, the lid, handle
and base silver, 30cm. high.
(Christie's) $3,509

A George II plain baluster
pint tankard, by Fuller
White, London, 1748, 5in.
high, 12oz. (Christie's)
$434

A New York Yacht Club
Trophy flagon, by Whiting
Manuf. Co., circa 1892,
10in. high, 35oz.10dwt.
(Christie's) $880

A William III plain cylindrical
tankard and cover, by Thos.
Brydon, 1695, 6½in. high,
24oz. (Christie's)
$6,729

A George II baluster tankard ,
by Thomas Mason, 1743, 8in.
high, 30oz. (Christie's)
$5,505

A Charles II plain tankard,
circa 1670, letter G a coronet
above and three fleur-de-lys
below, 8in. high, 37oz.
(Christie's) $7,865

A Charles II large cylindrical
tankard, 1679, maker's mark
IC a mullet below, 7.5/8in.
high, 41oz. (Christie's)
$9,914

A James II slightly tapering
cylindrical tankard, 1686,
maker's mark SD, pellet
below, possibly for Samuel
Dell, 7in. high, 24oz.17dwt.
(Christie's) $33,048

SILVER

A Continental lidded tankard on leaf-capped berry feet, with presentation inscription and date 1771, 6¼in. high, 20.25oz. (Christie's) $2,304

A tankard, the domed lid with a pineapple finial, by Wm. Hollingshead, Phila., 1760-85, 10½in. high. (Christie's) $3,080

A silver cylindrical tankard, by John Brevoort, N.Y., circa 1740, 6¾in. high, 26oz.10dwt. (Christie's) $2,860

A Chinese tankard with bamboo-style scroll handle, 5½in. high. (Christie's) $341

A Queen Anne Irish tankard, by Philip Tough, Dublin, 1708, 23cm. high, 44.75oz. (Phillips) $4,290

A George III tapering cylindrical tankard, by Robert Sharp, 1791, 6¾in. high, 30oz. (Christie's) $4,604

A Charles II cylindrical tankard, 1677, maker's mark IA in dotted oval, 7.3/7in. high, 32oz. (Christie's) $4,626

An early George III baluster pint tankard, by S. Courtald, London, 1764. (Woolley & Wallis) $864

A William III provincial plain tapering cylindrical tankard, Norwich 1701, maker's mark HA, 6½in. high, 21oz.12dwt. (Christie's) $33,462

A circular tazza, by The Moore Co. for Tiffany & Co., circa 1865-69, marked on base with the 550 Broadway mark, 6.5/8in. high, 17½in. wide, overall, 41oz. (Christie's) $3,850

A Charles Boynton silver stemmed bowl, 12.5cm. diam., 5.75oz., maker's mark for London 1937. (Phillips) $273

A tazza with two scrolling strapwork handles, by Tiffany & Co., 1870-75, 6½in. high, 12.5/8in. wide, overall, 23oz.10dwt. (Christie's) $1,320

A Georg Jensen white metal tazza, the bowl cast on the underside with trailing vines laden with fruit, 19cm. high, 17oz.15dwt. (Christie's) $2,217

Pair of Victorian shaped circular comports on rising circular bases, by R. Garrard, London, 1880, 9in. diam., 42.25oz. (Christie's) $2,112

A Continental 19th century parcel gilt tazza with three applied caryatid handles, 8¾in. high. (Christie's) $480

A Georg Jensen miniature tazza, designed by J. Rohde, 4.8cm. high, together with a similar tazza. (Christie's) $502

A pair of pierced and engraved circular tazzas with applied stylized foliate rims, 8½in. diam., 19.75oz. (Christie's) $240

A pair of Victorian silver gilt comport dishes, by Robert Garrard, 1857, 25cm. diam., 14.5cm. high, 73oz. (Phillips) $2,016

A four-piece tea service, by John B. Jones Co., Boston, circa 1838, each piece globular with applied relief foliate decoration on the body, teapot 9¼in. high, gross weight 84oz.10dwt. (Christie's) $1,430

A six-piece tea service and tray, by Gorham Manufacturing Co., comprising a kettle on stand, a coffee pot, a teapot, a covered sugar bowl, a cream pitcher, a waste bowl and a large two-handled tray, kettle 13in. high, tray 31¼in. long, gross weight 374oz. (Christie's) $16,500

A Tetard Freres combined tea and coffee set, the teapot, 18.5cm. high, the coffee pot and cover, 22.5cm. high, wooden tray, 67.2cm. long, stamped on tray Prodbon E., Paris. (Phillips) $1,440

TEA & COFFEE SETS

An 'Aesthetic Movement' style teaset, in the manner of C. Dresser, total weight 14oz., Birmingham, 1907. (Phillips) $576

A Victorian four-piece coffee and teaset of Gothic style, the arched panels with classical figures, by Hayne & Cater, 1847, 68oz. (Phillips) $2,700

A Victorian four-piece matching coffee and tea service of pear shape and with basket-weave bodies, by Robert Hennell, coffee pot, teapot and milk jug 1859, sugar bowl 1857, 79.5oz. (Phillips) $3,861

A Hukin & Heath plated teaset, designed by C. Dresser, teapot 11.5cm. high, with design lozenge for October 1872, numbered 2109. (Phillips) $216

A three-piece tea service, by Colin and J. W. Forbes, N.Y., 1810-20, gross weight 51oz. 10dwt. (Christie's) $1,100

Three-piece teaset with fluted decoration, approx. weight 16oz., Sheffield 1906 and 1912. (Peter Wilson) $239

TEA & COFFEE SETS

Part of a five-piece tea and coffee service, by
Tiffany & Co., N.Y., 1907-47, coffee pot
9¼in. high, gross weight 125oz. (Christie's)
$2,420

A Victorian four-piece tea and coffee set, makers
E. & J. Barnard, London, 1852, coffee pot en
suite, maker D. & C. Hands, London, 1845, 69oz.
all in. (Woolley & Wallis) $1,937

A three-piece tea service, by Tiffany & Co.,
N.Y., teapot 9in. high, gross weight 71oz.
(Christie's) $1,760

A three-piece tea service, by John Targee, N.Y.,
circa 1810-14, teapot 9in. high, gross weight
61oz. (Christie's) $2,420

A James Dixon & Sons electroplated three-piece
teaset, designed by Dr. C. Dresser, registration
mark for 25 April 1880, teapot, 10.4cm. high.
(Christie's) $6,336

A three-piece tea service, by Fletcher &
Gardiner, Phila., 1813-25, teapot 9in. high,
gross weight 87oz. (Christie's) $6,600

A George III matching four-piece coffee and tea service, the baluster bodies highly embossed in the revised rocaille manner, bearing the mark of John Wakefield, coffee pot 1819, teapot, sugar and milk, 1820, 103oz. (Phillips) $2,700

A plain octagonal pear-shaped tea and coffee service, in the Queen Anne style, by Sebastian Garrard, 1920, height of tea kettle 13¼in., gross 158oz. (Christie's) $3,775

A five-piece tea service, by Gorham Manufacturing Co., circa 1865, comprising two teapots, a covered sugar bowl, a cream pitcher and a waste bowl, teapot 8in. high, gross weight 110oz. (Christie's) $2,640

TEA & COFFEE SETS

An American tea and coffee service, by Geradus Boyce, New York, circa 1825, coffee pot 12in. high, gross 157oz. (Christie's) $1,730

A three-piece enamelled demitasse service, by Tiffany & Co., N.Y., bearing the touch mark of the Pan-American Exposition in Buffalo, 1901, coffee pot 9in. high, gross weight 37oz.10dwt. (Christie's) $24,200

'Como', a Christofle electroplated four-piece modernist teaset, designed by Lino Sabattini, circa 1955, teapot 22cm. high. (Christie's) $2,674

A Russian fluted vase-shaped tea and coffee set, each on a spreading circular foot with scroll feet and shell and scroll border, height of coffee pot 9in., 182oz. (Christie's) $5,618

A six-piece tea and coffee service, by Bigelow, Kennard & Co., Boston, circa 1901, kettle 12in. high, gross weight 168oz. (Christie's) $4,180

A six-piece tea and coffee service with a plated tray, by the Mulholland Bros., Evanston, Illinois, 1916-19, coffee pot 9¼in. high, tray 25¼in. long, gross weight 170oz. (Christie's) $3,850

A Victorian four-piece plated tea and coffee set in fitted mahogany case. (Parsons, Welch & Cowell) $468

TEA CADDIES

A George III octagonal tea caddy, by Henry Chawner, 1791, 13oz. 8dwt. (Christie's) $2,516

A Liberty & Co. silver and enamel tea caddy of oval section, Birmingham hallmarks for 1907, 9.3cm. high, 5oz.2dwt. gross weight. (Christie's) $316

A Victorian silver mounted glass tea caddy, Chester, 1900. (Reeds Rains) $316

A George III shaped oval tea caddy, by Robt. Hennell, London, 1782, 4.75in. high, 14oz. (Woolley & Wallis) $4,000

A Ramsden & Carr silver tea-caddy and spoon, London hallmarks for 1931, 10.9cm. high, 13oz.7dwt. gross wt. (Christie's) $2,524

A George III shaped oval tea caddy, by Wm. Plummer, 1784, 14oz. 15dwt. (Christie's) $2,044

A Dutch oblong tea caddy, Sneek 1737, maker's mark illegible, probably FE for Feddeiedes Edema, 6oz. 5dwt. (Christie's) $1,156

A Victorian tea caddy, maker George Fox, London, 1874, 5in. high. (Hobbs & Chambers) $800

A Queen Anne plain oblong tea caddy, maker's mark overstruck with another, perhaps that of Thos. Farren, 10oz. (Christie's) $2,974

TEA KETTLES

A pyriform kettle on stand, by Grosjean & Woodward for Tiffany & Co., 1854-65, 11.5/8in. high, 30oz. (Christie's) $990

A Dutch tea kettle, stand and lamp, by H. Nieuwenhuys, Amsterdam, 1751, 13½in. high, gross weight 69oz. (Christie's) $6,600

Late 19th century rococo Revival hallmarked silver kettle on stand, by Tiffany & Co., 10¼in. high, approx. 24 troy oz. (Robt. W. Skinner Inc.) $600

George II English hallmarked silver kettle on stand, by E. Wakelin, 11¾in. high. (Robt. W. Skinner Inc.) $3,400

An F. Minsfiberg kettle-on-stand with ivory handle and ivory finial, 29.2cm. high. (Christie's) $2,689

An Edwardian part-fluted tapering oval tea kettle with ebonized wood handle and finial, by Henry Wilkinson & Co. Ltd., London, 1908, 12in. high, 37.5oz. gross. (Christie's) $716

A Victorian inverted pear-shaped tea-kettle, stand and lamp, by D. & C. Hands, 1856, 15½in. high, 72oz. (Christie's) $2,656

A George III plain circular tea kettle, stand and lamp, by John Scofield, 1787, 12½in. high, gross 55oz. (Christie's) $2,359

A tea kettle on stand, retailed by Starr and Marcus, N.Y., circa 1910, 14½in. high, 53oz. 10dwt. (Christie's) $1,210

TEAPOTS

A George II Scottish bullet-shaped teapot, by Wm. Aytoun, Edinburgh, 1736, assaymaster Archibald Ure, gross 22oz. (Christie's) $2,831

A William IV shaped circular teapot, by Paul Storr, 1836, 5¼in. high, 27oz. (Christie's) $1,859

A rounded rectangular teapot, probably by Israel Trask, Mass., circa 1813-25, 6½in. high. (Christie's) $165

A Victorian silver oval drum teapot in 18th century style, London 1858, makers Hands & Son, 19½oz. (Parsons, Welch & Cowell) $323

A Victorian oval half fluted silver teapot, London 1898, makers Barnard Bros., 25¼oz. (Parsons, Welch & Cowell) $231

A fluted oval teapot, marked 'Revere', 6in. high, gross weight 15oz.10dwt. (Christie's) $1,430

A pyriform teapot with a domed hinged cover, by Peter Van Dyck, N.Y., circa 1720-35, 7¾in. high, 25oz. (Christie's) $93,500

An urn-shaped teapot with a domed cover, by Bailey & Co., Phila., circa 1848-65, 10¾in. high, gross weight 37oz. (Christie's) $1,100

A Dutch silver pear-shaped teapot on rim foot, Amsterdam, 1722, 5¼in. high, gross 9oz.10dwt. (Christie's) $3,460

A George III plain oval teapot, with beaded borders, 12.5cm. high, 1782. (Phillips) $734

A square teapot, the hinged cover with a green stone finial, by Tiffany & Co., N.Y., 1877-91, 5in. high, gross weight 15oz. (Christie's) $16,500

A George III circular teapot with ivory finial and scroll handle, by Paul Storr, 1809, 6¼in. high, gross 40oz. (Christie's) $4,131

TRAYS & SALVERS

One of a pair of George II shaped circular salvers, by David Willaume II, 1743, 13¼in. diam., 118oz. (Christie's) $85,924

A silver tray, by Howard & Co., N.Y., circa 1900, 18¼in. diam., 78oz.10dwt. (Christie's) $1,430

A George II shaped circular salver on scroll feet, by John Swift, 1751, 22¾in. diam., 136oz. (Christie's) $7,550

One of a pair of George III shaped oval salvers, by Thos. Hannam and John Crouch, 1776, 15¾in. long, 80oz. (Christie's) $5,287

A Victorian octagonal gallery tray, by Martin Hall & Co. Ltd., Sheffield, 1877, 19½in. long, 84oz. (Christie's) $4,089

A George III two-handled oval gadrooned tray, by John Newburn, 1809, 26½in. long, 104oz. (Christie's) $2,988

A George II shaped circular salver, by George Wickes, 1739, 13in. diam., 43oz. (Christie's) $3,635

An oval tray on eight claw and ball feet, by Omar Ramsden, 1923, 22¾in. long, 85oz. (Christie's) $2,478

A George II salver, by John Kincaid, London, 1744, 17in. diam., 71oz. (Christie's) $4,400

SILVER

TRAYS & SALVERS

A large silver gilt shaped circular salver, on four curved openwork vine tendril feet, by Wm. Cripps, 1750, 22½in. diam., 157oz. (Christie's) $29,743

One of a set of five Regency Sheffield gilt salvers engraved with the Royal Arms for the period 1801-16, 26cm. diam. (Phillips) $3,744

An early Victorian presentation circular tray, by Joseph & Albert Savory, London, 1845, 76oz., 18.5in. diam. (Woolley & Wallis) $1,192

One of a pair of silver bread trays with open foliate handles, by S. Kirk & Son Co., Baltimore, 1903-07, 14¼in. long, 44oz. (Christie's) $1,430

One of a pair of William and Mary silver gilt salvers, circa 1690, 11¼in. diam., 82oz.10dwt. (Christie's) $220,000

A two-handled tray, chrysanthemum pattern, by Tiffany & Co., N.Y., circa 1882, 30in. long, 262oz. (Christie's) $6,600

A George IV shaped circular salver, by William Pitts, 1822, 22½in. diam., 202oz. (Christie's) $7,865

A small salver, square, with cusped corners and a molded rim, by Jacob Hurd, Boston, circa 1740-50, 5¾in. square, 5oz. (Christie's) $8,800

A set of six George III silver gilt dinner plates, by Eliz. Godfrey, London, 1761, in the George I style, 9½in. diam., 89oz. (Christie's) $7,700

629

TUREENS

A George III two-handled
oval soup tureen and
cover, by Paul Storr, 1807,
12¾in. high, 176oz.
(Christie's)
$28,314

A tureen designed by Henning
Koppel, the cover stamped
HK H 10 Georg Jensen 925
S 1034, 72cm. long, 105oz.
(Christie's) $31,460

A George II two-handled
gadroon edge oval soup
tureen and cover, 40cm. long,
by Edward Wakelin, 1754,
95oz. (Phillips)
$7,007

One of a pair of George III
sauce tureens, maker Samuel
Hennell, London, 1811, 7½in.
wide, overall, 62oz. (Hobbs &
Chambers) $2,359

A covered soup tureen, with
domed oval lid, by Bailey &
Kitchen, Phila., 1833-46,
15½in. high, 16in. wide, 127oz.
(Christie's) $3,520

A Victorian oval plated soup
tureen and cover, 11½in.
wide. (Parsons, Welch &
Cowell) $257

An early Victorian two-
handled soup tureen and
cover, by B. Smith II,
1837, 12in. high, 197oz.
(Christie's)
$7,865

A George II soup tureen and
cover, London, 1759, maker's
mark probably that of Wm.
Reynolds, 17in. long, 117oz.
10dwt. (Christie's)
$18,700

One of three early 20th century French covered tureens,
by Olier et Caron, Paris, 11in.
long, 130oz. (Christie's)
$2,860

A George III small two-handled coffee urn, by Thos. Daniell, 1785, 15in. high, gross 34oz. (Christie's) $2,974

A Victorian plated tea urn of fluted urn shape, makers James Dixon & Son, 17in. high. (Parsons, Welch & Cowell) $154

A George III two-handled vase-shaped tea urn, by Paul Storr, 1802, 20½in. high, gross 122oz. (Christie's) $10,626

A plated coffee urn with applied lion mask ring handles, 13in. high. (Christie's) $550

A William IV melon-fluted two-handled tea urn on a square base, by J. W. & E. H., Sheffield, 1837, 18in. high, 145oz. (Christie's) $3,580

A two-compartment caviar container of urn-shaped form, by Omar Ramsden and Alwyn Carr, 1903, 25.5cm. high, 27.75oz. (Phillips) $2,145

An Old Sheffield plate vase-shaped tea urn, 17¼in. high. (Christie's) $464

A coffee urn, with a conical cover, by Samuel Kirk & Son, Baltimore, probably 1846-61, 16½in. high, 56oz.10dwt. (Christie's) $3,520

A George III two-handled oval tea urn, by Samuel Hennell and James Taylor, 1814, 13¾in. high, gross 143oz. (Christie's) $4,247

VASES

A WMF Ikora patinated metal
vase, shouldered ovoid shape
with short cylindrical neck,
23.6cm. high. (Christie's)
$462

A tall silver vase, made by H. G.
Murphy and R. M. Y. Gleadowe,
25.5cm. high, 29.5oz., maker's
marks for London, 1935.
(Phillips) $3,024

A vase-shaped pitcher, in
the Japanese taste, by
Gorham Manuf. Co.,
Providence, 1885, 9in.
high, 40oz.10dwt.
(Christie's)$6,600

A WMF Ikora patinated metal
vase, elongated ovoid shape
on stepped circular foot,
31.6cm. high. (Christie's)
$462

A Cartier two-handled silver
vase, London import marks
for 1930, on ebonized stand,
29.2cm. high, 60oz.15dwt.
(Christie's) $1,584

A silver twin-handled vase,
16.6cm. high, 12.5oz.,
stamped E.J.B. maker's marks,
Birmingham, 1909. (Phillips)
$403

A Quezal vase with silver
overlay decoration, 9in.
high. (Christie's)
$604

A WMF Ikora patinated metal
vase, ovoid shape, inlaid with a
figure on horseback in silver,
gilt and dark gray, 20.2cm.
high. (Christie's) $593

An urn-shaped vase with
two cast mask handles, by
Shreve, Stanwood & Co.,
Boston, 1860-69, 13in.
high, 24oz. (Christie's)
$715

VINAIGRETTES

A George III gilt lined purse vinaigrette with wrigglework decoration, by S. Pemberton, Birmingham, 1816. (Christie's) $255

A Victorian gilt lined engine-turned book vinaigrette, by Edward Smith, Birmingham, 1857, 1½in wide. (Christie's) $240

A William IV 'castle-top' vinaigrette, by Nathaniel Mills, Birmingham, 1836. (Phillips) $489

A William IV vinaigrette, the cover chased in relief with a ruined building, by Taylor & Perry, Birmingham, 1835. (Phillips) $800

A miniature Regency silver vinaigrette, maker IL, Birmingham, 1817, 0.75in. long. (Woolley & Wallis) $75

A Victorian 'castle-top' vinaigrette, the cover decorated with a view of Windsor Castle, by J. Tongue, Birmingham, 1844. (Phillips) $428

A George IV rectangular purse shaped silver vinaigrette, by Clark & Smith, Birmingham, 1824, 1.25in. long. (Woolley & Wallis) $159

A cylindrical double-ended pill box/vinaigrette, 3oz., London, 1917. (Peter Wilson) $70

An oblong 'castle-top' vinaigrette chased with a view of Litchfield Cathedral, by N. Mills, 1843-4. (Christie's) $1,652

A William IV tartan engraved silver vinaigrette, by N. Mills, Birmingham, 1837, 1.5in. long. (Woolley & Wallis) $126

A Regency rectangular vinaigrette, the gilt interior with a pierced engraved grille, maker possibly Wm. Shaw, London, 1813, 1.15in. long. (Woolley & Wallis) $100

An early Victorian 'castle-top' vinaigrette, the cover chased with a view of Windsor Castle, by Francis Clarke, Birmingham, 1838. (Phillips) $459

One of a set of four George III silver gilt two-handled wine coolers, collars and liners, by Paul Storr, 1813, 11in. high, 689oz. (Christie's) $371,800

A large plated two-handled ice bucket with ornate rim, 11in. diam. (Dickinson Davy & Markham) $150

One of a pair of George III two-handled vase-shaped wine coolers, by Matthew Boulton & Plate Co., circa 1825, 9½in. high. (Christie's) $6,729

A Victorian silver gilt two-handled vase-shaped wine cooler, by A. Benson and H. H. Webb, 1893, 12½in. high, 106oz. (Christie's) $3,775

One of a pair of Queen Anne cylindrical wine coolers, by J. Bodington, circa 1710, 9½in. high, 216oz. (Christie's) $390,390

One of a pair of Old Sheffield tapering bucket-shaped wine coolers with applied ram's mask and ring drop handles, 7½in. high. (Christie's) $892

A German two-handled wine cooler, by Hermann Julius Wilm, Berlin, circa 1855, 15¼in. high, 327oz. (Christie's) $12,397

One of a pair of Old Sheffield two-handled campana shaped wine coolers, each with a detachable collar and inner liner, 8¼in. high. (Christie's) $1,453

One of a pair of Old Sheffield plate two-handled fluted campana shaped wine coolers with detachable liners, 10½in. high. (Christie's) $1,162

WINE LABELS

A George III rectangular wine label, incised 'Vidonia', by S. Meriton II, circa 1775. (Phillips) $189

An early 19th century wine label of cast openwork fruiting vine design, possibly Irish, circa 1820. (Phillips) $422

A George III wine label, incised 'Champagne', by Margaret Binley, circa 1765. (Phillips) $142

A Victorian cast wine label, title scroll incised 'Red Constantia', by Rawlings & Sumner, 1843. (Phillips) $573

A George III shaped oblong wine label, incised 'Lisbon', by B. Bickerton, circa 1765. (Phillips) $221

A Victorian stamped-out hunting horn wine label, incised 'Port', by G. Unite, Birmingham, 1857. (Phillips) $474

A George III crescent-shaped wine label, by Benjamin Tait, Dublin, circa 1785. (Phillips) $205

A George III oval thread-edge wine label, by Phipps & Robinson, circa 1790. (Phillips) $189

A George III cast scallop shield wine label, 'Sherry', by Wm. Eley, 1814. (Phillips) $458

A George IV Irish wine label, incised 'St. Peray', by L. Nolan, Dublin, 1825. (Phillips) $474

A George III Scottish wine label, incised 'Rum', by W. P. Cunningham, Edinburgh, circa 1795. (Phillips) $205

A George III bead-edged wine label, incised 'Burgundy', by S. Barker, circa 1790. (Phillips) $347

A rectangular silhouette on paper by John Buncombe, of Catherine Reynolds of Newport, circa 1785, 90 x 70mm. (Phillips) $226

A rectangular conversation piece by Wm. Welling, of a husband and wife taking tea, signed and dated 1874, 280 x 380mm. (Phillips) $4,832

A gentleman standing full-length profile, by Augustin Edouart, cut-out on card, signed and dated 1836, 10¾in. high. (Christie's) $495

A full-length profile of a family group, by Augustin Edouart, signed and dated 1825, cut-outs on card, 13in. high. (Christie's) $1,573

Pair of early 20th century silhouettes, 'The Bull Fighters', by Wilhelm Hunt Diederich, 9½ x 13in. (Robt. W. Skinner Inc.) $450

An oval black silhouette by John Buncombe, of a lady, circa 1800, 95mm. high. (Phillips) $143

Pair of early 19th century bronzed silhouettes by F. Frith, signed and dated 1844, 10½ x 8½in. (Parsons, Welch & Cowell) $512

A gentleman profile to left, by John Miers, on plaster, oval 3½in. high. (Christie's) $131

SPECTACLES

Late 19th century spectacles with papier-mache case decorated in the Chinese taste. (Christie's) $99

A pair of brass framed Chinese spectacles, with folding sides and quartz lenses. (Christie's) $260

One of two pairs of late 18th century burnished steel turn-pin sides spectacles. (Phillips) $496

A pair of Georgian silver blue-tinted spectacles with double turn-pin sides, London, 1825, possibly by J. Hobbs. (Phillips) $496

An 18th century pair of steel ring side spectacles with tinted lenses in a leather case, 5in. long. (Christie's) $229

A pair of 18th century burnished steel green tinted protective folding sides spectacles with circular lenses. (Phillips) $434

A pair of folding spectacles with tortoiseshell frame, by Theodore Hamblin Ltd., together with another three pairs and a quantity of gilt spectacle parts. (Christie's) $130

A pair of 16th century leather nose spectacles, 9cm. wide (Phillips) $2,480

A pair of silver turn-pin sides 'D' cup blue smoke lenses, together with another three pairs. (Christie's) $382

A pair of 19th century brass and tortoiseshell folding-sides spectacles with deep clouded brown quartz lenses, in shagreen case, 6½in. long. (Christie's) $336

A pair of 19th century brass and horn folding-sides spectacles with horn ear pieces and brown quartz lenses, in brown stained sharkskin case, 17.8cm. long. (Christie's) $367

A pair of Chinese brass framed turn-pin sides spectacles with brown tinted quartz lenses, in a brown stained sharkskin case, 6¾in. long. (Christie's) $183

A gray stone figure of a lion, some earth encrustation, Tang Dynasty, 19cm. high. (Christie's) $1,258

An 18th century soapstone seal carved with a recumbent dreaming figure, 11cm. wide. (Christie's) $2,202

A dark stone figure of Guanyin, seated in dhyanasana, Tang Dynasty, 39.5cm. high, mounted on black marble stand. (Christie's) $14,157

A Romano-Celtic stone shrine, carved in relief with a figure, possibly dedicated to a tree deity, 25.5 x 18.5cm. (Phillips) $1,530

A Sumerian brick fragment impressed with four lines of cuneiform —'Ur Namma, King of Ur, who built the temple of Namma', 27 x 29cm. overall. (Phillips) $290

A Polynesian sandstone head, with disc-shaped headdress. (Phillips) $428

An 18th/19th century polychrome and gilt soapstone rectangular tea caddy and cover, 14.5cm. high. (Christie's) $1,101

A Roman pottery oil lamp, 13cm. long, complete with original limestone mold, Christian, North African, 5th century A.D. (Phillips) $130

Little Lady with Handbags, carved limestone figure, by Wm. Edmondson, Tennessee, circa 1935, 13in. high. (Christie's) $4,400

A carved stone figure of Hercules, partly draped with lion's skin, holding golden apples of the Hesperides, 40in. high. (Robt. W. Skinner Inc.) $800

A naturalistically colored stone carving of a chimpanzee, 53.5cm. high. (Phillips) $460

Early 19th century stone-ware architectural bust, modelled in the form of a Naval officer, 18in. high. (Peter Wilson) $564

An 18th century soapstone figure of the 145th Lehan, 12.5cm. high. (Christie's) $1,179

A Buddhist stone stele, dated to the 2nd year of Zheng Guan of the N. Wei Dynasty, 36cm. high. (Christie's) $943

A 19th century sandstone life-size figure of a young maiden, signed E. Morton, 66in. high, complete with a sandstone plinth, 28in. high. (Reeds Rains) $2,635

A late 19th/early 20th century Italian alabaster group of two Bacchic putti supporting an urn, by E. Battiglia, 91cm. high. (Christie's) $3,030

One of a pair of 5th century A.D. large stone figures of chimera, heavily carved from a matt gray material of lime-stone type, approx. 55.5cm. high. (Christie's) $157,300

A sandstone head of rounded form, on a long cylindrical neck, 27cm. high, perhaps Romano-Celtic. (Phillips) $229

A late 17th/early 18th century Brussels Genre tapestry depicting four children with a dog, 3.4 x 2.8m. (Phillips) $8,352

Late 17th century Flemish tapestry woven in blues, reds, browns and green wools and silk, 8ft.11in. x 10ft.7in. (Christie's) $8,591

Late 17th century Flemish tapestry woven in wools and silk, 100 x 142in. (Christie's) $4,373

A 17th century Flemish tapestry woven in fresh and well-preserved colors, 11ft. x 14ft.11in. (Christie's) $7,810

A 17th century Brussels verdure tapestry woven with Eurydice being bitten by a serpent, 11ft. x 16ft.6in. (Christie's) $12,320

Early 18th century Brussels tapestry woven in silks and wools with fishermen and ladies in a landscape, 9ft.10in. x 9ft. (Christie's) $12,320

A Flemish verdure tapestry woven in brown, green and blue wool, 9ft.3in. x 4ft.5in. (Christie's) $1,874

A 17th century Spanish armorial tapestry woven in greens, blues, yellow and orange wool, 11ft.1in. x 9ft.10½in. (Christie's) $4,998

Late 17th century Brussels tapestry woven in wools and silks, restored, 14ft. x 9ft.4in. (Christie's) $8,591

Late 16th century Flemish tapestry woven in silks and wools, 101 x 91in. (Christie's) $6,248

A Flemish tapestry cartoon painted on canvas, 112 x 159in. (Christie's) $5,935

A 17th century Brussels verdure tapestry, depicting a dog and animal beside a river, framed by trees and foliage, 2.92 x 2.46m. (Phillips) $5,184

An 18th century Aubusson pastoral tapestry, depicting a hunting party with equestrian figures, ladies, hound and falcons in a foliate landscape, 2.33 x 2.75m. (Phillips) $3,456

A tapestry woven in fresh colors in wools and silks, 56 x 85¼in. (Christie's) $5,467

A 17th century Brussels tapestry woven in well preserved silks and wools with Bacchus seated in a gilded chariot, 9ft.1in. x 12ft.4in. (Christie's) $28,160

A late 19th century Japanese panel of k'o-ssu tapestry worked in pastel silks and gold thread, 0.77 x 0.22m., and companion. (Phillips) $664

Late 18th century needlework pocketbook, silk yarns worked in a variant of the Queen stitch, probably New England, 4¾ x 4in. (Robt. W. Skinner Inc.) $550

An 18th century crewel embroidered pocketbook, Mass.. (Robt. W. Skinner Inc.) $9,000

A 19th century Chinese picture, the whole embroidered in colored silks and couched gold thread with a fiery dragon, cosmic and other symbols, 69 x 97cm. (Phillips) $862

A 19th century French shawl designed with curled cones, the center with medallion, the border with niche designs, 3.40 x 1.64m. (Phillips) $323

A 17th century Biblical needlework picture, England, 12 x 16in. (Robt. W. Skinner Inc.) $2,500

A late 19th century Chinese embroidered picture, 89 x 24.5cm., and two others. (Phillips) $573

A Chinese coverlet of ivory silk embroidered in colored silks, 2.30 x 2.10m., knotted fringe. (Phillips) $554

A Japanese wall hanging of deep grey silk embroidered in shades of green, pink and ivory, 1.52 x 0.93m., lined. (Phillips) $1,132

A 19th century Chinese picture of a kylin, the whole embroidered in colored silks and couched gold thread, 56 x 53cm. (Phillips) $924

A coptic woven linen square in black, red and cream, 15 x 18cm., contained in a cotton bound folder, 4th-5th century A.D. (Phillips) $142

A 17th century needlework cushion, silk and metallic yarns in a variety of stitches, England, 8 x 10in. (Robt. W. Skinner Inc.) $3,000

An 18th century style pictorial needlework wall hanging, circa 1880, 22½ x 26in. (Robt. W. Skinner Inc.) $600

An embroidered wall pocket of ivory cotton and silk yarns worked in chain stitch, 4½ x 11in. (Robt. W. Skinner Inc.) $650

A silk needlework picture, by Mary Flower, Phila., 1768, 23in. wide. (Christie's) $187,000

A 17th century crewel embroidered panel, America or England, 20 x 37in. (Robt. W. Skinner Inc.) $300

An undyed linen panel with crewel work embroidery in multi-colored wools, 2.18 x 1.74m. (Phillips) $634

Early 20th century flatweave saddle cover, S. Caucasus, N. Persia, 4ft. x 4ft. x 7½in. (Robt. W. Skinner Inc.) $400

A late 19th century Chinese coverlet of yellow silk, embroidered in pink, blue, green and ivory silks, 2.60 x 2.14m., fringed and lined. (Phillips) $1,201

Late 19th century Soumak bag face, S. Caucasus, (minor wear), 1ft.7in. x 1ft.6in. (Robt. W. Skinner Inc.) $650

One of a pair of 17th century needlework stumpwork pictures, England, 5¼ x 4¼in. (Robt. W. Skinner Inc.) $2,300

A Chinese needlework picture, the ivory silk ground embroidered in shades of blue, brown, ochre and ivory, 36cm. square. (Phillips) $286

A late 19th century Chinese k'o-ssu picture of fighting warriors on horseback and on foot, with companion, 1m. x 0.25m. (Phillips) $656

Needlework picture, 'Shepherdess of the Alps', N.Y., 1800, 12½ x 15¼in. (Robt. W. Skinner Inc.) $1,800

A late 19th century Chinese k'o-ssu cover, the center worked in pastel silks on a gold thread ground, 1.84 x 1.44m., lined. (Phillips) $1,771

Late 18th century silk embroidered picture, New England, 21 x 19in. (Robt. W. Skinner Inc.) $3,500

A printed velvet curtain designed by C. A. Voysey, 262 x 239.5cm. (Christie's) $3,965

An Arts & Crafts linen cover embroidered in red and ivory linen, 1.46 x 1.58m. (Phillips) $453

French 'Bouvet a Plat' or coachbuilder's router in cormier wood by Mines de Suede. (David Stanley Auctions) $635

A 13½in. panel raising plane, by I. Dogdell, with replaced sole fence and offset handle (spur chipped) round topped iron, by R. Moore. (David Stanley Auctions) $418

A mahogany staircase saw with 7½in. blade. (David Stanley Auctions) $53

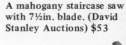

A hand-operated diamond cutting machine with copper cutting wafers. (David Stanley Auctions) $93

An early R/H side axe, 11½in. edge, with star decoration, sharply cranked handle. (David Stanley Auctions) $85

A beech plough by Gabriel, with brass thumb screw at the end of the stems. (David Stanley Auctions)
$1,085

An ultimatum brace by Wm. Marples with boxwood infill, handle and head with ebony ring. (David Stanley Auctions)
$2,402

A 19C two-handled French floor plane. (David Stanley Auctions) $141

A shipwright's large ash brace with 18in. sweep and 2in. fixed center bit. (David Stanley Auctions) $217

An early goosewing axe with 18½in. blade, two smiths marks and simple decoration. (David Stanley Auctions)
$141

A Swiss jewelling and wax lathe lacks tool rest. (David Stanley Auctions) $58

A Stanley No. 196 circular rebate plane. (David Stanley Auctions) $775

Pair of mahogany steel tipped trammels with knurled brass tightening screws, 9in. overall. (David Stanley Auctions) $178

A 2½in. quirked ogee plane by Crow. (David Stanley Auctions) $88

A screwstem plough with boxwood stems and nuts, by J. Miller, Clayton St. (David Stanley Auctions) $108

Early 25½in. try plane with flat iron handle. (David Stanley Auctions) $558

A mahogany sash fillester with boxwood fence and stem wedges. (David Stanley Auctions) $178

A beech button chuck brace with rosewood head and neck, by Deanes, London Bridge. (David Stanley Auctions) $68

A Stanley-Marsh No.100 miter machine, lacks saw. (David Stanley Auctions) $31

A mahogany A square with lead bob. (David Stanley Auctions) $55

A bookbinders plough complete with cutting press. (David Stanley Auctions) $124

A 'Peter Rabbit' chickmobile, hand car, No. 1103, circa 1935. (Christie's) $605

Volkswagon 'Beetle' cabriolet with fibre glass white body, 5 h.p. Briggs & Straton engine, 6ft.6in. long. (Peter Wilson) $1,339

Early 20th century lithographed tin wind-up toy, Japanese 'Chick-Chick', 10in. long. (Robt. W. Skinner Inc.) $240

Lead model Mickey and Minnie Mouse barrel organ group. (Hobbs & Chambers) $58

Four Disney stuffed figures, comprising a velveteen Mickey Mouse and Pluto; two corduroy 'Widgets', late 1930s-40s. (Christie's) $440

A printed tinplate station, by Carette, circa 1912. (Christie's) $332

A pale golden plush covered teddy bear with embroidered snout and slight hump, 15½in. high, with Steiff button. (Christie's) $1,337

A restored and repainted early Marklin three-funnel tinplate battleship, German, circa 1910, 17in. long. (Christie's) $679

A gold short plush covered teddy bear, slight hump, 15½in. high, circa 1926. (Christie's) $269

TOYS

Painted and lithographed tin wind-up sedan, circa 1930, 11½in. long. (Robt. W. Skinner Inc.) $500

A Victorian carved wooden rocking horse. (Parsons, Welch & Cowell) $755

Lehmann 'Naughty Boy' tin wind-up toy, 1904-35, 4.5/8in. long. (Robt. W. Skinner Inc.) $275

A late 19th century glazed and cased model of M. Osborne's — The Butcher's Shop, 46.5 x 43.5cm. (Phillips) $1,072

Two early 20th century jointed teddy bears, one with blonde mohair, 19in. high, the other yellow mohair, 16½in. high. (Robt. W. Skinner Inc.) $350

Spot-On — 2A Presentation Set. (Phillips) $1,072

Lehmann 'Paddy and the Pig' tin wind-up toy, 1903-35, 5½in. long. (Robt. W. Skinner Inc.) $300

A 19th century carved and painted wood horse pull toy, mounted on wooden base with wheels, 11in. high. (Christie's) $495

A 20th century wind-up toy, French celluloid spherical artist, 4in. high, and a Japanese mohair pup in basket, 6in. high. (Robt. W. Skinner Inc.) $110

TOYS

Lehmann 'Zig-Zag' tin wind-up toy, 1910-45, 5in. long (Robt. W. Skinner Inc.) $550

A 19th century carved wooden rocking horse, painted piebald with leather bridle, material covered saddle and gray horse-hair tail, 7½ hands high. (Christie's) $1,494

Lehmann tin wind-up 'Li La', Germany, circa 1903, 5½in. high. (Robt. W. Skinner Inc.) $500

Max lithographed tin Amos and Andy, N.Y., 1930, 11½in. high. (Robt. W. Skinner Inc.) $650

A Marklin monoplane in cream and green, fitted to a double bogie, plane 20cm. long. (Phillips) $286

A bisque-headed jack-in-the-box, modelled as a smiling clown, in paper covered wooden box with pull string for lid, 4¾in. high. (Christie's) $597

Late 19th century hide covered horse pull toy, Germany, horse 24in. long, height on platform 27in. (Robt. W. Skinner Inc.) $500

Spot-On — 145 L.T. Route-master Bus (transfer Radiator), (M), boxed. (Phillips) $543

Blonde mohair jointed teddy bear, 1910, 17in. high. (Robt. W. Skinner Inc.) $275

Spot-On — 156 Mulliner Luxery Bus (pale blue/silver), (M), boxed. (Phillips) $600

Dinky model Guy van, 'Weetabix', No. 514, boxed. (Hobbs & Chambers) $662

A 'Nora Wellings' pre-war fur fabric monkey, 11½in. high. (Reeds Rains) $56

Early 20th century embossed die cut Santa sleigh with reindeer, Germany, 15¾in. long. (Robt. W. Skinner Inc.) $200

Spot-On — 110 2B A.E.C. Major Brick Lorry (E to M), boxed. (Phillips) $257

Spot-On — 'A' Presentation Set T1, comprising Bentley Saloon, Consul Classic, Triumph TR3, Isetta, Austin A40. (Phillips) $185

A Peek Freans biscuit tin 'Castle' made of four different sections, manufactured by Huntley Bourne & Stevens, 1923. (Phillips) $371

A Marklin tinplate clockwork constructor racing car, 1935, red, No. 7. (Hobbs & Chambers) $446

Two No. 116 Ives Union Stations, together with platform cover, circa 1928. (Christie's) $1,760

American Flyer Manufacturing Co., Model No. 560 spring-driven monoplane, 54cm. long, span 60cm., boxed. (Phillips) $257

Early 20th century Walbert lithographed tin wind-up ferry boat, 13¾in. long. (Robt. W. Skinner Inc.) $200

Spot-On — Presentation Pack of four Sports Cars (E to M), boxed. (Phillips) $314

Gama tinplate 300 friction Cadillac in red and black, (M), boxed, 31cm. long. (Phillips) $786

Spot-On — 110/4 4000 gallon Auto Petrol Tanker (M), boxed. (Phillips) $572

A German tinplate horse-drawn open carriage finished in cream and green, the felt covered tinplate horse supported on a flywheel setting the horse in motion. (Phillips) $1,430

Fleischmann, tinplate clockwork liner No. 67, 51cm. long. (Phillips) $1,144

1911 Rolls-Royce 40/50 h.p. Silver Ghost two-seat roadster, coachwork replica of H. J. Mulliner 'Balloon Car' by Wilkinson, Reg. No. R 1064, Chassis No. 1582, Engine No. 1582. (Christie's) $143,820

1925 Talbot-Darracq 12 h.p. four-door tourer, Reg. No. HU 1651, Chassis No. DC 4803, Engine No. 48042. (Christie's) $8,109

1930 Chrysler 77 four-seat roadster, coach-work adapted by Rustless Iron Corp., Reg. No. JT 5518, Chassis No. R2058W, Engine No. 30332941. (Christie's) $39,150

1934 Lagonda M45 4½ liter four-seat tourer, Chassis No. Z11165, Engine No. TB 2915. (Christie's) $29,070

1957 BMW 503 V-8 two-door four-seat Cabriolet, Reg. No. 262 EBK, Chassis No. 69201, Engine No. 30242. (Christie's) $32,130

1968 Jaguar E-Type 4.2 liter two-seater fixed head coupe, Reg. No. WGK 711G, Chassis No. IE 21899, Engine No. 7E 18189-8. (Christie's) $19,125

1955 Bentley R-Type four-door Sports saloon, Reg. No. PXU 283, Chassis No. B532X, Engine No. B262. (Christie's) $12,240

1938 Humber Imperial drophead Coupe, coachwork by Thrupp & Maberly, Reg. No. EVH 871, Chassis No. 6001265, Engine No. 6001248. (Christie's) $9,180

1934 MG KI Magnette Supercharged four-seater Sports tourer, coachwork by Corsica, Reg. No. JB 3717, Chassis No. KO 354, Engine No. 539 AKD. (Christie's) $71,145

1925 Rolls-Royce 40/50 h.p. Silver Ghost four-seater tourer, coachwork replica of Barker by E. R. Reeves, Reg. No. XY 82, Chassis No. 122AU, Engine No. TU 144. (Christie's) $74,970

1935 Lagonda Rapier Sports two-seater, Reg. No. BYN 857, Chassis No. D11438, Engine No. D3186. (Christie's) $8,874

1917 Haynes Light 12 Model 41 Type T four-seater tourer, unregistered, Chassis No. 21225, Engine No. 21225. (Christie's) $30,600

1935 Hillman 20/70 De Luxe four-door saloon, Reg. No. BMM 18, Chassis No. 10491, Engine No. 20/10496. (Christie's) $3,060

1947 Daimler DB18 four-door saloon, Reg. No. JK 9366, Chassis No. D50189, Engine No. 11057. (Christie's) $2,295

1933 Marendaz Special 13/70 two-seater-tourer, Reg. No. JB 1477, Chassis No. 4242, Engine No. 4242. (Christie's) $9,180

1926 Rolls-Royce Twenty foursome drophead Coupe, coachwork by Salmons, Reg. No. OX 20, Chassis No. GOK 64, Engine No. G1606. (Christie's) $21,420

1966 Maserati Sebring two-door GT fixed head coupe, coachwork by Vignale, Reg. No. NGP 280D, Chassis No. 101/10/091, Engine No. 101/10/091. (Christie's) $9,945

1928 Rolls-Royce Twenty Prince of Wales Cabriolet, coachwork by Barker, Reg. No. UL 6654, Chassis No. GFN 35, Engine No. DGA. (Christie's) $36,720

1973 Alfa Romeo Montreal two-door Sports coupe, Reg. No. WAM 142, Chassis No. AR 1426322. (Christie's) $7,344

1959 Bentley S1 four-door Sports saloon, Reg. No. 976 HYP, Chassis No. B52 GC, Engine No. 5688 or 5G88. (Christie's) $9,945

1971 Mercedes-Benz 280 SL roadster, Reg. No. WBH 3995, Chassis No. 11304422001195, Engine No. 1309. (Christie's) $13,005

1965 Aston Martin DB5, fixed head Coupe, registration no. BOP1C, 'Supperlegra' 2995 cc. engine. (Peter Wilson) $14,452

1933 Austin Seven two-door saloon, Reg. No. AMG 347, Chassis No. 176032, Engine No. M176710. (Christie's) $3,060

1934 MG Midget PA Sports two/four-seater, Reg. No. ATU 634, Chassis No. HA 0403, Engine No. 1956A 135P. (Christie's) $13,005

1960 Jaguar MK IX four-door Sports saloon, Reg. No. CSV 156, Chassis No. C775119 D/N, Engine No. N/C 9283/8. (Christie's) $11,475

1928 Rolls-Royce Twenty four-door Sedanca De Ville, coachwork by Thrupp & Maberly, Reg. No. GJ 7623, Chassis No. GKM 52. (Christie's) $39,780

1928/9 Rolls-Royce Phantom I Experimental Sports tourer, coachwork replica of Jarvis by Keith Bowley, Reg. No. XV 2332, Chassis No. 56WR. (Christie's) $68,850

1965 Ferrari 275GTS two-seater Spyder, coachwork by Pininfarina, Reg. No. GGJ 4C, Chassis No. 07395, Engine No. 213. (Christie's) $67,320

1929 Rolls-Royce 20/25 two-door Sportsman's coupe, coachwork by Thrupp and Maberly, Reg. No. UW 793, Chassis No. GX 012, Engine No. 55M. (Christie's) $30,600

1927 Bentley Red Label Speed Model 3 liter four-seater tourer, coachwork by Vanden Plas, Reg. No. YE 7477, Chassis No. LM 1330, Engine No. LM 1332 55. (Christie's) $41,310

1926 Vauxhall 14/40 four-door saloon, coachwork by Mulliner, Reg. No. YP 9827, Chassis No. LM 3885, Engine No. CH 3884. (Christie's) $9,180

1928 Bentley 4½ liter four-seater, Sports tourer, coachwork replica of Vanden Plas, Reg. No. YX 1916, Chassis No. MF 3172, Engine No. MF 3172. (Christie's) $70,380

A molded copper 'North Wind' weathervane, in the form of a cherub's head blowing stylized air, 23in. high, 56½in. long. (Christie's) $18,700

Copper car weathervane, Prides Crossing, Mass., circa 1914, 3ft.8in. long. (Robt. W. Skinner Inc.) $6,250

Late 19th century 'Racing Horse and Jockey' weathervane, U.S., 17in. long. (Robt. W. Skinner Inc.) $3,100

A molded copper weathervane in the form of a running horse, by Harris & Co., Boston, circa 1878, 20in. high, 26in. wide. (Christie's) $1,320

'Mayflower' silhouette weathervane, attributed to E. G. Washburne & Co., N.Y., circa 1920, 36in. long. (Robt. W. Skinner Inc.) $1,900

An American 19th century cast iron horse weathervane, 26in. high, 35in. wide. (Christie's) $16,500

'Foxhound' weathervane, L. W. Cushing & Sons, Waltham, Mass., circa 1883, with traces of gold leaf and weathered verdigris surface, 27in. long. (Robt. W. Skinner Inc.) $12,500

A hollow gilt copper and cast iron weathervane in the form of a bull, American, 1885-1890, bull 39in. long, 23in. high. (Christie's) $3,300

A locomotive and tender copper weathervane, America, circa 1882, 61 in. long. (Robt. W. Skinner Inc.) $185,000

A gilded centaur weathervane, probably A. L. Jewell & Co., Waltham, Mass., circa 1860, 30¼ in. high, 40 in. long. (Robt. W. Skinner Inc.) $130,000

Late 19th century trotting horse weathervane, made by J. Howard & Co., 40 in. long. (Robt. W. Skinner Inc.) $9,250

Early 19th century gold leaf dove figure, America, 13 in. high, 23 in. wide. (Robt. W. Skinner Inc.) $1,300

'Flying Horse' weathervane, A. L. Jewell & Co., Waltham, Mass., circa 1870, 35½ in. long. (Robt. W. Skinner Inc.) $7,000

Cast iron and sheet iron cock weathervane, U.S., circa 1860, 22 in. high. (Robt. W. Skinner Inc.) $2,100

'Colonel Patchen' full bodied copper running horse weathervane, America, late 19th century, 40½ in. long. (Robt. W. Skinner Inc.) $1,200

Late 19th century ewe weathervane, molded sheet copper body and tail with cast metal head, 29 in. wide, 18 in. high, America. (Robt. W. Skinner Inc.) $1,100

WOOD

A Maori wood feather box of elliptical form, 32cm. long. (Phillips) $900

A 19th century carved wood dragon, articulated from head to tail, legs move, Japan, 27½in. long. (Robt. W. Skinner Inc.) $700

A beechwood sculpture, carved as reclining woman, in the style of Hagenauer, 43.4cm. long. (Phillips) $216

A large wood head of Guanyin, Ming/early Qing Dynasty, 58cm. high, wood stand. (Christie's) $2,044

A North Italian late 18th/early 19th century walnut panel. (Parsons, Welch & Cowell) $1,087

Late 17th/early 18th century Buddhist sculpture of Amida Nyorai, 48.4cm. high. (Christie's) $1,249

A carved wood figure of Guanyin seated, probably Ming Dynasty, 73cm. high. (Christie's) $4,719

Pair of giltwood wall lights of Regency design, 37½in. high. (Christie's) $1,239

One of a pair of late 17th century Italian giltwood lions, 22½in. high. (Christie's) $4,686

WOOD

Mid 19th century burl wood bowl, circular, with a molded rim, American, 24in. diam. (Christie's) $1,980

Five carved and painted wooden ducks, various carvers. (Christie's) $770

A wooden fretwork jig-saw puzzle, in the style of Jan Toorop, 39.4cm. long. (Christie's) $712

Mid 19th century painted wooden splint basket, probably Pennsylvania, 11in. wide, 7½in. high, 8in. deep. (Christie's) $825

A carved walnut figure of St. Lucy, traces of original polychrome, the reverse hollowed, 44.5cm. high, probably S. German. (Phillips) $720

A Regency rosewood book-rack with spindle-filled super-structure and one drawer, 16¼in. wide. (Christie's) $2,946

Probably 19th century carved and stained maple figure of an eagle, American, 34½in. high. (Christie's) $8,250

A group of Yoruba wood figures, comprising a soldier, a native bearer, an Oba and two Colonial officials. (Phillips) $1,759

An Australian fruitwood vase of elongated shape, with silver shield-shaped plaque, 17¾in. high. (Christie's) $139

Late 19th century carved and painted wooden boxer figure, America, 18in. high. (Robt. W. Skinner Inc.) $2,200

An Egyptian wood building clamp incised with hieroglyphs — Seti I, 19th Dynasty, 1318-1304 B.C., 26 x 12cm. (Phillips) $690

An Egyptian anthropoid wood sarcophagus, 174cm. high, late Dynastic-Ptolemaic Period. (Phillips) $4,896

A Hagenauer carved wood and metal bust of a woman in profile, 12½in. high. (Christie's) $1,344

One of a pair of giltwood wall brackets with D-shaped tops, 13½in. high. (Christie's) $1,487

A 19th century carved and polychromed wood head of a young woman, Spain, 10¾in. high. (Robt. W. Skinner Inc.) $550

A Baule wood male figure of elongated form, standing on a rectangular base, 48cm. high. (Phillips) $270

A mahogany latticework waste-paper basket on bracket feet, 14½in. wide. (Christie's) $5,104

A New Guinea lime spatula, 34cm. high, and a bamboo comb, 27.8cm. high. (Phillips) $165

19th century sailor's pine art carving, 14in. high. (Robt. W. Skinner Inc.) $350

Early 20th century gilt wooden trade sign in the form of a fish, American, 57¼in. long, 17in. high. (Christie's) $4,400

A 19th century European carved and painted wood Blackamoor, painted in polychrome and gilded, 56¾in. high. (Robt. W. Skinner Inc.) $1,400

A 19th century N. American carved pine wood doll torso with holes in the head for wig. (Christie's) $235

A 19th century carved walnut panel with a coat-of-arms and motto Le Main Tiendrai, 46in. wide. (Christie's) $2,478

A polychromed Yosegizukuri wood figure of Daruma, 51cm. high. (Christie's) $1,093

A Senupo wood rhythm pounder carved as a female figure on a circular base, 112cm. high. (Phillips) $390

Early 20th century carved wooden relief fishing scene, probably Maine, 18 x 24½in. (Robt. W. Skinner Inc.) $1,500

An African wood staff, the finial carved as a human head with elongated ringed neck, 44cm. high, and a wooden snake, 57cm. long. (Phillips) $75

A Solomon Island wood bowl
of oval section, 44cm. long.
(Phillips) $390

A New Guinea lime spatula,
37.5cm. high. (Phillips)
$630

A mid Victorian black and
gilt japanned tole hubble-
bubble, with metal label of
Lowe, London, 10½in. high.
(Christie's) $346

Pair of decorated border
woodcut blocks by Eric Gill,
of naked maidens among
foliage, 18.6 and 18.9cm.
high, excluding bases.
(Christie's) $2,019

Penobscot figural polychrome
wood club, pommel in form
of wolf's head, 48in. long.
(Robt. W. Skinner Inc.)
$425

Pair of Italian gilt and silvered
blackamoor figures. (Parsons,
Welch & Cowell) $2,160

A Continental carved wooden
tankard with hinged cover,
8in. high. (Prudential Fine
Art) $2,184

Northwest coast wood carving,
Nootka, of a reclining seal,
possibly a net float. (Robt. W.
Skinner Inc.) $475

Pair of late 19th century
miniature clogs with leather
uppers. (Peter Wilson)
$55

INDEX